LOCKS & CREAM CHEESE

by

Rosemary & Larry Mild

AmErica House
Baltimore

First printing

ISBN: 1-58851-702-0
PUBLISHED BY AMERICA HOUSE BOOK PUBLISHERS
www.publishamerica.com
Baltimore

Printed in the United States of America

For Margarita + Roberto

Mysteriously yours,
Rosemary + Larry

This book is dedicated with love to Alena, Craig, Ben, Leah, and Emily – our five grandchildren from whom we derive so much inspiration.

And to the lovers of cozy mysteries everywhere with whom we enjoy a special camaraderie.

TABLE OF CONTENTS

CHAPTER 1

MURDER AT MARCHE HOUSE

Tuesday, October 14, 1980

Four unloaded freighters strained at anchor like Dobermans pulling at leashes. A stark moon chiseled their silhouettes over Maryland's Chesapeake Bay. Gusting breezes coaxed frothy whitecaps from the murky bay surface. Atop a cliff on the western shore, a shadowy figure shrouded in black turned away from churning waters to face the old mansion. The black haversack slipped from a tilting shoulder to the ground. Gloved hands removed a folded grappling hook tied to a length of throwing line. With most of the line coiled in one hand, the other hand spun the hook in a wide circle until the momentum peaked. At that instant, the hook flew to the balcony above, over the rail, bursting open to hang fast on a wrought iron baluster.

The figure yanked hard on the paid-out tether and, after tying the bitter end to the haversack, began to scale the coarse stone wall to the balcony. The lithe frame swung over the broad iron rail one leg at a time and bounced to the floor, freezing all motion, listening like a stalking alley cat. Hearing no sound, the intruder hoisted the haversack of tools to the balcony and moved with them to the double French doors.

A gloved hand slowly tried the ancient brass knobs to coax them open, but the glass-paneled doors were locked. An experienced eye discerned the lack of foil strips on the window panes--an antiquated alarm system at best. The top inside pane of the right-hand door yielded to a sharp wrap with a small peen hammer, allowing the removal of the remaining shards with gloves.

One hand slipped inside the top of the door, locating two small plastic boxes, one above the other. The bottom one, shaped like a candy bar, contained a long, narrow magnet screwed to the door. A gloved hand quickly inserted a wedge of cardboard just large enough to maintain the precise spacing between the door magnet and the second box. This box contained the door frame's magnetically activated switch. The intruder bound the two boxes together with duct tape. A small screwdriver released the two wood screws holding the magnet to the door. A few more quick screw turns freed the switch from the frame above it. The switch and magnet now dangled away from the door and frame, suspended there by the stiff wiring. A long arm reached inside and down to the catch to release one double door from its mate.

The intruder stepped inside and flicked on a flashlight. Its beam revealed a high-ceilinged Victorian room with a canopied four-poster bed. A mahogany highboy filled one corner. The light scanned silk-covered walls, passing over several richly framed oil paintings to settle on one in particular: a turn-of-the-century portrait. The masked intruder pulled a small photograph from a hip pocket and compared it to the stately lady peering out of the frame. It matched perfectly. A toothy smile of relief breached the knit ski mask.

Shedding the gloves and stuffing them into the haversack, deft fingers checked carefully for security devices that might be concealed behind the carved, gilded frame. Discovering none, the figure in black lifted the support wire from its wall pin. The wire provided a convenient means to attach the frame to a pair of rings on the haversack.

The flashlight fit neatly into a pocket. The intruder had taken care to make no noise, and yet a foreign sound floated up beyond the door to the hall, like someone walking on carpet. The footsteps came closer and stopped. The door rattled on its hinges. Its brass knob turned slowly, its movement gleaming in reflected moonlight.

Just twenty minutes earlier, Willard Aigue had opened the front door to the Marche House mansion to make the last of his nightly security rounds. Since old Hubert Marche had died last year, no one lived in the place. Willard and his wife, Norma, served the Marche estate as caretakers, grateful for the perk of living in the three-room cottage at the top of the road.

Willard arrived earlier than usual this night because he wanted to fix the French doors that led from the Missus' bedroom to the balcony. They rattled in the wind, and the loose hinges kept setting off the silent alarm, which was not so silent down at the cottage. It didn't bother him much; he'd simply turned down his hearing aid. But each time it happened, Norma threw a fit for half an hour afterward, and he couldn't rightly blame her. He planned to tighten the hinges tonight and take care of the problem once and for all.

He clipped the ring of house keys to his belt and swung his box lantern around the grand foyer in wide sweeps and then in the direction of the dining room. Working his way cautiously through the dark, silent mansion, he pointed the beam across the expanse of each room, checking windows and doors along the way. Eighteen minutes later, he reached the top of the wide, curved staircase that led from the grand foyer to the second floor.

After checking out the first bedroom, Willard stopped in the hall before the Missus' bedroom. He turned the knob and pushed the door inward. About a quarter of the way open, it met with resistance, and he could push no farther. Startled, he pushed harder. He saw a hand gripping the door from the inside, the thumb curled tightly around the door's edge.

Willard dropped the lantern. Grasping the knob with both hands, he pulled the door shut against the jamb, catching the vulnerable thumb in an unexpected vise.

"Ow! Oh, man, you son-of-a-bitch!" a voice shouted.

Willard pulled the door toward him with the force of all his weight, but the strength of the intruder beyond was too much for his seventy-year-old body, and the knob slipped from his grasp. The towering black figure lunged at him and thrust him backward against the staircase rail. Willard screamed as he felt his body hurled through space, downward, downward....

The thief peered over the railing, but could see nothing in the dense darkness. The flashlight flicked on. The old man appeared grotesquely illuminated in the bright beam. His limbs splayed out, distorted, in crumpled work clothes. Willard lay face up in a widening pool of blood.

The thief, after descending a few of the stairs, decided against taking a closer look, and instead, ran back through the open bedroom door, shouldered the haversack and sprinted for the open French doors. Untying the grappling hook from its tether and using double lengths of its line, the intruder swung from the balcony and rappelled down the stone wall. Once on the ground, the fleeing figure gathered in the line and darted down the stone steps of the cliff to the bay shore road below. The car started quickly and sped off into the night. The painting lay covered and cradled safely on the rear seat.

Willard lay immobile on the marble floor, unaware of either coldness or hardness at first, but acutely aware of pain. It wasn't excruciating pain. It felt more like pressure, except that he couldn't move. He lay there for more than an hour while his body's heat drained out of him. Fear and shivering cold dominated his whole being. He knew full well death awaited him; only a matter of time now. A blurry shadow moved into view. It was a man, one he didn't recognize. And then he heard Norma, but he couldn't turn his head to see her. He wanted to see her. He wanted to live.

"Officer, will he make it?" she asked.

"Don't know, ma'am, but I've got an ambulance on the way. They'll get him to the hospital."

Norma's fearful face appeared suddenly before him. "He's trying to say something. His lips are moving," she said.

The man's face came closer, too. "Sounds like he's saying *dumb*."

Norma nodded. "That's what it sounds like to me, too."

Willard tried to shake his head. He couldn't move. He rolled his eyes to tell them no, but neither of them understood. His eyes came to their final position and froze there. The police officer took his pulse and shook his head slowly, and Norma knew she had lost her man. She buried her head in

Willard's chest and sobbed until the uniformed officer gently pried her loose and led her away.

Willard Aigue was buried four days later.

CHAPTER 2

ICONS AND EYESORES

Thursday, October 23, 1980

The population of Black Rain Corners, Maryland, hovered around 2,100, allowing for the usual rate of births, deaths, marriages, divorces, and an occasional runaway. Just passing through on the shore road, Black Rain Creek Drive, one would never imagine the 830 homes. Like so many other communities nestled beside the Chesapeake Bay, winding lanes and woodlands hid dwellings along numerous by-waters. The inhabitants comprised those who made their living locally as well as those who commuted to Washington, Baltimore, or Annapolis.

Town Hall sat on a corner across the street from Gander Creek, just before it emptied into the bay. The part-time mayor's office occupied the second floor, and the makeshift hall of records and clerk's office sprawled across the first story of the converted Victorian home. A red-brick structure next to it housed the volunteer fire and police departments. The county established a token police presence here in the early seventies when a rash of break-ins targeted a dozen or so upscale homes. They had hoped to use the improved response time as a deterrent.

The local police force consisted of one full-time county officer and part-time Paco LeSoto. He'd retired from the Baltimore police force four years ago and bought a tiny bachelor bungalow in Black Rain Corners. The town paid his salary and created the title of inspector in the process. The residents thought the title especially appropriate because of his intense attention to detail, and he actually enjoyed being addressed as "Inspector."

Paco sat at his desk in pink shirt sleeves, his collar open, a checkered red and pink bow tie clipped over one collar stay. A gray tweed sport jacket hung over the back of his chair. Using an eye loupe, he pored over an antique Derringer pistol, which lay on a cloth smeared with Cosmoline. Two paper towel sheets protected the desk surface. He worked a small bit of foreign matter from beneath the mother-of-pearl grip with a tweezer and admired the latest addition to his personal gun collection.

Officer Frank Mullins burst into the room and tossed a folded newspaper down on Paco's desk. "Hey, Inspector. Seen this morning's crab-wrapper yet?" His index finger prodded an article at the bottom of page one. "They went and did it again."

"Did what?" Paco asked.

"Called you Inspector Taco LeSoto."

"Was there a byline?"

"Yeah, your buddy."

"He's certainly no friend of mine. Did he at least get the rest of the story right?"

"See for yourself." Frank pushed the paper closer. "You think he did it on purpose?"

Paco folded the Derringer back into its cloth and deposited the gun in a small tool kit. He wiped the desk clean with the paper towels and discarded them before picking up the *Annapolis Journal-Gazette*. Frank sat down at the duty desk across from him.

The article gave a fairly accurate account of a teenager finding a gilt frame and canvas stretcher in a dumpster.

"...Inspector Taco LeSoto released the youth last night after determining he had nothing to do with the burglary of the Marche House painting."

Paco finished reading and then looked across at Frank. "Yes, I think the man does it quite on purpose. Probably some kind of redneck."

He buttoned his shirt, reclipped the dangling tie, and stood to don his jacket. "Well, that's about all the abuse I can take for today. I'm going home to feed the twins."

"Twins?" Frank repeated. "Oh, you mean your birds, the macaws."

Paco smiled and slipped out the door.

Meanwhile, ninety miles to the north, a steel-gray '79 Toyota sped toward Black Rain Corners.

"Simon? Honey? You haven't said a word for the last fifty miles. When I said I'd drive, that didn't mean you were free to desert me altogether."

"Huh? What's the matter, dear?" His wife had retrieved him from deep concentration. He'd been mulling over some electrical engineering glitch from the office, a timing problem. His mind simply wouldn't purge itself of the workplace at day's end. The four-hour drive south on I-95 had been an opportunity not to be wasted.

"Well, if I'm going to do all the driving, the least you can do is keep me company," Rachel said, her lips pursing in a mock pout. "I don't like talking to a wall."

"What wall is that, dear?" The small crease of a smile grew on his face.

"As if you didn't know. That secret place you engineers hide behind when you want to think."

"Oh, that wall. Well, I'm here now. What do you want to talk about?"

"Oh, everything and nothing. I just enjoy your company." As they sped along, her eyes feasted on the fall colors: gold maples and crimson Bradford pear trees. "And I'm excited about going home. You, too?"

"Thrilled, simply thrilled," he said. "My first visit to my new father-in-law."

"Darling, if I didn't know you better, I'd say you were scared to spend time with my family. They can't be nearly as forbidding as that mathematical world you live in. All those stuffy algorithms and such."

He laughed. "At least I don't have to make small talk with algorithms. Besides, I already met everyone at the wedding, didn't I? And I thought I behaved quite well."

"You did, darling. You were charming. But you spent a grand total of three hours with them. You didn't get to really know anyone."

"True. But I did talk to your father for a little while, and he made me feel like so much meat being inspected."

"Daddy's not like that, dear. Actually, he's a real *mensch*."

"But he's a psychoanalyst. It's like he knows what I'm going to say before I say it. I felt so...so transparent." Simon thought for a moment. "Yeah, that's it."

"I suppose the thought of a psychoanalyst can be a bit unnerving, if you didn't grow up with one." Rachel broke into a sly grin. "Actually, my ex was scared to death of him. But then again, my ex was terminally insecure. But, really, Daddy's not scary at all. He doesn't go around ego-snooping all the time, trying to climb into people's heads." She took a box of Tic-Tacs from her purse and popped one in her mouth. "But he does love helping people."

"Is he going to help me whether I like it or not?" Simon asked. "Rachel, I met a man who was very formal, very proper, and very serious-minded."

"Well, that's not all bad, is it? But I admit the wedding probably wasn't the best place to get to know him. Too much tension and hype and everything."

"Well, what's he like, then?"

Rachel broke her train of thought for a few minutes while she pulled up to the toll booth and handed the unsmiling collector a dollar bill from the coin box clip. She pulled away from the booth in a rush to gain the outside lane. Hmm, how to describe Daddy to Simon? Then it came to her.

"He's like an elegant white feather with every quill and filament in place. Watching him move, he appears to dart from desk to file to phone or wherever, as though he were carried randomly by the wind, but he is truly propelled by his mind's purpose."

Simon sat straight up in his seat. "I suppose he wears a halo as well?"

"Now that you mention it, he..."

"A good thing I know when you're joking. I suppose you can describe the rest of your family in equally fine imagery?"

"Let's see, there's Aunt Freddie. She reminds me of a wine glass. Waterford crystal, I think. She was quite a looker in her time."

"I remember Freddie," said Simon. "Nice lady. Wasn't she the busty-lusty legal beagle with great legs and a warm smile?"

Hesitating long enough to pull into the right lane and let a tailgater pass, Rachel laughed. "I don't know if she'd approve of the lusty part, but you've got the rest right. She's super-smart, too."

Freddie, a widow, had been a legal secretary at a prominent Annapolis firm. Rachel's father, Dr. Avi Kepple, invited his sister to move into his house when she was forced to sell hers. It seemed a natural thing to do. He had plenty of room, and the Kepple house had become desolate after his own wife died.

Simon asked, "Doesn't Aunt Freddie have a son or something?"

" 'Or something' would be about right. Victor's been bleeding her dry for years. He's a compulsive gambler and carouser extraordinaire. Nobody in the family knows for sure, except Daddy, maybe. But we think she was forced to sell her house to keep Vic out of jail."

"Victor sounds like the salt of the earth. I'm glad he didn't come to our wedding."

"Believe it or not, there's a decent side to him. At least there used to be when we were growing up. He sells insurance when he actually works. In fact, he can be quite charming at times."

"Oh, yeah? Remind me not to buy a whole-life policy from him. Got an icon for a con artist?"

"Sure thing. He looks like a mustard pretzel. Thin, scrawny, poor complexion like salt bumps, and a little jaundiced with age."

"Ah! Nothing like good looks to make up for a nasty personality."

"Of course, his royal highness shows up from time to time to sponge a week or two off my father."

"Isn't Avi afraid that Victor will pull one of his shenanigans on him?"

"I don't think Vic would dare. He knows Daddy has his number. There's some kind of unwritten yet binding agreement between them that they be honest with each other. Whatever decent side there is to Vic has been Daddy's influence."

"Will Vic be there today?"

"I don't know."

"So how come your dad never remarried? Your mother's been gone for so many years."

A shadow of sadness crossed Rachel's face. "That's always bothered me, frankly. He's always had so many women friends, some really chasing him."

"I didn't mean to upset you by asking."

"No, no, you didn't, dear. It's a natural question."

Still, Simon felt uneasy and quickly changed the subject. "So...anybody else in the house I need briefing on?"

"There's Molly, of course, Daddy's housekeeper and cook. Let's see, her icon would be a large beach ball with an apron. She's in her sixties, about four foot eight, and just as round as she is tall. Truly a body with neither a neck nor a waistline at all. She's got watery blue eyes that bulge."

"A regular Miss America," he said, chuckling.

That wasn't all, Rachel mused to herself. Molly's soprano voice had a grating edge that got more and more shrill whenever she tried to persuade Avi to see something her way. And that's what drove Avi crazy: She *always* had something to say. Often he took refuge in his den and turned the classical music way up just for a little peace and quiet. Rachel giggled.

"Actually, Molly's a treasure. Her housekeeping won't win any awards, but she more than makes up for it as a gourmet chef. Her presentations are fit for a lord."

"She sounds like a combination of Julia Child and the Pillsbury Doughboy. I love her already. Is there more?"

"Well, yes. She's Mrs. Malaprop incarnate. Aunt Freddie's forever trying to correct her Mollyprops--that's what Daddy calls them--and sometimes Molly's feelings get hurt. She's a very sensitive human being."

"By the way, what time are they expecting us?"

"Expecting us? Oh-oh. I forgot to let them know we're coming. Got a busy signal when I called from the office yesterday. Then my boss came in about that new book I'm editing. I never did call back."

"Then they have no idea we're coming?"

"I've got to find a phone."

"See that sign?" Simon pointed. "Maryland House, only three miles. You can call from there. Hey, babe, if no one answers, do we turn around and go back to New York?"

"Well," she said with an impish smile, "we could always rescue the weekend by driving straight to the Washington Hilton for a mini-honeymoon."

Simon's face lit up. "I'll go for that. Can't we just keep driving?"

"No, of course not. I can't imagine them not being home. And I promise you, you'll have a great time." Keeping her eyes on the road, she reached over and gave his thigh a firm squeeze.

At Maryland House, she pulled nose-in to the curb opposite a pay phone and left the engine running. "I'll just be a minute," she said as she slammed the car door.

Simon watched his forty-year-old wife of seven months tuck herself into the snug transparency of the phone booth. She dropped the coins and rapidly pecked out the most familiar number in her repertoire. While she waited for an answer, she smiled out at him. She looked away as she began to talk.

With a measure of pride, Simon surveyed the petite athletic figure leaning against the glass door. Rachel's mature beauty affected him to the core. Her facial features were chiseled, classic, and sharp. The nose had perhaps too much of a downward turn to deny her Jewish heritage. Straight brown hair fit like a knitted cap around her head and stopped just below her tiny ears, leaving her long nape bare and full of interest. Simon liked that curved place where neck met shoulder.

Rachel bounded out of the booth and reached the car in seconds. She found the door opened for her. "They're thrilled we're coming. Can't wait to see us." She hugged her husband quickly before putting the car in reverse.

She began to back out of the space when Simon asked, "How's the gas doing?"

"We're low. I'll pull up to the pumps. I could use the little girl's room, too."

Simon baby-sat the gas hose while Rachel disappeared inside the large brick building. He was standing curbside when she reappeared ten minutes later with two soft drinks and two packs of snacking crackers. "I'll only be a minute, hon," he said as he disappeared into the same building.

Rachel set the refreshments down on the roof of the car while she opened the door. She moved them to the floor console between the seats before sliding in behind the wheel. Removing the wrap from the crackers, she popped one into her mouth and crunched away. She reached for her drink.

"Hey, lady, whatcha doin' in there?" A deep male voice bellowed at her from just outside the car door. Her drink fell to the floor, spilling, and she coughed, sending a splatter of dry peanut butter crackers to the windshield and dashboard.

She swallowed hard, the last of the cracker crumbs sticking in her throat. "You get away from here this instant, or I'll call my husband." Her voice sounded less authoritative than she intended. She pushed the door latch down. But the window was already down. The stranger merely pulled the latch up again and swung the door back. The man had a chunky body that bulged out of his black shirt and black trousers. His massive square face appeared gray with the scars of close shaving.

"No, lady, *you* get outta *my* car." Deep-set raccoon eyes glared at her. "Otherwise, shut up and get in the passenger seat. I always do the driving."

Rachel's jaw dropped open. And she wanted to scream, but nothing came out. She tried to yank the door from his hand, but his grip proved too strong.

"Out, lady...out." He stood there, waiting.

A friendlier, more familiar voice came from behind him. "What are you doing over there, hon? Who is that man?"

Rachel took in her surroundings once more. "Oh, my God!" she whispered. She saw Simon standing next to their '79 Toyota Corona. The car she sat in looked exactly like theirs: same model, same steel-gray color, even the same velvety gray upholstery. She'd gotten into the wrong car. "Sorry, mister," she said meekly. She hastily gathered up her paper cups and crackers.

"Just get out," the man repeated. "You've caused enough trouble. I should make you clean up that mess on my floor."

Rachel moved as fast as she could, even spilling half of the second drink while she ejected herself from the stranger's car. As she moved away, she heard him cursing. "Dumb broad...crazy dame...clumsy ditz." Afraid to look in his direction, she heard his engine roar into motion. The tires screeched twice as he lurched backward and then burned rubber out of the parking lot.

Rachel leaned on the hood of their car for a moment and held out what was left of the refreshments to Simon. As he took them from her, he offered, "Are you all right? Want me to drive some?"

"No, thanks, dear, I'm okay," she said weakly. She slid into the driver's seat and buckled her seat belt. "Simon, how could I make such a stupid mistake? If I'd been paying attention, I'd have noticed that our jackets weren't on the back seat."

"Don't blame yourself, hon. It could've happened to anyone."

"But he really scared me. He looked like a thug in one of the old Edward G. Robinson movies. The black outfit, the white tie. Mafia chic, I guess I'd call it. Dear, nothing like that has ever happened to me before." Despite her distress, Rachel pulled the car onto the highway, picked up speed and headed toward her Chesapeake Bay hometown.

Simon was eager to get her mind off the whole episode. "I've been sitting here thinking about all those neat icons you have for everyone else. You must have one for me, too."

"Could be," she said.

"Hey, you're gonna stop there and not tell me?"

"Of course, I'll tell you. You're a great big teddy bear with dreamy brown eyes and curly brown hair."

Rachel glanced at her husband. The bushy brows and horn-rimmed glasses gave his round face a scholarly look. His six-foot, 180-pound physique bordered on the muscular.

"And you know what? You're a *mensch*, too. That's one of the reasons I married you." She noticed that his lips had formed a smile, but he looked as though he'd succumbed to a daydream. Afraid she'd lost him to work again, she tested him to see if he was listening.

"I have this new author. He says he's going to rewrite the Bible. The man's got a new twist: he'd like to do it in stone. My boss wants to give him a contract, but there's one problem. He can't--"

"--find an efficient way for you to edit stone tablets. You thought I was daydreaming again, didn't you?" Simon loved to finish her punch lines. He shifted around in his seat, and she saw him break out in one of his "Gotcha!" grins.

She laughed back at him. He had set her up. Twenty minutes later, she tried again with another ploy. This time he was gone.

"Simon? Si-mon..."

CHAPTER 3

COUSIN VICTOR

"Molly, would you pick up the phone? I can't get down these confounded stairs fast enough." Freddie Moskowitz enjoyed the best of health for someone in her early seventies, but she couldn't do anything as quickly as she wanted to these days.

Molly Mesta waddled toward the phone in the den, picked it up, and took a deeper breath for all of her hurrying. "Good morning, Dr. Kepple's residence. Oh, Rachel! It's so gorgeous to hear your voice. You want me to wake your father? Oh, no, I can't do that. He needs his rest. His work is all mental, you know. You're coming home? Wonderful! I'll tell the doctor the minute he wakes up. Bye."

"What was that all about?" Freddie asked.

"It's Rachel. She and her husband are on their way here. Comin' in about 1:30. Rachel and Simon Mendelsohn, now that's a nice name."

"Yes, she's found herself a fine young man. Sensible, too."

"Oh, my, what's this?" Molly stuck her hand behind the telephone table and extracted a single Bicycle-pattern playing card. It had been lodged there with only an edge exposed. She turned it over: the deuce of diamonds. A long-distance telephone number sprawled across the card in green ink. She pulled open the drawer in the little table and dropped the card into it.

"Whatever did you find, Molly?"

"Just a phone number, Miss Freddie."

"It looked like a playing card from here."

"It was."

Freddie lowered her eyes, and a pained look crossed her face. She changed the subject. "Molly, what's all the rattling out in the kitchen? Who's out there making all that noise?"

"It's Greta Polaski, Miss Freddie. She's come over to help me prepare for the Hysterical Society meeting."

"The *Historical* Society, Molly."

"Yes, ma'am!" Molly scooted through the free-swinging dining room door, just in time to avoid her backside being swatted. She nearly collided with Greta, taking down the Royal Worcester china from the top shelf of the glass-front hutch.

On the top rung of the step stool, Greta made a precarious picture. The shy, frail lady cooked and kept house for Mrs. Raphael next door. She claimed she'd never seen her seventy-third birthday, but Olivia Raphael wasn't fooled. Greta had to be eighty, if a day.

Greta loved to talk, and Molly listened loyally. "Wasn't that a beautiful funeral they had for Willard Aigue? I didn't know he had all that many friends and such. He and Norma, poor dear woman, made such a nice quiet and friendly couple, they did."

"I agree, a goodly service by the parson," Molly said. "It's a horrible way to go. And the thief got away Scotch free--with only one painting, though. I wonder how much it's worth. Pricey, I bet ya."

"Don't know much about that," Greta said. "But the paper says some kid from Deale got arrested for trying to sell the solid-gold frame to an antique shop. The kid told them he found it in the dumpster down at the inn the night Willard got hisself killed."

"Did they let him go?" Molly asked.

"Yeah!" she answered.

"Careful with those dishes," Molly warned. "They're replaceless." She knew the history of the china by heart. Fifty years ago, the doctor and his bride had the set custom-made during his postgraduate work in London.

"They're so beautiful," Greta said, examining a dinner plate. It had a wide blue border embellished with gold filigree and tiny hand-painted orange dots. Greta climbed down the step stool. Thin and veiny, Greta looked like a stick standing next to Molly's great bulk. "I'll get the cups and saucers later."

"The doctor's late wife," Molly said, "she actually designed the pattern in 'em."

"What ever happened to her?" Greta asked, shakily handing the last stack of plates to Molly, who put them on the pantry counter.

"Some kind of cancer, I think. Died off in her forties. He's been alone over thirty years now."

"He never wanted to remarry?"

"No, he forewent that."

"What a shame. You been with him all that time?"

"Oh, no, I never knew her. I've been here goin' on twenty-four years. How about you?"

"How many times I got to tell you? I came to Miss Olivia's when Mr. Raphael died six years ago, leaving her alone with her grandkid." Greta emitted one long sigh. "Now she and the doctor are both alone. Looks to me like they'd make a good match."

"I know he likes her, but he likes his freedom even more," Molly said. "Besides, I'll bet you marrying a lady with a nine-year-old grandchild ain't exactly his idea of romance, uh-uh, no, sir. What happened to Caitlin's parents, anyway? I ferget."

"Got themselves killed in a car crash when she was little."

The back door rattled, prompting both women to look up. They saw a round face squashed against the glass, large eyes in clear-framed glasses peeking in below the curtain.

"Speak of my little devil," Greta said as she pulled back the door.

In bounced Caitlin. Her single long braid flopped on her back as she bounced. "Can I play with Shana? May I, please? We'll be quiet, honest!"

"If it's okay with Miss Molly," Greta said. "But don't you go teasing that dog now and getting her barking, you hear?"

Greta looked over at Molly, who nodded, then said, "You're not in school today?"

"I have off. Isn't it neat?"

At the sound of her favorite playmate's voice, Shana came trotting from the sunny spot on the hallway floor, leaped onto the ceramic-tile kitchen floor, and skidded to a scratching halt in front of Caitlin. The full-grown golden retriever at five had lost none of her puppy playfulness. Her tail thudded heavily against a cabinet door.

Molly sat down on the stool to peel a basketful of Granny Smiths just as the front door chimes began their three familiar tones. She glanced at Greta hopefully.

"Stay where you are. I'll get it," Greta said. She had hardly opened the door when she found a clipboard and pen thrust in her face.

"Sign here, ma'am."

She scribbled her name quickly without asking why and handed the paperwork back to the man in the olive jacket and delivery cap.

"Have a nice day." He had spun around and gone halfway down the walk before Greta found the large cactus plant sitting by the door. It stood a good three feet high and about eight inches across, a single pale green column full of forbidding spines. A plastic spear stuck in the soil held an envelope with a card.

Greta tried to approach the plant from at least two sides and gave up. "Hey, Moll, wait'll you see this crazy thing."

Molly lumbered down the front hall. "Lordy me, what in heaven's name? What are we suppose to do with a thing like that? It's not even pretty. I've never cared much for cactuses. They're stuckulents, you know."

"No, I didn't know," Greta said, looking puzzled.

"Let's get it in the front door, and the doctor will tell us where he wants it when he gets up." Struggling, the two women managed to drag the cactus into the foyer. "Now," Molly said, "let's reward ourselves with a cup of instant coffee while I get out my intergredients for the apple-brandy spice cake. So much company's coming this weekend, I got a whole slew of sweet tooths to bake."

"I'll put the kettle up," Greta said. They slid into captain's chairs to wait for the hot water. "Who do you suppose the plant's from?"

"From a patient, I bet. A grateful patient, that's who. They're always sending him stuff." Molly didn't know where to put all the knickknacks, *tchotchkes*, and artwork any more.

"Aren't you the least bit curious about the cactus, Molly?"

"I can wait, but if you insist...."

Molly waddled down the hall to the foyer, slid the card out of its envelope, and peeked. "Uh-huh." She tucked the card back in and returned to the kitchen.

"Well?"

"Well what?"

Sssss-wheeeeeee! The kettle whistled. Molly turned off the burner and poured two neat cupfuls.

Just then the door to the dining room swung open, and the doctor stuck his head in. "Good morning, ladies." Avi shook a little silver bell in his hand to emphasize his presence. He returned to sit at the head of the dining room table, where a place had been already set for him with sterling silver and everyday Delft.

"Morning!" both women responded in chorus.

"How about poached eggs and toast this morning?" Molly asked.

"I believe I'll skip the eggs. Do we have any more of that oat cereal in the cupboard?"

"Horse food? Yes, I think there's some left. It's better for you, anyway. Not so many cholesteroils."

"Ahem! Thank you, Molly. That will be fine." He pointedly picked up the morning paper. Dr. Avi Kepple's robust manner seemingly added inches to his medium height and compensated for his slightly underweight frame.

"Hi, Dr. Kepple." Caitlin's small face appeared around the door.

"Caitlin! Come in, dear. No school today?"

"Nope, teachers' meetings, and Grandma gave me a book she wants me to read. I just started it."

Avi laid down his paper. His thinning hair was white, edged in gray, yet he looked a decade younger than his seventy-six years. He removed his gold-rimmed glasses and wiped a spot on the lens with his napkin before replacing them.

"Tell me about the book, Caitlin."

"Well, it's about a girl my age, and she has problems with her teeth. They're growing in all wrong, and she can't even talk right. It's called..."

"Overbite?" Avi asked.

"I don't think so. Her jaw is crooked."

"Does she have to have an operation?" Avi asked.

"The doctors say she might need several and a series of braces, too."

"That sounds ominous," Avi said. He leaned closer, to listen and to observe Caitlin. As a psychoanalyst, his ability to understand rather than just hear endeared him to his patients. He squinted while listening, crinkles forming at the corners of his hazel eyes. His eyesight had been faulty from birth.

"And what happens to the girl?"

"She's having a hard time and doesn't want to go to school. The other kids tease her a lot. That's as far as I've gotten."

"How do you suppose it turns out?"

"I'm sure she has the operations and winds up with all those nasty braces, or there wouldn't be any point to the book."

"But surely she won't have to wear them all her life, will she?" Avi interjected.

"Of course not. That's the idea. It's one of those happy-ending stories. Right?"

"Do you think Grandma had a good reason for getting you that book?"

"Of course," she said. "But Grandma didn't need a book to tell me all that. I listened at the door in the doctor's office."

"Let me know how the real story turns out, won't you?" A sparkle appeared in Avi's eyes, and the start of a smile grew across his face.

"Sure . . . thanks. I'm gonna play with Shana now. Bye." She ducked back into the kitchen.

"I'll take you up on the poached eggs, Molly," Freddie called from the sunroom. As Freddie came up the hall on her way to the table, she bent over to pluck the card from the cactus planter and handed it to Avi.

"Ah, Francine Meadows. Such a nice note, and how gracious of her to send me a little something. So what *is* it?"

"There, in the hallway, that...thing. Will you look at it? It's huge. It can't stay there. We'll be falling all over it," Freddie said.

Avi strained to look over his shoulder, and when the cactus caught his peripheral vision, he did a double-take. He pushed his chair back and quickly walked into the foyer.

"Oh!" he groaned in mock despair as he surveyed it. "Oh, brother! Who'd be without it?"

His sister laughed. It was Avi's favorite expression whenever he received something outlandish.

Caitlin bounded into the foyer and placed herself directly in front of the plant. Cocking her head, she said, "That's a saguaro, Dr. Avi. It's an endangered species."

"How do you know, Caitlin?"

"We studied it in social studies, our unit on the Southwest."

"Really? But shouldn't it have arms?" he asked.

Caitlin spoke like a miniature schoolteacher. "It takes forty years to grow an arm. How old are you, Dr. Avi?"

"Seventy-six." He knew what was coming next.

Caitlin scrunched up her freckled face and placed an index finger on her lips as she calculated. "That means you'll be 116 years old," she said. "Sorry, Dr. Avi. Well, maybe you'll still be alive. You're pretty healthy."

Avi burst out laughing. But his mind was off in a more Freudian direction. Why would the newly divorced Mrs. Meadows give him such an obviously phallic gift?

Molly waited by the table in the dining room.

"Why are you still standing there, Molly?" Avi asked.

"That cactus sure is strange, if you ask me. Yes, pretty strange. And, oh, Doctor, I've got something to tell you. Miss Rachel called while you were still snoozing. She and Simon are on their way here. They're comin' about 1:30 for the weekend."

"Wonderful! That's great news, Molly. Now how about some breakfast?"

"Comin' right up, Doctor."

She put up the water for Freddie's eggs and arranged slices of honeydew melon on the breakfast plates, garnishing them with mint leaves from the garden. Then the front door chimes rang again. Greta had already climbed back up on the step stool.

"Caitlin, honey, would you get the door for me, please?" Molly asked.

"So who's the plant from?" Greta's curiosity persisted.

"Ms. Meadows from over on Orchard Street."

"You mean that snappy-dressing divorcee who's always looking up her nose at folks?" Greta asked.

"Yeah, that's the one. The doctor fixed her head up fine, and her lawyer got her lots of acrimony."

Caitlin reentered the room and knelt down on the floor to hug Shana. "Who was at the door, Caitlin?" Molly asked.

"Oh, just some guy in a sweat suit. He said he belonged here and forgot his key. But, really, Molly, I've never seen him before, so I didn't let him in."

"Oh-oh. What did he look like?" Molly asked.

"Well, he was wet and smelly...skinny with black, curly hair. He was nasty to me, too."

Just then the back door swung open and crashed against the wall stop with a bang. The wet and smelly creature stood there, bellowing. "Let me at that little twerp. I'll murder her."

Shana instantly jerked to her feet. Alert, with her tail stiff behind her, she began barking at him. Cowering, Caitlin kept Shana between the angry creature and herself.

Molly enjoyed every minute of this. "Caitlin, this is Cousin Victor, and he *does* live here. At least, he visits for a few days every now and then. He's Auntie Freddie's son. Victor, this is Caitlin Neuman from next door."

"Oh?" Victor said, as though he expected more of an explanation.

"Sorreeee!" Caitlin said, not at all apologetic. "I think I'll go home now." She edged around Victor's back, stuck her tongue out so only the others could see, and slid quietly out the back door.

Molly had trouble keeping a serious face. "How about some honeydew, scrambled eggs, and biscuits for you, Victor?"

"Sure, just as soon as I get showered."

"That you, Victor?"

"Yes, Mother."

"Would you come in for a moment? We need to talk about something." Victor pushed through the door to the dining room.

"Did you have a nice jog, dear?"

"Yes, Mother. It's a great day to be outdoors."

"Of course. Although I've never understood this running business. Everyone out for a run looks so uncomfortable, so...well, pained. What's the fun in that?"

"No pain, no gain, Mother."

"If you say so, dear, but I still don't get it. Well, then. We do have some good news: Rachel and Simon are coming. They'll be here this afternoon."

"Wonderful." Victor scowled, knowing the second shoe was about to drop.

"They'll be needing Rachel's room, so I hope you won't mind moving to the den for a few days." Freddie saw the miffed look on her son's face. "Now, now, the pull-out couch won't be uncomfortable at all. You like to take naps there, don't you?"

Avi decided to put an end to his sister's pleading. "Thank you, Victor. I always knew you were a good sport, someone we could count on."

Relieved, Freddie said, "I'm glad that's settled. Run along and have your shower now. You're all wet. You'll catch a chill."

"For God's sake, Mother, lay off. I'm fifty-one years old."

Victor cut across the dining room to the front hall and paused to look in the den, his habitat for the next four or five days. He leaned his forehead on the door frame and sighed deeply. He wasn't much of a reader and the room bore all the gloomy atmosphere and smells of a scholar's retreat. He saw a spacious room, perhaps sixteen feet by fourteen, each wall lined with oak bookcases. A couch, a desk and chair, a recliner, four cherry-wood end tables, and an imported oriental rug filled out the room. He sighed again and headed for the staircase.

Over breakfast, Freddie and Avi discussed what to do about the accumulation of gifts from appreciative patients.

"Freddie, where can we display that sculpture of the ballet dancer? It's actually not very Degas, but I suppose some would call it art."

"I know just the place for it. In the sunroom, where that plant just died. There are some white water marks on top of the spindled table. It would cover them perfectly." She stopped to listen to make sure Molly was out of earshot. "In fact, we have water marks on most of the tables in the house. Avi, she over-waters the plants and doesn't mop up the spill-over. Nothing I say makes any difference."

"I suppose not."

"And what about that monstrous cactus?"

Avi thought for a minute. Finally he said, "Let's put it in the den for now." Together, he and Freddie slowly maneuvered the cactus through the den door and hoisted it onto an end table, where it seemed to overwhelm its small perch.

Their silent satisfaction at finding a roost for the latest gift was broken by a shrill cry from the kitchen and Molly's scolding voice.

"The doctor's not going to be happy about this, not one bit, uh-uh, no sireee." Avi rushed to the kitchen, and as he pushed through the swinging door, he saw Greta on the step stool, unsteady and sobbing. Tears hovered on her gaunt cheeks. A Royal Worcester cup lay on the floor, shattered and scattered beyond recognition.

Victor came down the stairs carrying two lumpy soft-pack suitcases, a black sock and a T-shirt hanging out of one; the other closed on several inches of shirt sleeve. Once in the room, he threw both bags on the floor in front of the sofa and swore.

Freddie stuck her head in the door. "Shush, Victor, someone will hear you."

"And what of it, Mother? It's nothing they haven't heard before."

"What's your problem, Victor? We're guests here."

"You're not just a guest, Mother. You have your own permanent room, somewhere to lay your head and a place to put your things. I'm forced to live out of these damn suitcases for the next four days."

"You eat and sleep here free, enjoying the unquestioned generosity of your dear Uncle Avi. Yet you show him and his children no respect. Make an effort, son, if not for your sake, then, please, for mine."

"I'll try, Mom, really I'll try."

"Thank you, Victor. You can be such a dear when you want to." She liked it when he called her Mom. It made her feel closer to him.

"Eh, Mom?"

"What, dear?"

"Can I have the keys to your car? I want to run down to the inn for a couple of hours and then I have a job interview over in Washington."

Her shoulders stiffened. "The inn first? How many more scotches, Victor? And how many more card games that you can't cover?" Tears welled up in Freddie's eyes. She pulled a hanky from her waist pocket and dabbed at her face.

Victor had been prepared to retort with another smarting remark, but seeing his mother's tears took the sharp edge from his voice. He gathered her into his arms and hugged her. "I don't have any money to drink and gamble with," he whispered in her ear.

"That didn't stop you last time."

"Things are different now. Give me a break, Mother. I'm trying to straighten out my life."

"I'd like to believe you." Freddie reached into her pocket once more and this time drew out a ring of keys. She pressed his fingers around the keys while he kissed her affectionately on the cheek. He slid slowly out of her grasp and out the front door.

CHAPTER 4

OPEN ARMS AND CLOSED DOORS

"Is this one of those hick villages you can't get to from here? It's one o'clock already, and we've been driving for hours." A sharp turn had jarred Simon awake. "I'd offer to drive, Rachel, but I haven't the foggiest as to where we are."

"Simmer down, Simon. Everything's under control."

It had been half an hour since Rachel had left the interstate. The southern Maryland roads proved to be well maintained stretches of divided highway, flanked by sweeping expanses of tobacco farms and pastel clapboard houses. Now she slowed and swung into the left lane, blinker clicking away as she rounded the corner of the turnoff. Split rail fences edged fields of tall cornstalks, paling and withering, a few ears spared from the late summer harvest. There were other reminders of fall: a bite in the air, a rickety roadside wagon with pumpkins and berry jams for sale. Rachel continued to drive a little too rapidly for the narrow, winding roadbed to suit her husband, and a little too intently to suit her own fatigue.

"We're only minutes from Black Rain Creek. In fact, there it is ahead of us." She indicated a pair of signs where the road ended in a tee. Captain Asher's Crab House sign led to the left; the Inn at Gander Pointe sign to the right, only three miles. "I can smell the seafood already," she said.

"Really?"

"No, silly, but I can sure remember what it tastes like." Rachel closed in behind a local farmer on his tractor and impatiently tried to edge around him and the hay wagon he towed.

"Take it easy. We're not in that much of a rush to get killed, are we?"

"Okay, okay, you're right." She braked gently to a comfortable distance behind the farmer and relaxed.

The road grade rose slightly, and for the first time, Simon noticed water on the left, tall cattail reeds, and wetland grasses. The dark, murky surface of the waters caused the high afternoon sun to glare like an intense fire, and the mirror effect fascinated him. "Wow! It's like an oil fire without smoke."

"That's Black Rain Creek. It's got a shallow, muddy bottom that churns up in the rain into hundreds of bubbling springs. Isn't it beautiful? The water is never clear--just plain murky, and the tides make it brackish. It's too shallow for boating, so it's a perfect watershed for fish and fowl alike. I really miss all this."

The tractor turned into a dirt lane, pulling the hay wagon out of their line of view. Before them stood the inn. A wide white verandah wrapped around three sides of the three-story, wood-frame building. A more modern, two-story brick extension sprawled behind it and elled to the left. The inn overlooked the narrow goose-neck shape where the creek struggled to meet the Chesapeake Bay. The sign on the front lawn read "FINEST LAID BACK LODGING & THE BEST SEAFOOD YOU EVER ATE." A much smaller sign on the pole out at the road displayed "BLACK RAIN CREEK DRIVE."

"You can actually smell the cooking from here," said Simon. "I didn't realize how hungry I was."

"You poor dear. Molly will fix you something. She'll feed you whether you want it or not. It's her way. Say, that's strange..." Rachel abruptly pressed her foot to the brake. "That looks like my cousin Vic up there on the verandah, talking to that man in the black suit." She slowed to the road's shoulder and tooted the horn, but the two men ignored her.

"Oh-oh! The black suit just pushed your cousin against the wall." Simon watched as the man grabbed Victor's shirt collar in his fist. Rachel tooted again. This time the aggressor turned toward them. His raccoon eyes scanned the road in search of the horn's source. He was dressed entirely in black with a solid white tie, rather peculiar attire for this area, she thought. And then it came to her.

"Oh, my God, Simon. That's the man from Maryland House. The guy whose car I got into. And it is definitely Vic." Her cousin seized the opportunity to avoid further confrontation by stepping through the front door of the inn and disappearing inside. The man scampered down the stairs and into a nearby car, a gray Toyota Corona like theirs. He drove right past them and disappeared in the curve of the road.

"This scares me. Should we stop and see if Victor's okay?" Rachel asked.

"I don't think he's hurt or anything. Why don't we give him an opportunity to explain later," Simon said.

Both disappointed and relieved, Rachel pulled away from the gravel shoulder onto the road again, and in another quarter mile, she turned into one of three narrow lanes that climbed steeply away from the creek bed. Trees grew more abundantly here. A tall hedgerow appeared on the right and left, seemingly endless, except for breaks allowed for driveways and mailboxes.

"How do you know whose driveway is whose?" Simon asked. "They all look alike."

"See that big green reflector on the tree up ahead? Daddy had that put up years ago. It works great, especially at night."

A seldom-used wrought iron gate, intended to go between two majestic stone posts, was folded back against the perfectly clipped hedgerow. A two-car garage sat opposite a circular asphalt driveway. Rachel rolled to a stop beside the garage.

Shana began barking from her pen in the backyard even before Rachel opened the car door. Goldens had been a part of the Kepples' family life since Rachel was eleven. Shana-mania became number three, after Oedipus Rex and Siggy. Shana raised herself onto her hind legs, her paws resting atop the chain-link fence. Rachel ran to the pen, leaned over the fence, and hugged Shana, letting the dog lick her cheeks freely.

"Did you miss me, girl, did ya, huh?"

Simon stood by the car and tried to view the house from there. It was nearly impossible to see anything but a mass of brick, so he sauntered across the driveway down to the start of the front walk, a long, slightly curved path of tan and mauve stone.

From his new perspective, Simon began learning about his father-in-law. The Kepple house welcomed visitors with an aura of warmth and friendliness. About fifty years old, the traditional two-story abode of pearl-gray brick spread under a succession of charcoal hip roofs, several of which looked like afterthoughts.

The stone walk up to the house ended at a three-step stoop. Recessed panels of leaded glass arched above the broad door of gleaming chestnut. A stunning brass replica of a golden retriever's head served as a door knocker. Black shuttered windows provided a smart contrast to the brick.

The door swung open and Avi emerged. "Simon, my boy, welcome!"

Avi approached Simon as if to shake his hand, but decided to embrace him instead. This unexpected and genuine affection took Simon by surprise. He hugged his father-in-law back. Aunt Freddie waited at the door with a grand smile on her face.

"Leave the bags for later," Avi said. "There's plenty of time for that." Together, with Avi's hand on his back, the two men climbed the steps to Freddie.

"Come in. Come on in." Standing one step above him, Freddie grabbed Simon by the shoulders and planted a large kiss square on his cheek. "Simon, dear, it's so good to see you again." She led him into the foyer, took both his hands in her own, and held him at arm's length. Simon tactfully managed to free himself from her tight grip.

They heard a loud screech of delight from Molly, so everyone could safely assume that Rachel had come in through the kitchen door.

"Simon, dear, you must be starved," Freddie said. She led him to the dining room and went to the kitchen door to greet her niece, but met Rachel already coming through it, running, arms out, to her father.

After the silent embrace, She laid her head on Avi's shoulder. And then she saw Freddie waiting patiently for her turn. This embrace was different; full of chatter and squealing, something Avi couldn't abide.

"Enough now, let's have lunch. We'll talk. Molly made sandwiches and noshes." Avi picked up his little silver bell and, as always, took pleasure in his ritual of ringing for her to serve them. Molly had set an elegant table right after breakfast, and on cue, she swept into the room carrying a large silver tray. Slices of rare roast beef, juicy turkey, glazed ham, and Danish Havarti lay across flaky croissant halves and thick slabs of seeded rye. Hearts of palm, alfalfa sprouts, radishes carved into roses, and marinated mushrooms appeared on a second silver tray. Molly's one concession to prepackaged food, potato chips, filled a china bowl. On the buffet sat a platter of fudge brownies and bunches of green grapes.

"Oh Molly, I can never forget how fabulous a chef you are, but when I'm actually here, everything's even better than I remembered it."

"Rachel, honey, wait till you see what I got in store for tomorrow night's shindigger: all my especialties."

Rachel pointed her nose toward the kitchen. "Mmm, I can tell." She turned to her father. "What's going on tomorrow night, Daddy?"

Avi put down his roast beef sandwich and dabbed dramatically at his mouth with a linen napkin. "It's a long story." He got up from the table and fumbled for a set of keys in his pocket. Selecting one, he undid the lock in the heavy buffet and slid open the middle drawer. He folded back a layer of table linens and removed a blue velvet jewelry case, which he carried back to the table and set in front of him.

"You remember Hubert Marche died, oh, about a year ago," he said. "Well, this July, the Marche family offered Hubert's mansion and its contents as a museum to the township. The mansion is now officially the Marche Museum."

"How exciting," Rachel said.

"And expensive," added Simon.

"Exactly," Avi continued. "However, the bequest came with a small stipend for a part-time curator and some caretaking for the grounds--hardly enough to keep the doors open. Anyway, the township council asked for volunteers to form a local Historical Society and a number of the more prominent citizens were recruited."

"Including you, Daddy?"

"Including me."

"Daddy, this is something totally new for you."

"It is that. I thought it would be fun at my stage in life to be involved in the arts. And with my shortened workday I do have the time. Of course, just creating a Historical Society did not solve the financial crisis. We had to raise money somehow."

Rachel helped herself to a fistful of potato chips. "So, Daddy, how did you raise the money?"

"Well, your Aunt Freddie came up with an excellent idea: to hold an auction. Various treasures in the mansion were auctioned off with an unusual stipulation: that they remain in the museum. The museum benefitted, and there were substantial tax advantages for the buyers." Avi fiddled with the case in front of him, obviously enjoying the suspense he'd created.

"And that velvet case?" Simon guessed no one else would play Avi's game.

"I thought you'd never ask." Avi worked on the reluctant catch until the lid sprung noisily open to reveal a glittering mass of light and color on a bed of white satin. Everyone stood and edged closer for a better look. It was a magnificently bejeweled gold key four inches in length, with a fleur-de-lis thumbpiece. The long, graceful shaft ended in a squarish filigree resembling an oriental brushwork character. Its teeth would fit the pawls and stops of some intricate lock. A single-eyed, gold link dangled from the end of the thumbpiece, obviously meant for a chain.

"The diamond in the center of the thumbpiece is estimated to be just over two carats," Avi said. "The three perfectly matched rubies at the leaf tips come to another carat. The scrolled shaft and teeth are alloyed for strength. The key is believed to be at least two hundred years old." He paused, enjoying the limelight.

"It's gorgeous. What is it worth?" Rachel asked.

"Up to now, we've only been able to guess, but tomorrow night we'll have an expert look at it. I paid thirty-five thousand, but I'm told it's worth a good deal more. Of course, the actual transaction is contingent upon expert appraisal and certification."

"What's it to? What could such a fragile-looking key possibly open?" Simon asked.

Avi shrugged his shoulders. "I wish I knew, my boy, I wish I knew."

"Were there many objects like this in the auction?" Simon was already beginning to enjoy his weekend stay here.

"About a hundred of the most valued small articles were auctioned off, but none quite so interesting as this one. In fact, several of the new Historical Society members did some research on it. That's why I'm looking forward so much to tomorrow night's meeting. They'll be reporting what they found."

The door chimes rang, and Molly cut through the dining room to answer them. Avi took a look at his watch. It was too early for his four o'clock appointment.

"Doctor," Molly called, "there's a delivery man out here with a humonstrous box."

"It's a special security display cabinet," Avi replied. "Have him bring it in the den. I'll be there in a minute to show him where to install it."

"Daddy, I thought the key would be kept in the museum."

"It will be. But first they have to upgrade the security system, and then the insurance people have to approve it. Meanwhile, I'm the custodian of this piece. Since the robbery up at Marche House, several hundred of the remaining objets d'art are stored in an Annapolis bank vault. Please excuse me now while I take care of this business."

Avi followed Molly to the den, where the delivery man had pushed a hand truck with the case on it. It was sixteen inches square and thirty-six inches tall. Avi directed the man to the proposed location, shoving aside Victor's two hastily packed suitcases.

The delivery man placed the cabinet eighteen inches in front of a bookcase, centered on the window wall. As he opened the access door, he began to explain the features of the case. "The top is made of thick, clear glass. All of the remaining sides are steel, dressed to look like oak. A combination door gives you access to the velvet display shelf under the glass as well as the floor-mounted hardware below." Pausing to hook his thumbs inside his gray coverall pockets, the delivery man looked up at Avi. "Sir, I'll need to drill some holes and run some stove bolts up through the basement floor and cinch them down inside the base, if that's okay with you."

"Can you drill the holes between the bookcase and carpet? I don't want any holes in the carpeting."

"Sure thing, sir."

"Good. When you're ready, the basement is down the hall, second door on the left."

The delivery man continued his spiel. "If you're wondering about the glass, whether it's strong enough..." He took a hammer and struck a sizable blow to the display window. "It's practically indestructible. And nice and clear, too, for excellent display. One of our business cards is on the shelf. See how easy it is to read through the glass?"

Avi nodded and removed the card. The delivery man pulled a small key from an envelope taped to the side of the case. "You'll need this to change the combination to one of your own." He demonstrated, using a ten-left, twenty-right, thirty-left, forty-right combination. Avi wrote down the current combination on the business card and laid it down on top of the case. He would select a new combination later, he decided, when he secured the key for the day. He thanked the man and left him in the den to complete his work.

Avi rejoined the others at the dining room table. Molly peered over Rachel's shoulder at the jeweled key. On seeing Avi, she picked up several plates and carried them back to the kitchen.

"Molly, has Greta gone home yet?"

"Yes, sir, she felt real bad about the cup, Doctor. She'll be back tomorrow night to help with the Hysterical Society."

"*Historical* Society, Molly." Freddie just couldn't let Molly get away with that, no matter how many times she tried.

Avi grinned. "Good, thank you, Molly."

Rachel closed the jewelry case and handed it to her father, who returned it to the buffet drawer.

"Remember, no one knows where I keep it but the four of us," Avi said as he secured the drawer once more.

"Daddy, who are they going to get for a part-time curator way out here?"

"We already have one, Olivia Raphael. She's also consented to chair the Society for two years." He turned to Simon and explained. "Olivia has a master's in art history and her undergraduate degree was in archaeology. She teaches both over at Georgetown University several nights a week."

The door chimes sounded again and Avi consulted his watch. He waited for Molly to announce his patient. "It's Mrs. Whitley. I showed her to your office, Doctor."

Avi left and Molly stayed to chat, taking her time picking up the empty sandwich tray. "That lady . . . oh, she's a knock-up, that one. Wears her dresses cut so low, she ought to be abreasted."

Simon sputtered trying to hold back his laughter, and Rachel faked a kick to his shin. But she giggled, too.

"Molly, stop that infernal gossiping," Freddie said. "Don't you have something to do in the kitchen?" Molly slunk unhappily out of the room.

"Aunt Freddie, weren't you just a little harsh with Molly?"

"Perhaps, but she must learn her place around here."

"Aw, Molly's almost family."

"She knows that all too well."

Half an hour later Molly stuck her head through the door. "The cabinet man's all done screwing. He's leaving now. Wants somebody to sign him off."

"Okay, Molly. I'll take care of it." Avi left the room.

"Aunt Freddie," Rachel said, "is Victor in town? I mean, is he visiting you?"

"Yes, dear. Why do you ask?"

"We're not sure, but Simon and I thought we saw him arguing with some man down in front of the inn. We honked the horn, but whoever it was ignored us."

Freddie looked dejected and spoke hesitantly. "Victor's fallen on some hard times, and your father has been kind enough to let him stay here until he gets back on his feet. He was staying in your room, but he moved to the den when he heard you and Simon were coming."

"Could the man have been Vic?"

"I don't know, dear. He left here right after breakfast and borrowed my car. He said he was going to the inn and then to Washington to see a man about a job."

"Has he given up his Atlantic City cronies?"

"Oh, yes. He made me a promise. He's learned his lesson quite well."

Obviously, Rachel thought, you haven't learned yours, yet.

First, they heard the front door close, and then the door to the den.

Aunt Freddie, a tremor in her voice, said, "He's back."

CHAPTER 5

MANSION IN THE SKY

Freddie paused at the den door. Her knuckle went silently to the wood several times before she actually knocked. "Victor?"

"Go away, Mother. I want some time to myself."

"Victor, we need to talk."

"Not now, Mother!"

"Yes, dear, now!" She heard the springs of the recliner adjusting to eject her son, and seconds later, he unlocked and opened the door. She sat down on the sofa.

"What's so important that it must be now?"

"Victor, you're being terribly rude. Hiding and sulking in a room away from your cousins doesn't exactly repay your Uncle Avi's kindness. You promised you'd do better. Rachel and Simon came all this way and you're ignoring them. You're here as Avi's guest."

"And you never let me forget it, do you?" Victor bowed his head and intoned, "We are eternally grateful." The sarcasm knifed through Freddie and caused her to remember a lifetime of difficulty with her only son.

"You will stop this nonsense this instant or..."

"Or what, Mother?"

"Or...or get out. Leave!" She trembled as the rage within her rose to meet his insolence. She began to cry and, as usual, Victor came over to sit beside her and comfort her.

"I'm sorry, Mother, but I've just had the worst of days."

Freddie's breast heaved a breath of relief as she regained her composure. "Did your interview go badly, dear?"

"Very badly. I didn't realize that the application meant actually buying a franchise. I misunderstood. I thought I'd applied for franchise manager. He expected me to put up a lot of money."

"Did the interview take place over at the inn?"

Victor stiffened with surprise. "Er, why, yes. I asked the guy to meet me there instead of in Washington. How'd you know?"

"Rachel mentioned that she saw you there arguing with some man when she passed by earlier this afternoon." Freddie was trying hard to read her son's expression. His spade-shaped face with its narrow chin and murky brown eyes betrayed nothing.

"Oh, that. The guy was really pissed, coming all the way over here for nothing."

"Victor, dear." Her voice dissolved into saccharine sweetness now.

"Yes, Mother." He knew what to expect.

"You're keeping all your promises?"

"Of course, Mother." He quickly wrapped her up in his arms. "Of course," he repeated over her shoulder.

"Good, I'm glad we talked. Now, let's go greet your cousins."

"Okay, okay." He removed the key from the inside of the door and locked it from the outside. Freddie took her son's hand and led him down the hall to join the others.

In the sunroom, while everyone else chatted, Molly stood by, leisurely watering the plants: ivies in woven baskets; philodendron in planters of slightly corroded brass; and African violets in English porcelain bowls--the soil in each already soggy before she started.

She felt at home listening in; she belonged to this family, didn't she? She considered it her right--no, her duty--to know what went on in the house. How else could she be useful to her employer? Yesterday she'd heard Avi mumbling to himself that he couldn't find a pile of letters he had to answer. And she'd instantly told him: "In the upper right-hand drawer of your desk, Doctor." He'd given her a strange look, but she ignored it.

"Watch what you're doing, Molly," snapped Freddie as she entered the sunroom with Victor. "You're getting the carpet all wet."

Shana stood up and greeted Victor by sniffing his male parts. He, in turn, pushed her away. "Get down, you horny mutt."

Avi seized Shana by the collar and scolded her in a tone that only brought on more affection.

"You shouldn't scold her for that, Doctor," Molly said. "It's her natural inspiration."

"Nevertheless, put her out, please."

Rachel jumped to her feet. "Wait, I've got a better idea. We'll take Shana for a walk. Victor, would you like to join us?"

Victor looked over at his mother before answering. He wanted in the worst way to say no, but dared not defy the determined set of her chin. "Yeah, okay, why not?"

Shana led Rachel, Simon, and Victor down Locust Lane to Black Rain Creek Drive at the base of the hill, and they crossed over to the creek side, following the rocky shoreline eastward, toward the bay. The late afternoon sun gently warmed their backs.

Simon spoke first. "So, Vic, how's the insurance business?"

"Pretty bad right now. The company I worked for merged with a bigger one, and they didn't have room for as many agents. And what's worse, the market's been sluggish for over a year, which makes it pretty tough to make a living when you're working straight commission. So now I'm shopping around for a new profession."

"How's it going? Any ideas or nibbles?"

"Not really, Simon. It's so easy to get discouraged. No one wants to hire someone in their fifties."

"I know. That's true in my profession as well. It wasn't always that way. An engineer with thirty years' experience used to be really sought after. Today they value experience only if it's been acquired in the last five years. It's ironic: technology is moving too fast. Whole inventories can become obsolete if companies stop to market anything."

Rachel asked, "Vic, were you down at the inn earlier today?"

Victor decided to be honest. "I'm afraid so."

"What was that scuffle all about? It looked rather unpleasant. You don't have to answer if you don't want to," she added.

"A small misunderstanding. At least small on my part, large on his. He made the trip over from Washington for nothing. He expected up-front money for a deal."

Simon had the leash, and suddenly Shana began to bark and chase wild Canada geese along the reeds. Knowing she was incapable of overtaking them, Simon gave her rein and ran along behind her for about a hundred and fifty feet before pulling her up sharply. Puffing and sucking wind, he sat down on a rock at the water's edge to wait for the others. The trek had taken him round the bend and out of sight of his wife and cousin, and the terrain and surroundings had abruptly changed.

A short wooden pier jutted out of the craggy rocks into the dark water. Several planks were missing altogether and the pilings were rotting away so that the entire structure rolled in rhythm with even the gentlest wave. A short rickety flight of wooden stairs led from the pier to the road above. On the inland side of the road, scaling the heights of the cliff, a half-dozen flights of stone steps led to a stone-walled overlook.

Simon had to shield his eyes with his hand to look up at the mansion above and beyond the wall. A small cloud crossed the sun's path long enough for him to take in the immense beauty of the structure. He saw a clever marriage of antebellum plantation and English manor house. Black slate covered the gently sloped roofs. White paint adorned the upper walls of wood. Coarse sandstone stood as a foundation. The overall effect seemed magnificent, yet somehow sinister framed in the scattered clouds. Windows abounded, telling him there must be twenty to thirty rooms up there. Many of the stained glass windows gave off hues of azure blue, rose, or lemon-yellow.

The small, helpful cloud floated away, and the sun returned to pain his sight and force him to squint. He turned away in time to see the others catching up with him.

Shana plopped herself down on the large flat rock next to Simon, panting, content just to watch the birds well out of her reach. Despite his morning jogs, Victor was breathing so heavily he could say nothing. Instead, he pushed the dog off the rock and sat down in her place. Shana meekly slunk down onto the sandy soil.

"It's okay, Shana," said Rachel, stroking the golden's head. "He didn't mean it."

"I didn't?" Victor asked.

Simon disregarded Victor's remark. "What's that place up there?"

"Oh, I see you've discovered the castle of Black Rain Corners," Rachel said, quite pleased.

"Then that must be Marche House."

"You got it--the residence of the late philanthropist Hubert Marche. He endowed the museum," she said.

"I know that," Simon answered, "but where did all his wealth come from?"

"Tobacco, I suppose. There's a bunch of it still being grown on the other side of that hill."

"It's so formal-looking for this country setting. Whatever possessed a tobacco farmer to build a place like that?" Simon asked.

"I don't think he did. He inherited it from his father. Oh, now I remember. His father was some kind of French aristocrat, probably rich to start with."

"Ever been inside?" Simon asked.

"No, but I've always wanted to go," Rachel said. "Vic, you've been there, haven't you? Didn't you use to chum around with Martha Marche?"

"Yes and yes. Marti Marche and I were friends in high school, at least until a rich new family with a bunch of kids moved into town. Then, just like that, I wasn't good enough for the Marches. Marti eventually married Felix Thornberry. He's a lawyer. They live in Washington now, although Felix spends a good deal of his time here in town. A nice sort, Felix, but, professionally, he's an ambulance chaser."

"So what's it like inside, Vic?" Simon asked.

"Fabulous, of course. Oh, I went there a number of times. Mostly in the kitchen or the game room, and even a few times in Marti's bedroom. Once I got lost and wandered down this long hall with paintings and drapes from floor to ceiling. The great man, Hubert, found me admiring the paintings and sent me home. I was crushed, but I still do have fond memories of the place."

"Is it still furnished so lavishly, Vic?" asked Simon.

"I've no way of knowing for sure, but I don't see why it wouldn't be. After all, they *are* turning it into a museum."

"I think we'd better start back now. I just felt a few drops of rain." Simon held his left palm up and out in front of him.

"We won't melt," Rachel said. "I'm content just to be back home in the peaceful surroundings of the Chesapeake."

Shana pulled hard on the leash. She had spotted a pair of mallard ducks bobbing on the waves. Without warning, she bolted over the rocks down to the water and plunged in up to her neck, jerking Simon along behind her. He succeeded in braking at the water's edge, just short of soaking his shoes and pants. The leash slackened and the next thing they knew Shana had emerged from the muddy bay shaking an icy, mucky spray all around her. Victor, still seated on the large, flat rock, caught the brunt of it. He was about to swear, but thought better of it. He joined the others in laughing at himself, something he hadn't experienced in many years.

"Molly will not be thrilled with this. Shana'll need a bath," Rachel said.

"If we don't get back soon, we'll all get a bath, like it or not," said Simon. The clouds were moving faster now, gathering in a dark warning. A gentle, fizzy sprinkle began.

As they crested the hill and pushed their way between the hedges directly into Avi's backyard, Molly waited for them at the door. She laughed when she saw Shana. "Come here, girl, I'll take care of you." Shana patiently leaned against the chain-link fence of her pen while Molly worked on her, hosing off the mud and stench of the bay, then ruffling and fuzzing up the fur with old towels.

"Okay, girl, you're done. Go in the kitchen now," Molly said. But Shana wasn't ready to settle down. She raced through the kitchen, straight to the front hall, and threw her body down, head first, on the luxurious oriental rug, rolling over and over. Molly sighed. She knew that Shana would always have the last word, or roll.

"In a minute, hon," Simon called. "I can't hear a word you're saying with the water running." He stood at the sink brushing his teeth. He had to bend his knees almost ninety degrees to see himself in the mirror. "A bathroom for Munchkins," he muttered, eyeing the toilet. A tall person had to assume the fetal position to use it.

But Simon found Rachel's bedroom a pleasant refuge, wallpapered in small Williamsburg-blue flowers. A print of Van Gogh's *Man at the Gates of the Public Garden* hung on one dormered wall. He would like to have taken a closer look, but decided to steer clear under penalty of a bumped head.

He discovered Rachel already in bed, sitting with Moss Hart's *Act One* propped open. Her Minnie Mouse T-shirt pulled down over her knees gave her a childlike sweetness.

"Now, what were you saying when I so rudely interrupted you?" He sat down on her side of the bed and squeezed her calf.

"Just thinking how nice Vic was this afternoon."

"And how nasty he was to Aunt Freddie at the dinner table."

"I wonder what makes him tick. I don't think even Daddy knows."

"Well, I do. You don't have to be a psychoanalyst to know that he's a fifty-one-year-old spoiled brat who's too lazy to find a decent job."

"Oh, and now I suppose you'll want to hang a journeyman's shingle below my father's?"

"I hadn't thought about that. Do you think he'd mind?"

Rachel laughed. "It could be a new specialty: engineering the mind. But seriously, dear, I do feel sorry for Aunt Freddie. She's such a good person, and she's worked so hard all her life. As much as I used to care for Vic, if he were my son, I'd have strangled him by now. I can't stand leeches, especially when they're able-bodied."

"Why are we whispering, sweetheart?"

"Well, for one thing, Aunt Freddie's room is on the other side of that wall and Vic is in the den just below us."

"Does that mean we can't fool around?" Simon got up and walked to his side of the bed. "And not for the whole weekend?" He slipped under the comforter. "A whole long weekend?"

Rachel looked over at the pitiful, sheepish expression on her husband's face. "Of course it doesn't mean that," she grinned. "Not unless you insist on making noise, that is." She slid down to kiss her husband's furry chest, when the phone rang. It only rang once, but she picked it up anyway.

She heard Victor's voice. "It's late and I don't want you calling here. What the hell do you want from me, man? I'll come up with it as soon as I can." And then he hesitated. "Rachel? Is that you? Get off. This is a private conversation."

CHAPTER 6

BUBBA'S DELI
Friday, October 24, 1980

Bubba's Deli and General Store, with its view of both the creek and the bay, sat on the corner of Maple Run Lane across from the Town Hall. This junction of the shore road and Maple Run, the middle road heading up and away from the creek, served as the town center. Bubba's prospered in a modest sort of way, being the sole store of any type for nineteen miles. A supermarket could hardly have survived serving the paltry number of families, so Schlemuel and Bertha Bubbashlufsky filled the niche famously. Schlem made a trip to Baltimore every other day to pick up produce and specialty products in his Dodge Ram pickup. Black Rain Corners residents could order almost anything from the big city by phone, and Schlem would cart it back for them. The profit margin wasn't his first priority.

Schlem and Bertha had emigrated here from Poland right after World War II. Their forty-eight-star citizenship flags hung side by side on the front door. Their deli, pale blue clapboard trimmed in yellow gingerbread, emanated a quaint Hansel and Gretel charm. No electronic scanners here, either.

Out front, Schlem had just finished culling the produce bins, tossing the spoilage into a carton, when he heard grating gravel behind him. Olivia Raphael and Caitlin pedaled up on the gravel apron, braking in front of the store.

"Hi, Mr. B." Their two voices chimed in almost perfect sync.

"Good morning, ladies. A *bissel* cool for biking, is it not?"

"No, sir, Mr. B, it's a most perfect day," Caitlin said as she dismounted her bike and leaned it up against a utility pole.

Olivia parked hers the same way. "There's no holding Caitlin back this morning, so I thought a brisk ride and breakfast here might be just the ticket."

"Well, now, something special my Bertha can fix you?" They walked through the sprawling store to a jalousied room at the rear. The wooden sign over the archway read KOSHER STYLE DELICATESSEN. Three small Formica tables with padded tubular chairs dominated the deli floor space. Boxes and cans of Kosher products lined the shelves. Customers stepping through the archway instantly embraced a deliciousness. Heavenly scents filled their nostrils: warm bagels and braided *challah*; wickedly rich soft cheeses; whitefish salad; and bright-orange lox.

"Can I have scrambled eggs and a cinnamon-raisin bagel with cream cheese and jelly, please?" It was Caitlin's favorite breakfast here.

"A good choice. And you, Mrs. Raphael?" asked Schlem.

"Nova, cream cheese, tomato--hold the onion--on a lightly toasted bagel."

"Milk and coffee?"

"That'll be fine." Olivia pulled her chair closer to the table.

"I tell Bertha." Schlem turned toward the kitchen just as his wife came through the doorway.

"I hear, I hear, you don't have to tell me." She set down a small plate with two thin slices of spiraled cake. "A little something extra," she said, "still warm from the oven."

"Yum! What is this, Mrs. B?" asked Caitlin.

"*Mund* cake. Ground poppy seed, diced apple, sugar, cinnamon." She left the room to fix their order, shuffling along in her slippers as if her feet perpetually hurt.

Olivia noticed Schlem lingering at the table. She saw a world map of worry woven into the wrinkles of his face. "Is anything wrong, Mr. B?"

"No, not wrong, Mrs. Raphael, but...uh...I have small question, if you don't mind my asking."

"Go ahead, Mr. B. Don't be shy."

"Well, thirty-two years ago when we come over from old country, we bring only few valuable things we can carry. We turned them to cash when we needed them. Most those things are gone now; the cash we got we put in the business. But there's one piece from my *zeyde*, my grandfather, I can't give up." He hesitated.

"Go on. Tell me more," Olivia said.

"It's true? You're going to be the curator of the new museum?"

"Yes, Mr. B, that's true enough."

"My oil picture--you'd be willing to look at it, maybe?" he asked.

"I'm not authorized to purchase any new items for the museum yet. We're just getting started and we're extremely short on financing. I'm sorry."

"Oh, no, Mrs. Raphael, not to sell it. I wouldn't want to do that."

"Then, Mr. B, what exactly would you like from me?"

"Just to look, please."

"I'd be glad to, but all I could do would be to venture a guess as to its worth."

"I get it from apartment upstairs. I bring it to you and you see."

Bertha brought the food out on a tray and set it before them with the single word: "Enjoy!"

Schlem waited patiently until they had finished eating. He cleared the table first and returned with a framed miniature oil painting. He stood before Olivia, shyly holding the six-inch by four-inch portrait in front of her.

Olivia took the painting in her own hands. "She's charming, exquisite even. What did you call her? Sadie?"

"No, *zeyde*. It means grandfather. I think it is his mother when she was little girl."

Olivia studied the painting. The solemn Victorian-era child appeared to be about ten years old and wore a yellow party dress with a lace collar. Olivia looked closely at the skilled brushwork, the light and shadows, and the rosy flesh tones. "This artist painted very professionally, but where did the frame come from? Certainly not from Europe. It's too crude to adorn an oil of this quality."

Schlem turned an unusual shade of pink. "I am guilty of that. I make frame from old scraps of molding I find out back. In old barn from behind the store."

Olivia apologized for her bluntness. "You know, Mr. B," she said, "I think you have a valuable painting here, but you might want to get it reframed if it's a family heirloom." She ran her fingers over the frame. Something about it intrigued her. It bore the *ess* shape of inch-and-a-half cavetto molding, and the corners were mitered well enough. A horizontal row of wheat sprigs, hand-carved in an alternating left-right pattern, ran along its length. From the unpainted reverse side it appeared to be very old wood. She couldn't tell for sure. Where had she seen that pattern before?

"Would you mind terribly if I borrowed the painting for a few days? I'll be very careful with it."

"Take it, please," he said, his face glowing with pleasure.

Caitlin grew bored with all this art talk. "Mr. B, can I go out back and sit in your antique car?"

"Sure, but you be careful, and wipe your feet before you get in." No one could pay Schlem a higher compliment than to ask to see his pride and joy. He reached into the nearest refrigerated case and cut a piece of halvah for her.

"Thanks, Mr. B." Caitlin happily accepted the wedge of gritty candy made from honey and ground-up sesame seeds, cradling it in a napkin as she hurried out.

Schlem owned a 1938 burgundy Buick in mint condition. Occasionally, he would use it to make home deliveries, but mainly he liked to show it off in antique auto parades, where he rode high and proud.

Schlem walked slowly with Olivia to the front of the deli, where he left her and began helping the next customer. "Coming right up--a dozen cheese blintzes...."

Olivia headed out the front door to retrieve Caitlin, only to find Molly Mesta standing in front of her.

"Hi, Mrs. Raphael. You're up early."

"Yes, good morning, Molly. How did you get here?"

"The doctor dropped me off and went on to get his head trimmed at the barber."

Olivia smiled. "Yes, the doctor is very careful about his appearance."

"Uh-huh! I told him he dresses for style. I dress for conversational. Can't pay attention to all those trivials, you know." Molly's abundant figure was stuffed into a lavender house dress and covered with a woolly beige sweater that she could just barely button. She carried an enormous straw purse that looked like a refugee from a Mexican bazaar.

"Yes, I'm sure." Olivia stepped aside to allow Molly to enter. "Oh, Molly, is there something I can bring tonight?"

"No, ma'am."

"Do you think the doctor would like me to come early and act as hostess for him?"

"Don't know, ma'am, but the doctor sure knows how to self-host."

Olivia was suddenly embarrassed and excused herself. She went to find Caitlin.

"Molleeee!" Bertha screeched. She came shuffling out from behind the counter and the two friends embraced warmly. But the line of customers grew steadily, so Bertha went back to work, and Molly picked up a shopping basket to collect her groceries for that evening. Schlem and Bertha were so busy that when the phone rang, Bertha beckoned for Molly to answer it.

"Hello! Bubba's Deli...Molly here. Oh, hi, Shirley. No, I don't work here. Just helping out. They're rushed now a mile a minute. I can take your order. Two pounds corny beef...six knockwish...three half-sours from the barrel." Molly scribbled for several more minutes. "Got it! Schlem will deliver it later today. How ya been?"

Molly held her hand over the phone. "Order for Shirley." She ripped the top sheet from the pad and handed it to Bertha. Taking her hand away from the mouthpiece, "You don't say...She's pregnant? With triplets? You gotta be a horse to have that."

"Molly, don't gossip so much. It's a business phone," Bertha whispered.

"Gotta go now, Shirl. Bye."

Molly hung up and finished her shopping, checking off the items on her list: "shlivered amonds, onones, cramberries, water chessnuts, mushroons...."

Schlem helped her carry the brown bags to the parking lot, where Avi already sat in the car waiting for her, passing the time with the large-type edition of the previous Sunday's *New York Times*.

"Good morning, Schlem."

"Morning, Doc. Nice day."

"Yes, thank you for helping." Avi pulled the trunk release and Schlem deposited the bags there. Molly squeezed into the car next to Avi. He shifted into gear and moved out onto Black Rain Creek Drive, turning left onto Locust Lane. Ahead, he saw Olivia and Caitlin walking their bicycles up the hill.

"Good morning," Olivia called as Avi crept past them. Avi and Molly both waved from the car.

Olivia walked a few more steps, pushed her bike to the edge of the road, and then stopped in her tracks. She removed Schlem's painting from her bicycle basket and stared at it.

Caitlin kept walking until she realized her grandmother hadn't kept up with her. She turned around and saw Olivia with the tiny painting in her hands, balancing her bike against her hip. "What's wrong, Grandma?"

"Now I know where I've seen it before," Olivia murmured, lost in her own thoughts. She tucked the painting back in the basket and continued up the hill.

CHAPTER 7

THE GATHERING PLACE

Freddie came through the kitchen door shaking her head. "I can't understand it," she said.

"What's wrong, Miss Freddie? You look presturbed."

"Disturbed or perturbed, Molly. There's no such word as presturbed."

"Yes, ma'am. But what's wrong?"

"The mailman's been here, but my magazine didn't come." Freddie took a cup and saucer down from the cupboard and began to pour coffee.

"Well, maybe you forgot to renew your inscription."

Freddie Moskowitz just bit her lip. Coffee sloshed onto the saucer as she turned her head and looked over the top of her glasses at Molly. Absolute innocence resided in Molly's face. So she resumed pouring, straight into the cup this time. Actually, with Avi ministering to his eleven o'clock patient and Vic still asleep, Freddie sought out Molly's company.

"Did you get everything you needed for tonight, Molly?"

"Yes, ma'am, 'cept for them silver paper doilies. I couldn't get a replica of them."

"I see. We'll just have to do without. Did you meet anyone down at Bubba's?"

"I spoke with Mrs. Raphael. Caitlin was with her."

"And what did Olivia have to say?"

"Nothing much. Just a bunch of questions about the doctor. I think she has a crush with him."

"Maybe you're right, but what did you tell her?"

"Nothing, I widestepped her questions."

Before Freddie could test her self-restraint one more time, Victor entered the room. He bent over his mother and kissed her on the cheek. "Morning, ladies."

"Morning's past, dear, as if you didn't know." His mother pointed to the cupboard. "Get yourself a cup from up there."

"I had a tough time falling asleep last night. I heard Uncle Avi up late, too. But that sandwich and milk you left me sure did the trick, Molly."

"Happy to reprieve ya."

From behind her, Victor reached his arms around as far as they would go and gave her a quick, friendly squeeze. She squealed and slipped away from him like a greased sow. Snickering, he poured from the coffeepot and set it down again.

Victor opened the refrigerator. "The cream's buried in back. I guess I'll skip it." He closed the door. "Sure is a lot of food in there. What's it for?"

"You know perfectly well, it's for the meeting tonight."

"Seems a shame, all that great food for a bunch of old Historical Society stiffs."

"Victor, you're incorrigible. And you're wrong. They're responsible citizens who care about their community and its history. They're also Uncle Avi's friends. Besides, some of them are younger than you are."

Victor laughed. "Okay, okay. You got me on that one. I should've kept my big mouth shut." His mother smiled to herself. She'd won that round, a rarity these days.

In the spacious lobby of the Inn at Gander Pointe, a brass chandelier hung from the two-story ceiling, hovering above a cozy circle of overstuffed easy chairs and potted green fakery. The registration and cashier's counters stood to the left of the columned entranceway. Through the glass doors and straight ahead, one could just make out the maitre d's station for the Chandelier Room, the inn's three-star restaurant. High paneled walls and double-storied windows encircled the lobby's staircase to the second floor, where three period-decorated suites were to be found. A wide arched passageway next to the registration counter led to the more modern accommodations in the next wing. Flanking the passageway were the lounge and bar to the left, and to the right, behind a wall of glass, a large heated swimming pool and exercise room.

Lenora Worthington strode into the familiar lobby dressed in an elegant black silk suit. A marcasite butterfly pin adorned one shoulder. Lenora wore only black for its dramatic effect. With shoulder-length jet black hair, smooth white complexion, and gray eyes, black worked for her. Tortoise-shell frames held large square glasses with thick lenses. She laid her black Gucci purse down on the registration counter and began thumbing through it for a scrap of paper with the confirmation number on it.

"We have a reservation, but--"

"Yes, Mrs. Worthington, we have your creek-side room all ready for you." The desk clerk pushed the registration card across the counter. "It's nice to have you staying with us again. Will Dr. Worthington require any assistance with your luggage?"

"No, thank you. He took the hand cart out to the car with him." She picked up the pen and filled in the necessary particulars.

"Lennie!" The deep-throated sound assaulted Lenora from the entranceway. She turned to find Martha Thornberry poised behind her, arms outstretched to deliver her trademark unavoidable hug.

"Marti, how nice to see you," Lenora said automatically. "And please don't call me 'Lennie.' You know how I feel about that."

Lenora eyed Marti's purple cashmere sweater and slacks, the designer scarf swaddling her throat, the heavy gold bracelets entrapping her wrists. Lenora knew Marti spent great sums on her clothes to compensate for wispy hair the color of burnt toast and a sallow complexion. Sometimes she found Marti bearable. Right now, Lenora just wanted to avoid the woman's rapid-fire, in-your-face speech. If left unchecked, Marti's verbal tsunami would splash forth and spill over her.

"Oooh, Lennie, the weekend's going to be so much fun. I adore getting in bed with history." She laid her hand on the back of Lenora's head. "I don't know how you manage it--I'd kill for hair like that." Lenora smiled weakly and backed up two steps.

"Marti!" a male voice whined. "If you refuse to get the bellboy, you could at least hold the door for me." Felix Thornberry struggled through the swinging front doors with two large suitcases. He dropped them both to the floor and flopped into the nearest easy chair. Flushed from the effort, he pulled down on the zipper tab of his windbreaker and flung it open, exposing his soccer-ball paunch. He smoothed the creases of his khaki slacks over his stocky legs.

"You handled it just fine, Felix, dear. You always do. Oh, there's Bucky. My, you're looking fit these days, Bucky."

"I'm *very* fit for an old geezer."

At seventy-six, Buckminster Worthington still jogged two miles each day with Lenora and maintained an ideal diet. He loved setting the pace for his sixty-one-year-old wife. Bucky stood there beside the luggage, looking every bit the Philadelphia psychoanalyst in a dark suit, conservative tie, and a head of pure white hair.

"So, my dear, where have they parked us?" Bucky asked his wife.

"Same room as last time, 203, overlooking the creek."

"Maybe we can get a room nearby and visit later," Marti said.

Lenora half-smiled politely. She took Bucky's arm, and he trailed the cart behind him while they went through the passageway to the elevator. She whispered to her husband: "Why do I always have a sense of foreboding when I'm around that woman?"

"There does seem to be an aura of trouble about Martha Thornberry," he agreed. "I just can't put my finger on what it is. But," he grinned, "don't expect her to stop calling you 'Lennie.'" With that, they disappeared into the elevator.

Back at the registration desk, the clerk told Marti, "Room 206 is as close as I can get you. It's diagonally across the hall."

"Yes, with a view of the leaf pile you call a hill out there. Oh, well, if you can't do any better, we'll take it."

"Yes, ma'am, I'm sure you'll be happy with your choice."

"By the way, has my stepsister, Heidi Hemming, checked in yet?"

"Yes, ma'am, several hours ago. I believe she and her young man are in the recreation area just now."

Marti turned to her husband and crooked her finger to beckon him. He picked up the bags, and with a strained and fatigued look, approached the arched passageway. Before he even opened his mouth, Marti told him, "Quit your bitching, Felix, and get these bags upstairs."

"But..."

"But nothing, Felix! Take our things to the elevator. I want to see if I can find Heidi." Marti tried looking through the steamed-up glass leading to the workout room and pool, but she couldn't identify anyone beyond.

On the other side of the glass, Ernest Lord fumbled while trying to secure additional ten-pound weights to the weight-lifting machine. He spent much of his working life as a gemologist and antique appraiser in a seated, hunched position. Thus, exercise had become an obsessive religion with him and the machines his sacrificial altar. His hard, lean body reflected his fidelity to that end. Despite his forty-two years and thinning hair, he'd remained a reasonably attractive man. He wore sweats and sneakers and a hotel towel around his damp neck. He'd removed the locking key to add the extra weights and now he needed to replace the key. It would not go into the next hole, no matter what orientation he tried.

"You have to push down on the load before that key will fit." The confident voice came from a tall, muscular man, who stepped down from his perch on the Stairmaster. "I had the same trouble myself earlier. Here, I'll show you." He pushed his hand down on the rack of weights and slammed the key home where it belonged. No sooner done, he shoved this hand in front of Ernest. "My name's Derrick, Derrick Powers. I'm into aerobics, health consulting, and body training."

Only a brief pair of bikini bathing trunks concealed any part of his sweating body. Wavy blond hair crowned a friendly face and smile. A band of equally blond hair stretched across his bulging chest.

"Thank you, Eric. I'm Ernie Lord. Do you work here at the hotel?"

"It's Derrick, Ernie. Naw, I'm just on a busman's holiday. Here for the weekend with my girlfriend. Gonna try out the Jacuzzi now. Oh, if you ever need a personal trainer..." He reached down to retrieve a business card when he realized that he only had his trunks on. "Oh, well, I'll catch you later."

Derrick turned and headed toward the pool door.

Ernie called after him. "Hope to see you here again tomorrow." Perhaps Derrick would throw him a few free crumbs of fitness advice.

Derrick held up a hand in half-consent. "Maybe so. Have a good evening, Ernie."

On the other side of the pool doorway, Heidi Hemming sat sleepily in the hot, frothing Jacuzzi. She slouched down until only her face escaped the churning water. Above the bubbles she actually perspired; below, the tension flowed from her forty-three-year-old body. She enjoyed talking to the lovely woman who'd shared the Jacuzzi with her only minutes before. Heidi had found her to be intelligent, beautiful, and in some unfamiliar way, exciting. Raising her body up one step, she turned her head toward the far end of the pool and watched the younger woman pull her svelte frame through hardly disturbed water as she free-styled lap after lap with seemingly effortless strokes. Heidi lazily slipped back to her former depth in both water and pleasant daydreams.

Danielle Lord continued her laps until she had counted an even two dozen. Then, deliberately avoiding the pool ladder, she nimbly slithered from the water, worming her hips about to alight on the tiled ledge. She pulled up on the straps of her Lycra swimsuit to better cover her abundant breasts, perhaps a little too abundant for her long, lithe frame. One hand smoothed her auburn pixie hairdo free of water.

Danielle laid a thick towel behind her, arched backward, and stretched out on the ledge, allowing her thoughts to wander. Ernest Lord, her husband of the past eleven years, was an energetic lover, but pretentious and self-absorbed, quite convinced that he alone possessed the formula for totally satisfying her. Thus, she often gave herself over to fantasies. But just now she couldn't get the full-figured blond woman in the Jacuzzi out of her head. She had introduced herself as Heidi. Perhaps they could be friends. Perhaps more. Maybe she would rejoin her after the next set of laps.

The door to the pool opened, and Derrick Powers stepped through, catching the attention of both women. Danielle abruptly sat up, unconsciously threw her shoulders back and bent one leg in a more flattering pose. Her gaze fixed on his muscled biceps: well-molded but not repulsively overdeveloped. This was a gorgeous man, an Adonis. His chest hair continued south as if purposely groomed to force her eyes down below his belly, where a tuft of blond curls met his brief swim trunks. She felt a warmth stirring deep inside her. Eye contact--and more? She couldn't be sure what flashed between them. Suddenly embarrassed by her obvious pinup girl pose, she feigned disinterest and lay back on the towel.

Heidi called to Derrick and he descended into the whirling Jacuzzi, taking a seat on the far side where he could keep a casual, if not concealed, eye on the bather across the pool. All the while he maintained an enthusiastic conversation with his companion.

Despite Derrick's efforts, Danielle felt the weight of his scrutiny. Embarrassed even further, she slid back into the pool and swam a dozen additional lengths. Ten minutes later she emerged again to resume her former perch. This time Derrick hesitated in mid-sentence. Heidi noticed.

"Sweetheart!" she said, standing up to reveal the fullness of her skimpy orange knit bikini. "Be a dear and get me a towel." She ambled up the steps without touching the railing.

"Of course, love." Derrick dutifully hoisted himself out of the Jacuzzi, brought a large fluffy towel to her body and began drying her off. Eyes half-closed and weak on her feet, Heidi absorbed the sensuality as the towel soaked up the water. But, suddenly, he stopped. "I wouldn't mind swimming a few laps, love," he said.

"If you must," she snapped. "It's time for my beauty nap, anyway. I'll meet you in the room in half an hour." She disappeared through the doorway.

Derrick dove into the pool and proceeded to swim ten energetic laps. No denying it, he was showing off, moving quickly, smoothly, efficiently. And when he finished, he sprang to a perch beside Danielle.

She literally applauded his efforts and returned his inquiring smile.

"I'm Derrick. And...by the way, you have beautiful green eyes."

Laughing, she held out her hand. "Hello, Derrick, I'm Danielle, Danielle Lord."

He took her hand in his and kissed it, continentally. "Was that your husband I met in the equipment room?"

"I'm sure it was. He doesn't like the pool at all. He's a real spoilsport. All he thinks about is business and body fitness."

Derrick smiled. "Nothing wrong with body fitness. I'm kind of hooked on that myself. What business is he in?"

"Gems and antiques, appraisals, mostly. We're here for the Historical Society meeting this weekend."

"Heidi--my friend--is attending that meeting, too."

"Oh? I'm supposed to be attending it with Ernie, but somehow, now that we're here, I'm not in the mood."

"Do I detect the sound of a neglected woman?"

"No! Of course not. And, sir, aren't you coming on a little strong? You're obviously attached."

"Guilty as charged, on both counts. Heidi and I have been dating for a couple months, but I admit I'm a confirmed bachelor and, frankly, Danielle,

I'm not much good at long-term relationships."

"Shame on you," she said lightly. "Does Heidi know that? She seems like a very nice woman."

"The subject hasn't come up yet. I suppose it will, eventually. But let's talk about you. You're a stunning woman. Can I persuade you to join me for drinks later?"

"Maybe...but maybe not. It's going to look rather odd if I don't show up at the meeting tonight."

"Why is that? Can't you plead a headache?"

"Yes, but I doubt anyone would believe it. You see, I'm a history buff and I write historical romances."

"You write history in the buff? Sounds exciting. Can I watch?"

She flushed and chuckled all at once. Ernie was never this playful. She lowered her head and mulled over an answer to Derrick's invitation.

"Well, I guess I could concoct a headache for tonight, as long as I show up for the rest of the activities over the weekend."

"Excellent! Let's meet in the bar at, say, 6:30." But he couldn't just leave it there. He fished for a compliment. "Was it the prospect of drinks or me that convinced you?"

"Neither! Don't be so conceited, sir. However, your technique for drying had a most enticing effect."

"You're joshing me."

"Yes," she said quickly, "of course, I am."

"Well, then, I'll go get a few towels."

"Don't you dare! I really am joking. Really." To prove her point, she jumped up and slid into her pool slippers. Quickly pulling on her pink terry beach robe, she tied the belt with exaggerated determination, as if the tight knot itself would fend off evil spirits and unwelcome advances.

"Ooookay, Mrs. Lord," he drawled. "I'll just have to give you a rain check. In the meantime, I'll see you in the bar at 6:30."

"No, better make it 7:15. Ernie will still be watching his damn football game at 6:30," she said.

Derrick nodded and let the glass door slip shut behind him.

CHAPTER 8

BAR TALK

"...On the fifteen, the ten, the five. Touchdown!" The TV announcer's voice grew hoarse with unexpected jubilance.

"Way to go, Terps!" The boisterous cheering for the University of Maryland team rose explosively throughout the smoke-filled lounge. Local fans congregated here in the Inn at Gander Pointe to watch the Terrapin home games on the huge TV mounted over one end of the bar.

Derrick Powers ogled a barmaid with shoulder-length raven hair. He watched her melon-shaped buns shift back and forth inside a confining mini-skirt as she wiped down the table opposite their booth. Heidi, his companion, chatted on about less interesting matters as she rummaged through her purse for a few bills to leave on the table. Derrick's smirk of amusement went unnoticed.

The barmaid finished and turned to face them. "Kin I get ya anything else, folks?"

"Oh, my, it's 5:30 already," Heidi said. "No, nothing for me. I've got to get dressed now." She dropped the folded bills on the table and stood to leave. "You coming, dear?"

"No, love," he replied. "You go ahead. I'll be along in a little bit." He blew her a gentle kiss, and she turned and left. "I'll have another Michelob Light," he told the barmaid. "At the bar," he added. She made a few token wipes at surface wetness and moved on to the booth in the darkest corner of the room.

"Hi, Vic, honey...Mr. T," she said. "Kin I get you guys another round?" She wiped her hands on her tiny white apron and tucked a wisp of hair behind one ear.

"No, I'm still good here." Felix Thornberry cupped both hands around his glass of Miller draft.

"I'll have another one of these, sweetheart." Vic held up the Heineken bottle so she could see the label.

"Vic...uh...honey?"

"Yeah, babe. What's up?"

"Hon, kin we talk a little bit later?"

"Sure, babe, any time you say."

Her hand brushed his lightly as she retrieved his empty bottle from the table. She headed straight to the stand-up station at the bar and called out her order to the bartender. While waiting for it, she leaned back against the massive expanse of mahogany and brass and idly tuned in on a conversation between the men seated on the first two bar stools. Without realizing the impact of what she heard, she soon became engrossed in what they said.

The man closest to her leaned on one elbow, his back to her, pudgy fingers folded about a half-filled glass of mostly ice. His voice sounded familiar. He spoke in a low, gravelly voice to a man with olive skin and shiny straight black hair. The second man spoke softly and with a proper British accent.

"You ain't interested in the game?" the gravelly voice asked.

"Quite right, I don't comprehend the first thing about American football," the British accent confessed.

"You play poker, then?"

"Uh...no, sir, I don't indulge in games of chance," the man responded.

"Any idea where I might find a game?"

"I'm not at all local, sorry."

"Where you from?"

"Islamabad, Pakistan."

"Then what're you doin' here, man?"

"I'm a buyer and seller of rare antiquities." He reached into the top pocket of his beige suit jacket and extracted a business card, which he handed to the man in black. "The name is A. A. Ahm," he said.

"A. A.?"

"I am also known as Ahmed."

"Hey, my initials are A. A., too," said the man in black. "Asher Allen Flowers. But that's a circumstantial coincidence, ain't it?"

"Surely!"

"My friends and colleagues call me Ace, though."

"How do you do, Ace." Ahmed extended his hand, and Ace took it.

"You say yer inta iniquities. What are they, man?"

"Antiquities are rare things, valued either for their history or their beauty, sometimes both."

"Does that include rocks and things?"

"Rocks?"

"You know--ice, diamonds, rubies, gems, and things," Ace answered excitedly.

"Ah, yes, sometimes," said Ahmed. "But that is more my father's specialty. I deal mostly in paintings. Turn-of-the-century masters in particular."

"Supposin' I had something rare, like you said. Would ya ask a lot of questions?"

"That...would depend," Ahmed said, trying to decipher the expression on Ace's gray face.

"Yeah, like where it came from and all?" Ace Flowers suddenly sensed the barmaid's presence and spun around to face her. "Well, now, look who we have here." His faint grin froze into a leer.

"You!" she exclaimed. She tried to back away, but thudded against the bar rail. His hand swiftly reached out and grabbed her wrist. With a rigid arm, he yanked her toward him.

"Stop, you're hurting me. Let me go," she cried into the noise of the room.

"You'd better remember what I told ya." He leered a second time and relaxed his grip.

The girl wrenched loose and disappeared behind the bar. He headed after her, but a massive hand of steel gripped his neck and shoulder blade, rendering him helpless.

"I think not!" Derrick Powers said, spinning the tough guy around to face him. He shoved him backward against the bar stool.

Ace Flowers clenched both fists and had every intention of retaliating, until he caught sight of Derrick's powerful frame.

"You friggin' bastard," Ace mumbled. Then he beat a hasty retreat to the men's room.

Ahmed slid his slight frame off the stool and moved several spots down the bar adjacent to the next occupied stool. "I say, is this seat taken?" he asked the tall man in the dinner jacket seated there. The man seemed surprised, as though jarred from deep thought.

"Might I join you?" Ahmed tried again while he hoisted himself onto the high stool.

"Why not? It's a free country, isn't it?"

"Why, yes, I suppose it is," Ahmed Ahm replied and turned toward the bartender. "Harvey's Bristol Cream, please." He fiddled with the single button on the jacket of his tropical suit until it fell open. Ahmed released his collar and loosened his tan-striped tie as well.

Derrick took the stool on the left side of Ahmed Ahm, and the barkeep set a mug and a bottle of Michelob Light before him. As Derrick reached for the mug, Ahmed noted the purple bruise on his left thumb. He turned back to take a sip of his sherry.

"You some kind of salesman?" the man in the dinner jacket asked.

"In a manner of speaking, sir," Ahmed replied, offering his business card once more.

"I too am interested in objects d'art. My name is Ernest Lord." He handed his own card to Ahmed.

Ahmed read: Ernest Lord, Ph.D. Gemologist and Antiques Appraiser. "Ah, Dr. Lord, I'm sure my father would thoroughly enjoy exchanging information with you. I think you call it swapping notes."

"Your father? I don't understand."

"In our family, my father is the expert on rare gems and jewelry," Ahmed said.

"And your field of expertise?"

"Oil paintings, particularly nineteenth and twentieth century."

"You've come a long way. May I assume your presence here is in the pursuit of business?"

"Oh, yes, actually my father's business. However, I seem to be having trouble making the necessary contacts here."

"I see," said Ernie," glancing up at the TV to catch the score.

Ahmed continued to enjoy their conversation, but he found himself getting drowsy. He drained the last of his glass and got up to leave.

"Well, sir, it's been pleasant," Ernie said.

"The pleasure has been all mine, Dr. Lord."

With the drapes of his room drawn tight, the doused lights and sweet sherry conspired to send Ahmed into a deep sleep in the easy chair by the window. His jaw hung open and an audible snore came from the dry roof of his mouth. But an hour later, a single knock at the door awakened his senses. His woozy attention locked immediately onto the narrow slit of light beneath the door. Foot shadows lingered only for a second and then disappeared. Ahmed jumped to his feet and moved quickly. He swung the door open and stuck his head out in the direction the footsteps had taken, but found no one in the hall. The only sound was that of the elevator whining its way to the first floor.

His foot struck something on the carpet: an envelope bearing the inn's logo. He shut the door again. Using the letter opener from the desk, he tore into the sealed flap of the envelope. A single sheet of house stationery bore the following hand-printed message:

Got a portrait of society dame done around turn of century, a John Singer Sargent. Well catalogued. Similar pieces go for a mil at auction. Asking a hundred thou. If you're interested:

1. Telephone bar downstairs in 10 minutes, and let ring only twice. Then hang up.

2. Repeat exactly ten minutes later. Doesn't matter if phone is answered or not.

3. First thing tomorrow morning a messenger will deliver a mailing tube to your room. You'll find the painting rolled inside, together with documentation.

4. Park your rental car next to the woods at the far end of the parking lot behind the inn. Meet there 11:30 Saturday night.

5. If you want the painting, bring cash in small denominations. Fifties or less. If you don't want the painting, just bring it along with you.

6. We'll be watching you. If you cross us, you'll never live to reach the airport.

Ahmed moved across the room and dropped down on the bed beside the night table and its phone. He read the note several times before committing to the deal. Then, with a trembling hand, he made the two phone calls.

Expecting to learn the identity of his cohort in crime, Ahmed hastened downstairs to the bar. Instead, the crowded bar left him with no clue. The ruffian bloke called Ace sat in a booth up front arguing with another man. The waitress had moved in with two men he'd noticed earlier in the corner booth. Ahmed's drinking acquaintances remained on their bar stools, relaxed and absorbed in Maryland football. Ahmed approached the bar. He needed another sherry.

CHAPTER 9

NIGHT OF LEGENDS

A sitting stone lion, actually a Chinese gate guardian, propped open the front door of the Kepple home. Avi and Freddie, clad in evening wear, stood in the foyer greeting members of the Historical Society. Spindly Greta waited behind them to collect wraps.

Ernest Lord arrived first, carrying a zippered briefcase. His formal attire wafted the smoky fumes of the sports lounge at the inn. Only a Tic-Tac covered the bourbon-and-branches he'd consumed there in the past hour. As prearranged, Avi had requested him to perform a preliminary appraisal of his key before the other members arrived.

"And where is your lovely wife this evening?" Freddie inquired.

"I'm sorry to say Danielle won't be joining us. She has a nasty headache."

"I hope this doesn't mean we'll be denied the pleasure of her company for an entire weekend," Freddie said.

"Oh, I don't think so. But she's been working so hard on her new novel that I guess it's beginning to catch up with her. She sends her apologies and hopes she'll be recovered enough to be with us tomorrow."

"Oh, good," Freddie said. "It's not often we get to meet with a published author here in Black Rain Corners. Please send her my best."

"Thank you, Mrs. Moskowitz." Ernie turned toward Avi as gracefully as possible. He wanted to avoid further elaboration of Danielle's "condition." She had been begging off from their activities as a couple with increasing regularity, and his excuses on her behalf were wearing thin. He extended his hand to Avi, who shook it warmly. "The key, Doctor, I'm so anxious to see it."

"Of course," Avi said, motioning to show the way.

Ernie followed Avi to the closed den door. Victor responded to the third knock and stood in the doorway with the tails of his bow tie undone.

"Hi, Uncle Avi. What's up?"

"Sorry to disturb you, Vic, but Dr. Lord needs to see the key. May I present my nephew, Victor Moskowitz...Dr. Ernest Lord."

"Nice to meet you," Victor said. "But if you'll excuse me, I really must find someone to help me with my bow tie."

Avi walked to the display cabinet, distractedly picked up the manufacturer's business card with the penned-in combination numbers on it, and laid it down again. He'd get to that later. He spun the dial through its sequence and removed the open velvet case holding the key. Switching on the high-intensity light at the desk, he waited for Ernie to take a seat there and then put the open case and key in front of him. "I think you'll be comfortable and undisturbed right here."

"Thank you...most unusual...a unique piece." Ernie removed a jeweler's loupe, metric calipers, color filters, a small Polaroid camera, and numerous other implements from his briefcase and was soon totally engrossed in his work.

Seeing no point in hovering over Ernie, Avi closed the den door and found Victor at the hall mirror still struggling with his tie, his whole body tense with frustration.

"Here, let me help you, Vic. I think after sixty years I've finally mastered these elusive little suckers." Avi quickly produced a perfect bow. "There you are. Quite handsome, if I do say so myself."

Victor managed a sincere grin for his uncle. Avi returned to the front door and the next arrivals.

Felix Thornberry wimped out his usual fingertip handshake for Freddie and Avi as if he feared someone might actually squeeze his hand too hard. His wife, however, could not abide such tentative behavior.

"Freddie, dear," Marti cooed, smothering her with a hug. "That gown does wonders for your figure, and puce is surely your color."

Marti moved to encompass a shrinking Avi. She stood toe-to-toe, less than six inches from his face. "And you, my dear Avi, you look so distinguished and sexy. How do you do it? I must have your secret. The Historical Society is such a good idea."

Avi backed away, but she followed relentlessly, leaving him less ground than before. "And that marvelous key of yours is going to create quite a sensation. I'm so excited for you." Felix stood idly beside his wife in embarrassed silence.

Heidi impatiently waited her turn, then abandoned it, and blew a kiss at her greeters. She made her way past them to the bar, where Molly awaited her wishes.

In desperation Avi took both of Marti's hands and steered her toward the sunroom. "Marti, you remember Rachel and my new son-in-law, Simon. He's an engineer. Not used to shindigs like this. Maybe you could make him feel a little more at ease." Avi pulled out his handkerchief and wiped his brow as he returned to stand beside his sister.

"So the fly escaped from the spider's web, masterfully, as usual," Freddie murmured, turning to greet their next arrivals. "Lenora, how are you? I saw several of your new paintings--the "Scenes on the Bay" exhibit--at a gallery in Annapolis. They're wonderful. Quite surprising, actually. I thought you only did abstracts."

"Thank you, Freddie. It's my first venture into scapes."

"Lenora," Avi said, "you're a radiance of beauty tonight. If it weren't for that elderly goat you call a husband, I'd..."

"You'd what, you old libertine, you." The voice coming up the walk belonged to Buckminster Worthington. Having shared this type of humor for many years, the two best friends and professional colleagues embraced for a moment. Like Avi, Bucky now limited his practice to perhaps a dozen patients.

"Hah, what do you mean, old? Your birthday's eleven days before mine."

"I'll ignore that remark," Bucky said, laughing.

"I see you've got your summer place rented out for the winter again," Freddie said.

"Sometimes I wonder if we use it enough to warrant the trouble of even keeping it," Bucky added. "It's so far to travel from Philadelphia on a summer weekend."

"But our roots are here, sweetheart," Lenora said.

"See that Molly fixes you a proper drink." Avi showed them down the hall. When he returned to Freddie's side, Trixie and Quentin Marcus had reached the door.

"I'll have one of those too," Quentin said.

"One of what, Quentin?" Avi asked.

"One of those drinks you offered Lennie and Bucky," Quentin replied.

"Now, Quentin, honey, you know you shouldn't be drinking when you're making a research contribution to the meeting."

"None of that now, Trixie-Pixie."

Avi broke in. "It's wonderful to see you both in such great spirits, considering your recent loss. Trixie, we're all going to miss your father."

Trixie's teased red-blond hair gave her an Orphan Annie look. The freckles on her pallid face bunched up as she tried to fend off tears. Avi squeezed her hand and Freddie reached out with both arms to hug her.

The spacious Kepple sunroom extended from the living room to the back of the house and gave the illusion of being round. A semicircle of French doors with crystal knobs separated the sunroom from an opulent flower garden beyond. An enormous curved sectional sofa sat a few feet in front of the French doors.

Molly had covered the pecan coffee table with her cocktail hour delights: plump shrimp and red and black imported caviar. Rye rounds, sour cream, chopped onions, and capers surrounded the colorful fish roe. She also operated a makeshift bar in the pantry off the dining room.

"Molly, be a dear and mix me a Bloody Mary," Heidi cajoled. Molly poured gin and V8 juice into a glass. Adding a sprinkle of fresh-ground pepper and a twist of lime, she stirred her creation with a tall stalk of celery and handed the glass to Heidi.

"Here's your Bleeding Mary, ma'am."

Heidi had taken only a sip when she heard this. She giggled first, set the glass down, and then began to cough violently. Molly came out from behind the bar and slapped Heidi on the back. Heidi kept coughing. Molly hugged her in Heimlich fashion.

Avi came running to the dining room. "What's wrong?" Heidi couldn't answer.

"Miss Heidi's drink went down the wrong pipe," Molly said. "I tried to give her the Hamlet maneuver. You know, artificial restitution."

Heidi finally stopped coughing. "It was something Molly said that made me laugh."

"Somehow that doesn't surprise me," Avi said, handing her a glass of water. "Now drink this slowly, very slowly."

The front door banged open. Caitlin bounded in, her single braid flying, with Olivia Raphael close behind.

"Wait a minute, child, not so fast. Remember, you're a guest here. I could have left you home with a sitter, so I'm counting on you."

"Uh-huh!"

"Now, behave yourself and mind Molly and Greta."

"Yes, Grandma." Caitlin rushed straight into the kitchen to play with Shana.

Olivia checked her appearance in the hall mirror, straightening the jacket of her ivory satin suit. In her early seventies, she looked much younger, despite her carefully waved white hair.

"Hello, everyone," she said. "Sorry I'm late. Let's all be seated."

She took some notes from her purse and searched for a place to lay them down. Noting that Avi had removed the huge *Webster's International Dictionary* from its *libre* stand, Olivia commandeered the stand as a podium--exactly as he intended.

"Welcome to the first official meeting of the Black Rain Corners Historical Society. This is indeed a momentous occasion." Olivia's froggy, seductive voice captivated her audience.

She reminded them that the Society had been chartered by the Black Rain Corners Town Council to convert the Marche mansion and its furnishings into a nonprofit museum. The Society assumed responsibility for seeing that it did not become a burden to the council and the taxpayers. The Marche family had also established a trust to help maintain the place and finance small stipends for a few employees. Heidi Hemming, Hubert Marche's stepdaughter, had been designated a permanent Society member in her capacity, first, as a personal representative of Hubert Marche's estate; and second, as a co-trustee of the Marche Museum Trust. Olivia would serve for eighteen months as the first curator. Reappointments or new appointments would be subject to the bylaws of the Society and confirmation by the town council.

"Oh, yes, the bylaws," Olivia said. She passed out small gray booklets to everyone. "The world couldn't know two more unassuming and gentle people than the Aigues." She spoke of Trixie Marcus' parents, who had been the trusted resident caretakers at Marche House. "Where's the justice? Willard's death is a terrible tragedy, not only to the family but to the entire community."

Olivia paused during the murmur of assent before explaining, "Norma Aigue will continue to live in the cottage, rent free. Her nephew has agreed to move in with her to take care of the grounds and act as handyman, and Norma will do light cleaning. A cleaning service will be used, as required, out of operating funds. We plan to be open to the public two days a week at first, Wednesdays and Sundays, as long as we can find volunteer docents from among our members. I myself would be delighted to volunteer."

"Olivia, what do you know about the stolen painting?" Bucky asked. "Do you think we'll ever get it back? The papers have been very pessimistic, not to mention sketchy about the details."

Freddie held up the *Annapolis Journal-Gazette* for October 15th. A photo of the painting dominated the front page. The caption said the photo had come from the museum's insurance files.

"It's no accident that the details are sketchy," Marti said. She was Heidi's stepsister and quite eager to contribute to this meeting. "The county police are being ultra-cautious about releasing information to the press. Let's face it, folks, when a John Singer Sargent is stolen, that's big news. The police are afraid it'll get sold underground and never be recovered."

Rachel edged forward in her chair. "Who is the portrait of?"

"My grandmother, Sophia Marche," said Marti. "The thief removed the portrait from my mother's room on the second floor." She leaned down to get a better look at the paper. "This black and white photo doesn't do the painting justice. But, still, you can see, she's such a grand lady. Gorgeous, in fact. I always admired it."

Indeed, the alluring young woman stood regally in her low-cut ball gown, gazing sadly out from the photo. She stood beside a table graced by a vase of sumptuous roses.

"I remember it, too," Heidi said. "I always wondered why Sophia looks so sad while being painted for posterity. Why would she want to look so unhappy?"

"Perhaps she didn't want to. Perhaps Sargent caught some deeper mood or expression," Lenora suggested.

"Can it be worth so much that a thief would commit murder to get his hands on it?" Felix asked.

"The value of the painting is estimated at just under a million dollars," Avi said. Felix whistled through his teeth.

"That's not surprising," Olivia said. "Sargent died in 1925. His art is world-famous. It could easily be the most valuable painting in Marche House."

Avi removed a magnifying glass from his vest pocket and unfolded the handle. He leaned over the picture and concentrated the magnifier on the corner beneath Sophia's hand.

"What do you see?" Lenora asked.

"Her hand," Avi said. "It's resting on some kind of box on the table, but the details aren't clear." He glanced up. "Do either of you ladies remember what that box looked like?" Both Marti and Heidi shook their heads.

"I never paid any attention to it," Marti admitted.

"This is the first time I've even noticed it," Heidi said.

Victor edged his way into the group. "Here, I remember the painting. Let me have a look, too." He took the magnifier from his uncle and studied the box for a minute. Then he looked up, his pock-marked face expressionless.

"Well?" Avi said.

"Well, what?" Victor asked.

"What do you make of it?" Avi demanded.

"I can't make it out, either." Victor handed the magnifier back to his uncle and retreated from the group. Avi thought he detected a flicker of recognition hovering in his nephew's dark eyes.

"I know we're all in a state of shock right now," Olivia said. "And that's to be expected. Willard's death and the theft--such violent acts--make us all feel vulnerable. But maybe we ought to get back to the business at hand. The robbery raises serious questions about the museum's security system. It's so ancient it creaks. That's something we have to look into, and soon." She looked up for a reaction. They all watched her intently and nodded in silence.

While Olivia spoke, Ernest Lord quietly entered the sunroom and took a seat on the sectional to her right. He held the velvet case in his lap.

Greta peeked out of the kitchen door and then slipped back inside, whispering to Molly: "Shouldn't we be serving the hot hors d'oeuvres now?"

"I can't do that until I get the IOU from the doctor," Molly replied. "I tried to get his attention before, but he just invaded me."

Back in the sunroom, Olivia continued. "During my first term as curator,

I won't be permitted to acquire any new pieces for the museum. Thereafter, excess revenues may be considered for that purpose. A five-dollar admission fee has been suggested. Not necessarily cast in stone, but a good starting point. The museum land and improvements remain the property of the trust and can never be sold." She cleared her throat.

"Also," she went on, "4,073 specifically inventoried items can never be liquidated for cash. Should the museum ever become a serious burden to the community, the entire museum property and the supporting trust will revert back to the Marche family estate. The town council would be responsible for all debts incurred. That's why we'll be so closely managed by them. Now I'd like to call upon our treasurer, Dr. Buckminster Worthington, for his report."

Avi took that moment to duck into the kitchen and give the nod to Molly. She and Greta emerged with silver trays of steaming crab puffs, stuffed mushrooms, bacon-wrapped water chestnuts, and coconut-covered mini-drumsticks.

Bucky began. "Good evening, everyone. The museum's financial situation involves both good news and bad news. The bad news is that our coffers contain only $56,238.19. We have debts outstanding for cleaning, $3,400; roof repairs, $11,512.48; miscellaneous printing: pamphlets, posters, and so forth, $517.03. And now that we have to upgrade the security system, we may be talking in the neighborhood of $50,000 or more.

"I guess we should be thankful that only one painting was stolen. However, there is some good news, my friends. Thanks to Freddie's brilliant idea, the Adopt-An-Artifact auction netted us pledges of $173,678. These are tax-deductible gifts." Freddie beamed and blushed as spontaneous applause filled the room.

Bucky spelled out the details. Upon completing the terms of these pledges, a benefactor's plaque would be installed next to the auctioned artifact. In addition, a benefactor would be allowed to borrow his or her artifact for a forty-eight-hour period once each year.

"I'm told that one of the largest pledges has come from our gracious host," Bucky said. "Avi told me earlier this evening that he also intends to bequeath the two large oils hanging in his dining room to the museum upon his death. The painters are renowned local Chesapeake Bay artists." Enthusiastic applause filled the room as Bucky sat down.

Avi stood up. "Thank you, Bucky. I'm delighted to be the benefactor of the magnificent jeweled key. Dr. Ernest Lord has just performed a preliminary appraisal. Ernie, why don't you tell us about it?"

Pleased that Avi had not stolen his thunder, Ernie took the podium slowly to draw out the drama of it. "Ladies and gentlemen," he began, pausing to adjust the knot in his tie. "I have agreed to serve on the Historical Society as the group's authority on antiques and gems. I have been able to estimate the value of the key in the vicinity of $60,000 to $63,000. My findings are contingent upon some remaining chemical and X-ray tests and, of course, based upon a continuing market for similar objects d'art." More applause filled the room.

Avi took the case from Ernie, opened it, and handed it to Victor seated next to him. "Vic, would you do me a favor and show the key to the other members?"

"I'd be happy to, Uncle Avi." As Victor moved from guest to guest, ohs and ahs and gasps of wonderment filled the room.

"Boy! I'd like to get a good gander at the box or door that goes with that key. Woweee!" Marti fairly shrieked.

After ten minutes, Victor returned to Avi with the key. Avi took the case from him and closed it as Victor settled back down in his chair. "Thank you, Vic. Now that everyone's seen it, I'll run it back to its display cabinet." He headed quickly for the den and Olivia resumed the podium.

"We do have a special treat tonight. Three of our members have become so intrigued with Avi's key that they have done some fascinating research into its origin. What we're unsure of is just how much is fact and how much has been conjured to fit the facts. At any rate, I have chosen to call them legends. Tonight we will hear three reports, from widely diverse sources. Meanwhile, why don't we take a little break?"

Avi strode back into the sunroom as the guests floated about with food and drinks in hand. "Vic?" He stopped abruptly in front of his nephew. "I just picked up a call for you in the den. A rather rude individual insisted that you call him back immediately." He held out a small scrap of paper. "Are you in any kind of trouble?"

Victor's hand shook slightly as he took the number from Avi. The pleasant expression he had worn all evening eroded from his face. "No, Uncle Avi, it's nothing, just a business possibility."

"At this hour of the night?"

"Yeah, kind of strange, but you know how it is. That's how some people do business. I'll take care of it now." An apprehensive Avi watched Victor hasten to the den.

CHAPTER 10

LEGEND I: GEMS OF DESTINY

The last rowdy football fans had left the Inn at Gander Pointe bar. The pre-dinner cocktail crowd had also migrated from their bar stool perches. Cozy red vinyl booths flanked both ends of the walnut-paneled lounge. An escapist aura emanated from the soft recessed lighting. A solitary figure on a bar stool hunched over a highball.

Danielle Lord sat out of view in a rear booth, sipping a Singapore Sling, savoring the sweet mix of sloe gin and grenadine. Ernie and Heidi had been sitting with her, sharing half-hearted small talk. Now they and three other couples had departed for the Historical Society meeting. Danielle toyed with a tiny paper umbrella, having little expectation of running into Derrick Powers again. Alone and feeling deserted, she wondered whether she'd behaved like a fool making a date with him in the first place. Perhaps she should have gone to the meeting with Ernie after all.

"It seems like such a lonely place for so stunning a lady. May I join you?"

Danielle tilted her head to see Derrick's chiseled features looking down at her. "Please!" she said. A shock of blond hair fell fetchingly over his forehead as he broke into a sweet smile. That disarmed her completely. He seemed so genuinely interested in her, and he didn't fit the stereotype of the narcissistic iron-pumping Adonis.

"I see you arranged to have one of your headaches, too," she said.

"Yes, in a manner of speaking, yes." He laughed as he slid into the booth across from her. "But I can hardly feel pain any more."

"That's strange," she said. "I'm pain-free also."

The bartender appeared at their booth and wiped away the wet rings of past drinks. "Can I get you something?"

"Bring the lady another, and I'll take a Michelob Light." Derrick relaxed, put his hands on the table and interlaced his fingers.

"That's a beautiful cocktail ring you're wearing," he said. She held her hand closer so he could see. Derrick took her hand in his, pretending to study the rather small emerald more closely. But then he looked up into her eyes; two more luminous emeralds already locked onto him. Her lips parted as though there was something she wanted, yet should not, could not ask for. She moistened the dryness with her tongue.

The drinks came, and the bartender quickly took the ten dollar bill lying on the table and left. They hardly noticed him. This game was new to

Danielle. She imagined Derrick as an experienced aggressor, but, really, he hadn't come on too strong. Well, yes he had, but hadn't she given him just the right amount of encouragement? She felt shame in that and excitement, too. She hadn't the least idea what would happen. She only wanted it--something--to happen.

"Everyone! Please, everybody! May we come to order?" Olivia had allowed the break to run just a few moments too long. "We have a lot of ground to cover tonight and I think you'll all find the legends most fascinating." Slowly, she regained the full attention of the members.

"About four weeks ago, Avi asked me to examine the key for him in connection with the artifact auction. In doing so I was reminded of something I'd seen years before. It wasn't the fleur-de-lis handle or the setting of the gems. It was the unique scrolling on the shaft and the choice of gems. I had found similar items in a catalogue of artifacts from a part of British India that is now Pakistan. The descriptions below the pictures were by a man I once had the pleasure of working with at Princeton. His name is T. T. Ahm."

Olivia paused to take a sip of White Zinfandel. "Dr. Ahm was my thesis adviser and a visiting professor. I've traced his whereabouts to a small museum in Islamabad and sent him a color photograph of the key. I couldn't even be sure he would remember me, but in two weeks I had my reply. I would like to read it to you now."

Dear Mme. Raphael,

Of course I remember the bright young mind and comely girl so quick to question and so full of ideas and principles. I could never forget our endless discussions over tea. You overflowed with curiosity, optimism, and assurance. Oh, how I envied that assurance. I look back on those lovely days with fondness, and cherish the memories we made. Ah, just to stir the honesty and idealism once more, but, alas, we are no longer availed of life's youth.

We are now both grandparents. I was so sorry to hear of the loss of your child and then your life's mate. I am sure you and your granddaughter carry their spirits close to your hearts. I, too, have been blessed with much family and together we have tasted both the bitter and sweet of life's fruit, but I shall not burden you with my tribulations here.

More to the point, I have examined the photograph very carefully, and I agree that the key might well have come from my part of the world. Perhaps it would be more beneficial for me to tell you a story and let you draw your own conclusions. I cannot validate much of the story. All I know is that legend and fact appear to fit like hand in glove, and one does not have to struggle to make the match.

Picture, if you will, a wealthy family of six living in a northern Moslem province of British India: a mother, a father, a son, and three daughters. According to popular theory, this family possessed an elaborately decorated box in which the unprotected destinies of their children resided until they were to reach the age of maturity. The box was decorated with rubies to signify daughters and a diamond to signify one son. Although the scrolling would appear to be quite ordinary and typical among many families, a more careful examination would reveal initials of the children clandestinely woven into the design. I could find no significance in the fleur-de-lis design; however, its use as decoration is quite common in this region. I am of the opinion that it is not related to the French fleur-de-lis at all.

An elaborately decorated key for such a box would be worn by the mother, around her neck on a gold chain. It could easily be her most valued possession, safeguarded by a mother's strength and savored by a mother's love. Legend has it that a thief broke into their home and became fascinated with the jeweled box. The father surrendered the box to save his family, but the mother had to have the key ripped from her neck.

Here the tale becomes even more bizarre. A British sailor known to have jumped ship for the sake of a Hindu woman had, in desperation, turned to thievery in order to survive. Weeks later, he was caught trying to fence this loot in the Grand Bazaar. He and the loot were turned over to the British constabulary in a nearby seat of provincial government. When the case came to trial, the evidence was nowhere to be found. Although the sailor was thus exonerated, he still had to face the Royal Navy on charges of desertion.

A few previously fenced baubles were returned to the family, but they never saw the box or key again. Thus, they believed the destinies of their children were imperiled and, indeed, a tapestry of irreversible tragedy was woven through their lives. The son died in a fall from his horse, the two younger daughters succumbed to cholera, and the eldest, fearing the worst, took her own life. So very sad it was.

The box and key were to surface some four years later in London. There the very same constable, who had unsuccessfully tried the sailor, attempted to sell the missing items to a pawnbroker. The sale supposedly broke off when a third party, a Frenchman, disrupted the negotiations to deal directly with the retired constable. Angered at being excluded from the transaction, the pawnbroker advertised a description of the box and key, because he sensed they were stolen property. The former sailor came forward to accuse the ex-constable, and both were returned to India for trial. The sailor received a short sentence; the constable a considerably longer one.

The later portion of the story comes from a newspaper account clipped by my late father. He also dealt in artifacts and objets d'art. Neither the

Frenchman nor the box was ever found. According to the account, only a first name could be found for the Frenchman, Jacques, for his last name had been obliterated by an inkblot in the pawnbroker's transaction books.

I have written to my son, who is currently in London on business of mine and will be on his way to your country in a few days. I have asked him to look into the pawnbroker's establishment for any further clues.

Who can say if your key is the one that unlocks my story with no ending? In any case, should your museum wish to sell this wonderful artifact, I am sure I can find a ready buyer for you. Should you decide to keep it, I am sure that the story I have told can only enrich its stature in your collection.

I trust that these words find you in the best of health and within reach of enlightenment.

I am most humbly yours,

T. T. Ahm

Olivia laid the letter down on the podium and blotted her teary eyes with a white monogrammed handkerchief from her purse. A hush gripped the room, as though the legend could not end here. Where was the box now? Could Avi's key actually be the very same one? Who was the Frenchman, Jacques?

Freddie had more pressing concerns on her mind. She turned to Avi. "Have you seen Victor?"

"Uh...yes. I gave him a phone message just before Olivia read her letter from this Ahm chap. He took the call in the den."

"I think I'll see if everything's okay."

Freddie hurried to the den and pounded on the door. "Victor, honey, is anything the matter? Why aren't you joining us?" The doorknob turned with a clicking sound, but the solid door would not budge. Freddie couldn't tell whether it had just been locked at that moment or if it had been locked all along. A mother's instinct believed he wanted to hide from her.

"Victor, honey, it's me. Why won't you let me help you?" Freddie thought she heard a sound. Maybe not. With her ear to the door, she listened intently for her son's movements, but heard only the eager conversations from the sunroom. The rug proved too thick for any light to appear under the door. After glancing about to see whether anyone watched, she stooped down and put her eye to the keyhole. But the key inserted on the other side of the lock prevented her from seeing anything at all.

Frustrated, Freddie went through the kitchen to the back hall. She unlocked the door to the garage and flicked on the light. Her green Chevy Chevette and Avi's blue Cadillac Coupe de Ville sat side by side. The hoods of both cars felt cold to her touch. Satisfied that neither car had been driven all evening, she re-locked the garage door.

Freddie slipped out the kitchen door and walked around to the side of the house. Looking up at the narrow den windows, a chill shot through her. Here too, in the bright moonlight, she had difficulty seeing whether the den had a light on. If so, it could be no more than a night-light. She walked slowly back inside, straight to the den door, and pressed her ear against it once more. Total silence.

Reluctantly returning to the sunroom, she encountered Rachel and Simon talking with Bucky. Rachel stopped mid-sentence.

"Aunt Freddie, you look worried. Is anything wrong?"

"No, dear. Why do you ask?"

"Well, Auntie, when the prettiest lady here isn't smiling, something is usually wrong." Rachel put her arm about Freddie's shoulders and walked her away from the two men.

Simon pursued his animated conversation. "I've been told," he declared, "that owning a boat is like having a hole surrounded by water into which you shovel money. There's a fellow I know...."

Bucky sighed. He'd heard this one before, always by non-boat owners.

When Rachel had pulled Freddie far enough to the side, she tried again. "What's wrong? Is it Vic?"

"No, of course not. Well...yes...Oh, dear, I don't know what to do." Freddie's voice broke.

"Then it *is* Victor. Is he up to his old tricks again?"

Coming to his defense once more, Freddie said, "He tries so hard, and it's not easy for him at his age."

"Do you think he's fallen off the wagon?" Rachel asked.

"I'm afraid he has, although I haven't actually seen him drinking. But all the signs are there. For one thing, he's been quite sullen lately. He wants to be alone all the time. Sometimes he lies on his back in the dark for hours. That's just not normal, Rachel. He has an extremely short attention span and he lies to me constantly. He has no compunction about that."

Freddie stopped for a moment, her head down. "He must think I'm really stupid," she whispered. "Either that or he doesn't care what I think. He's always going to meetings, but won't tell me what they're about, and he gets phone calls at all hours from very uncivil individuals. Tonight he's disappeared altogether."

"Disappeared? What do you mean?"

"Well, your father sent him to the den to take a phone call, and he never came back."

"That's hardly disappearing."

"No, but I went to the den and found it locked. I knocked on the door, and he didn't answer. As far as I could tell, there were no lights on and no sounds in the room."

"That's easy enough. Maybe he went for a drive or a walk."

"No, I don't think so. Avi's and my car are both here, and Vic's muddy running shoes are still in the back hall."

Rachel appeared puzzled. "What about his own car?"

"He doesn't have one right now. He managed to total his Dodge a few months ago and hasn't been able to afford to replace it."

"Vic's a grown man, fully capable of taking care of himself. Perhaps someone came and took him for a ride."

"I don't think I like the sound of that."

"Oh, Aunt Freddie, you know what I mean." But Rachel wished she had phrased it differently. And now that she had inadvertently planted the thought in her aunt's mind, it didn't seem quite so far-fetched.

CHAPTER 11

LEGEND II: IN GENEVE'S OWN WORDS

Olivia plucked a stuffed mushroom from the tray on the cocktail table and popped it into her mouth whole. She slid her jacket sleeve barely an inch up her arm to check her diamond watch. As if reading her thoughts, Molly appeared and prepared to announce dinner, but she never got the chance. A huge bulk of fur upstaged her by squeezing past into the sunroom. Shana had had enough of the kitchen and her companions.

"Shanie!" Molly called, trying to grab her collar, but the exuberant dog rushed to Avi, leaving his black tuxedo trouser leg swathed with bronze-gold fuzz.

"Dog!" Avi commanded. "Sit!" Shana tried, but she was too excited. Joyfully wagging her whole behind, the plume of tail grandly swept over the hors d'oeuvres tray, sending crab puffs and bacon-wrapped water chestnuts flying. Guests ducked, a few laughed. Olivia chuckled with relief that her outfit had dodged the line of fire. A breathless Caitlin came running from the kitchen, giggling. She glanced anxiously at Olivia.

"I'm sorry, Grandma. She just got away from me. And she was being so good, too." Shana managed to inhale a crab puff before Caitlin pulled her away and led her back into the kitchen.

"Dinner is served, Doctor," said Molly, unruffled, as though nothing at all out of the ordinary had happened.

"Good, we're all starved," said Avi.

"And it's an excellent break point for our legends," Olivia said. "We have two more. Lenora will read hers between dinner and dessert. And after dessert we'll have Quentin's contribution."

The candlelit dining room table glowed with elegance, graced by a white Belgian lace cloth, Royal Worcester china, and Waterford goblets.

"Avi," said Marti, "isn't Victor joining us?"

Avi sighed. He had hoped no one would be unkind enough to bring up this awkward situation. But the empty chair could hardly be ignored.

"Apparently not, Marti, I believe he's gone out for the evening." Avi preferred that explanation to another possibility: that he was sulking in his room, behaving like a boor.

The guests dove into the first course. "Avi, this cream of asparagus soup is out of this world." Lenora said. "And I don't normally even like asparagus."

Soon Molly swept in with flawlessly broiled filet mignon; buttered noodles tossed with garlicked bread crumbs; fresh green beans with almonds; a salad of romaine and endive, mandarin oranges and French dressing; and steaming popovers. All conversation ceased as they savored each bite.

As the guests slowly sipped their red Bordeaux and finished off their last morsels, Olivia brought them back to business. The guests straightened up in their chairs, each one fighting the urge to doze off.

"Listen, everyone. Lenora is next. She's been doing research on her own. Some of you may not know that Lenora's mother once worked for the Marche family, and she has an interesting story for us."

Lenora pushed her chair back and brought out a small bedraggled silk book that might have once been white. She held it up for everyone to see. "This is my mother's diary. Actually, it's one of many volumes she wrote during her short lifetime."

Lenora found her place in the little book and looked up, a somber expression on her face. "My mother, Geneve Dulac, died at the age of forty-six. I knew her only eleven years, but even as a child I thrilled to learn about my family history, and I read just about everything she wrote. Although quite a statuesque woman with strawberry blond hair, she dressed rather plainly. Her romantic French ancestry made her such an interesting and perfectly dear lady. I've selected this volume from the year 1912 because it deals with her employment at Marche House." Lenora held up the open book to show them the pages.

"It was June 28th," she explained, "a week after she had announced her engagement to Robert Dulac, my father. She had visited him at his house in Norfolk, Virginia, for three weeks and had just returned to the employ of Sophia Marche. Geneve served as Sophia's private secretary as well as her confidante."

June 28th

I can't remember enjoying a visit with Papa so much. We made it a festive occasion. Robert's proposal of marriage and my acceptance have pleased the family no end. I returned to Marche House today just bursting with this news. My heart beat all aflutter. That is, until I reached Sophia's door and found it locked. I could hear her moving about inside, so I called to her and pleaded with her to let me in. She told me no. "Go away," she said. I could hear the tears in her voice.

"Is it Monsieur Cartier? Has he hurt you again?" I asked.

"But, yes!" she cried in two great sobs. I begged her to talk to me, if only through the locked door. But she just kept sobbing. Then she recovered some small measure of her composure to say, "You cannot help me tonight. Leave me, please, I implore you."

I left her, but reluctantly. I feared for her safety. Her husband, Cartier, is a brutally jealous man with a ferocious temper. He will beat her for so much as a flirting smile, an unexplained gesture or for no reason at all. I shudder to think of what he might do if he discovers that she has taken a lover, a discreet affair with a foreigner.

June 29th

Today Sophia opened her door to me. At first she tried to hide behind her oriental folding fan, but it proved to be too much of a hindrance for her to converse with me, so slowly she lowered her shield of shame. I saw what he had done to her beautiful childlike face. Red, puffy bruises marred the delicate lines of her left cheek, and the eye above it has been sorely blackened.

"I'm so ashamed," she said. Sophia was such a petite lady and looked even smaller in her despair. She sat down on the chaise and lowered her head, allowing her lovely brown curls to fall around her fair, bruised face, hiding it once more.

I sat beside her with my arm around her shoulder and tried to console her. "Do you want to tell me about it?"

"Yesterday Cartier found an envelope addressed to me in a male handwriting. A corner of it had protruded from under my desk blotter. He demanded the note, and I told him I had destroyed it because it was clearly not meant for me. He didn't believe me and insisted that I tell him who had sent it." She began to cry again. "I wouldn't...I couldn't...He hit me...knocked me to the floor...and left me there."

"Why do you stay with such a brute of a man?" I asked.

"Cartier didn't always behave this way. He can be kind and gentle and generous, too. But all that seems so long ago now. And where would I go? I could never leave my darling Hubert. My son is the center of my life."

Where indeed? She dictated a letter to her lover, and I posted it in care of his friend, Daniel Marisse, in Calais, France. Afterward, she sent me away while she rested. I began a long letter to my Robert. I'm so proud of him studying to be a doctor at Johns Hopkins University.

July 3rd

A packet arrived for Sophia today and I picked it up at the postmistress's in Black Rain Corners. I hurried back to Marche House and ran up the stairs to Sophia's room. The two of us basked in the excitement as she carefully undid the wrappings. An unknown admirer, she told me, but we both knew Jacques had sent it.

There was no note...

Lenora heard whispers and restless stirrings. She stopped her reading and looked straight at Avi.

"Sorry for the interruption," he said. "I just asked Olivia if the name in the London pawnshop wasn't Jacques as well. It's quite a coincidence, you know."

"It certainly is," Olivia said. "Perhaps it lends credibility to both stories."

Lenora agreed and began to read from the diary again.

...There was no note, only the initial J written on a card. Sophia pulled away the wrapping with such tender care, as though the paper was as significant and precious as its contents. We both gasped seeing the contents within. Her hazel eyes flashed with reflected light as they widened with pleasure.

The packet contained a box, finely tooled, of what I believed to be tropical koa wood and finished to a splendid sheen. The elaborate swirling grains wound to four natural knots symmetrically spaced on the cover, front and two sides. The wood was carved with many flourishes and (I couldn't be absolutely sure) there seemed to be some initials carved into the design, almost as if they were meant to be hidden in the scrollwork. In the center of each hollowed-out knot was a finely carved fleur-de-lis covered with gleaming gems, a large diamond in the center and a ruby set into each of the three petal tips.

Again, a noticeable stirring filled the room as the listeners acknowledged the description of the box and its configuration of jewels. Lenora read on.

Sophia pressed the box, which was roughly the size of my rabbit-fur muff, to her breast and squeezed her eyes tightly shut as though she were trying to will her heart into it. It all seemed so sad to me--to be in love, but forced to remain apart from your sweetheart. Just above the jewels on the front of the box was a gold escutcheon limiting the passage of all but the most unusual key. Except there was no key. A look of anticipation registered on Sophia's face, and then she took a deep breath and opened the box. The key lay within. And what a key, for it matched the box's design, gem for gem, on a smaller scale. The key's tab formed the shape of a fleur-de-lis, a ruby in each major petal, a diamond at the crest.

A momentary smile replaced Sophia's troubled countenance. "I know," she said, "I'll keep his letters in it and they'll be safe from Cartier and his jealous prying."

No sooner had she uttered those words than she ran to the wicker chest at the foot of her bed and thrust her whole arm into its depths, feeling for a precious bundle she was certain would be there. Without having to look for it, she joyfully retrieved a packet of at least thirty letters tied in a wide brocade ribbon. She ran her thumb across the edge of the stack, gently flicking the individual letters like the strings of a harp. She paused, deep in thought, then pressed the lot to her lips and said, "Yes, it will be perfect, and when I look at it, I will think of J."

I held the cover of the box open as she placed the packet of letters inside and slowly turned the key. I knew then that I was a part of her conspiracy to deceive her husband. I do not condone it. I'm a good God-fearing woman, but my mistress is kind and mistreated, and if ever a man deserved to be cuckolded, Cartier would be my choice.

Sophia stood on tiptoe to place the box atop her chiffonier with the key still in the lock. She paused for a few moments and then ran her fingers down the high, narrow chest of drawers until it rested on the knob of the third drawer. I knew it contained her chains and necklaces. I watched while she selected a long, thin gold chain and tested it for strength. Taking the key out of the lock, she strung the chain through the loop at the top of the key's fleur-de-lis and fastened the simple clasp before slipping it around her graceful, smooth neck. Picking up the key, she pulled the bodice away from her bosom and dropped it in, as though the deep chasm there afforded extraordinary concealment. She suddenly became conscious that I was watching her every move, so she kissed me lightly on the cheek and motioned for me to leave.

The dining room became so silent it seemed that the guests were holding their breath, waiting for the tragic story to continue. Lenora leafed through some of the pages, reading only a few of the passages in their entirety and skipping others altogether. She found the passage she sought, cleared her throat, and began again.

July 14th

Sophia's face has healed without blemish. She is again lovely as ever and her spirit soars once more. Cartier has had a house guest for several weeks, but until supper the day before yesterday, he has kept Mr. Sargent entirely to himself. I thought him to be an Englishman at first, having encountered his trunk, marked "London," in the hall outside the guest bedroom. His polite conversation included something about being born to American parents during their stay in Florence, Italy. We learned that he is fluent in many languages, having called so many European cities home before the age of twenty.

Upon being seated across from Sophia, he was immediately drawn to her beauty and begged Cartier's permission for the opportunity to capture her on canvas. He claimed to be so intrigued by her exceptional features that he was motivated to return just once more to portraiture, his original profession. Today, at tea, Cartier relented and gave Mr. Sargent his permission.

July 25th

Sophia poses for several hours in the morning sunlight each day for the artist. She modestly told me he is a world-renowned painter. He is strict with her pose--chin raised, a quarter turn from front, subdued smile, and almost no cheek coloring. She has chosen a shimmering blue satin gown with daring neckline and taffeta petticoat. Her hand rests on a small mahogany table beside a crystal vase overflowing with pink roses. Her fingers caress a carved box, Jacques's loving gift. I don't know how she stands so still for so long. Mr. Sargent won't let either of us see the oil in progress. I'm surprised he tolerates my presence there at all, so I cannot complain.

August 9th

At last the painting is finished, unveiled to everyone's satisfaction at tea this afternoon. Cartier has ordered a most exquisite gilded frame to hold it. He is simply ecstatic over the result, and a contagious good feeling emanates throughout the household.

August 11th

Sophia received her first letter in more than a month today. I had just finished posting one for her, in care of Jacques's friend at the Calais address. The postmistress winked at me as I accepted the letter for Sophia. I viewed it as though she knew something more than the passage of a letter through her hands. Perhaps I am imagining it. I cannot find a way to divorce myself from this conspiracy. I have felt that way from the day it began in Paris two years ago. Sophia and I were strolling joyfully through the Louvre when Jacques offered to explain the Impressionist school of painting to her. They were inexorably attracted to each other in such an immediate way that I shall never understand it. She has often called upon me to cheat and lie for her. I deplore it, but I comply because her husband is such a malevolent man, so undeserving of sweet Sophia.

I had the letter in my hand as I climbed the stairs toward her room. Mr. Marche had just left her and we met at the middle landing. He smiled at me and even condescended a greeting. No small thing for him, a nod and "miss." Not "Miss Geneve," of course. He has never once deigned to call me by my given name.

I replied with "Good day, sir."

He passed me and suddenly, turning with a stern expression across his face, motioned toward the letter in my hand. "For Mrs. Marche, I presume?"

"Yes, sir," I replied.

"And who is it from?"

"I don't know, sir. The sender isn't marked on the envelope."

"Any ideas?"

"Probably one of her many lady friends on the Continent, sir."

"Har...rumph," he cleared his throat. "I see. Good day, miss." He continued on his way down the stairs, leaving me to wonder if Cartier Marche had begun to suspect his wife.

When I entered her room, I found Sophia in a melancholy mood.

"Was your husband so abusive today that I find you so low?"

"On the contrary," she said. "He was pleasant and quite chatty. He apologized for hitting me and said he missed me. He also mentioned hiring a nanny for Hubert to give the two of us more time together. A Miss Leslie Temple, I believe. I guess that's why I'm so sad."

I held the letter out to her. "Then perhaps this will cheer you up." She grabbed it from my hands and broke the seal. She read with an appetite fed by desire and denied by time.

"He writes so beautifully...He pledges his love over and over. He says he will come for me one day. He will make up for the indignities I have suffered at Marche House."

I left Sophia at her window seat looking out at the dark, misty bay, a haunting view, though she saw none of it.

August 23rd

Another letter from Jacques came today. Sophia read it five times before handing it to me to read. We're so close these days. She shares everything with me. I had to read it twice. He has bought a place in Normandy...Coming here in one month, plans to take her away for good...Says he'll write soon to give necessary details.

"Will you give up all this to go with him?"

"Of course, silly. What does all this matter?"

"And what of Hubert?" I asked. "Cartier will never let him go with you."

There were tears in Sophia's eyes. "I see so little of him now that he has a nanny. She lavishes so much affection upon him and she surely is a competent teacher. I have so little left to give him. Cartier has the boy wrapped around his little finger. He idolizes his father and cherishes every minute spent with him." Sophia went on and on trying to justify leaving little Hubert behind. "After all, he could hardly lead the kind of life we expect to live on the Continent."

This was a different Sophia emerging, one I didn't know.

September 9th

Today I checked with the postmistress, as I've done every day for the last two weeks. She told me that the gentleman of Marche House himself had picked up the solitary letter for his wife. Well, I knew I had to warn her and time was crucial. Abandoning all of my other errands in town, I turned the carriage around and mercilessly drove the horses up the hill to the house. I thought about what the letter might contain. Would it expose her liaison? What if Mr. Marche confronted an unsuspecting Sophia?

I left the carriage and the sweaty mares by the front door and raced for Sophia's room on the floor above. Her door was ajar, and I pushed it back to find Sophia sitting at her secretary, writing a note. Her calm face wore a pleased-with-herself smile, as though she hadn't a trouble in the world. When I tried to interrupt, she raised her other hand in a motion to postpone what I had to say. But I could not delay.

"Dear Sophia, please listen," I pleaded. "Cartier has intercepted one of Jacques's letters to you. I just found this out from the postmistress." As I stopped to take a breath, I realized that my declaration had not sunk in. She looked confused, not startled as I expected. When I repeated my news, her face became wan and drawn. Her eyes still conveyed her disbelief.

"But Cartier was just here. He said nothing about a letter. In fact, he was quite cheery. He even talked about going for a ride later and would I wish to visit my cousin Elizabeth for a week while he had some workmen in for noisy renovations. How could he have one of Jacques's letters? He would be thrashing me to a pulp this very minute if he did."

"Take my word for it, he does have one of your letters. Perhaps it is the very letter with Jacques's arrangements for you both. He would know when Jacques is to arrive. And...perhaps he is scheming to lay a trap for him."

"*Mon Dieu,*" she cried in the language of her birth. "What can I do?" Reality had begun to set in, and sobbing took hold of her desperation.

"You cannot confront him, nor can you afford to ignore him," I said. "We don't know where Jacques is and so we cannot warn him of the danger." There seemed to be no obvious solution. "Clearly, we must sleep on this and not act too rashly," I told her as I put my arms around her and tried to comfort her. "Perhaps you should go to your cousin Elizabeth. At least you'd be safe there while we think of what to do."

Sophia turned around to face me and looked into my eyes as she said, "Whatever would I do without you, my dearest friend?" I began to cry as well. The rest of the day became a shambles, accomplishing nothing.

I leave this evening to spend the weekend with my father, and if I am lucky, my Robert will be able to spend a few hours with Papa and me.

September 12th

I returned to Marche House this morning only to be informed by some workmen that the mistress of the house was not in. In fact, one of them handed me a note from Sophia telling me that she had indeed gone to visit her cousin Elizabeth in Alexandria, Virginia. I did not encounter Cartier until later that day. He seemed quite polite, cordial even. He strongly suggested that I return to my father's house until Sophia returned. He promised to send for me then. I could hardly refuse, so I packed my things once more and left for home.

October 1st

It has been nearly three weeks since I have heard from Sophia. I wrote her at Elizabeth's a week ago, but have received no reply. I'm very worried about her grave situation. I have an awful premonition about it.

Robert cheers me up and tells me not to worry. He managed to spend some free time with me today, a paltry three hours, I must confess, but he is such a dear delight to me. I've never known anyone to be so kind and considerate.

October 4th

An unspeakable tragedy has befallen my Sophia. Two men came to my father's door today and delivered a summons for me to appear at an official inquest on the 16th. When I asked the business of the inquest, the men informed me that there had been two deaths at Marche House. A carriage carrying the mistress of the house and a gentleman named Jacques Giraud had disengaged itself from its horses and run over a cliff on the Marche property. Mr. Giraud's body had been found, along with many of Mrs. Marche's belongings. The men understood that she accompanied him at the time. Her body had not yet been recovered, but they presumed it to have washed out to sea.

How horrible. How sad. My poor, dear Sophia. I shall never see her again. Thank God for Robert. I shall not have to worry about future employment. But no one can ever replace my dear Sophia as my true friend.

October 16th

Today I attended the inquest. I have never experienced such a terrible, macabre day in all my life. The details of the tragedy were laid out for everyone to understand. A pivotal cotter pin connecting the horse harness with the carriage turned out to be the cause of the accident. It had worked itself loose and fallen to the ground in the vicinity of the front door, where they had found it.

My testimony that Sophia had planned to run off with Jacques shocked the community, and as far as the onlookers at the inquest were concerned, apparently shocked Cartier as well, but it confirmed the theory that Sophia had been in the carriage. I did not simply blurt out this information. The magistrate extracted it painfully, question by question, until I had little recourse but to respond with the truth as I know it. Forgive me, Sophia.

October 17th

The inquest ended today, and I am glad to be done with it. My suspicions that Cartier had something to do with the two deaths were ruled groundless and the whole horrible calamity was declared an accident. I am glad and disappointed all at once. Sophia had sinned, but she was also good and beautiful. She certainly didn't deserve to die this way. May God forgive her.

Lenora looked up at the group as she closed Geneve's diary for the year 1912.

"What an extraordinary and heartrending story," Olivia said. "Is there more?"

"I could find only three other passages relating to the Marches," Lenora replied. "In January of 1913 Geneve found a news item announcing the marriage of Cartier Marche to Leslie Temple, Hubert's nanny. In May of 1913 Geneve found another news item stating that Leslie Marche had reported her husband missing. And in August, a three-month investigation into his disappearance was abandoned."

"Thank you, Lenora," Olivia said. "I found the diary to be deeply affecting. We may learn a lot from it." Eager voices agreed. "Now, everyone, let's relax. I imagine soon it will be time for dessert, and then we'll resume the meeting in the sunroom." Olivia noticed Molly poking her head through the swinging door. "Yes, Molly?"

"Excuse my nosing in here, but there's an important phone call for Victor, and he's not in his room. At least he didn't answer my knock. Does anyone know where he is?"

Freddie gasped, and her hand flew to her mouth. The others merely shook their heads.

CHAPTER 12

LEGEND III: A ROOM APART

Freddie abruptly pushed her chair back and jerked to her feet. Not that she had anyplace to go; she just didn't know what else to do. Avi set his napkin down, worked his way around the table to his sister, and put his arm around her shoulders.

"Victor's a grown man and can take care of himself."

"That's just what I told her, Daddy," said Rachel.

Avi continued talking to Freddie, even though he couldn't entirely suppress his own uneasiness. "There's probably nothing to worry about. I'm sure he'll be back in a couple of hours. You always said he's such a night owl." Freddie accepted his consolation reluctantly, and she and Avi took their seats once more.

The kitchen door swung open as Molly and Greta entered bearing the desserts. A breath of relief swept among the guests. They welcomed the distraction.

"Oh, Molly, your chocolate mousse, my absolute favorite," Olivia said.

"Thank you, Miss Olivia, that's tasty of you to say so. Believe me, it's a lot of work. It could do a person out. But little Caitlin, she's a good girl. She helped me separate the twelve eggs and only broke three." Everyone laughed. "She'll be an upright good cook some day. But don't forget to try my apple-brandy spice cake. It's a new addition to my repository." Molly's sensuous sweets consumed the next half hour.

"Avi," Marti said, "I'm warning you, if you ever let Molly leave, you'll lose all of us, too. All your friends, all your relatives. She's irreplaceable."

"I know, I know," Avi said, laughing."

"I'll second that," Quentin said.

"Ah, Quentin," said Avi. "Considering the circumstances, we hardly expected the two of you to be here tonight. We're certainly glad that you did come."

"Actually, Trixie insisted," Quentin said. "She felt her grandfather's contribution would be important to the group."

"In that case, let's resettle in the sunroom with our coffee to hear the last legend."

Quentin stepped up to the temporary podium, cleared his throat and began. "A few of you may remember Trixie's grandfather, Isaac Aigue, Willard's father. On his next birthday Isaac will be ninety-four years young. He distinguished himself as a damned good carpenter and builder for over seventy years, too. Of course, he's retired now, a remarkable man, decidedly alert most of the time and still possessed of a fine sense of humor. Unfortunately, old Isaac is confined to his bed these days, enfeebled by a devastating bout with pneumonia last winter. Believe it or not, he insisted on apologizing for just being old. He's a grand old man, and we both love him dearly. However, as you might expect, he's subject to frequent memory lapses. I believe we caught him at an exceptional time."

Quentin reached into the side pocket of his sport coat and withdrew a small tape recorder and audio cassette. He set the recorder down on the cocktail table and pressed the PLAY button.

A crackly voice greeted his audience. "Hello, everyone, I'm Isaac Aigue. I sure wish I could be at your meeting to tell you folks everything in person."

A second voice, Quentin's, said: "We're sorry too, Isaac, but we surely do appreciate your talking with us for our members. Are you comfortable? Good, let's begin. Do you remember telling Trixie about some renovations you worked on up at Marche House?"

"Yes, son, I do. But I done that work more 'n sixty years ago." Isaac cleared his throat and coughed twice.

Quentin tried again. "Could you tell us what the work entailed, what you did there?"

"Well, I built a room for that mean-minded old bastard, Cartier Marche."

"What kind of room?"

"A room...a room with four walls." (Cough, cough.)

"Anything special about this room?"

"Oh, yeah, there sure was. I built a kind of secret room with a hidden door and no windows, none anybody could see, anyhow. That crazy man had the whole plan in his head. He wouldn't even let me put it on paper. He said he'd kill me if I ever told anybody about his room. And I didn't tell anybody either, not for over fifty years."

"How come you told Trixie then?"

"Well, young fella, when you've lived as long as I have, there ain't too many things or people that you're afraid of. Besides, by then, nobody'd even heard of old Marche for more 'n fifty years."

"I see what you mean. Tell us about the room."

"What do you want to know?"

"Well, for starters, where in the house was it located?"

"I can't remember exactly, but I know it was on the first floor behind a staircase. Side of the house that got the afternoon sun, I think. He had me make two long rooms a lot shorter to make a place for the new room. It's a very strange way to do things, not at all efficient, and a heap more expensive than a regular room woulda been. Never seen nothin' like it before or since."

"What made it so strange?"

"Like I told you, I created this space between the two rooms. According to his plan, I removed the old flooring and foundation and redone 'em from the ground up. Then he had me make four new walls, a ceiling, and a floor that don't touch the old ones. Now I calls that strange, don't you?"

"Sure. Tell us about the door. Where was it located?"

"Hmm...Wha?" (Snore...snore.)

"I do believe he's fallen asleep, Trix. What'll we do now?"

"Grandpa Isaac, wake up. Please, Grandpa, only a few minutes more. It's no use, Quentin, he'll be out of it for at least a half hour."

Click, click. The tape recorder had caught the sound of itself being turned OFF and then ON once more.

Quentin's voice asked: "Did you have a nice nap, Isaac?"

"What nap? I just tole you 'bout the room."

"Sure, Isaac. Tell us about the door. Where was it?"

"Hmm...I can't remember exactly where it was, but I do recollect you had to push on it and pull out a holding pin before the spring released the door."

"You mean you pushed on the door to make it open?"

"Nope, you pushed on the piece of molding until you saw the pin, and then you slid the door sideways while you pulled the pin."

"Where was this molding?"

"I don't rightly remember that. Sorry."

"Was it inside or outside of the house?"

"Oh, inside, of course. He wouldn't let me touch a thing on the stonework outside."

"Where'd you put those invisible windows you spoke of before?"

"Windows?...Oh, they weren't exactly windows, more like skylights. They couldn't be seen from the second floor because the outside balconies covered them. I left some space between them and the next floor to let in the light."

"I see. Roughly how big was the secret room?"

"I, ah...cuppa."

"What's that?"

"Cuppa, cuppa?"

"I believe Grandpa Isaac wants his coffee now."

Quentin turned off the tape recorder and said, "I'm afraid that's all we were able to get out of Isaac. I can't help wondering what this room was all about."

"Thank you, Quentin," said Olivia, "for that illuminating and exciting contribution."

"Yes, indeed. But why did Cartier Marche need a secret room?" Avi asked. "What was he going to do with it?"

"It sounds as though he planned to hide someone or something there," Heidi said. "But who? Or what?"

"Sophia is my guess," Lenora said. "But the poor thing ran off and got killed before Cartier had the chance to imprison her."

"Did she run off? They never found her body, you know." Felix spoke out, surprising even himself.

"Oh, Felix, you're much too sinister in your thinking." Marti just couldn't abide her husband taking an intellectual part in the discussion or, even worse, saying something original.

"He could be right, Marti," Bucky offered. "That is a distinct possibility."

"Why would the room require that type of construction?" Avi asked.

"I think I can answer that," said Simon. "It's probably safe to say Cartier had a prisoner in mind when he had it built. The separate foundation and double-walled construction were undoubtedly for sound isolation. No cry for help could get past such a barrier."

"Perhaps he only planned to hide her there until Jacques went away," Heidi blurted out.

"That's not beyond the realm of possibility either," Bucky replied.

"Do you suppose he actually intended to imprison his beautiful wife?" Felix asked.

"Who else, silly?" Marti asked.

"I dare say he might have had Jacques in mind," Bucky said.

"Now that's a refreshing thought. Take revenge on your wife by getting rid of her lover," Heidi said.

"But what about my key?" Avi asked. "Do you suppose it's the very same one that fits the jeweled box? And if so, could the box still be in the secret room?"

"Either there or at the bottom of the bay, having gone down with the ship--or carriage, so to speak," Rachel said. "It could easily have been among Sophia's unrecovered belongings."

Avi nodded. "Or recovered by someone else between then and now."

Olivia finished the last sip of her coffee. "I believe we've opened the proverbial can of worms here, or Pandora's box, to put it more elegantly. Instead of just learning all the answers about Marche House, we've wound up asking even more questions about it. I've got a suggestion. On Sunday afternoon, let's say at 1:30, I will open the mansion to any and all of you to conduct a thorough search for Cartier's hidden room. That should give everyone plenty of time to organize their thoughts. And I'll give you all a guided tour of the mansion at the same time."

"Now that sounds fabulous," Rachel said. "Almost like a treasure hunt."

"Before we call it an evening, though," Olivia continued, "I think I can contribute one more piece to the puzzle." She set on her lap a small white and gold Godiva chocolates shopping bag. "Don't get your hopes up, everyone, the chocolates are long gone. Anyway, I have something much better to show you." Cautiously unwrapping a large packet of tissue paper, she withdrew Schlem Bubbashlufsky's miniature portrait.

"Yesterday down at the deli, Schlem showed me this oil of his great-grandmother when she was a child. The painting is quite good, done in the tradition of European portraiture, but the atrocious frame, Schlem's handiwork, is probably of more interest to us. He found this cavetto wood molding in the ruins of a carpentry shop out in back of his property fifteen years ago. I'd like to draw your attention to the repeated sprigs of wheat lying back and forth along the double ess shape every five or six inches. It's quite unusual today, especially since it had to be fashioned by hand."

Olivia tucked the painting back into the bag. "I found a few more pieces in Schlem's tool shed. With his permission, of course. He's so thrifty that he didn't want to throw any of them away. He's kept them all these years. The molding resembles the trimwork you'll see throughout Marche House. Moreover, I now believe it to be the residue from Mr. Aigue's 1912 renovation. This may be of some help when we get around to our sleuthing on Sunday. So, with everyone's permission, I declare this meeting of the Black Rain Corners Historical Society to be adjourned. Oh, Molly, I'd love another cup of your delicious coffee. Is this another of your secret recipes?"

"Sure is, Miss Olivia." Molly took the silver coffeepot to the podium and refilled Olivia's cup.

"I wouldn't mind a little of that, Molly, if it's not too much trouble." Ernie pushed his cup and saucer toward her.

"No trouble at all, sir. It's no inquisition."

Now everyone had gone. Only Olivia remained, having sent Caitlin home with Greta. Olivia looped her arm through Avi's and guided him casually, yet deliberately, into the living room to the sofa, chatting lightly all the way.

Molly followed close behind them. "Doctor, I left a plate of cookies and a thermos of coffee for Victor on the floor in front of the den. I knocked, but the door didn't answer so I just left the tray to find him."

Avi smiled. "That's fine, Molly. Thank you, you're very thoughtful. Everything was extraordinary tonight. You can turn in now. Good-night."

"Good-night, everyone." She headed upstairs to her room.

"Good-night, Daddy. I love you." Rachel bent over her father and kissed him warmly on the cheek. "You too, Olivia." The two women brushed cheeks.

"Good-night, Dad, uh...Avi." Simon stood just behind his wife, uncertain of how affectionate to be. "Good night, Olivia." He decided to keep it verbal.

Avi said, "See you in the morning. Sleep well, both of you."

Olivia blew them two silent kisses. No sooner had they left the room than they heard her say, "They make such a lovely couple."

Avi and Olivia sat cozily on the couch.

"Avi, what a successful evening. The Society is really charting new territory, and I'm thrilled we're both a part of it."

"I am, too. You know, Olivia, this is an odd place for me to be, figuratively speaking. I've never in my life, and certainly not in my profession, been involved in such intrigue before."

"I know. I'm beginning to feel like a character out of Jane Austen. But why not, Avi? It's good for us. And I'm assuming the police will catch the murderer and recover the Sargent."

"Probably, Olivia, but I've got something else on my mind. This business of Victor is disturbing."

"Yes, it is. It does seem rather strange, his disappearing so early in the evening and not even telling you he was going out."

"Indeed. Well, I'll just have to wait till morning to see what happened. I confess I'm pretty uncomfortable with him as a house guest." Avi was silent for a moment. "So we'll see each other at the museum on Sunday. Maybe we'll even be done there in time to fit in our gin game."

"Oh, yes, we must. You've been on a roll for a week now, and I intend to win back those two dollars."

"Nope, that's not going to happen, Olivia." They both laughed and embraced warmly. She stood to leave, and Avi got up, too. It was understood that he would see her home.

She took his arm and they strolled outside onto the asphalt driveway. Olivia felt a chill and quickened her step, so Avi followed suit until they reached her front porch. Taking the key from her, he unlocked the door, and in the dim light of the night they kissed with the confidence of years of comfortable love.

Upstairs in the Kepple home, Rachel and Simon got ready for bed. She pulled the comforter aside and sat down next to him as he pulled off his shoes.

"You know," she said in a low murmur, "I heard Olivia say we make such a nice couple. But, really, she and Daddy are precious together."

"I take it this is a long-term relationship."

"Forever. Mother and Olivia met at the grocery store when her daughter and I were both five." Rachel grinned. "We were both having tantrums in the produce section at the same time and our mothers started commiserating with each other. That was the beginning of a lifelong friendship of our two families. It was "Aunt" Olivia and "Uncle" Harry. Our families did everything together: beach, picnics, vacations."

"So what's keeping your dad from marrying her?"

"He feels he's just too set in his routines and has too many aches and pains to saddle her with. If Uncle Harry had died ten years earlier, things might have been different."

"But what happened during all the years after your mother died and Harry was still living? Didn't your dad date?"

"Only half-heartedly," Rachel said. "But then he went to Paris for a psychoanalytic convention. And when he came home, he was walking on air, like a high school kid in love. He had met someone, a French lady psychoanalyst, and they had this little fling during the convention."

"His couch or hers?"

Rachel giggled. "Does it matter? Anyway, they even talked about her leaving her husband. Daddy offered to help her establish a practice here in Maryland, and I guess they would have gotten married. But she decided against it. Told him it would be too big a cultural adjustment for her, with the language difference and everything."

"That's a shame. It might have been a good match."

"Maybe, but there was another reason she didn't come."

"Oh?"

"Her husband had a gun. He suspected something and told his wife he'd kill whoever it was."

Simon started laughing and couldn't stop. He laughed so hard he fell back on the bed. Rachel giggled some more. "Shh, they'll hear us."

"What a great story!" Simon stood up and walked to the dormered window seat, where he'd left a neatly folded pair of pajamas. As he shook out the pajama legs, something caught his eye outside at the front gate.

"Hey, Rachel, come here. Quick!" Through the branches of a maple tree, he saw a woman enter the driveway. She took a few steps, glanced up at their bedroom window and, seeing someone there, retreated out of the driveway into the shadows. "See that?"

"Yes, but barely," said Rachel. "I thought it might be Olivia, but why would she be turning right leaving our driveway? Her house is on the other side."

Heidi stepped out of the elevator on the second floor of the inn. The long evening had made her drowsy and she just wanted to crawl into bed. But her eyes boinged open as she spotted the man entering her room halfway down the hall. "Derrick!" she called in a loud whisper, afraid to disturb other guests.

But the door closed behind him.

She turned the key, pushed the door open, and almost collided with a wall of muscle. Derrick stood just inside, his back to the door, shoving his shirt tails into his trousers. He wheeled around to confront her, a startled look on his face.

"Oh, hi, sweet stuff, have a nice meeting?"

"Don't 'sweet stuff' me, you insufferable bastard."

"What? What's wrong, honey?"

"Don't play dumb with me. Look at you."

Derrick looked down at his torso and held his arms out, palms up. "What do you mean?" he said, shaking his head in exaggerated confusion.

"I saw you sneak into the room half-dressed."

"Sneak? Half-dressed? My shirt tail came out. That's all. What kind of federal case are you making here?"

Heidi wrenched a wooden hanger off the rod in the closet and approached him swinging, shouting. She no longer cared who heard her. "Do you always misbutton your shirt that way? I'm surprised you even had time to pull your pants up. Who was she? Where is she now?"

"All I did was get dressed in a hurry to go get some ice. So I'm sloppy. That doesn't mean I'm out dickie-dunking on you. I spent the evening watching TV in bed."

"So where's the ice, you liar?" She glared at him.

"I forgot the bucket and came back to get it when you came in. Honest, hon." He shook her wrist and the hanger fell to the floor. Slipping his hand about her waist, he attempted to pull her closer to him. She stiffened, struggled, and tried to escape, but his grip tightened. Feeling her finally relax, Derrick boldly stole a long kiss, his lips too hard on hers, his tongue probing, until at last her lips parted, yielding.

Heidi wanted to believe him, and feeling his arousal against her, she thought maybe she had been wrong. Her arms went around his neck. He effortlessly picked her up and laid her down on the bed. She let him undress her slowly and deliberately. He would prove his fidelity soon. That was what she wanted to believe.

Ernest Lord, returning from the Society meeting, had just missed the elevator that carried Heidi upstairs. Taking the next one, he found his wife in bed, ear cocked toward the wall.

Danielle had heard the ruckus next door, every word of it, and found it enormously entertaining. Her book lay open at her hip, and she held a finger to her lips, motioning Ernie to join her.

She looked lovely to him, so refreshed, so desirable, and so innocent.

CHAPTER 13

LATE FOR BREAKFAST
Saturday, October 25, 1980

Molly's domain, the sunflower-yellow kitchen, basked in bright morning light, and the aroma of brewing coffee--three parts Folgers and one part chocolate macadamia nut--delighted a second sense. Harvest gold, the newest shade in culinary appliances, complemented the oak cabinetry and the blue and yellow Spanish floor tiles. The breakfast nook, at one end of the kitchen, overlooked Molly's autumn flower beds: an array of yellow, white, russet, and purple mums. A pedestaled table and four captain's chairs nestled in the curve of the bay window.

The mixer hummed and whirred as Molly whipped up the batter for banana pancakes. For all her awkward appearance, her heavy roundness, she achieved a model of efficiency within her own milieu. No wasted motion, no open cookbook, and no hesitation. She'd committed this love of cooking to memory out of affection for the Kepple family.

Freddie poked her head in. "Coffee smells good, dear."

"Be ready in a few minutes, Miss Freddie. Can I start a stack of banana pancakes for you?"

"Pancakes? Oh, no, I couldn't possibly after that sumptuous meal last night. Just toast, and one slice at that."

"Okay, Miss Freddie, toast it is." Molly's voice conveyed a barely veiled disappointment. "How about your tweed bread, then?"

"That'll be fine, Molly." Freddie couldn't find fault with this perfect description of whole wheat.

Molly popped a slice in the toaster. From the refrigerator, she removed a saucer of buttered noodles from the previous night's feast and slid them into Shana's food dish. The dog attacked it with the familiarity of a gourmet accustomed to rich dining. As she chomped, a large clump of noodles fell to the floor. Shana vigorously tried to lick them up. The more she licked, the more she spread them over the gleaming tiles. She swiped at them with her paw, but they stubbornly stuck there, just long enough to be discovered by Avi.

"Molly, I keep telling you not to feed the dog our table food. The vet says it's too rich for her. She'll get sick. Besides, she's too fat. I suppose she's already had filet mignon."

"Just a tad, Doctor. Only a few bites left. How 'bout some banana pancakes?"

"Thanks, Molly, but last night's dinner just about did me in. I'll just have some cold cereal and toast." Her attempt to change the subject hadn't escaped Avi's notice, but he decided to give up on the lecture about Shana's diet. No amount of talking made any difference.

Rachel and Simon greeted Molly with a musical "Good morning," and she tried once more to peddle her pancakes. However, they preferred coffee and a bran muffin to share.

Molly set down a large tray of cereal, toast, muffins, and assorted spreads. She added a steaming stack of pancakes, despite all the refusals, before returning to the kitchen.

Simon relented and decided to try one...and then another. "Fabulous!" he said. "So light and fluffy. When're you going to make me some of these, hon?"

Rachel feigned deep concentration. "In our next life, maybe, if I'm not too busy."

Simon laughed. "In that case, I'd better eat a few extra now. Where'd you ever find Molly, Avi?"

"She worked for a colleague of mine who'd gotten married. He called to let me know that, after twenty years with his family, Molly was available." He lowered his voice to a whisper and told the story of her interview. Avi learned that she had left school after tenth grade to support herself. She'd bragged about her years of experience: "After all, I worked for royalty folks over in Georgetown."

Avi stopped as soon as the door swung open and Molly appeared with a tray of cheese Danish and asked, "Will there be anything else, Doctor?"

"No, Molly. Oh, maybe so. Would you remove the tray from the hall outside the den, please?"

"Yes, Doctor, right away."

Freddie stirred sugar into her coffee deliberately, her head bent over her cup to hide her distress. "Does anyone know what time Victor came in last night? I waited and waited and even fell asleep with the lights on." She looked searchingly at each of them, but they all shook their heads.

With Victor's snack tray in hand, Molly returned to the dining room. "Strange," she said. "Victor didn't touch the snacks. Not even the decapitated coffee. Not a drip of it. That's not like him."

"No, not like him at all," Freddie said. The color began to drain from her face. She slid her chair back and started for the den. She knocked on the door, gently at first, then firmly, and finally, a desperate pounding--all the while calling, pleading: "Victor? Victor, honey? Vic, dear?...Please open the door."

Avi came to her side. "Perhaps he isn't in there. Maybe he stayed at the inn last night."

But Rachel doused that hope. She got down on one knee and peered into the keyhole. "No," she said, "he's got to be in there. The skeleton key's still in the door." She rose to her feet and put her arm around her favorite aunt. "You mentioned that Vic still had a drinking problem. Do you suppose he hit the bottle last night and passed out? That would explain why he doesn't hear us."

"I don't know whether I want you to be right about this or not," Freddie said. "I need him to be safe, first and foremost. Then I'll deal with him falling off the wagon."

Her niece took the initiative. "As I see it, we have two choices. One, we can wait him out and see if he emerges. And two, we can break into the room."

Freddie turned to her brother with pleading eyes. "He may be ill. Can we, Avi? Break in, I mean."

"Of course, Freddie. I'll go get the other key."

"That won't do any good, Dad," Simon interjected. "Not if the key is still in the door from the inside."

"Can't you take the door off the hinges?" Rachel asked.

"No good, either," Simon replied. "The pins are on the inside too, and the screws are hidden by the door jamb."

Molly hovered behind them and offered to call old Mr. Thomas, the handyman. "He's well reversed in that sort of thing," she said.

"No, not yet. I suppose we could just break the door down and the repair expense be damned," Avi said.

Simon shook his head. "That door is very old and very solid. Breaking it in would be no simple task."

"I got an inspiration that might work," Molly offered. "Saw old Mr. Thomas do it once."

"Do what?" asked Rachel.

"He stuck contract cement on the end of a stick to turn a key on the other side."

"Might just do the trick," said Simon. "Depends."

"On what?" Rachel asked.

"On whether that contact cement is still in our glove compartment."

"I think it is. I'll get it for you."

"The penlight, too," he called after her as she trotted to the front hall and out the door. It was no more than a minute before the door burst open again with Rachel extending the tubes of two-part contact cement.

"Molly, can you get me a few of those long fireplace matches, an old jar cover, and some paper towels?"

"Coming right up, Mr. Simon." Waddle or not, Molly was off and back in a hurry with each of the items. She watched Simon squeeze equal amounts from both tubes into the jar cover. Breaking off the incendiary tips of the matches, he stirred the two globules until two colors and two consistencies merged at the end of the first matchstick. Then he wiped the stick clean with a paper towel.

"Hold this for me, will you?" He handed the penlight to Molly, who directed its beam into the keyhole. It took a number of Simon's instructions before she properly focused the beam on the elusive key.

Turning the matchstick slowly, Simon collected a small bubble of the mixed contact cement on the end of it. Careful not to touch the sides of the lock or the mechanisms inside, he applied a controlled amount of glue to the exposed cylindrical end of the skeleton key's shaft. Another quick rotation permitted him to separate the matchstick from the deposited blob of cement and back out of the keyhole without pulling any significant tail from the gooey residue.

"Whew," said Simon. "And that's not even the hard part."

"So what's the hard part, then?" Rachel asked.

"Well, once the two dabs of cement are dry--one on the key and one on the end of the stick--we'll have to line their ends up very carefully before making final contact. Once they're stuck together, well, good luck. There's no second shot at it."

No one said a word. Freddie held her breath to the point where she thought she would choke or faint. When Simon assured himself that the cement on the stick was no longer tacky to the touch, he said, "Time to have a go at it."

"Want to change places?" Rachel offered.

"No, better not...a little lower with the light, please...more... hold it."

This time Simon entered the keyhole more slowly and with a great deal more care. He checked his alignment one last time and then brought the two objects together with a small jerk. He let his breath out in relief and inspected the joint once more. "Hmm, not too bad. Could have been a little more centered, but it will have to do."

"Come on, Simon," Rachel urged, "you're too much of a perfectionist. What now?"

Simon jiggled the stick lightly to test the response of the key. Positive. It adhered to the matchstick. He began to twist the stick as close to the keyhole as he could reach. He jiggled the stick and key combination against the far side of the escutcheon, trying to sense the alignment that would pass the key clear of the lock. It turned easily at first until the key encountered the bolt mechanism.

Simon felt the strain increasing as he continued to turn. No longer any need to look, just feel. Perspiration ran down his face. The matchstick itself showed signs of fatigue. Just before the mechanical stress reached the breaking point, he reversed the rotation. The key and the attached stick moved freely again and he tested them in a continuum of positions.

"Hot damn! Good!" He'd passed the critical juncture. Only a slight twist more and he'd have it. Pushing the stick against the key as far as it would go, he then used a second stick to poke the first one free of the lock. At last the matchstick and key thudded to the floor. He quietly pulled the second stick back through his side of the lock and pulled himself to his feet before letting out a triumphant "Yahoo!"

Avi handed Rachel the second key, and she turned it easily in the lock. She tried the doorknob and, sure enough, it unlatched and swung inward. "You did it, sweetheart," she said.

"A fine job, Simon," Avi said with visible relief.

The room was nearly dark; the only light came from the three narrow-slotted windows, and even that was limited by an enormous shade tree outside. Avi stepped past his daughter and son-in-law. When Freddie tried to enter, Rachel, fearing the worst, held her aunt and prevented her from going any farther.

Avi called out: "Dear God!...Molly, get my bag! Quickly! From the office!"

Victor lay on the oriental carpet face down, as though he'd just rolled off the opened hide-a-bed couch. His clothes reeked of urine. The carpet smelled of whiskey, although neither a bottle nor a glass could be seen. "Simon, over here, give me a hand," Avi called. The two of them managed to turn the body over.

Victor's eyes glared wide open, as though filled with the fright of his last thoughts. Avi tried for a pulse. Found none. And when he looked up, Molly stood there with his medical bag. He ripped away Victor's soiled, rumpled dress shirt and black bow tie and removed the stethoscope from his bag. He listened with hope where he already knew there was none. And while he listened at Victor's chest, he noticed some bruising on his nephew's abdomen.

Deciding to leave Victor there on the floor, Avi reached up to close the lids over the eyes of terror. There were signs of puffiness above one of them. He shook his head slowly and got to his feet. "May he find eternal peace and comfort in the hands of God."

The sobbing of his sister in the hall became a screeching. "Vic-tor! Don't leave me, my darling. Please, please, dear God, let him live." With that, she collapsed in Rachel's arms.

Enlisting Simon's help, they carried Aunt Freddie to her room on the second floor. Molly went along to open doors and help where she could.

Avi sank into the recliner to think about what he should do next, but then realized he faced the body on the floor. He got up, pulled the rumpled top sheet off the open sofa-bed and spread it over Victor. Resuming his position in the recliner, Avi placed his hands on his knees.

"Well, Vic, old boy, you couldn't live like a *mensch*, so I guess you just couldn't die like one. You had a good mind that you failed to put to good purpose; opportunity and affluence that you chose to squander; and a loving family that wanted so much more from you and for you. It wasn't easy, but we found something to love in you, anyway. Such a waste."

Molly reappeared in the den doorway. "Is there anything I can do, Doctor?"

"Is Freddie all right, Molly?"

"I don't know, Doctor. She's lying on her bed crying. She keeps shouting things. Rachel is with her."

Avi reached into his bag, studying and rearranging bottles until he found the one he wanted. He shook two pills from it and handed them to Molly. "See that she takes these with water. I'll be up to check on her in a little while." Molly passed Simon in the front hall.

"Oh, come in, Simon," Avi called. "I'm just trying to sort things out in my mind. Perhaps you can help. I feel terrible that you're being subjected to this nightmare. Here it's your first visit to us and..." He shook his head, his shoulders slumped in defeat.

"Glad to do what I can, Dad."

"I'm afraid it's been so many years since I've treated the physiological side of a patient, I'm having difficulty determining the actual cause of death. Ordinarily, finding a body of Victor's general health in a locked room would suggest some sort of natural cause. Heart failure, for example."

"What's different in this case, Avi?"

"Two things, Simon. One, Victor's mental state."

"You mean suicide?"

"A definite possibility."

"What else, sir?" Simon still struggled to find a comfortable way to address his new father-in-law. It would be a long time before he would settle on "Dad" for good.

"Well, there are bruises on his body, as though he received a beating from someone in the last few days."

"Then you think this is a matter for the authorities?"

"I'm afraid so, son." Avi picked up the phone on the cherry wood table next to him and dialed 911.

CHAPTER 14

THE INSPECTOR

Inspector Paco LeSoto and Officer Frank Mullins waited for someone to respond to the doorbell at the Kepple home. Frank shifted from foot to foot as he eyed the polished chestnut door with its dog's head knocker. The things some folks spend their money on, he mused. It wasn't often he got called to Locust Lane.

Although Paco had become his supervisor, Frank remained the only full-time county policeman at the Black Rain Corners station. Paco, after retiring from the Baltimore police force, Detective First Class, had found himself too strapped for cash to live on his pension and Social Security, so he lent his big-city expertise to the town about eighteen hours a week. Both men answered to the Police Central office over at the Anne Arundel county seat.

As Molly cautiously opened the front door, Paco presented his shield and business card. "I'm Inspector LeSoto and this is Officer Mullins. We're responding to a call from Dr. Kepple."

"Yes, the doctor is expecting you." Molly pulled the door open all the way, and the two policemen stepped into the front hall.

Molly found the inspector kinda cute, though a bit underfed at five foot nine, perhaps a hundred sixty pounds sinking wet. He impressed her as a natty dresser, too: gray tweed jacket, leather loafers, sharply creased slacks, and yellow shirt with a gray bow tie. The temples of his horn-rimmed sunglasses pierced a full head of coarse salt and pepper hair.

"And you are?" Paco asked.

"I'm Molly, Dr. Kepple's homekeeper. He'll be with you in a little jiffy."

"Thank you," he acknowledged, pushing the sunglasses onto his forehead.

Molly was immediately struck by the inspector's gaze as it leapt about his new surroundings in hyper fashion. Unnerving yet seductive. Nobody could lie to keen hazel eyes like that. He would be a man who could wheedle dark secrets from reluctant suspects.

Officer Frank Mullins stood physically forbidding at well over six feet in his crisp blue uniform. Molly pictured him as the strong silent partner.

Avi stepped out into the long hall opposite the den with an outstretched hand. He waved them in.

"Hello, I'm Dr. Kepple. My nephew is in here." He ushered them to the den door. "We discovered him about an hour ago locked in this room."

"Have you touched *anything* in the room yet?" Paco spoke softly in his most officious tone. Then a thought amused him: perhaps the doctor was entitled to professional courtesy. He would be dealing with a psychoanalyst, a professional in mind games--nothing he couldn't handle. Paco repeated the question as they followed Avi into the den.

"Except for the fact that we turned him over to see if he could benefit from any medical attention."

"We?"

"My son-in-law, Simon and I."

"Oh. Did you actually administer any?"

"No, Inspector, he was already dead. I simply covered him with the sheet from the sofa-bed."

"Just how did you determine that he was already dead?" Paco bent over and picked up the matchstick and key combination from the carpet with a cotton-gloved hand. He wore only the one glove, on his left hand.

"Finding no pulse, I verified his death with my stethoscope. From the temperature of his body and his general coloring, my guess is he died some time late last night."

"What's this thing?" Holding the key and matchstick by the stick end, Paco slipped the gadget into a clear plastic bag that he retrieved from his pocket.

"You see, when we tried to get in the room, we found the door locked from the other side and the key still in the lock. We couldn't take the hinges off the door because they're on the inside too. My son-in-law devised that ingenious gadget to push the key out from our side of the door. Then I was able to use an extra key to get in."

"I see. What about the windows?" Paco asked.

"They're sealed and, besides, they're too high up on the wall for anybody to climb through."

Officer Mullins was busy with his notepad, taking down both Paco's questions and Avi's responses. He stopped for a moment and knelt down on one knee to examine a damp spot on the rug. He brought a finger's rub to his nose. "It's whiskey, maybe some kind of brandy," he said. "Must have spilled a full glass to be still there, but I don't see either a glass or a bottle anywhere around." He tore off a piece of paper towel from a roll in his kit, laid it down on the damp spot, and patted it with a wooden tongue depressor to absorb the remaining wetness before depositing the towel scrap in another evidence bag.

"Good work, Frank," Paco said. "Tell me, Doctor, how many other people were in the house?"

"Well, besides myself, there's Rachel, my daughter, and her husband, Simon. They're visiting from New York for the weekend. Then there's Molly, my housekeeper, and my sister, Freddie. She lives here with me and is also the deceased's mother. I guess that's five. And, of course, the deceased, Victor, made six."

"The deceased lived here too?" Paco inquired.

"Yes, but not on a regular basis. He'd visit us for a few days now and then, and this stay, somewhat longer. He'd fallen on hard times financially."

"Anybody else you can think of?"

"No one living here. However, we did entertain the entire Historical Society here last night. We held our meeting during cocktails and dinner."

"What exactly is the Historical Society?"

"We're a new organization formed to administer the Marche Museum, the old mansion up on the hill."

"That so? You mean the place where the caretaker was killed?"

"Yes."

"Officer Mullins answered the first call, and then the criminal investigation team from the county took over."

"I see," said Avi. "Have they found Aigue's killer yet or the painting?"

"Not that I know of, Doctor. I'll need a list of your members and their addresses and phone numbers. I'll want to talk with all of them."

"Of course, Inspector. They've planned a tour of the museum for the afternoon. I could have them meet here for brunch tomorrow morning. I'll call the inn and make sure everyone comes early enough."

"I'll put together a menu of the guests for him, Doctor." Molly stood in the den doorway.

"Thank you, Molly." Avi watched Paco bend over the body and pull back the sheet. Molly gave an involuntary shiver, turned away, and retreated to the kitchen.

Paco motioned to Frank, who removed a flash camera from his briefcase. Some forty flashes later, Paco agreed that Frank had sufficiently recorded the state of the body and the room's environs.

Paco examined the torn shirt and the bruises on Victor's chest. "Was the shirt damaged before or during your examination of him?"

"I tore the shirt away to get my stethoscope to his chest. It was already soiled."

"And the bruises, what do you make of them?"

"If I were to venture some kind of guess, I'd say they were sustained in a beating."

"I agree, but who from? Would these be the unusual set of circumstances you spoke of on the phone?"

"Exactly!" Avi watched as Paco donned a second glove and systematically went through each of Victor's pockets, removing keys, handkerchief, penknife, loose change, checkbook, and wallet. He opened the wallet and found sixty-five dollars in it. Mullins held Ziploc clear storage bags for each item extracted.

"It looks as though none of his personal effects have been disturbed. Would anything else at all be missing from the room?"

A sudden dread descended upon Avi. "My key," he murmured. With the shock of Victor's death, he'd completely forgotten about the jeweled key. Even worse, he'd never changed the combination on the security cabinet. As softly as the words "my key" had escaped his lips, they didn't escape the attention of the inspector.

"Another key? What's going on here?" Paco asked sharply.

"This one is an antique, Inspector. It belongs to the museum. Here, I'll show you." Avi approached the display cabinet with apprehension. He could almost hear his own heartbeat, and his breathing came fast, swelling almost audibly. But he forced himself to take control, not to hyperventilate. In the presence of the inspector Avi felt vulnerable. He must suppress his anxiety.

Avi turned on the cabinet light, and looking through the glass, saw the blue velvet case resting safely on its shelf. He emitted a small sigh of relief, for that's the way he had placed it back in the cabinet last night. "It's in its case. I'll open it and let you see for yourself."

"Good idea, Doctor," Paco said. "But I'd appreciate your putting those on first."

Avi slipped into the pair of surgical gloves that Mullins offered and began spinning the dial through the steps of the installation combination. Sensing the ultimate click, he swung the windowed lid up and removed the velvet case. He swallowed hard as he depressed the clasp and felt the top pop open.

"Good God, it's gone!" Avi stared in disbelief at the impression in the white satin, outlining where the key had lain.

"What was this key, and why is it so important to you?"

Avi didn't speak for a moment. He wanted to collect his thoughts and regain his presence of mind. "With your permission, Inspector, why don't we all sit down, and I'll explain. You, too, Officer. Inspector, this is a dreadful turn of events. Not the same kind of shock as Victor's death, you understand, but a serious situation for me."

"Oh? Why is that?"

"Well, the key is extremely valuable for two reasons. For one, it's gold and encrusted with gems, a diamond and three rubies. It also has considerable historical value, having come from the estate of the late Hubert Marche. It's now part of the Marche Museum collection, and I'm quite certain it's irreplaceable."

"And may I ask how this jeweled key came into your possession and why it's in your house instead of in the museum?"

"I don't actually own the key."

He stopped abruptly as he saw Paco's left eyebrow arch. "Well, I do and I don't. You see, I bought the donor rights to it at a fund-raising auction for the new museum."

"What does that mean?"

"Well, Inspector, it means I own it, but I don't get to keep it permanently. It's in my keep, on loan, awaiting its ultimate display location in the museum."

"What's it worth, anyway?" Paco bent over the display cabinet and inspected it without touching anything. He toyed with the idea of picking up the velvet case, but decided against it. Everything would have to be fingerprinted. "There's no sign of forced entry here. So," he repeated, "what's it worth?"

"Well, I paid thirty-five thousand. However, last night Dr. Lord appraised it at more than sixty thousand."

"This Dr. Lord--another medical doctor?"

"No, sir." Avi went on to explain Ernie's background and function in the Society.

"I see. Are there any photographs of this key?"

"Dr. Lord took some last night and the insurance people probably have some."

With quick, darting movements, Paco made a complete tour of the den. He scanned the titles of the books tightly packed into the bookcases. The professional journals piled on the table next to Avi's recliner. The family photographs filling one wall. The plants--the densely leaved philodendrons, the pepperomia, and the cactus, so tall and fat it looked ridiculous. He gingerly fingered one of the thorns.

"Never seen a cactus quite like this, this big, I mean, not in anybody's house, anyway." Paco deliberately made an effort to abate the tension.

"Neither have I, Inspector. I just received it as a gift from a patient, and frankly, it's not something I would have chosen." He sensed that the inspector was trying to reach some sort of decision while he scanned and evaluated what he saw.

"The key was insured, then?" Paco asked.

"I believe it was. Under a blanket policy the estate turned over to the museum. I have no idea to what extent, though. We'll have to check on that."

"Under the circumstances, I think we'll have to treat this investigation as a robbery-homicide, at least until more questions are answered."

"And what will that mean to the members of my household?" Avi already knew, but needed to hear the answer anyway.

"Two things: the den is off limits to everyone except my people and, until further notice, the members of your household will have to make themselves available for questioning."

"Of course. We'll cooperate in any way we can."

"Doctor, you said the door to this room was locked."

"Yes."

"Those windows up there...I know you already said so, but you're sure there's no way to open them...no way anyone could have gotten in?"

"Not that I know of. They're glazed into immovable frames. They're an integral part of the wall, I believe."

"Hmm. Odd construction. And you say the door was locked from the inside with the key left in the lock."

"Yes, I told you that earlier."

"Of course, you did. I know it may sound silly to ask, but is there any other way in or out of this room, sir?"

"No, none."

"Were there any signs of a struggle in the room when you entered?"

"Not that I could determine. But I did note those bruises on Victor's body. I'm not an expert in that kind of thing, obviously, but they didn't look exactly fresh. Other than that, I didn't see any signs of foul play. He was just lying there, face down."

"We'll check out the bruises during the autopsy. You say he was lying face down?"

"Yes, I told you I turned him over. He must have fallen off the couch."

"Who actually entered the room with you?"

"Just my son-in-law, Simon. The others waited at the door."

"Others?"

"My daughter, my sister, and my housekeeper."

"What was the state of your nephew's general health?"

"I don't really know. If he'd had a physical recently I don't know about it. However, he gave the appearance of being in fair health, possibly a bit underweight. He jogged almost every day. His mother may be able to tell you more."

"Where is she now?"

"Upstairs resting. My sister, Freddie, has been dealt quite a blow. She's a sensitive, deeply feeling woman who simply doted on her son, the center of her universe."

"Do you know of any enemies he might have had?"

"He was a boozer and a gambler. I think he knew I had his number and he felt ashamed. At the same time, I know he respected me." Avi paused, let out a deep sigh and moistened his lips. "I suppose Victor hid a good deal from his family. Actually, he preferred to be close-mouthed. I never stopped trying to draw him out, but he never felt comfortable enough to confide in me. I'd call it a complex on-again, off-again relationship. I do feel he had that semblance of integrity that somehow went wrong, allowing his weaknesses to get the better of him. He recently lost his job as an insurance agent and it left him feeling hopeless. If he'd been willing to confide in me, I think I could have helped him."

"In what way, Doctor?"

"Restore his self-confidence, for instance, to get him back on track with another insurance position. He needed to develop some defenses to deal with his overprotective mother as well. He was actually good at what he did. He wanted to accept my help, but he had difficulty admitting that at his age, fifty-one, he couldn't handle his own life."

Avi shook his head. "I know when I'm out of my depth. You asked about his enemies. Whether his creditors could have been called enemies or not, I have no idea. You see, he gambled compulsively, incurably so."

"Would you happen to know any of these creditors?"

"No, sir."

"There are some things we should attend to now. First, is there a funeral parlor you would prefer?"

"Uh...yes. Hoffman's. I'll make the call."

"That won't be necessary. You see, the body will have to be transported to the morgue in Baltimore. I'll make the call to the medical examiner's office myself. I've got some special instructions for them."

"Thank you, Inspector, but I will have to call Hoffman's, too. Freddie and I will have to meet with them to choose a casket, discuss the burial, all those painful details."

"Of course, Doctor. Now if you'll excuse us. Officer Mullins and myself will conduct a thorough search of the room. I'm putting in a call to the mobile crime unit and they'll be here soon to dust for fingerprints. We'll want to get everything off to the lab. Oh, in about an hour I'll want to resume my questioning, perhaps your son-in-law next."

"Yes, I'll tell him." Avi started up the stairs toward Freddie's room. Rachel and Simon were just coming out, and Rachel closed the door.

"She's sleeping now, Daddy." Rachel spoke in hushed tones. "Those pills of yours are certainly effective."

"Yes, they're quite strong." Avi turned around and followed the two of them back down the stairs, and Rachel led them straight to the kitchen, where they slid into the captain's chairs at the oak table.

The kitchen seemed uncharacteristically quiet. Molly silently arranged fresh-cut yellow and purple mums in a ceramic pot. Shana lay curled up on her corduroy beanbag, subdued, as though she actually understood the reserved behavior of the day.

"Coffee, Doctor?"

"Please, Molly, for all of us."

Molly placed the flowers in the middle of the table and proceeded to serve the coffee, along with a plate of warm sugar cookies, glad to have something specific to do for her family.

No one spoke for several minutes until Rachel could stand it no longer. "What did they find, Daddy?"

"Inspector LeSoto is calling it a robbery-homicide."

"But why homicide? And what's missing?"

"Rachel, don't say anything to your Aunt Freddie, at least, not now. But it looks as though Victor has been beaten. And then there's the matter of the jeweled key."

"What about the key?" Simon and Rachel raised the question in near unison.

"It's missing."

"Oh, no!" Rachel gasped.

"Case and all?" Simon asked.

"No, the empty case is still there."

"How could the thief, the murderer, whatever he is, possibly have gotten in with the door locked from the inside?" Rachel said.

Molly stood next to Avi, poised to refill his cup, but she decided to theorize first. "Doctor, if you don't mind my asking. If the thief did beat Victor up, why would he want to hurt him when he got away with the booty, anyway?"

Avi looked up into Molly's face and acknowledged her astuteness. "Well, perhaps Victor was reluctant to give it up and the thief took to persuading him."

"Oh," she said, and moved over to pour more coffee into Simon's cup.

Simon tried another tack. "How could anyone get into the display cabinet? Is it damaged?"

"No. It isn't damaged," Avi said, pausing for a moment to straighten his tie, stalling for time. Indeed, he wished he had a better answer for Simon than the bald truth.

"I put the key back in the security cabinet myself." Avi stopped talking and pressed his lips together. He dreaded what he knew would be his son-in-law's next logical observation.

"Didn't you say the empty key case was in the locked display cabinet and..." Simon was interrupted when Paco pushed his way through the swinging door.

"Doctor, the ambulance will be here in half an hour. They'll remove Mr.

Moskowitz and keep him at the morgue until the medical examiner's people are ready for him. One problem, though, the examiner's office has quite a backup. Won't get to him until Monday morning. That means you can't schedule a funeral until Tuesday morning at the earliest."

"I see, thank you." It crossed Avi's mind that he had other family members to notify. So many unpleasant tasks to tackle.

"Mr. Simon?"

"I'm Simon Mendelsohn. What can I do for you?"

"I'd like a few moments of your time...in the sunroom, perhaps?"

"Certainly!" Simon followed Paco out of the room.

"Will he want to talk to me too, Daddy?"

"Oh, you bet he will."

In faded jeans, soft flannel shirt, and penny loafers, Rachel looked more like a preppy teenager than a successful New York editor, and her wary expression enhanced the image. She'd never been questioned by the police before.

"What's the inspector like?" she asked.

"He's the perfect gentleman doing his job, and a good one, it seems to me. He's very thorough. Just answer his questions. He'll recognize the truth when he hears it. He appears to be very perceptive."

"What are we going to tell Aunt Freddie when she gets up?"

"As little as possible, my dear, as little as possible. She's so distraught. She doesn't need to know about the bruises. She'll undoubtedly find out later. But for the time being, the robbery is sufficient cause for the police involvement as far as she's concerned."

"Was poor Victor actually beaten to death?"

"I don't think so. The bruises didn't look fresh. More like a few days old. That is, they didn't really look severe enough to have caused his death. But I could be wrong."

"Why did this happen, Daddy? Why?"

"I just don't know."

Rachel had nothing further to ask her father at this point. She was too bewildered, too shocked to put it all together just yet.

The doorbell chimed, and Molly hastened to answer. She returned a moment later to the kitchen to whisper: "Doctor, the ambulance has come for Victor."

Simon held the front door open to allow the two attendants to roll a gurney into the den. Molly and Rachel stood in the foyer, suspended in time, until the attendants reappeared, pushing the covered gurney. Just as it passed them, with Officer Mullins following, a strap came untied and Victor's left arm dropped to a dangling position below the gurney.

"Oh...ugh!" Rachel shuddered and turned away. But not wanting to miss anything, she quickly turned back again. In watching Victor leave for the last time, she felt a sadness and yet an excitement that embarrassed her.

As the ambulance attendant retied the strap, Molly's eyes thoughtfully rested on the reshrouded hand. "Not a nice way to go out, uh-uh, not one bit," she murmured.

Officer Mullins bummed a ride with the ambulance to the south county police station in Edgewater. He would run the evidence, each piece sealed in plastic, by the lab later on. Meanwhile, there was paperwork to be done and the crime unit people needed to do their thing as well.

Avi's two o'clock appointment arrived. He had tried to call the patient to cancel, but couldn't reach her, and now he tried to present as calm a demeanor as the day would allow. As he ushered the patient into his office at the far end of the house, Rachel could hear her questioning Avi. "An ambulance? How terrible. Who--" He closed the door.

Molly sat down at the kitchen table next to Rachel while they waited for the inspector to finish with Simon. In another ten minutes the two of them came through the door, and Molly got up.

"Can I get you a cup of coffee, Inspector?" Though Paco was slow to answer, Molly poured ever so quickly. He could hardly say no. The plate of cookies remained on the table, but for the inspector she had better things in mind. "How about a nice dish of my chocolate mousey, Inspector?" Before he could respond, a crystal goblet appeared before him. He tentatively tasted a spoonful.

"This chocolate mousse is out of this world, ma'am."

"Molly is an expert chef," Rachel said. She and Simon excused themselves to go and check on Aunt Freddie, who'd been asleep for several hours now.

"Ma'am, you can cook for me any time."

"Thank you. My name is Molly, Molly Mesta. Well, Inspector, you're good at your policing and I'm good at my work, so you can call the dessert professional curtsy." Molly coquettishly held onto the end of her apron as she spoke, her watery blue eyes bright from the unexpected gallantry.

Paco smiled, slid out from his seat and bowed deeply. "And I, fair maid, am Paco LeSoto, formerly of the Baltimore Police Department."

"I'm not a fair maid. I'm a darn good homekeeper and cook." Molly chuckled at her own joke.

He winked at this short, stocky, plain-looking woman who had stirred his digestive juices. "Ah, Molly, my dear, you are so much more. But alas, I must return to my work." He started for the door, and she handed him Avi's guest list from the night before, together with the addresses and telephone numbers.

She also tucked into his hand a small white paper bag filled with half a dozen sugar cookies.

"Oh, Inspector! Are you..."

"It's Paco. My name is Paco, dear woman."

"Paco, then. Are you through with the den? Can I straighten up in there?"

"My men are probably finished, but I'm not quite through. What did you have in mind?"

"Well, I thought I would close up the couch, dust, vacuum the floor, and water the plants, if it's okay by you."

"We've covered that part of the room pretty thoroughly, so I don't see any problem with it, especially if you do me one favor."

"What's that, Paco?"

"Put a fresh bag in the vacuum cleaner before you start and let me have it when you're done."

"Sure. Be glad to." The housekeeper suddenly felt a new dimension of importance: helping the police solve a crime!

Paco headed for the den, where, as he suspected, the crime unit technicians had already packed up and gone. He'd declared this room a crime scene and yet he wasn't a hundred percent sure which crimes had been committed.

Crime scenes passed through Paco's life like so many acquaintances, some dwelling longer than others, a greater number becoming more intimate with time, and a few choosing to remain eternal mysteries. The bloody ones left a stain on his soul, but he was grateful for the conundrums, the challenges they provided him. Every scene had its own personality, something of those who created it and a little more of their failings. Only the crime scenes knew exactly what had happened. It required considerable stroking and understanding to lay bare their failing memories.

Paco scanned this room, very much the doctor's retreat, the open sofa-bed an intrusion. He proceeded to check each of the books on the shelves, this time more thoroughly. He opened them one by one and spun the pages with his thumb, looking for everything and nothing in particular. All these volumes--perhaps one would speak to him. *The Complete Works of Sigmund Freud, Treating the Troubled Family, Psychoanalytic Studies of the Adolescent*. These professional texts Paco expected. But he was struck by the sweeping range of the doctor's tastes: *French Impressionism*, *Great Palaces of Europe, Presumed Innocent* by Scott Turow, *Exodus* by Leon Uris, *The Complete Plays of William Shakespeare, The World's Greatest Operas*.

Molly pushed the vacuum cleaner in one hand and carried her watering pitcher in the other, a dust cloth tucked in her slacks waistband. She began to make up the sofa-bed, when a six-ounce glass tumbler rolled out of one of the sheets and dropped to the floor. She bent over and reached out to grab it, but she felt a hand push her arm away.

"No, Molly," Paco said. "I'll get it. The crime unit missed it." He scooped up the glass with his cotton-gloved hand and held it at eye level, noting a series of ever-so-faint sipping rings and what could be a residue trace at the bottom. "Hmm," he said. "But there should be a bottle as well." After tucking the glass into an evidence bag, his eyes scanned the small room. His mind sank deep into the associative process.

Molly began to dust, humming as she worked. Paco found her voice pleasant, but the humming abruptly stopped. When he turned around, he found her poking in the sand and dirt of each plant in the room. He watched her carefully for a few minutes as she poked away with a letter opener. She suddenly felt self-conscious and looked up at him.

"Pray tell, my good woman, what do you think you're doing?"

"Poking around."

"That's obvious, but what for?"

"The jeweled key, Paco. I thought it might be hidden in the dirt of one of these pots."

"What made you think that?"

"I saw Victor's hand when they were taking him out. His fingernails were all dirty."

"That's good thinking." Had Victor tried to hide the key from the thief, Paco wondered. Standing beside her, he gently took the letter opener from Molly and continued poking in the dirt. She sat on the couch to watch him. He dug far more meticulously then she had, but even so, he found nothing. He returned to Avi's books with renewed enthusiasm, and she watered the plants with renewed generosity.

Then the inspector spied *Lost Horizon* on the shelf, James Hilton's parable of the time-frozen paradise of Shangri-La. As a boy, Paco had enjoyed the novel and its struggle with discontent. A smile emerged while reaching for an old friend. But the book didn't feel quite right in his hand. And when he tried to flip the pages, he found that it was the mere shell of a book, hollowed out to conceal a flat, nearly emptied half-pint of Hennesey Cognac. A partial roll of Certs breath mints and a small plastic prescription bottle containing a solitary pill shared the cache.

Paco examined the bottle's label: for Victor Moskowitz, Pettibone's Apothecary, a northwest Washington address. "Valium: 5 mg, take 1 tablet every 6 hours as needed for anxiety, no more than 4 in 24 hours, 1 refill." The bottle had originally contained 120 pills. Paco frowned. The doctor's name had been obliterated. Why?

Paco shaped his lips as if to whistle and then uttered one word: "Deadly."

CHAPTER 15

DIRTBAGS

The high-pitched whine wound down and groaned to a halt, leaving the Kepple den in a welcome quiet. Molly carefully removed the squat folding bag from the upright vacuum cleaner, placed it in a plastic bag from supermarket produce, and sealed it with a tie-wrap.

"There!" Molly said, trying to get Paco's attention. He stood across the room, engrossed in reading. She noticed that his expression softened as his eyes perused the pages, stopping at familiar passages and allowing small smiles to escape. Molly found herself drawn to his sharp bony features, his wavy salt and pepper hair, a bumper crop for a man so close to her own age.

"There what?" Paco suddenly turned to face her.

"Your cleaner sweepings, Inspector."

"Oh, yes, thank you, Molly. There's so much to be done here."

"Me too. I've gotta start dinner now."

Avi passed by the den door on the way to seeing his patient out. He reappeared a minute later. "Inspector, forgive me for eavesdropping, but if you want to continue working in here, you're more than welcome to join us for a bite to eat."

"Oh, that won't be necessary. I can come back in the morning."

"Nonsense, I insist. You'll join us then?"

"Thank you, you're most gracious."

"Molly, you'll set another place for the inspector."

Paco continued to flip through one book after another until he sensed Avi watching him. He decided to postpone the search and instead continue his questioning of the family members. "Do you think I could have a few minutes with your daughter now? Where might I find her?"

"I believe she's in her room. I'll get her for you."

"That won't be necessary. I can ask my questions there if you don't mind. You see, I'd like to have a look at the second floor at the same time."

"If you'll follow me, Inspector." Avi led the way upstairs to Rachel's old room. He knocked gently and waited for her response before entering. "The inspector would like a few words with you. Would that be all right?"

"Yes, Daddy, I'm just writing some notes...Oh, Inspector, please sit down." She gestured to the dainty ruffled chair in front of the vanity and then turned her own desk chair to face him. "We could go elsewhere if you like."

"No, this will be fine, Mrs. Mendelsohn."

Avi wasn't sure whether he should stay or leave, so he sat down on the bed and just listened.

Outwardly, Rachel retained her usual self-confident demeanor, but she couldn't help but be aware of his eyes. Commanding and unfathomable, she thought. "What can I do for you?" she asked, her voice betraying an edginess.

"Well, for openers, what kind of a relationship did you have with your cousin? I mean, were you close? Did he ever take you into his confidence?"

"Vic wasn't the confiding kind, at least, not since we were kids, anyway. He is--I mean, he *was*--a very private person, a poker face and all. I suppose it comes with the territory."

"The territory?"

"His gambling."

"I see. Did you notice any strange behavior or personality changes in recent weeks?"

"Actually, until yesterday when we came home to visit my dad, I hadn't seen Vic in years. Two or three, at least. In fact, he even missed our wedding last March."

"Was there a confrontation over that?"

"No, he just didn't show up, which bothered me a little. I thought it tacky of him not to even call."

Paco listened intently and turned to Avi. "Doctor, where did Victor spend his time away from the house?"

"I suppose he spent some of it looking for honest work and the rest looking for his gambling cronies."

"And where would that be?"

"Down at the inn, I believe."

"Do you think he might have been there yesterday or the day before?"

"I just don't know."

"I do, Daddy. We saw him there on the verandah on Thursday when we drove past on our way here. We watched a man roughing him up." She nervously spun the pen in her hand. "Not badly, really, but he did have Vic by the collar. We tooted the horn, but the guy just kept at it. Then Vic pulled himself away and went inside the inn. The other guy ran to his car and drove away."

"And then?"

"We decided not to stop, just to come straight here. I asked Vic about it later and he denied having any problem."

"Did he identify this man?" Paco asked.

"No. Vic lied to us about him, though. He told us the man had come all the way from Washington to sell him a franchise and was angry because Vic didn't have any money to buy one."

"How did you know Victor lied?"

"We had already encountered this same man on the trip down from New York." Rachel shuddered at the thought. She related the incident to Paco.

"How do you know for sure it was the same man?"

"The way he dressed. He looked so...so thuggy. Black suit, black shirt, white tie. We recognized his car, too."

"I see." Paco suppressed a smile, made a few notes, and continued. "Speculating that Victor did owe money, would either of you know how large a sum we're talking about?"

Avi thought for a moment. "My guess is that it was considerable. The last time my sister had to bail him out, seven years ago...."

"Bail him out?" Paco interrupted.

"Of his debts, Inspector. Not jail. He's never been in jail that I know of."

"I see. Please continue, Doctor. Seven years ago?"

"Freddie had to sell her home and move in with me." Avi removed his glasses and rubbed his eyes. "I believe that figure was $27,000. I would have disowned him for that. But not my sister."

"Daddy! They might have killed him for that kind of money."

"So I wouldn't have disowned him, then." Avi felt a pang of guilt for speaking so flippantly.

"Did he get a lot of phone calls, Doctor?"

"More than you'd expect from a house guest. In fact, he had two last evening."

"Did he take either of the calls?" Avi didn't have a chance to answer. A moaning sound came from Freddie's room, and the questioning waited while they determined whether it would subside. They heard the moaning again, followed by low-level sobbing. Avi stood up. "You stay here, Rachel. I'll see to your aunt." He left the room hearing Rachel's anxious voice say that she couldn't answer the last question.

He knocked softly on the half-open door. Freddie lay on her side in bed with her feet pulled tightly up into the fetal position. She still looked meticulously dressed in her beige slacks and paisley silk blouse, exactly the way they had left her so many hours earlier. She tried to sit up, but instead fell into his lap, burying her face there, and Avi held his sister like a hurt child, rocking her back and forth--something he had not done in years.

"Oh, Avi, what am I to do? He was my only child. You don't know what it's like to lose a child. You can't. No one does."

"You're right, Freddie, I can't know in the same way you do. But you are not alone. There are so many others like you. I see them all the time in my practice and I do my best to help them. And in most cases I do help them."

"Avi, I can't go on. What is there to live for now?"

"You can go on for a family that loves you. You can share in all our blessings."

She felt a new hand on her back and turned to see Rachel sitting close to her. "I love you, Auntie. I need you and Daddy needs you."

"That's true, Freddie, I've come to count on you a lot these days."

"Nonsense, Avi, you don't need me. I know what a social animal you are."

Avi had to laugh, but shook his head. There was no winning this one. "I have to go downstairs now," he said. He was unaccustomed to sitting in such an awkward position for so long. "Would you like to rest some more?"

"You go ahead. Rachel will stay with me for a few minutes, won't you, sweetheart?"

"Of course, Aunt Freddie, I'll stay as long as you like." She hesitated. "There's a police inspector here, Aunt Freddie."

Her aunt's body jerked to attention. "What's a police inspector doing here?"

"Don't you fret any, Auntie. It's just a routine matter in an unexpected death. However, Daddy did invite him to supper tonight."

"Oh, for God's sake, was that necessary?"

"Perhaps not, but Daddy's key is missing from the den also, and everyone is concerned."

"Surely they don't think my Victor had anything to do with it?"

"No, Auntie, he never left the room. At least, I don't see how he could have. But..." Rachel took a deep breath before continuing. "The inspector would like a few words with you. He promised it wouldn't take long. Would it be okay if he came in now?"

"Now?" Freddie's lips tightened into a thin line and she locked her arms across her chest. "I don't see that I'm being given any choice in this, am I?"

Rachel opened the door and Paco cautiously stepped in. "I'm Inspector LeSoto, Mrs. Moskowitz. Please accept my condolences over your loss."

"Thank you," Freddie murmured.

"Ma'am, I know this is very difficult for you, and I'll only take a few minutes of your time. I understand your son was unemployed and..."

Freddie broke in, her voice filled with anger. "It was only temporary. He was trying hard to get back on his feet."

"I'm sure he was, ma'am," Paco said softly. "I'm sorry to have to bring this matter up, but I understand he liked a card game now and then. Can you tell me who was financing his poker and pocket money while he was unemployed?"

"What difference could it possibly make now?" Freddie asked. Rachel stirred uneasily on the edge of the bed. Paco waited. Freddie could see he wasn't going to let her off the hook. She began again. "I assumed he still had some commission money left from his insurance job. I don't know why they laid him off. He was a good salesman." Her face brightened. "He routinely surpassed any quotas they gave him. He looked so nice in his suits and ties and he had a beautiful smile, too. Didn't he, Rachel?"

"Of course, Auntie."

Paco persisted. "But weren't you even a little suspicious of where the money was coming from? He'd been out of work a few months, hadn't he?"

"Yes. He...he..."

"What is it, ma'am?"

"My son was very upset Friday. He didn't want to tell me why. I started crying because I worried about him. Then he finally admitted he had one of his creditors after him."

"Do you know who?"

"He said it was the Sandman."

"The Sandman? Do you know his name?"

"No. Vic said he was some kind of collector. Maybe Felix Thornberry knows. I...I don't want to get him in trouble, but he might know something. He played cards with Vic occasionally."

"Did your son tell you anything else?"

"No. We had a bad argument. I wanted him to go to the police. I suggested that this Sandman person might want to kill him. But Vic called that ridiculous and said he could handle the Sandman himself."

Freddie remained very quiet for several minutes. Paco watched her, knowing more would come.

"Then...Vic told me he had to get away for a few weeks, just to play it safe. I became frightened. I had no idea where he could possibly go without money, but he clammed up after that and stormed out of the house for the rest of the afternoon." She shook her head. "Ever so strange. That night, the night of the meeting, he got all dressed up and looked so handsome in his dinner jacket and black tie. I naively thought everything would be all right again." Freddie's shoulders sank in defeat and she started sobbing. "But then he disappeared right in the middle of the meeting..."

"Ma'am, thank you, you've been very helpful," Paco said. "I'll be on my way downstairs now." He quietly left the room.

"Rachel," Freddie said, covering her face with her hands, "where did we go wrong? Edgar and I tried so hard to be good parents."

"You *were* good parents, Auntie," Rachel said, handing her the tissue box. "You and Uncle Edgar gave Vic the finest education, all the best opportunities."

"I know, but somehow I feel responsible for the way he turned out."

Rachel bit her lower lip before answering. She had often talked to her father about her aunt. She recalled Avi saying, "Freddie's guilt--it's her most cherished obsession, and no one can talk her out of it. She wears it like a second skin."

"Auntie, you were a good mother. Victor made his own choices, took the path he wanted. Now it's time for you to let yourself be happy. You're entitled, Auntie."

"Maybe so," Freddie whispered. Rachel's impassioned thoughts aroused a new determination, the resolve to survive this nightmare.

Rachel watched her aunt straighten up, gather in her emotional burdens, and head for the bathroom to repair the tear-torn damage to her face. With a soapy washcloth, Freddie wiped away the smudged mascara and corralled a few silver hairs in disarray. She firmly took her niece's arm and accompanied her downstairs.

Avi, Simon, and Paco were already seated at the dining room table when Rachel and Freddie appeared. Paco held Freddie's chair for her.

Molly entered, bearing a large platter of juicy lamb chops. She selected the two choicest chops, along with garnishes of sliced oranges and watercress, and set them carefully on Paco's plate. Surprised at the portion, he looked up into her face as she stood beside him. He wasn't quite sure, but he thought he detected a wink in the corner of her right eye.

She moved on to serve Freddie next, and then the others. Occasionally, she emerged from the kitchen to replenish one or more of the serving platters, and as the silverware appeared on the individual empty plates, she removed them from the table. When she removed Paco's, he brought his fingertips to his lips as a silent compliment to her culinary artistry. Mistaking his gesture for a kiss, she flustered, bumping into the swinging door on her way out.

CHAPTER 16

DOUBLE EXPOSURE

Bucky walked past the busy maitre d' station in the restaurant of the Inn at Gander Pointe. He scanned the dining room for his wife and the rest of their party. Along the rear windowed wall, Felix Thornberry stood up and waved him to their table. Bucky waved back and stepped down into the Chandelier Room. Its low ceiling seemed ill-fit for the mismatched collection of elaborate crystal chandeliers. Not exactly the Plaza or the Waldorf. But soft lighting danced on the prisms, creating a reasonably romantic ambiance that delighted the local patrons. Bucky observed that the others had already started their dinner.

"Well, Bucky, where have you been so long? We said seven o'clock sharp."

"Sorry, Felix, I've been on the phone with Avi. Some bad news, I'm afraid."

"What news?" The words came from several lips.

"Victor was found dead in the den this morning."

The reaction moved slowly around the table in soft, nondescript word bites accompanied by sighs and gasps. That is, until Marti asked what everyone wanted to know: "How?"

"They won't know for several days until an autopsy is performed. The present consensus is that he died of a heart attack sometime last night."

Lenora spoke first. "Poor Freddie. She's really had a tough time of it. First Edgar and now Victor."

Heads nodded, but Marti responded, "She's probably a lot better off without either of them."

"What a cruel thing to say," Heidi scolded.

"Well, neither of them was worthy of licking her boots," Marti said.

"It's her husband and son you're talking about. Have a little respect for her if not for the departed. I know you never liked Edgar, but I did." Heidi could feel the anger and contempt welling within her.

"Oh, stop it, you sanctimonious twerp," Marti snapped.

Heidi began to cry. "I'll bet you've even said nasty things about Willard, too."

Suddenly, Marti felt pangs of contrition. "No, Willard was a lovable old man. In no way did he deserve what happened to him."

"Enough, you two," Felix said.

Lenora noticed that Bucky had remained standing with a troubled look on his face. She knew him. He had more to tell. "What else, dear?"

All eyes turned toward Bucky. His Adam's apple rose and fell as he swallowed.

"Avi told me that the jeweled key is missing. It's been taken from its display cabinet."

"My God, you can't mean it!" Ernie grabbed the arms of his chair with such force that he almost lifted his whole body from the seat. No doubt the missing key affected him more than Victor's death. The key represented an irreplaceable treasure. After all, he hadn't known Victor.

"Yes, indeed, I do mean it," Bucky said, with a sidelong glance at Ernie; the scientist's reaction was not lost on him. "Avi had to call in the police. Inspector LeSoto, I believe he said his name was. He's at the house now. There's going to be an investigation."

"Then it's robbery," Felix blurted out.

"Of course, it is, you dodo." Marti wasn't going to miss an opportunity to put her husband down. "Do you suppose it's the same thief that took the John Singer Sargent?"

"It's entirely possible," said Bucky. "Maybe they'll get a lead on Aigue's murderer, too."

"But if it's robbery, then Victor may have been murdered as well as poor Willard," Felix said. Silence fell. Plates of crab-stuffed flounder, clams casino, and trout amandine began to cool as the entire group looked to Bucky for confirmation.

"No one has mentioned the word murder yet. We don't even know for sure how Victor died. Inspector LeSoto does want to question each one of us individually."

"When?...Where?" Felix was the first to seize upon the significance of the request.

"Well, Avi has simplified the task somewhat. He's invited us all to brunch at his house tomorrow morning at 10:30 before our scheduled afternoon trip to Marche House. I told him I would pass the word along. The inspector will talk with us then."

Derrick scowled. "Do they think we had something to do with the robbery and murder?"

"I don't know any more than you do, Derrick. But given the circumstances, I should think we're all suspects. We may have even been in the house when it happened."

"Oh, perish the thought, Bucky." Heidi clanked her fork down on the plate. "Do you know what I'm going to do, Derrick?"

"No, Heidi, dear, how should I know?"

"I'm going to the house to pay a condolence call on the family and see if there's anything I can do for them."

"Aren't you going to finish your dinner?" Derrick asked.

"No, I'm not really hungry any more." Heidi picked up her purse, pushed her chair back from the table, and sprang to her feet. "Ta-ta, everyone." She waved her hand above her head as she dodged chairs between her and the exit. Derrick's mouth fell open, and he had to make a conscious effort to close it again.

He recovered enough to turn his attention to Lenora. She looked so exotic: her black wool dress fell in soft folds over her breasts and hips; her diamond-clustered earrings barely brushed her long, pale neck with each tilt of her head. Odd how sensual she looked, despite her schoolmarmish glasses. Derrick watched Heidi leave, then placed his hand on Lenora's leg as he spoke. "I'll never understand that woman."

"Maybe you should try a little harder," Lenora replied. With two fingers, as if she were conveying an orange peel into a garbage can, she picked up his hand by the wrist and dropped it off into space.

Derrick turned his attention to Ernie Lord, who had just sat down in Heidi's chair to talk football with him. But Derrick had not given up on Lenora yet. He allowed his hand to roam behind him, back to the leg he thought belonged to her. He was surprised when his errant hand was gripped tightly and slammed onto the tabletop.

"Ow!" he yelped. Derrick turned to find that Lenora had changed chairs with her husband.

Eyes fixed firmly on her plate, she chuckled softly as she toyed with her lobster Newburg. The look on Bucky's face was enough to kill. Derrick hadn't prepared to tangle with a man half his size, twice his age, and possessing sufficient influence to destroy him socially. He decided to leave the table instead. But when he rose, Ernie tried to lure him into the bar for some serious college football on television. Derrick found some excuse and left the room.

Felix seized the moment. "I wouldn't mind watching a little of that game myself. Could you use a little company, Ernie?"

Lenora interrupted. She had another idea. "How about a few hands of bridge? You play, Ernie?...Felix?...Danielle?"

"Excuse me, dear. The powder room calls." The conversation waited while Danielle, a dark look on her face, made her way across the room to the lobby. Meanwhile, Felix waited for his answer.

"Sure, all of the above!" Ernie responded. "We could play bridge in the lounge and keep an eye on the football game. And all the rest of you are welcome too."

Frail slivers of moonlight escaped around the edges of the drapes into a deep darkness shrouding the rest of room 203. The Worthingtons slept together, in the buff, in one of the two double beds.

Lenora slid a Rubenesque leg out from under the spread. Her eyes squinted and strained to focus the four fuzzy red numbers on the clock-radio. After leaning on one elbow, the fuzz cleared long enough for her to determine the time: 11:45. She'd slept for only an hour. The bridge game had broken up early. Her head dropped to the pillow once more, and she pulled the covers back around her body. Eyes closed, she made an effort to find sleep again, but her full bladder would not permit it.

Lenora swung both legs out from the covers and sat on the edge of the bed. Reaching for her glasses, she bumped the tissue box, and in turn, the glasses fell onto the thick carpeting behind the night stand. She continued to grope unsuccessfully for the glasses until she could wait no longer. She arose from the bed and edged her way along the wall to the other side of the room. There were two doors, each with a thin band of light beneath. She inched toward the bathroom and its reassuring night-light.

Finally feeling the door handle, she pushed against the door itself. But it wouldn't budge. Grasping the handle firmly, she pulled it toward her, and this time it gave way freely. She staggered through the doorway toward the light and let go of the door handle. Groping wildly for something familiar--the towel bar, the sink--she heard the massive door squeak closed behind her, ending in a definitive "thunk."

A sixth sense beckoned her back to the security of the door she had just come through. One step...another...the door...and now to find the handle. But where? Her hands slid desperately over the metal surface of the door until her fingers finally clutched the handle. At that moment the realization gripped her. She was locked out of her room, in the hall, naked!

First she knocked. No response. Then she pressed her lips to the edge of the door and called out softly. "Bucky! Bucky, dearest!...I'm locked out in the hall...Please let me in!" She had to assume he was sleeping on his good ear and that his hearing aid was on his night stand. "Buck-eee!" she called, a little louder now, and then she felt sudden panic. Was that a door opening down the hall? She couldn't be sure.

She helplessly sat down on the carpet with her back to the door, knees tucked tightly under her chin, arms hugging her legs. The industrial grade carpeting scratched her soft bottom. A chilling cold gripped her. It wouldn't be long before someone saw her.

Slowly, her fear-fogged brain began to clear and her courage returned. She tried to remember the layout of the hall from prior trips over the years. She knew there was an old-fashioned fire extinguisher somewhere on the opposite wall. But she'd look ridiculous walking around the hallway clutching an extinguisher. And what about her bare backside? There was that rubber mat in front of the elevator, but it was dirty and probably too heavy to even pick up, much less wrap around her. Ah, the window across from the elevator had floor-length drapes. That might work.

She got to her feet and slowly felt her way down the hallway until, at last, she reached the elevator. Across the hall, she could just make out the wide, tall window. She could see blobs of lights--streetlights, she guessed--and fuzzy blurs of moving car headlights. What a relief; she was getting close. With hands outstretched, she felt the hard, cool glass and, to the right of it, the coarse drapery material. She tugged at it firmly, fully expecting the track clips to give way. They didn't. She yanked harder. They creaked, but the drape held fast.

Noise across the corridor. Thunk. Clunk. Whirrrr. The elevator! Quickly pulling the drape around her, she stood deathly still and peeked out. Whirrrr ...clunk. The doors rolled back noisily as two people stepped off. The taller one, a man, walked off at a hurried pace. The second person, a woman, stood in front of the elevator, making use of the window's light to search in a large handbag for her room key.

"Pssst!...Pssst!" Lenora whispered. "Over here, behind the drape...Sorry, didn't mean to frighten you."

"What? Who's there? What do you want from me?"

"I've locked myself out of my room and I don't have any clothes on."

"What on earth...Is that you, Lenora?"

"Yes! Who are you?"

"It's me, Heidi."

"Oh, thank God. I locked myself out. I need to get a key. And I can't go to the desk like this."

"Lenora, how in heaven's name did you do that?"

"It was sheer stupidity. My glasses fell off the night stand. I'm blind as a bat without them, and I took the wrong door to the bathroom."

"Wow!"

"Can't you get me something to put on? A robe, a coat, anything? I'm freezing out here."

"Sure, dear. But you've got to admit this is crazy. It isn't like you, Lenora."

"You're telling me? I can't believe this is happening."

Heidi finally found her key. She hurried to her room and reappeared a moment later with a short white robe. She held it up as Lenora slipped into it. Lenora began to chuckle, a giggle at first, and then a near-hysterical laugh. Heidi joined her.

"You know, Lenora, you're damned lucky it was me coming out of the elevator. A stranger would have reported you to the front desk by now."

"I know. I can't believe that man didn't see me." Suddenly, Lenora was no longer laughing, but shaking and sobbing the big tears of stress release.

"Come to my room. I'll go to the desk for another key."

"I don't think they'll give it to you, will they?"

"They will when I explain. Or maybe the desk clerk can come up with me to unlock the door himself." She led Lenora back to her room to the straight-backed chair next to the bed.

"Wait here. I'll be right back," Heidi said.

Lenora was about to sit down, unaware that Derrick lay on the nearby bed. When she felt a corner of the robe's hem open, she casually brushed it shut with the back of her hand. Startled to find another hand there, she used sheer instinct to find a face to go with the stray hand. With a tightly clenched fist, and a fierceness driven by the night's frustrations, she lunged forward. Her fist hit something soft and fleshy and slid onto something hard.

"Aww!" She knew she'd scored a hit. Turning back toward the open door, Lenora fled the room for the relative safety of the hall. She held her hand over her mouth to keep from crying out. How was it that letch kept cropping up everywhere? She leaned against the wall and sobbed. Derrick had upset her and rendered her oblivious to the sounds of the elevator.

Heidi reached out to touch her, and Lenora jumped with fright. She then noticed the elderly night clerk.

"I'm such a nuisance, a pain actually," Lenora whispered. "And you're a princess to help me like this." She hugged Heidi. "Good-night. We'll talk tomorrow."

The night clerk limped ahead to Lenora's room and unlocked the door, leaving it open for her. "Thank you so much. There will be a tip waiting for you at the desk in the morning." she said. He smiled and shuffled toward the elevator. She went into the room and closed the door.

Bucky will never believe this, she thought, as she shed the robe, climbed into bed, and snuggled close to her husband's backside. Oh, no! Another sensation struck her at that moment. She hadn't been to the bathroom yet.

Forty-five minutes earlier, in the Thornberry room across the hall, Felix and Marti were having a marital row.

"You still haven't explained what happened the last time we were here," said Felix. "Were you messing around with Quentin again?"

"Absolutely not! He was simply being a gentleman and saw me to my door. I asked him in and we had one drink together. I do *not* have a thing for him. In fact, I wouldn't give you a quarter for Quentin."

"Then why was his tie on the chair?"

"How should I know? Maybe it fell out of his pocket. He wasn't wearing it when he came in. I thought..."

"What's that noise?" Felix broke in.

"What noise?"

"In the hall." Marti took off the chain and opened the door a crack. She peered around the edge and began to grin broadly.

"Oh, this is precious. It's even delicious," she said.

"What on earth are you talking about, woman?"

"Come have a look for yourself."

"Buck-eee...Buck-eee!" They saw a nude Lenora pounding on the door across the hall.

"Let me see this. Oh, man. Now that's a good-looking woman." He got down on his knees to watch while Marti leaned over him.

"Shh! She'll see us," whispered Marti.

"Hey, I never noticed it before, but there's a security camera on the wall down by the elevator pointed up this way. I bet she's on camera," he said.

"I bet she is, too. She's locked herself out of their room without a stitch. I love it. It's perfect."

"She sure is."

"No, you dirty old man. I mean she's on videotape. They usually keep a tape of those security cameras, don't they?" Marti closed the door, quietly.

"I guess so. What of it?" Felix asked. "What did you close the door for?"

"You'll see--tomorrow. Besides, you've had enough excitement for one night. Next thing you know you'll be wanting sex from me."

CHAPTER 17

MORNING BECOMES ELECTRIC
Sunday, October 26, 1980

Marti lay with the left side of her face on the thin hotel pillow. She hadn't slept much except toward morning, when sheer exhaustion took over. She sprung one eye open, then the other. Why am I up so early? she asked herself. Oh, yeah. The purpose came to her in a flash, and an impish grin grew on her face. She stretched her limbs and threw back the covers.

Chilled by the sudden breeze of the flying bedcovers, Felix whimpered and rolled toward her with a bundle of comforter in tow and wound up on his stomach, his right arm covering the sheet where her body should have been. Marti reached over and patted his behind until his combined whimper and gurgle turned into a steady moan of satisfaction. He turned over again and went back to his snoring. She dressed hurriedly and let herself out of the room.

Furtively scanning the hall from left to right, Marti hoped she wouldn't encounter anyone until she completed her mission. At 6:25 Sunday morning she found the elevator and lobby empty. A gray-haired clerk stood with his back to her behind the registration desk.

"Sir! Ahem, sir!" she called and he turned around to face her.

"Well, I'll be...If it ain't Martha Marche herself."

"Ev? Everett Pucket, is that you? Haven't seen you since high school."

"Hey, yep, it's me all right. Older, meaner, sassier, and better looking."

"You are just that, Ev. A few gray hairs, but nothing else has changed." Marti didn't really mean it. He looked old and weather-beaten, and now he sounded like a country yokel. She wondered whether it was a deliberate affectation.

"You look a mite purtier than I remembered," he said.

"Thanks, I'm Marti Thornberry now, but what are you doing behind that desk?"

"Well, since I bummed up my leg I can't be a waterman no more. Working an oyster boat just got too damn hard. And Social Security disability ain't quite payin' the bills, so I come down here to be the night manager."

"Tell me, Ev, would an extra hundred dollars help any?"

"Oh, no, Marti, I couldn't take no charity from you."

"Oh, it wouldn't be charity, Ev, I can guarantee you that. There's a favor I need done. Do you think you could handle it?"

"Maybeee! What would I have to do for that kind of money?"

"Well, first of all, you'd have to be discreet about it. Can you keep a secret?"

"Sure 'nuf, but it ain't illegal, is it?"

"Of course not. I wouldn't be involved in anything illegal, would I?"

"No, I reckon you wouldn't." He grinned.

"Do you think you could get hold of last night's tapes from the surveillance cameras on the second floor and make a copy for me?"

"Well..." He eyed her suspiciously. "I don't know about that. Sure, the two video recorders are in the hall closet behind the desk here. But what would you want with the tapes? Nobody ever looks at 'em. They're boring."

"It's for a practical joke, Ev. For a good friend of mine."

"It must be a mite good friend, a hundred dolla' friend." He hesitated for just a moment, then ducked under the barrier bridge at the end of the desk. Selecting a key from his master set, he opened the tape recorder closet. He pressed STOP and then EJECT on each machine and handed her one of the two emerging cassettes.

"Don't you need copies?"

"Naw, we just keep recording over the top of them. It's time to put new ones in, anyway."

Marti laid the tape down on the registration desk and rummaged through her purse for her billfold. She selected two crisp fifty dollar bills and handed them to Ev. "Thank you," she said, leaning over to give him a peck on the cheek.

"Appreciate it, Marti. The kiss, too."

Marti scooped up her things from the desk, managed one last wink for Ev, and headed for the elevator.

Felix was still asleep when she entered their room, unaware that she had been gone at all. Well, she'd fix that soon enough.

Because the inn made a successful business of renting videos in the lobby, each room TV had a built-in VCR. Marti slipped the cassette into the VCR and pressed the PLAY button...An empty second floor hall...several nondescript passersby...more empty hall...more strangers. Marti kept using the FAST FORWARD button on an intermittent basis until she noticed the time-of-day and date annotation imposed on the upper left of the screen. Then she fast forwarded to 11:30 p.m. the previous evening before pressing the PLAY button again. There she saw the titillating events she was looking for.

Too triumphant to contain herself any longer, Marti tried to wake her husband. She shook his foot, but he pulled it up under him. She pushed his fanny until he rolled from side to side on his stomach.

"Yuh...ah...yuh! Marti, for God's sake, what the devil are you doing?

You're rocking the daylights out of me."

"Get yer lazy bones out of that bed. I want to show you something."

"What's so important that it can't wait for a respectable hour? What time is it, anyway?"

"It's ten after seven and time to get up."

Felix fought back the urge to say something he might regret later and struggled to sit up. It was then that he noticed the silent screen at the foot of the bed. His vision locked onto the beautiful bare form feeling her way down the hall doorway by doorway. "Wow! That was last night," he said.

"Sure was."

"What's it doing on TV, honey?"

"I bribed the night manager for a copy of the surveillance tapes."

"Are you crazy? What are you going to do with it, Marti?"

"Well, for starters, I'm going to give Miss Snooty Puss a copy and sit back and wait for the fireworks."

"That might be considered attempted extortion, hon."

"Not if I don't ask for money, it isn't. It's more like revenge for the way she looks down her nose at me."

"Just be careful, hon. We don't want any trouble."

She smiled and ignored his warning. "Which of these should I wear to the Kepple brunch today?" She held up a long-sleeved gray knit top in her right hand and a red one just like it in her left.

"Well, the gray one looks like the top half of long johns and the other one sure looks like red flannels, dear."

Marti said nothing, shoved both tops into the second drawer, and selected a sweater and slacks outfit instead. "That's the last time I solicit your opinion," she said.

Felix chuckled to himself. Success at last.

Simon sat on the rear stoop of the Kepple home. He had a firm hold on Shana's collar and attempted to fasten her leash, but his thumb couldn't seem to budge the halyard clip at the end of it. Rachel came out and sat beside him.

"Here, let me do that," she said. "That is, if it won't offend either your masculinity or your mechanical aptitudes, sir."

"Be my guest, O great slayer of dragons."

She took the leash clip, pushed the thumb button to one side before sliding it back and open, and clipped it to Shana's collar.

"Well, you certainly made that look easy," Simon muttered. He bent over to adjust the legs of his gray and blue sweat suit and stood up beside her. "Which way?"

"Let's go to the right this time, farther up Locust Lane to the top of the hill."

"Is it much of an incline? I'd prefer an easier time of it, if you don't mind."

"It's quite gradual, honey, and I'm sure you'll appreciate the view from the top." Rachel began to jog in place, and Shana's patience gave way with a major yank on the leash, sending Rachel forward. "Easy, girl!" They waited for Simon to catch up with them.

Coming through the gate, they found Shana sniffing and pawing at what looked like a piece of white cloth. Rachel knelt to pick it up and showed her discovery to her husband. "Look, dear, a woman's handkerchief with the monogram R." She shook the dirt and dust off it, gently fingering the scalloped lace border.

"It's in surprisingly good condition," he said. "The lace isn't even torn. Which means it couldn't have been here long. Is it yours? Could you have dropped it yesterday on our walk?"

"No, I don't even own any handkerchiefs. I'm a Kleenex girl myself."

"This is odd," he said. "There are high-heel footprints all the way up to the hedgerow and down to the driveway again." Simon poked at the ground with a stick, brushing against a half-buried Styrofoam coffee cup bearing the logo from the inn. The cup spilled over, dumping a soggy mess of nearly a dozen cigarette butts, all of them liberally smeared with salmon-colored lipstick.

"Obviously, somebody's spent time here," Rachel said. "You know what? I'll bet it's that woman we saw from the upstairs window Friday night."

"You don't think it's anyone from the Historical Society?" he asked.

"Couldn't have been," she said.

"Why not?"

"All the members were at the meeting. No one even came late, except Olivia--but only by a few minutes, and she doesn't smoke. This woman spent a lot of time here, waiting for someone or something. It takes a long time to smoke so many cigarettes. Look, there are more high-heel footprints in the mud up by the maple tree."

"Yeah, and most of them are in the area behind the tree," Simon added. "It looks like the person tried to hide there. There are tire tracks, too."

Rachel looked up into her husband's face. "Do you think we ought to tell the inspector about this?"

"I don't see why not. It might be useful to him and explain a few things. He should be at the house by the time we get back."

The sky was darkening rapidly. "It looks like it's going to pour," Rachel said. "Won't the rain obliterate everything?"

Simon grabbed one of the empty trash cans from just inside the Kepple gate and turned it upside down over the butts and several of the clearer heel prints. "There," he said. "That should hold it for a little while, anyway."

"God, I love it when you get so scientific."

He chuckled, the creases around his eyes crinkling behind his glasses. Shana pulled on the leash, ready to move on, so up the hill they trudged, glancing sideways at each break in the dense hedgerow. Simon marveled at old stately homes embellished by luxuriant landscaping. He saw huge locust trees arching their branches over the lane, forming one of nature's finer canopies in russet and gold.

They slowed down when the colonnade of trees gave way to an autumn meadow. Bedded with dried tobacco rubble, it fell gradually away from the lane where they stood. The land dipped down to the edge of the creek bed far below. And across the meadow, overlooking the chalky edge of the tallest cliff, stood a noble structure of white wood and sandstone.

"Is it...?"

"Yes, it's Marche House," Rachel said. "It looks different from this angle, doesn't it? Isn't it simply beautiful from here?" They looked beyond to the Chesapeake Bay, so wide at this point that they couldn't see the other shore. Freighters and tankers sat at anchor, waiting their turn to be unloaded up in Baltimore.

"It certainly is a magnificent view," he said. "But look at those huge black clouds now, how fast they're coming in from the bay."

"Oh, boy, I think we're in for another drenching rain. Soon, too."

Simon noticed a narrow paved lane with switchbacks leading from the bay front road up to Marche House. As it ascended the cliff side, it swung around to the front of the house, passing over a bridge that extended out and over the shore road down at water's edge.

"That's quite a precarious approach. Is it the only road up?"

"For cars, yes. You saw the steps out back yesterday. And there's a footpath on this side. We passed the start of it about twenty yards back."

Just then lightning flashed once, then quickly again, and the rumbling sounds of thunder followed soon after. A few heavy drops of rain splashed down. Shana cowered close to Rachel.

"Let's go!" Simon shouted.

Shana led them, almost galloping, back to the lane and all the way home. By the time they reached the Kepple driveway, their hair had matted and their dripping sweat suits hung heavy and clammy against their bodies from the steady downpour.

They encountered Schlem's classic Buick parked next to the garage. He was delivering the brunch order from Bubba's, and Molly busied herself taking large brown bags from him at the kitchen door. A sharp, deafening thunderclap shook the air. In her fright Shana broke from Rachel and very nearly bowled Schlem over to get to Molly, where she cowered and trembled against the housekeeper's large round thigh.

"Poor Shanie, it's okay," Molly cooed. "She always gets like this when it thunders. Won't leave me alone. You're a Velcro dog, aren't you, Shanie?" And turning to Rachel and Simon, "Don't move a stitch, either one of you!" She pulled open the closet door, yanked out two massive towels, and tossed them at the newlyweds, who still stood shivering at the back door.

"What now?" Simon looked questioningly at his wife.

Without answering, Rachel pushed open the adjacent door to the basement stairwell and stepped inside, closing it behind her. It wasn't a minute before he heard a plop of soaked clothes and sneakers landing on the basement floor. She emerged with her towel wrapped and tucked to form a perfect sarong.

"Ta-dah!" she said. "Now it's your turn."

"Okay, but the result won't be nearly as fetching as yours." He ducked behind the same door and reappeared minutes later with his own terry wrapping. He could hear Schlem talking with Molly over the sound of her mixer, but no one else was close enough to see him, so he darted, hairy-legged and barefoot, up the staircase to their room.

While vigorously toweling off his curly head, he stepped to the window overlooking the front of the house and tried to visualize the woman they'd seen Friday night. What could she possibly have wanted? Was she armed? A spasm of dread flickered through his brain. Had he seen Victor's murderer?

CHAPTER 18

THE INSPECTOR'S TURN

Ssssss...tisss...sssss! Molly spooned the chopped mixture of white onions, sweet green peppers, and fleshy pink lox into the hot buttered skillet, then pushed and turned it with the nylon spatula. She tilted her head to one side questioningly. Had she heard a knock at the back door? She lifted the skillet off the gas flame and listened intently for several moments. Another knock. She slid the pan onto a cold burner and turned down the flame she'd been using.

"Keep your britches on. I'm coming." She wouldn't have said this on her way to the front door, and if Avi had heard her saying it at all, he'd certainly have reprimanded her. She gave the back door a half-hearted pull. A flush suffused her moon face. "Inspector! Oh, dear. If I'd of known it was you, I would've come rickety-split, yes, indeed, sir."

"Think nothing of it, dear lady," he said. "You must be very busy with all this unwelcome activity here."

His thick crop of hair had been combed into a dipping flourish. Paco had raised his right eyebrow until it nearly met the flourish. Arching eyebrows were a predictable adjunct to Paco's facial expressions, revealing reactions to different stimuli: the right brow indicated pleasure; the left, disbelief; both brows admitted surprise.

Paco closed his eyes, tilted his head back, and inhaled deeply. "It smells a little like heaven in here, and yet I can't discern what it is. Must be some of your culinary magic, little lady."

Molly blushed again. "Thanks," she said. "But it's just onions, peppers, lox, and eggs all confused in a pan. Would you like some?" Molly slid the skillet back over the flame. The sounds and smells of sautéed flavors burst forth and conquered the room once more.

"Oh, don't go to any bother for me, Molly." Leaning over the pan, he inhaled a second time.

"Sit down at the table there. You're not putting me in. I'll fix you a plate in a minute." Molly added the beaten eggs from the blender pitcher, and the sizzling subsided. She truly liked this man, Paco LeSoto. Oh, she liked most people all right, but somehow there was more to him. He's so polite to me, she thought. And he dressed up today. She tried not to be too obvious as she admired the sharp yellow bow tie sitting under his chin.

Obediently, Paco slid into a captain's chair and crossed his legs. His black and white jacket fell away to reveal a dark monogram on the lighter gray shirt pocket. His polished leather loafers gleamed. Mouth watering, he watched her dish most of the lox and egg feast out onto a china platter--the rest onto a smaller plate for him. A second platter of steaming hash browns came from the oven. Molly placed both on a tray and carried it proudly into the dining room, using her hip to swing through the door.

"Ah, Molly," Paco heard Avi exclaim, "such a beautiful breakfast."

"Thank you, Doctor."

Returning to the kitchen, Molly set the small plateful before Paco, adding an orange-cranberry muffin. After she poured a cup of coffee for him, he placed his hand over her free hand. He looked up into her face with the kindest of eyes and said, "Thank you, dear lady."

A chill ran through Molly's frame, and she had to force herself to say something. "You're a dear man, too." A nervous smile appeared on her face as she returned the coffeepot to the stove.

"Did I mention that cooking is a hobby with me? I absolutely love to experiment with new spices to bring out special flavors in foods."

"Paco, I'd never figure a man of your statue would like to cook."

"It's true, Molly. Maybe I'll cook a feast for you sometime."

She didn't answer. Deep vertical furrows creased her forehead; the lines of her mouth flattened out.

"What's wrong, Molly?"

"I know you mean well, Paco, and you're just making polite conversation, but you don't have to make promises to me."

"Dear Molly, I'm being very sincere. I'd love to cook for you. I'd love to be your friend. And I'd never patronize you."

She was silent for a moment and then answered slowly. "I'd like you to be my friend, too. I'd like that very much."

"Thank you," he said. He popped the last bite of muffin in his mouth and stopped in mid-chew when he saw no smile was forthcoming. Her thoughts were far away. Was it he who had caused this troubled look, or was it something else?

"Molly, if you'll forgive me, I must ask you a police-type question. You look distressed. You had the same expression yesterday when I asked you whether Victor had left the house Friday night. Could you possibly tell me what you were thinking then?"

"I'm not sure...Oh, yes. I was thinking that Victor couldn't of left the house after I put the snack out for him. He'd have picked up the tray and put it in the den or back in the kitchen when he went out. Or at least slid it over to the wall."

"Could it be that he didn't see it?"

"Uh-uh, no sireee, he would've flopped all over it. I left it on the floor in front of the door. I coulda put it on the shelf in the hall, but I thought he might miss it."

"What time did you leave the tray? And what happened to it afterward?"

"It musta been just before midnight. I picked it up again yesterday morning at 11:30. Nothing touched."

"Good morning, Inspector." Simon entered the kitchen. "Oh, by the way, now that it's stopped raining, there's something I want to show you out front at the gate."

"Oh, really?" Paco placed his fork on his empty plate and drained the last of his coffee. "Now let's get to it, sir."

Once outside the gate Simon went straight to the overturned trash can and set it upright once more. "I used the can to preserve what Rachel and I found here this morning."

"I see a Styrofoam hot cup with lipstick on it and a number of cigarette butts in and around it."

"Exactly, Inspector. Look at the high-heel prints. Someone spent a good deal of time here, perhaps waiting for someone to come out or something to happen. Curious, don't you think?"

"Yes, but I wouldn't attach too much importance to it just yet. On the other hand, there are more footprints leading to the macadam driveway." Paco paused for just a moment. "In fact, Officer Mullins found several high-heel footprints in the mud under the den windows."

"We saw her, Inspector."

"Saw her?" Simon had surprised Paco. Both eyebrows shot up.

"Yes. My wife and I saw her standing at the end of the driveway from the upstairs bedroom Friday night."

"Just what did you see?"

"Not very much else, because the woman noticed us in the window and left."

"Did either you or your wife recognize the woman? Could you describe her?"

"No on both counts, sir. The light was poor, and the tree foliage kept getting in the way. By the way, sir, we went out for a walk this morning, and my wife found this on the ground near the driveway." He pulled the lace handkerchief out of his hip pocket and handed it to Paco.

Paco examined the handkerchief. "It's not your wife's?" he asked, fingering the monogrammed R.

"No, she said it's not."

Paco nodded, carefully folded the new piece of evidence into a plastic bag and then made several more notes in his little book. Retrieving a pair of tweezers from his pocket he rescued the cup, which still contained several of the butts. He then slid it into a larger plastic bag he took from the trunk of his car. There he also found a can of Krylon clear spray fixative and sprayed the clearest set of shoe prints thoroughly to preserve it. Afterward, he turned the same trash can back upside down over the prints.

"That ought to hold it until I can have Mullins make a plaster cast of the prints this afternoon. Hmm...R...Rachel? Raphael?" The two men walked back inside.

In the kitchen, Avi had just finished giving Molly additional instructions for the morning brunch. "The guests should be arriving any time now. Inspector, where would you like to conduct your questioning?"

"Would the den be acceptable, Doctor?"

"The den will be fine. I'll have Molly bring a coffee service in for you and see that you're comfortable there. Molly!"

"Yes, Doctor, I'll see to it."

"I think I hear cars in the driveway. Yes, there's the doorbell now."

Molly ushered the Worthingtons in, followed by Heidi and Derrick. Stepping into the hall, Derrick peeked over the top of his dark glasses just enough for Molly to notice the black and purple bruise encircling his eye.

"Oh, that's a beauty you've got there, sir, quite a doozer. I'll bet that hurts."

"Hi, Molly," Heidi said, grinning. "This is Derrick. Ah, yes, some arrogant door jumped right off its hinges and hit him smack-dab in the eye last night." He nodded to Molly. His muscled shoulders appeared narrower, less powerful this morning. He looked sullen slumped over in his Ralph Lauren polo shirt.

Overhearing Heidi from the living room, Lenora burst out laughing. Then she noticed a stranger motioning for her and Bucky to come into the den. Paco introduced himself and bade them take a seat. He shut the door.

"I'm investigating both the unexplained death of Victor Moskowitz and the uncertain whereabouts of an antique jeweled key. And I would like your cooperation in clearing up these matters. I must ask you to relive Friday evening as best you can."

Lenora described the meeting as she remembered it. "And then I read selected passages from my mother's diary. The jeweled key was mentioned."

"Is the diary..."

The door opened briskly. Molly entered with a silver coffee service and set it down on the cherry wood table. Her chubby hand lifted a small pitcher from the tray. Ear cocked in studied concentration, she proceeded to water the plants.

When Paco could wait no longer, he said in a near-whisper, "Please, dear Molly, police business is such a delicate matter. It is essential that I ensure these folks their privacy. Thank you so much."

Unruffled by Paco's dismissal, Molly emptied the remainder of her pitcher into the dirt of the stately cactus and left the room.

Paco closed the door and took his seat once more. "And now, Mrs. Worthington, is the diary still in your possession?"

"Oh, yes, it's safe in our hotel."

"It's in the safe at your hotel, you say?"

Paco's voice was gentle, but Lenora felt his hazel eyes bore into hers. She looked back at him with a steady gaze, but her stomach felt suddenly queasy. "No, Inspector, not in any safe. In our room. I mean I just tucked it into the pocket of my suitcase and locked it. The suitcase, I mean. I guess I could have taken the diary to the desk and had them put it in the hotel safe. Do you have any reason to believe anyone will try to steal it?"

"No, ma'am. That is, I don't know. I'm just trying to ascertain if it also had some intrinsic value to a thief. Was there anything mentioned in the passages you read that could hold any monetary value for anyone attending the meeting? Or be a source of embarrassment to one of the Society members, perhaps?" Bucky and Lenora shook their heads very slowly. "Could you say the same for the letter read by Mrs. Raphael?" The same response. "And I suppose the same thing holds true for the tape that Mr. Marcus played?"

"I can't imagine any connection between the historical accounts and either Victor's murder or the robbery," Bucky offered.

"Perhaps not, Dr. Worthington, but may I remind you we haven't yet determined that it was, in fact, murder. But let's move on and discuss the deceased for a moment. Did either of you know Victor?"

"No," Bucky said, "not personally. We'd never met him before Friday night. We knew about him, of course."

"How's that?"

"Avi and I have been friends for so long. He's mentioned before that his nephew comes and goes. Victor's instability has been a source of concern to him for years."

"That's all he's said about him?"

"That and the fact that his sister has had a hard time dealing with Victor since her husband died."

"Nothing else?"

"That's all, sir," Bucky said.

"Okay, let's get back to the night of the meeting. Did either of you leave the group at all that evening, either from the sunroom or the dining room?"

"I don't believe I did, but didn't you powder your nose a few times that night, dear?"

"Why, yes, at least twice. Does that make me a suspect, Inspector?"

"Not necessarily, ma'am. Did you go near the den that evening?"

"Oh, no. I used the guest powder room at the other end of the hall."

"Then you apparently know your way around this house quite well."

"Uh, yes, that was not my first visit to the Kepple home, you see. And..."

"I do see. Thank you both for your cooperation."

But Lenora's glasses slid low on her nose as she leaned forward. Being dismissed like a schoolgirl unnerved her. "Inspector, please let me explain. We're close friends of Avi's. When we come to visit, the three of us generally chat here in the den over drinks. You know, music, theater, the arts."

Paco nodded. "Thank you," he said. "Have you yourself ever been to Marche House?"

"Oh, yes," Lenora said eagerly. "Hubert invited us to several dinner parties."

"Then you and your husband were friends of Hubert Marche?"

"Yes and no, Inspector," Bucky interjected. "Not friends, exactly. More like acquaintances. Hubert came to me as a patient for therapy about seven years ago."

"All the way to Philadelphia?"

"Yes. It would have been more convenient for him to see Avi, but Hubert worried about local gossip. You know how small towns are. He felt he'd have more privacy in Philadelphia."

Lenora's ample body snapped to attention. She slid to the edge of the sofa and faced her husband. "I never knew Hubert was your patient."

"Of course, you didn't, dear. You know I never discuss my patients."

"But I assumed the dinner invitations were strictly social."

Bucky merely shrugged.

"Why was Hubert Marche in therapy, Doctor?" Paco asked.

"I don't feel comfortable going into detail, even though Hubert is dead. But without betraying patient confidence, I can tell you he was obsessed with guilt. Something in his relationship with his first wife."

"And how long was he in therapy with you?"

"I saw him once a week for about two years, and then he abruptly stopped coming. Told my secretary business was too pressing for him to make the trip any longer. I was surprised. There was still much to be resolved."

"I see." Paco turned his attention to Lenora. "Mrs. Worthington, did you enjoy the dinner parties?"

"Oh, yes, there were never more than ten guests, and we had the most fascinating discussions, usually about art. The house was exquisite, of course, and he took us on a little tour on our first visit. I could even visualize what it was like when my mother lived there."

"I understand you're a fairly well-known artist in these parts, Mrs. Worthington," Paco said. "Do you two collect art as well?"

Bucky remained silent, but Lenora's eyes brightened behind her tortoise-shell glasses as she answered. "Oh, yes, we're extremely proud of our collection. In fact, I fell in love with the Sargent painting at Marche House."

Paco's bristly eyebrows shot up. "*Did* you, now?"

"Oh, yes. After all, it was a portrait of Sophia, my mother's employer and confidante. Bucky and I made him an offer, but Hubert wouldn't even consider it."

Paco noted a look of concern on Bucky's face. "What exactly was Hubert's reaction to your offer, Dr. Worthington?"

Bucky hesitated and then said, "He seemed a little cool after we broached the subject."

"At what point in his therapy was it?"

"Well . . . he stopped coming to see me at about that time."

"Did you receive any more dinner invitations after that?"

"Come to think of it, no."

"Mrs. Worthington," Paco said, "what was your reaction to the news that the Sargent painting had been stolen?"

Lenora flashed an alarmed look at her husband as if hoping he would rescue her. "I was shocked and horrified, as you can imagine."

"Have you any idea who could have stolen it?"

"Of course not," she answered, her voice angry now. "I just hope and pray it's found soon and not damaged."

"Thank you both," Paco said. "That's all I need for now. You've been extremely helpful. Would you send in Miss Heidi Hemming on your way out?"

"Of course, sir," Bucky said.

As they walked away, Paco could hear Lenora's barely audible whisper. "He made me feel so defensive. What have I done? I know I said too much."

"No sense worrying about it now," her husband answered.

For a few moments Paco seemed lost in thought while he sorted through what he had learned thus far. And then he noticed a tall blonde figure filling up the entire doorway. Or rather, he noticed a sky-blue angora sweater that seemed to roll like waves over the softness of full breasts.

"Miss Hemming? Please come in and make yourself comfortable. Yes, there will be fine. Is Hemming your married name? I understand you're the daughter of the late Hubert Marche."

"I'm not married. Never been. Heidi Hemming is my stage name. I'm an actress--well, an aspiring one, anyway. My real name is Helga Huddleson Marche. I'm Hubert's stepdaughter. You see, my mother was married previously." She self-consciously ran her fingers through her ash-blonde bob.

"Miss Hemming, could you tell me in your own words what took place at the meeting Friday night?" Paco cocked his head, listened intently, and asked: "Would you mind repeating that part about when you first saw the key?"

"Well, Dr. Kepple took the velvet case from Dr. Lord and opened it. It was the first time most of us had seen the key. Absolutely gorgeous. Then Dr. Kepple gave the case to Victor and asked him to circulate among the members so they could see the key up close."

"Did anyone handle the key or remove it from its case while Victor moved through the group?"

"Not that I know of, but I wasn't paying close attention when it got to the other side of the room. I can't be sure."

"Who returned the key to the den?"

"I guess Victor did...No! Wait! I remember now. Victor brought it back to Dr. Kepple, and he took the case from him and closed it."

"Did Dr. Kepple return it to the den right away or did he keep it with him?"

"Um, let me see. I think he got up right away and left the room."

"Did Victor follow him out of the room?"

"No, I think it was ten or fifteen minutes later."

"What was?"

"Ten or fifteen minutes later that Victor left the room. And that was the last time I saw him."

"Had you known him before?"

"Victor? Yes, as a child, but never very well. He was a lot closer in age to my stepsister, Marti."

"I noticed you arrived this morning with a young man. Was he with you Friday night? I didn't see him on the guest list."

"No, he wasn't here. His name is Derrick Powers. He's not a member of the Historical Society, but frankly, I expected him to come with me anyway Friday night. At least I'd hoped he would, since we were spending the whole weekend together. And Dr. Kepple told me it would be okay to bring him. But Derrick begged off and stayed back at the inn."

"I see. How long have you been dating him?"

"Only a few months. We met at a gym in Annapolis. I thought we were a little more than just dating, but I'm beginning to think I'm wrong."

Paco watched her nervously touch her upturned nose and then a rouged cheek. Somehow, the unlined cherubic face seemed oddly misplaced on such a voluptuous body.

"Sorry, Inspector," she said. "I'm getting off track, aren't I?"

"No problem, Miss Hemming. By the way, have you ever taken your friend through Marche House?"

"I...uh...no...well, just the one time about a month ago."

Paco waited in silence, hoping she would volunteer more details, but her cupid's bow lips pressed shut. He gave up. "Indeed. Thank you for your help. Would you ask your friend to step in here for a moment, please?" The inspector added a few more notes while Heidi brought Derrick into the room, and then Paco motioned her out.

"Ah, Mr. Powers, is there anyone at the inn who can vouch for your whereabouts Friday evening?"

"I spent a very pleasant evening chatting with a Mrs. Lord, Danielle Lord. Her husband attended the meeting here."

"Where and when did this chat take place?"

"Oh, let's see...from eight to ten in the bar and then we watched a little TV in her room until about eleven. After that everyone returned from the meeting." Derrick leaned back almost in a slouch, rested his right ankle on his left knee, and extending his arms along the back of the sofa. Paco noted the studied nonchalance.

"Mr. Powers, I see you're wearing battle scars. Would you care to comment on them?" Paco indicated his eye.

"What? Oh, the shiner. I'm afraid I ran into a door. Rather embarrassing thing, don't you think?"

"Ah, yes. I'd say that's a pretty nasty bruise you've got there on your thumb, too, Mr. Powers. Do you think you'll lose the nail?"

"It's quite possible, Inspector. I'm always doing something of the sort. I got it slammed between two barbells. I guess I'm getting clumsy in my old age."

"Funny thing, Mr. Powers, you strike me as being neither old nor clumsy."

"I'll take that as a compliment. But accidents do happen."

"Have you ever been to Marche House, sir?"

"I'm looking forward to going there this afternoon, Inspector."

"I see. Thank you, Mr. Powers, would you send Dr. Lord in next, please?"

"You mean that's all?"

"Yes, thank you." Paco enjoyed leaving his suspects guessing. A moment later, he was surprised to see Dr. and Mrs. Lord enter the room together. "Good morning," he said. "I had thought to question each of you separately, as there are some matters that might be personal. Are you sure you wouldn't rather have it that way?"

"Oh, Inspector, we have no secrets from each other." The words came freely from Danielle, who entered carrying a plate of two cheese Danish. She sat down on the couch, crossing her long legs with deliberate slowness. Her pleated tartan skirt rested above her knees.

Paco noted her feline grace, and how her perky breasts pushed impudently forward in her white silk blouse. Two sexy women in ten minutes, he thought. A dangerous thing, he reminded himself, allowing his mind to wander like this.

Danielle began to fidget, recrossing her legs the opposite way. Paco saw an expression of irritability creep over the gorgeous face. His every attempt to make eye contact failed. She now seemed depressed. He cleared his throat, marking time to refocus his thoughts.

"Dr. Lord, would you describe the meeting on Friday evening?"

Ernie's account did not vary from the others at first. But then he launched into a minute description of his appraisal process, as if he were addressing a large audience. "To summarize," he said, adjusting his tie and drawing out his words, "in my experience, the key is a treasure of exceptional proportions. Its disappearance is a catastrophe of great magnitude. I thought you might like these." He handed Paco copies of the appraisal papers and Polaroid photos he had prepared Friday evening.

"Excellent, they'll be most helpful. Tell me, Dr. Lord, would a piece like this be difficult to fence?"

"Intact, yes, because of high-profile recognition. However, I'm sad to say, with the gems removed, they could easily be sold on some secondary market. But you would know that better than I. Of course, the total value would be greatly reduced because of the lost historical significance."

"Of course. And now to a little more delicate matter. Mrs. Lord, I understand you didn't attend the meeting Friday night. Why was that, ma'am?"

"I had one of my nasty headaches. They're not migraines, just sinus, but they do take their toll, Inspector. And maybe you already know, I'm a novelist. I write historical romances, and it's been a bit stressful for me trying to meet my publisher's deadline." She took a large bite of cheese Danish.

"That's a very interesting profession, Mrs. Lord. And now, can you account for your time at the inn Friday evening?"

The sweet cheese pastry had settled firmly in Danielle's mouth when the question was sprung on her. She tried to swallow, but the bite was too large. She chewed furiously, covering her mouth with one hand. She raised one index finger to signal that she needed a minute. Paco poured her a cup of lukewarm coffee, which she first sipped and then gulped down. "Sorry, Inspector..."

"I understand. You can account for your time then?"

"Oh yes, I was in the lounge having a few drinks around eight."

"Were you alone?"

"No, I believe Derrick Powers was there also. And some other man who sat at the bar."

"Forgive me, but I must make sure I have this straight. Were you sitting alone in the lounge?"

"No," Danielle said, her anger mounting. Her tongue flicked slowly across her delicate upper lip and then across her lower one. "Mr. Powers joined me at my booth for a little while."

"I see. How long were you and Mr. Powers in the lounge?"

"Until after ten, I think."

"And then what happened?"

"Nothing happened," Danielle snapped. She looked uneasily at her husband. Then, in a much softer voice, "I returned to my room and watched TV until Ernie came back."

"Then you were alone during that period?"

"Well, no, not exactly." This time she evaded Ernie's eyes. "Mr. Powers was kind enough to see me to my door and stayed to watch a little TV with me." Ernie's gaunt cheeks puffed slightly and his sinewy neck turned as mottled red as a steamed crab.

"Thank you, Mrs. Lord. That coincides with what Mr. Powers told me. Thank you both. And if you'll send Mrs. Raphael in next, I'd appreciate it."

Just as soon as the Lords had cleared the den door, Paco could hear Ernie's accusing voice. "Sinus headache? Yeah, sure. How long is this going to go on, Danielle? I've just about had it."

"Lower your voice, for God's sake," she retorted. "We'll discuss it later."

It had been a mistake, Paco decided, to allow them in the den together, even though Danielle had pushed for it. He didn't like being the instrument of domestic agitation. In any event, the information would go no further if it had nothing more to do with the case.

"Ah, Mrs. Raphael. Won't you come in and have a seat."

"How can I help you, Inspector?"

"I'd like to have your version of what happened here on Friday evening." He waited while this lady with an aquiline nose settled into the recliner. "Take your time and try to remember as much as you can."

Olivia's version did not vary from the others he had heard. She had also brought along Dr. Ahm's letter for him to read.

"Has Dr. Ahm's son tried to contact you as yet?" Paco asked.

"Why, no. Now that you mention it, in all this terrible business I'd completely forgotten about him."

"I understand that Dr. Kepple walked you home that evening, after the meeting."

"Oh, he told you about that."

"Yes. Did you encounter anyone or notice anything unusual during that walk?"

"No, Avi just saw me to my door and bid me good night."

"Did you leave the house again for any reason?"

Olivia looked off into space for a moment. She sat in seeming ease, but her erect back and slightly narrowed eyes belied extreme concentration. "No, of course not. But now that you mention it, I did have a chill, a creepy feeling that someone was watching us. I didn't see anyone, though."

"I would appreciate it if you would keep trying to remember," Paco urged. "Any detail might trigger your memory."

"Perhaps. I'll certainly do my best. Maybe Avi can shed some light on it."

"Of course. By the way, ma'am, do you ordinarily carry a personal handkerchief with you?"

Finding the question unusual, Olivia cracked a smile and looked at Paco with a curious tilt of her head. "I do," she said, pulling a small hanky from the sleeve of her finely cut blue suit.

"Would there be a monogrammed R on it?"

"As you can see, it's an O for Olivia."

"Thank you, Mrs. Raphael. And now, if Mr. Marcus is here, would you send him in, please?"

The Marcus interview went quickly, but with a crucial difference.

"I saw the dead man later that night, maybe after everyone else did," Quentin said. Then he gasped. "Oh, no, why did I say that? Now you'll think I'm a suspect."

"Calm down, sir," Paco said. "I'm just trying to get all the facts right now. Where did you see Victor?"

"I was coming up the hall just after dessert had been served, when I spotted him coming out of the bathroom at the other end of the hall."

"And what time would that have been, Mr. Marcus?"

"Between 10:30 and eleven, I think. I looked at my watch as I came through the door. I pretended not to notice him and he didn't acknowledge my presence. He went straight into the den and shut the door. I guess my seeing him caused some embarrassment."

"Thank you very much, Mr. Marcus, you've been extremely helpful. And please accept my condolences over the loss of your father-in-law."

Paco summoned the Thornberrys next. Marti whooshed into the den in front of Felix. "We're the Thornberrys, Inspector." She shoved her right hand straight at Paco's midsection, barely giving him time to offer his own hand, and shook it vigorously. "This is all so unnerving. So much excitement and so much violence. First our caretaker and now Victor, and within two weeks of each other. I've never been mixed up in a murder before," she said.

"Until now she's just been plain mixed up," Felix quipped.

"What makes you think Victor was murdered, Mrs. Thornberry?"

"Well, isn't that why we're here? I mean the key's missing and everything.

I thought it was a robbery and murder."

"We're not quite sure, yet. Perhaps you can enlighten me with your version of what went on that evening."

Marti used more words to describe less of what happened than any of the others. Felix had to keep butting in to keep her on track. Paco listened, but found her entirely unenlightening.

"Did either of you know Victor personally?"

"Yes, sir," Felix answered. "Vic and I played poker Tuesday and Thursday nights in the card room down at the inn."

"You were friends, then?"

"No, not...not friends, actually," Felix stammered. "Just into the poker thing. We didn't see each other any other time."

"Can you tell me something about Victor's gambling habits?"

"Our games weren't anything heavy, just penny ante. Vic liked to play with us local guys to hone his skills. He always kept his debt paid up in the neighborhood, but word had it he was into the boys up in Atlantic City in a big way. Oh, yeah, he bet heavily against the point spread in sports, too."

"I see. Thank you. I might need to talk to you a little more about this at a later time," Paco said. Marti remained unnaturally quiet. She glanced at her watch and drummed her long, tomato-red nails on her knees.

"Is there something you'd like to add, Mrs. Thornberry?"

Marti jerked her head up, as if she wasn't expecting to be addressed. Her mouth opened, the thick crimson lips poised to spew forth something of value. She breathed in heavily. "No, Inspector...no...nothing." Paco waited, his left eyebrow arched. But she remained silent. He excused them, and they started out the door.

"Oh, Mrs. Thornberry?" She stopped in her tracks and Felix continued on. "I understand that none of Hubert Marche's relatives received any inheritance per se. You and your stepsister do receive a generous grant or stipend as long as you serve on the board of trustees to the Marche Museum Trust. Is that correct?"

"Yes, that's right," she said, stepping back into the room a few feet. "We're both trustees, but..." Now Marti's voice took on a strident quality. "Heidi is also the personal representative of my father's estate--something I'll never quite understand."

"Why is that, Mrs. Thornberry?"

"Because she's his stepdaughter. I'm his daughter, for God's sake. Heidi has no head for business whatsoever, and she doesn't know the museum and its inventory like I do. It just isn't fair. But it was like that when we were growing up. She played the soft, sweet, cute one and my father always seemed to like her best."

"What happens to the estate if the museum goes belly up?" Paco asked.

"Everything goes on the auction block. The majority of the proceeds would go to charity and the remainder would be divided among the family. There's no doubt Heidi and I will benefit more if the museum prospers."

"I thank you for your cooperation and time." Marti left the door open. She headed back into the dining room.

Paco scribbled earnestly in his notebook and then leaned back in the tapestried recliner, contemplating his English loafers as they rested on the matching ottoman. Avi appeared at the door. He looked drawn, his face a mask of controlled concern as he sat down on the couch opposite Paco.

"If you're done with the questioning, Inspector, could I interest you in some of Molly's famous lox and eggs?"

"Thank you very much, Doctor, but she's already indulged me a few pounds' worth in the kitchen."

Avi smiled, but his heart wasn't in it. "What happens now, Inspector? Any clues about the key's whereabouts? I'm embarrassed to ask you, but you can understand what I'm feeling. The key is my responsibility, not to mention my investment. As if it's not enough that we have poor Victor dead and my sister distraught, now I have to worry about the key too." His voice grew firmer as he unfolded his distress, peeling it off like a woolen sweater on a hot day.

Dr. Kepple had a vulnerability, a way of revealing what was truly on his mind that Paco found endearing. He began to size up the psychoanalyst. A formal man, Paco noted. Avi wore a jacket and tie even during Sunday brunch in his own home. And yet, his refreshing candor countered the formality. The two men sat for a moment, the only sound the final droplets from the plants hitting the rug.

Avi looked up in surprise and shook his head. "Oh, brother, she's still at it. And I've warned her so many times not to overwater those plants."

"Some things, some people never change, Doctor," Paco said with a sympathetic smile.

"I suppose you're right, Inspector. But..." and Avi's eyes twinkled. "It's a neurosis of my own making. I'm compelled to try. It's what I do."

"Spoken like a true professional, Doctor."

Molly loaded the dishwasher with the expertise of someone familiar with three-dimensional jigsaw puzzles. Paco watched for a moment and then held out his cup and saucer for her. He knew she could have retrieved it from the den herself, but he wanted to ask her a few more questions.

"Oh, hi, Paco." She took the cup and saucer from him and found exact spaces for them in the bin before closing the door and starting the heavy-duty cycle. "Well, have you got it all solved yet?"

"Oh, no, Molly, I need to ask many more questions. I'm not even sure of all the crimes yet. There's only one thing I am sure of."

"What's that?" Molly asked.

"We're dealing with two senseless deaths here. But as for the rest, I'm stymied."

Paco leaned back against the counter while Molly refilled Shana's water bowl. He wondered whether there was any connection between the two deaths. Gambling--a motive? Would organized crime have an interest in killing either one of these men? Victor was worth a lot more alive to them than dead, and poor old Aigue couldn't possibly have posed a threat to anyone. Paco sat down in one of the captain's chairs and gazed out the window. The thefts: Marche House was pivotal in both. Wasn't it a coincidence that the two pieces stolen were probably the most valuable of their kind in the entire place? Both thefts had required insider information, no question about that, and at least one person interviewed here today supplied such information.

He sat straight up and turned to Molly, as if his next thought were descending on him for the first time. "I'm not even sure I've identified all the players yet."

"How can you find the rest?" Molly asked.

"By identifying the inside player first," he replied. "What about Mr. Thornberry? Did he call Victor here very often?"

"Maybe once every week or two. Not very much," she answered.

"He seemed to know an awful lot about Victor's debts and his whereabouts. By any chance, did Victor tell his mother where he was going on Friday?"

"Well...I don't like tattlin 'bout members of the family, but they did have a disagreement Friday afternoon."

"Did it get nasty?" Paco asked.

"No, no, no! But they talked too loud and I overheard them. She'd been crying. Said she couldn't stand by and do nothing, and he said, 'It's just for a few weeks. It'll be our secret, Mother.'"

"Oh? Then Mrs. Moskowitz was telling me the truth." His fingers idly fiddled with the fringe on the embroidered place mat. "So if Victor was involved in both thefts, then the loot might already be in the hands of a fence."

"I have to muddletate on that," Molly said, her glassy blue eyes narrowing. "I sure don't think Victor would do anything like stealing. He liked to drink and gamble, but that was it. And he didn't take off after all."

"So you think he was just running from his debt?"

"Uh-huh."

"Molly..."

"Yeah?"

"Does Greta talk much about Mrs. Raphael?"

"Uh-huh, sometimes. What makes you ask? Is she a suspicion?"

"I was wondering if she had trouble making ends meet. Do they live on a tight budget, or did her late husband leave her pretty well fixed?"

"Oh, her ends come together very nicely. Although I heard Greta say Miss Olivia's broker called and told her she had a loss. I guess you have to expect that when you deal with somebody called a broker. I don't know if she needs fixing at all."

CHAPTER 19

THE MARCH TO MARCHE HOUSE

"Ohooo! Geeeez!" Trixie Marcus desperately grabbed the vinyl handle above her head with two hands as the Lincoln Town Car gobbled up the access road to Marche House. Momentarily, it had swung out to a jutting point 300 feet over the water to follow the abrupt cliff line and then swung back toward the great house again.

"Whoa, there! Take it easy on those curves, Olivia. We're not in that much of a hurry to get there, are we?" Lenora had indulged in one too many helpings of hash browns and eggs, and Olivia's driving had an explicit way of revisiting these sins.

"Well, I wanted to do something dramatic to get your attention," Olivia said. "And get you to appreciate this roadway up." She slowed down considerably for the last 500 feet. "Hubert Marche went to no small expense to provide this access road. That stretch over the water required a trestled bridge. I'm told it's quite an engineering feat."

"Still, you needn't have flown over that part so fast. My stomach may never catch up with the rest of me." Trixie's face had lost all its color.

"What's the matter, Trixie? Did the ride upset your tender tummy?" Marti, sitting comfortably up front, glanced over her shoulder.

Lenora, seated in the back on the other side of Felix, replied: "Marti, do you always have to be needling someone? Can't you bury the hatchet, at least for the rest of the afternoon?"

"I'm not the one whose mouth is always open, Lenora." The words left Marti's mouth before she had contemplated their impact.

Olivia marched up the worn white marble steps of Marche House long before the others had even opened their car doors. She needed to get away from them if only for a moment.

"Please, Marti, pu-leeese," she heard Lenora beg, and the bickering seemed to abate. Olivia found the bronze double doors locked. But she took a moment to savor the rural Maryland scenes portrayed in relief in eight panels: wild ducks, hunters with shotguns, marsh grasses, a rippling creek. Shielding her eyes from the bright noonday sun, Olivia turned toward the cottage a hundred yards away and saw Norma Aigue working her way along the flagstone path. Norma waved a large skeleton key in her hand. She would soon be there to let them in.

The cottage sat along the edge of expansive tobacco fields falling away southward to the water and climbing gradually back up to the tidy green tree line at Locust Lane.

Turning her head to the west, Olivia's eyes sought out the walking path through the fields of bleached cornstalks and high grass still bowing submissively from the recent drenching rain. Beads of light from the last droplets glistened on the faded October growth. A lone hawk soared majestically overhead. On the path Rachel and Simon led the pack of brisk walkers, with Derrick and Heidi just behind. Quentin struggled to keep up some fifty feet beyond the others.

Olivia sat down on one of the wrought iron benches under the portico, welcoming its momentary refuge. Six massive white wood Doric columns lined this classical porch. High above in the center hung a wrought iron gas lamp. A black ironwork fence, with vertical rails of finely molded ears of corn emerging from their husks, edged the portico and steps. The same pattern decorated the benches.

"Have a seat, everyone, until Norma and the others get here," Olivia offered. She wished that Avi and Bucky could have joined them, but she understood it was important that someone stay with Freddie, and Bucky felt he too could be of help there.

"Whoops!" Lenora reached for the railing as the four-inch-thick marble step shifted slightly under her weight. "It looks like the brass anchoring strap is missing from this step," she said.

A horn blasted. The arrival of a Buick Regal signaled the coming of the Lords. As they ambled slowly up the walk, Danielle lingered. "Ernie," she drawled excessively, "do y'all believe this? An Old South plantation here in lil ole Black Rain Corners. Look at those tall windows upstairs." She giggled. "Ah can almost see Scarlett O'Hara spying on us from behind a curtain up there. I've got to use this place in my next book."

"Okay, dear, sure, but how corny can you get? Besides, Scarlett's wind has already gone. Maybe you could begin your novel with 'It was a dark and stormy night.' I can just see you typing away perched atop Snoopy's doghouse."

Danielle smiled stiffly. "Well, aren't you the romantic one. Just you wait, I'll make something of it."

Norma approached and Trixie hugged her. "Hi, Mama."

"I didn't know you would be coming with the group today."

"I thought I'd surprise you, Mama." Trixie followed her mother to the door and watched her unlock the one on the right and swing it back inside. The seldom-tried hinges squealed, objecting every inch of the way. Trixie took one look at the grand foyer and shied backward. "I...I just can't go in. It's where my daddy died. I can't. I'll come back to the cottage with you, Mama.

Quentin, will you pick me up afterward? Please, honey."

"Sure, Trix. As soon as we're through with the tour," Quentin said.

"Trixie?" Marti said.

"Yeah."

"I'm sorry I've been such a bitch today. I should have remembered you just buried your father last week. I honestly don't know why I do it, hon."

"It's okay."

By now the entire group had assembled. Olivia stood on the top step in her blue tweed suit. "Gather 'round, everyone," she said, with a welcoming sweep of both hands. "I'd like to introduce Norma Aigue, Trixie's mother and our trusted caretaker." Olivia placed her hand on Norma's shoulder. "And dear Norma, I'm sure you know how we feel about your tragic loss of Will." Norma forced a smile.

"Don't come by too early," Trixie said to Quentin. "We need some time together." Norma kissed Trixie on the cheek, slipped the large front door key into her pinafore pocket, and the two of them headed off to the caretaker's cottage.

"And now," Olivia said, "let's start with a bit of Marche House history. Cartier Marche was Marti's grandfather. She has given me a term paper on her family's history that she wrote for a tenth grade English composition class. As she told me, with a little help from her dad. It's a good thing she saved it all these years." Olivia began to read.

"Cartier Marche was the only child of wealthy French parents, who were obsessively religious. Cartier, a throwback to more adventurous ancestors, rebelled against his constricted upbringing at an early age. His parents were disappointed that he did not choose the staid, safe life of a squire or clergyman. Nevertheless, they agreed to advance him a substantial portion of his inheritance so that he might seek his fortune in America.

"Cartier arrived in Maryland at age twenty to try his lot as a gentleman farmer. A year later, in 1899, he purchased a much smaller version of what is now Marche House from its antebellum owner. His modest beginnings grew rapidly, for he had become a shrewd farmer with an attentive ear to market needs--optimally shifting crop rotations between tobacco, corn, and feed hay. Proving to be a wise futures investor as well, he soon amassed a sizable fortune. In time he lavished improvements and additions upon the house, making it the crowning glory of his achievements."

"How odd," Lenora said softly.

"What's odd, Lenora?" Olivia asked.

"The front of the mansion. It looks like a Greek temple."

"Right you are," Heidi said, smiling. "It was my stepfather, Hubert, who added that portico and pediment after his father's death."

Olivia read on. "Cartier, returning to France to attend to the family estate after his father's death in 1907, met and married Sophia Raucheau. Within a year, she gave birth to Hubert. Sophia died in a carriage accident when Hubert was only four years old. Cartier married a second time: Leslie Temple, Hubert's young nanny. Cartier mysteriously disappeared soon after that, leaving Leslie to raise Hubert." Olivia paused and looked up. "We all learned those last details from Geneve's diary."

She scanned the page to find her place. "Hubert grew up to be a stylish and scholarly gentleman. Both father and son proved to be avid collectors of antiques. Hubert, the more astute collector, gave Marche House an international flavor, slowly and methodically developing the showcase it is today." Olivia stopped reading to gaze at the portico, then added in her own words: "Hubert became obsessed with the notion of permanence and immortality. Which is why we're lucky enough to have this museum." She folded Marti's term paper and tucked it into her handbag while the group applauded.

"My stepfather did something else I'm proud of," Heidi interjected. "He preserved his father's tradition of the working farm. Tenant farmers cultivate the land even now."

"A good point, Heidi," Olivia said. "And now, let's step inside."

They moved across the threshold one by one. Rachel gasped with delight. But then, upon noticing the masking tape left on the marble floor by the police, her gasp turned to dismay. She led the group around the taped shape where Willard's body had fallen to its last breath. She forced herself to look away, and the fascination with the room soon overtook her.

A shallow white wood dome crowned the grand foyer. Eight tiny hexagonal windows cast a blue-white light about the rim. A carved white wooden camellia at the peak supported a chandelier by multiple chains of brass. The six-foot spectacle in tiers of crystal tears tinkled in the unleashed breeze from the still-open bronze door.

A magnificently turned staircase, with white vase-shaped balusters, gracefully wound its way to the hall above. Rachel's eyes followed the wide mahogany railing as it continued along the second floor hall and turned back toward the front of the house to safeguard a spacious balcony filled with straight-backed gilded chairs. From this lofty vantage point, one could survey the social scene below.

Four oil paintings dominated the grand foyer walls. They depicted the traditional Maryland hunt: equestrians in reds, blacks, and whites; their mounts of chestnut, roan, and dapple gray; and tri-colored hounds. The object of the hunt could not be seen. The paintings hung above two floral Chippendale settees.

The group waited in expectant silence for Olivia to start the tour. "Everyone, please stay together. I haven't had the opportunity to prepare a formal docent's lecture tour, nor have I completed very much of the requisite research. So please bear with me, and I will answer whatever questions I can. If you will follow me into the parlor on our right...this is the sitting room, where the family entertained guests for tea or sherry."

To Rachel the room looked surprisingly cozy. The small pedestaled walnut tables had once held teacups and saucers of Limoges and Sevres. Sunlight filtered through the leaded-glass windows, displacing the gloom so typical of turn-of-the-century European parlors. Curlicued armchairs and fringed Victorian love seats were scattered informally across the floral carpet.

"Look at those portraits!" Simon exclaimed. "The frames alone are probably worth a fortune."

"I'm sure they are, Simon," Olivia said. "They're Italian, hand-carved. Gilded rococo frames always lend grandeur, even to children's portraits."

"Yeah, even where none might be deserved," Felix said. Marti ignored him.

"Are the portraits members of the Marche family?" Rachel asked.

"That's my mother and me in our white dresses with my stepfather. I was only nine when that was painted," Heidi said. "Marti, you should recognize the two ladies in the next one."

"Yes, I was eighteen. And that's my mother, Millicent, in the blue dress. She was Hubert's wife."

"His first wife," Heidi corrected.

"Yes, his first wife," Marti continued. "And in this one, the small boy is Hubert with his father. I'm not quite sure who the young lady in the last oil is, but I think it might be Leslie Temple Marche, my grandfather's second wife. She raised my father. I knew her only when she was a good deal older, of course. It's not a good likeness."

Olivia cleared her throat noisily and tried to pick up where she had left off. "The huge fireplace in this room is shared by the library through that door to the rear of the house, and backs up to another fireplace in the grand ballroom at my right."

Olivia beckoned for the group to follow her. "And now for the *piece de resistance*," she said. But it needed no introduction. Flanking the arched doorway, two six-foot pink marble muses reached out in welcome. On passing through the archway, Derrick rubbed the round bellies of both statues. Heidi giggled.

Danielle gasped. "It's a mini-Versailles Palace." She squeezed her way through the group and spun about the floor, waltzing and whirling with an imaginary partner and music confined to her ears alone. She stopped and began to clap her hands enthusiastically. "Wouldn't it have been wonderful to have lived in such times?"

"Absolutely, Danielle, you've caught the spirit completely," Olivia said. "The Marche family, especially Cartier, strove for the Versailles look, with a generous dollop of Italian Renaissance, I might add. A great deal of money was spent to that end."

She flipped a wall switch, and suddenly the ballroom lit up with the opulence of seventeenth century royalty. At intervals along the plum-colored walls were narrow panels of pink and white Italian marble and tall arched mirrors in gold leaf frames. Set between them were console tables; their rich tops of inlaid tortoiseshell and mother-of-pearl rested on gilded cupids and classical heads.

"Hey, guys," Danielle chirped, breaking the awed mood, "check out the ceiling. Do you believe it?"

The ceiling was painted in pastel motifs of flowers, fruits, and monogrammed coats of arms. Plaster medallions of carved petals and leaves held three crystal chandeliers.

"Hubert electrified these chandeliers," Olivia said, "as he did the entire house in the mid-1930's."

The parquet hardwood floor gleamed in readiness for the next ball or reception. A concert grand piano and velvet-covered straight-backed chairs filled one corner where the orchestra played. Two huge Arabian tapestries covered the end walls: a shaggy lion devouring its bloodied prey and a Bedouin leaning into the fierce wind as he pulled his dromedary across the blowing sands.

"Who's the gorgeous broad over the fireplace?" asked Quentin.

Olivia smiled. "The broad, as you put it, was Cartier Marche's first wife, Sophia Raucheau Marche. She was certainly gorgeous, and if you recall the legends, she died running away with her lover."

"What a waste. Such beauty." Quentin shook his head as he spoke.

"That pink velvet gown, that necklace and her ring." Danielle Lord turned to her husband. "Do you suppose any of it is still in the estate?"

Ernie tried to recall the pieces from the inventory he had been given. "I believe the diamond necklace is, but I'm not sure of the ring. As for the gown, I highly doubt it."

But something else bothered Simon. The portrait of Sophia by John Singer Sargent had hung in private obscurity in the boudoir of the lady of the house. This Sophia, rendered by a little known painter of the era, enjoyed a place of honor over the ballroom fireplace. Why? The thief must have known quite a bit about this house and fine art to have zeroed in on the painting upstairs.

Simon studied the oil: the face of an angel, staid in thoughts of quiet goodness, her soft brown ringlets falling on her rosy, full bosom. He was more enchanted by the woman than her trappings. "Those are the eyes of innocence and a face of purity. How could such a women be an adulteress?"

Rachel laughed. "Adulteress, dear? How Victorian of you."

"Boy-oh-boy, Simon," Marti said, "have you got a lot to learn about women. If you ever decide to get rid of him, Rachel, let me know. I'll be glad to educate him."

"Now what kind of remark is that?" Felix asked, his face falling into a pout.

"Never you mind, Felix," Rachel said kindly. "I intend to keep my man all to myself." She wrapped both arms about her husband from behind and gave him an affectionate squeeze. "But Simon, honey, don't be so hard on poor Sophia. Being married to a monster like Cartier would send any woman into another man's arms."

Olivia made a mental note of that remark. She would work it into her formal docent spiel. "Now if you'll follow me."

"Wait, Olivia! What's that tiny balcony above the library door?" Only Rachel had noticed it.

Olivia shrugged. "I'm afraid I don't know."

"It's the air-conditioning," Heidi said.

"Air-conditioning?" everyone repeated in disbelief.

"Yes," Heidi said. "Originally, servants were used to fan air across huge blocks of ice and force the air down into the room."

"Ingenious. It couldn't have been too efficient, of course. But for its day and age, quite remarkable," Simon mused.

They filed into the library, a shadowy room lined with built-in, six-foot-high black walnut bookcases. Between two small windows on the east wall hung a painting of a stormy English landscape. Above the bookcases, a coat of arms embellished the upper reach of the north wall. The musty scent of old leather-bound volumes filled the air.

"What I wouldn't give for this in my office," Rachel said, running her fingers over a mahogany and ebony oval desk. "It's the lions' feet that really get to me."

"Me too. That was one of my stepfather's favorite pieces," Heidi replied.

"It's a Thomas Sheraton writing table," Marti added.

Armchairs of carved walnut and rosewood lined the border of the hunter green carpet. Olivia paused at a round spindled table supporting a tooled-leather lamp. "Behold, ladies and gentlemen, Hubert's ingenuity at disguising modern conveniences." She opened a vertical panel in the lamp base: "*Voila*!" Inside nestled a telephone.

An oil painting of Sophia and Cartier in riding habit hung over the fireplace, she astride an English saddle and he standing beside her chestnut mare. "So dignified and elegant," Rachel said. "Not a hint of their troubled marriage."

Simon's attention was fixed elsewhere: on the proportions of the room itself. The library was much wider than the parlor and extended beyond and behind where he believed the wall of the grand foyer to be. His technical curiosity drew him to the wood trim in the library and he remembered it elsewhere in the house, too. About six inches below the ceiling, an-inch-and-a-half-thick white cavetto molding encircled the room. In other rooms the molding had appeared at chair rail height. What struck Simon as curious was the horizontal wheat pattern that had been etched and highlighted in gold leaf on the concave surface.

"Ernie, come look at this molding," he said, pointing up. "It's really strange, the way they chose to inscribe this pattern on a curved surface. It must have been extremely labor intensive, even for a fine craftsman."

"I agree, Simon. It had to have been done largely by hand," Ernie said. "But then again, we know Cartier spared no expense, and fine workmanship is evident in the other rooms, too. I'd sure like to know what kind of tools were used, though."

"I'd be interested, too," Olivia said. She had been listening intently. Simon's remarks triggered her memory, and for the first time that day she thought of Schlem's driftwood frame. Were they getting close to finding the secret room? Though her heart quickened in anticipation, she decided to hold her immediate thoughts for the time being and guide the group to the splendor of the dining room on the other side of the house.

"The perfect setting for lavish dinners. I can even visualize myself as a guest here in days of yore," Olivia said. The room was largely English Tudor. A wall of windows in tiny square panes faced the front of the house. Tall tapestried chairs surrounded a massive dark cherry table that could comfortably seat two dozen guests. The two richly colored stained-glass fixtures illuminating the table had been created by Louis Comfort Tiffany himself. Just below the oak-beamed ceiling, a narrow mural of country scenes traveled the perimeter of the room, beginning and ending at a columned fireplace of black and gray marble.

"What's on your mind, dear?" Rachel had noticed Simon's prolonged stare.

"Here's that unusual trimwork again, just below the mural. It seems to continue throughout the rest of the house." The cavetto molding extended from the dining room to a sewing room and an anteroom containing china and linen closets.

"You're right, Simon," Olivia confirmed. "That same molding goes all the way up to the second floor, as you'll soon see." She pushed the door open toward the rear of the house and held it until everyone congregated in the large work area. "The kitchen actually consists of four separate rooms: a pie and cake pantry on my right, a storage pantry next to it, this main food preparation room where we're standing, and the head housekeeper's room there on the left. Despite the stark appearance of these rooms, Hubert Marche saw to it that they were equipped with the very latest appliances--installed as unobtrusively as possible, just like the phone hidden in the lamp." She demonstrated by opening a gaily painted cupboard next to the sink to reveal a modern dishwasher. She proceeded to pop open other doors, drawers, and panels, revealing other appliances.

"Olivia, why would anyone want to conceal such a treasure trove of kitchen tools? Hiding them simply makes them less efficient to use." Rachel picked up a wooden spoon from a deep bowl and used the handle to scratch her forehead just above the hairline. Simon chuckled.

"Perhaps I can throw some light on that," Marti said. "Don't forget, my father wasn't the one doing the cooking. He was more concerned with the aesthetics of his house. He left the mechanics of the kitchen, housekeeping, and gardening to his staff, which was quite large."

"Where's the stoves and ovens?" Felix wanted to know. "They didn't bake all those pies and cakes in that fireplace, you can bet on that."

Olivia responded: "Hubert insisted that all the major cooking be done in the cook house, that little brick and stone annex just beyond the kitchen door. There was something about the smells of food that disrupted his work as well as his sense of aesthetics." Olivia swung open the kitchen and cook house doors and pointed. "But I can assure you, there are also two modern convection ovens out there with stovetop burners."

She then led them back to the grand foyer and up the stairs, and a hush settled over the group. As if of one mind, they sensed an unnatural presence in the house. Imperceptible at first; next, barely discernible, as it floated its way into their collective consciousness. And then, the eerie yet melodious chords reached out for their attention, subtly, softly from the stairs above the grand foyer. The music wasn't getting any closer as they climbed, but it *was* getting louder, and their awareness grew with each step taken.

"It sounds like a harpsichord, but there isn't one in the house--none that I know of," said Marti. She looked apprehensively toward Heidi, who gave her an agreeing nod. The strains grew louder again, emanating from nowhere and everywhere at the same time.

"It's Bach, a Bach fugue. And it definitely is a harpsichord," Lenora whispered.

"Yes, I agree on all counts," Olivia said. "But, ladies and gentlemen, that is not live music. And I don't buy any haunted house nonsense, either."

Ernie and Simon were the first to reach the top of the staircase. The melodious strains grew softer for a moment, then swelled again. But from where? Both men felt disoriented. Where to go next? Down the carpeted hall toward the ballroom balcony? Through the gallery of family portraits? In and out of the maze of bedrooms? Which way?

CHAPTER 20

SPINNING FINIALS

A single ghastly chord reverberated through the upper halls, adding to the general confusion. It came from everywhere at once. At the top of the stairs Olivia turned to face the others. She held up her right hand, motioning them to stop, then raised her index finger to her lips to call for silence--silence needed to track down the source of the hidden harpsichord. Now, eerie chords suggested ghostly origins. The reactions ranged from Marti's nervous giggle to Quentin's deathly serious expression.

Realizing that no stranger could get past the scrutiny of the group poised on the stairs, Simon and Ernie chose an orderly search of the upstairs bedrooms, beginning at the balcony end. The hunt went on ten, then fifteen minutes, sufficient time to agitate those left on the staircase.

"How long are we going to be imprisoned here?" Quentin whispered, shifting from foot to foot.

"Shhh!" Marti hissed.

With only three bedrooms left to search and one of them still cordoned off with yellow plastic police tape, Simon made a discovery. He found two thin brown wires emerging from the dumbwaiters on either side of the hall and running just under the carpet's edge toward the drapes of the cathedral window at the hall's end. Moving swiftly yet silently, Simon pointed for Ernie to open the dumbwaiter door at the left while he took the one on the right. Both men discovered small loudspeakers, the kind that normally unhook from a boom box tape recorder. But the music had stopped. This time Ernie pointed to the window seat behind the drapes and stealthily approached it. When both men were in position, Simon yanked back the drape in a dramatic flourish. There crouched a frightened nine-year-old trying to make herself as small as possible. She clutched a boom box to her stomach.

Olivia rushed to the end of the hall and stopped short. "Oh, my God! Caitlin Neuman, what have you got to say for yourself? You gave everybody quite a fright. And what are you even doing here? You're supposed to be in your room doing your math homework...Well?"

"I didn't want to miss everything. I felt left out. I didn't mean anything by it. I just wanted to have a little fun." Caitlin began to sob loudly.

"Where did you ever dream up such an idea, young lady?" Olivia held out her arms to her only grandchild.

"Gosh! That part was easy. The kids talk about Marche House being haunted and all, and I thought..."

"That's just the trouble. You didn't think. And do you know what I think, young lady?"

"Yes, ma'am. I mean, no, ma'am."

"I think you owe everyone here an apology."

"Yes, ma'am. I'm sorry, everybody. I didn't mean any harm."

Simon suppressed a smile. "I have to admit you were certainly clever," he said. "The way you got the speakers to reverberate through the entire dumbwaiter system. You gave us quite a chase."

Caitlin's downcast eyes flickered with relief, but filled with renewed anxiety when she lifted her head to meet her grandmother's frown. It conveyed only one message: *I'll deal with you at home.*

"Grandma?"

"Yesss?"

"Can I look in the room where the painting's missing?"

"From the door only," Olivia said. "The police don't want anyone in the room yet."

As the group filed into the master bedroom behind Olivia, Caitlin lingered in the doorway next to it. She saw the new pane of glass on the French door where the thief had broken in. The manufacturer's sticker had not been removed yet. But her quick scan of the walls did not reveal the location of the missing oil, so, holding onto the door frame, she ducked under the tape and leaned backward into the room, straining to see the near wall.

"Caitlin Neuman, what did I just tell you?" Olivia's commanding voice came from the adjoining or "conjugal" doorway that connected the lady of the manor's room to the master bedroom.

Surprised by the second reprimand, Caitlin dropped to the hard floor on her backside, feeling her embarrassment with both hands.

"Yes, ma'am," she called out. She waited until she heard the tour leave the master's domain and enter another bedroom beyond it. Then she scrambled to her feet and wandered into the master bedroom, Hubert's room. She intended to view the crime scene from the adjoining door, but she soon became drawn to the powerfully masculine environment. No man had found his way into their lives since Grandpa Harry died, and his things had disappeared long ago.

Caitlin moved about the room, touching this and spinning that. With great delight she discovered that the ornately carved finials on the chair backs spun freely on dowels, their glue no longer effective. Each playful spin whetted her curiosity and incited her spirit of adventure. She spun her way about the room, leaving no finial unturned on the bed, dressers, and chairs. At the conjugal doorway she hesitated long enough to view the crime scene as she peeked out across another band of yellow police tape. There she saw the faded rectangle of wallpaper where the stolen painting had once hung.

Turning back into Hubert's room to continue her explorations, she discovered a majestic highboy with a finial yet untwirled. Standing on tiptoe, her hand could just reach the tantalizing carved acorn. She tried to spin it, but it wouldn't budge. Stretching even taller, she tried once more. This time the finial moved freely and she heard a metallic click. Boinnnggg! Thunk! A panel sprang open between the two top drawers. A scream escaped from her lips. Standing there, excited, with a quick hand over her mouth, Caitlin contemplated her next move. She couldn't very well keep this discovery to herself, could she? And yet, wasn't she in enough trouble with Grandma already?

Just then Rachel poked her head in the doorway. "What are you doing in there, child? Is something wrong?"

"No, ma'am...I mean, maybe a little bit," Caitlin admitted. A sheepish look crept over her face.

"Well, now, suppose you tell me about it," Rachel said.

"I turned that pretty acorn on top of that dresser and this little hidden door popped open. I'm afraid to tell Grandma 'cuz she told me not to touch anything." She lowered her head and whispered, "I know I'm not supposed to be in here."

"It's probably not quite as serious as you seem to think, young lady. Here, let's have a look." Rachel reached into her purse and retrieved the penlight they had used to unlock Avi's den door. Peering inside, she wanted to shout. Instead, she slipped her hand deep into the compartment and pulled out a large, jewel-studded box. She set it carefully down on a nightstand before yelling to the others. "Everyone, come quickly. Caitlin's made a fantastic discovery."

Rachel waited for the entire group to assemble and explained. "It came from this hidden compartment in the highboy. The compartment door released when Caitlin rotated the finial at the top."

Caitlin glanced over at her grandmother long enough to perceive the steel eye of discipline descending. She looked away quickly and edged close to Rachel for protection. But a scolding was the farthest thing from anyone's mind, even Olivia's. The air fairly crackled with expressions of awe, appreciation, and speculation as the group huddled together to examine the artfully carved details, the gleaming precious stones, and the elegance of the burnished wood.

"Such magnificent craftsmanship...Why, this must be Jacques's box--his gift to Sophia!" exclaimed Olivia.

Rachel reached for the box and carefully, gingerly tried to open it, but the catch wouldn't give. "Darn! It's locked. We need Daddy's antique key." She suddenly looked crestfallen. "But what am I saying? His key is missing." She lifted the bejeweled box and found it much heavier than she had imagined. The contents noisily shifted within as she turned it about in her hands. "This is so frustrating. I'm dying to see what's inside," she said with a sigh. "Well, perhaps 'dying' isn't the most appropriate word."

Simon smiled. "Let's bring it back to the house with us. We'll call around and find a good locksmith to open it."

"Simon, suppose you take charge of the box until then," said Olivia, "but please be very careful. And don't drop it, for heaven's sake. Meanwhile, is anyone still interested in seeing the last three bedrooms?"

Following a chorus of yeses, the tour continued.

Tired of the tour and pleased with the diversion, Quentin took Felix by the elbow and led him back downstairs to one of the Chippendale settees in the grand foyer. Once they were seated, Quentin began, "A rather surly individual stopped me at the inn on Thursday. Apparently, he mistook me for you, but I set him straight."

"Surly? In what way? What did he look like?" Felix had a pretty good idea who the man was, but he wanted to hear it from Quentin. And just how much did his friend know?

"He looked like a hood, if you must know. And he spoke as if he came from a rough place in New York or New Jersey."

"Did he give you his name or say what he wanted?"

"No, but he was trying to find out where Victor Moskowitz lived. Who is this guy, anyway? He sounds like bad news."

"Oh..." Felix chose his words carefully. "Just some guy I played cards with a few times in Atlantic City. Did you tell him Victor lived at Avi Kepple's place?"

"No, Felix. I told him Victor usually hung out in the bar and he could find Vic for himself. That seemed to satisfy the guy, and he headed that way."

Felix hadn't planned to tip his hand to Quentin. Ace "Sandman" Flowers was much more than a card-playing buddy. More like a collector/enforcer for big-time gambler Mitch Brodie. He knew Mitch and Ace all too well because he had had the misfortune to run afoul of them once up in Jersey. Vic must have been into Mitch for quite a bundle for him to have sent his *numero uno* enforcer.

Quentin's steady, inquiring gaze made Felix uneasy, and he decided to come clean. "Ever notice the way I walk?"

"You...have a slight limp," Quentin said warily.

"Yeah," Felix admitted. "Well, let me tell you, it's not from jogging." He paused to let this sink in and then asked, "Have you told anybody else about the guy looking for Vic?"

"Who should I tell?" Quentin looked him straight in the eye.

"Well, Inspector LeSoto, for example."

"Why should I tell him?"

"It might be pertinent to the investigation of Victor's death." Felix didn't actually believe Ace or Mitch had anything to do with Victor's death; killing was not their M.O. Get the money or inflict pain on the welsher--more their style.

"Yeah, I see what you mean." The impression of withholding information from the police made Quentin feel uneasy. He'd better tell the inspector soon.

"Uh...Quentin?"

"Yeah, Felix."

"You been messing around with Marti again?"

"Not now or ever, man. We're just buddies. That's all."

"Sure?"

"Sure! Hey, they must be through upstairs. I hear them coming down now." Marti came into view at the bottom landing first.

"Hi, Marti, having fun yet?"

"Why, yes, Quentin, honey. Felix, Simon thinks he knows where Isaac's secret room is. Isn't that exciting news?"

"Yep! And just where does he think it is?" Felix asked as he and Quentin rose to rejoin the group heading back into the dining room.

Simon was just putting forth his hypothesis when they arrived. "There has to be another room extending behind the grand foyer. Just like the library does on the opposite side. Ah-hah! Here it is." Simon reached for a knob on a door painted to look like another wall panel. The door swung inward to reveal a small room that extended behind the grand foyer. Simon's face fell with disappointment. "Not much of a secret room, with a doorknob for access and two large windows to the outside, is it?"

"No, I'm afraid it doesn't fit the description old Isaac gave us," Quentin said, after a brief perusal of the new room. "I'd say this is some kind of den."

"Exactly," Heidi chimed in. "My stepdaddy converted it into a den from servants' quarters when I was still quite young."

"So much for the secret room then. I wonder where it is?" Rachel said.

"Don't worry, babe, we'll find it." Simon put his hands on her shoulders and gave her a reassuring squeeze. "We'll just have to come back here with tape measures and stepladders and measure everything inside and outside the house until we find our structural anomaly."

"But we only have until just after the funeral, don't we?" Rachel asked. "I kind of expected we'd leave for home Tuesday afternoon."

"We may have to adjust our schedule," her husband said. "I think it will be at least Wednesday or Thursday. We should call our bosses tomorrow morning and let them know we'll be late getting back."

Rachel looked admiringly at her husband. She felt delighted that he'd allowed himself to become so involved in family affairs and the museum, too. She found a certain excitement in his approach to things mechanical and ideas scientific. He looked at all of life as a new Rubik's cube, a puzzle to be solved. If only Simon could locate Avi's key. Finding it, and the secret room, too, would solidify her father's confidence in his son-in-law. She so wanted her daddy's approval.

"You sure know how to make a fella feel at home, Molly. I may never want to solve this case." Paco held the cup steady on the saucer while Molly poured spiced herbal tea from the china brewing pot.

"Say when."

"When," he replied. She set the pot down on the oak table and covered it with a crocheted cozy. Squeezing into a chair opposite him, she pushed the sugar bowl and the dish with lemon slices toward him.

"Aren't you going to join me, Molly?"

"No, sireee! Tea just isn't my bowl of soup. Not today, anyway."

Paco just smiled. "I see," he said.

"Won't your boss be disappointed in you if you don't solve this caper?"

Paco nodded and drew in a breath. "Not to worry, I'll solve it. By the way, are those Mrs. Moskowitz's shoes on the counter there?"

"Uh-huh. She got them full of mud and wanted me to send them out to be cleaned. I gotta put 'em in a paper bag and take 'em over this afternoon."

"Did she wear them Friday night?"

"I think so," she replied.

"Let me take them over to the cleaners. I go right by there on my way."

"If you're sure you don't mind, it'd be goodly of you."

"Molly, dear," he began hesitantly, "I don't like asking this type of question, but it is my job. Is there anyone in this household who wanted Victor dead?"

"Nobody liked Victor for any reason, but nobody disliked him all that much either. He sometimes treated Miss Freddie real bad, but she always let him do that. I'd be ferocious if he did that to me. I'd sure take him off his haunches."

"But you wouldn't kill him?"

"No! Killing him would 'complish nothing."

"And no one else here would?"

"Course not! They're resputable people. Although I once heard the doctor say he'd like to wring Victor's neck."

"Do you think he could have?" Paco knew the answer, but wanted to hear it from Molly anyway.

"That's absorbed. The doctor's a very fine man, a pillow in the community, too. I don't 'prove of these questions."

"Sorry, we'll change the subject now." Paco reached out and patted the back of Molly's plump hand. He pulled his hand away quickly when he heard the back door rattle a few times and swing open.

"Hi, Molly...Inspector! I'm surprised you're still here." Rachel trooped through the kitchen, followed closely by Simon, who laid their treasure, wrapped carefully in an embroidered linen pillowcase, on the table.

"Just tidying up a few details for my report," Paco said. "Did you enjoy your trip to the museum?"

"Oh, yes," Rachel said. "The house is absolutely magnificent. Such elegant furnishings. The only disappointing part was that we didn't find the secret room. Happily, we did find the jeweled box."

"The room's there, all right. I'm sure we'll find it eventually," Simon insisted.

"Secret room? Jeweled box? I thought we were dealing with a missing jeweled key here." Paco exclaimed with both eyebrows flying north.

"We...I mean, you are, Inspector. Hasn't anyone told you about the three legends?" Rachel asked.

"I know *of* them. How are they pertinent to my investigation?"

Simon replied: "That's hard to say, Inspector. There's Dr. Ahm's letter. That's the first legend."

"Ah, yes, Mrs. Raphael showed that one to me."

"Then there's Geneve's diary. That would be legend two."

"Which Mrs. Worthington has locked up in her suitcase at the inn," Paco added.

"And lastly, there's the tape of Isaac Aigue's secret room at Marche House."

"Of course, the tape. What's on it?"

Simon explained: "It's an interview with Mrs. Marcus's grandfather. He constructed a secret room at Marche House for Cartier years ago. Quentin played it for us Friday night. You know, I wouldn't mind hearing that tape again. Maybe there's even a clue everyone missed the first time."

Paco asked, "Does the tape tell you where to look for the secret room?"

"Vaguely. Not in enough detail for us to head right for it."

"Where is this tape now, sir?" Paco asked.

"I believe Quentin gave it to Olivia. That is, a copy of it, at any rate."

"I think I need to have another talk with Mrs. Raphael," Paco said, arching his left eyebrow slightly.

The dining room door burst open, and Avi appeared. "So this is where everyone is hanging out! Have I missed anything?"

"Sorry, Doctor," Embarrassed to be discovered socializing, Molly immediately pulled herself to her feet and headed to the stove, where her cream of broccoli soup simmered. Dipping in a wooden spoon, she sipped critically, then broke into a blissful smile.

Avi leaned over the table and poked at the linen bundle sitting there. "What's this?"

"It's the jeweled box that goes with your stolen key. At least, we think so," Rachel said as she began unwrapping it. And when it sat in plain view: "Isn't it exquisite?"

"It's breathtaking," said Avi.

"You can say that again," Molly said. "It's mind bungling."

"Well, isn't anyone anxious to see what's inside?" Avi rattled the clasp, then lifted the box, shook it, and tried the lid. "Oh-oh. How are we going to get it open?"

"Can't open it. We need your missing key to do that," said Simon.

"Perhaps I can help," Paco said. He reached into his inside breast pocket and brought out a long, thin bifold wallet. He spread it open on the table before him and withdrew three slender wire-like tools with peculiar-shaped ends. He inserted the first probe through the escutcheon and examined the mechanism within the lock. As Paco explored, his eyes left the lock and drifted off into space, where they became fixed somewhere in the glass-fronted cupboards behind Rachel and Simon. He worked as though his eyes had become an abstract extension of his probe, registering and displaying in his mind alone. After memorizing the chamber's entrails, he held the first probe in place while he used a second but different type of probe to individually trip each of the engaging pawls in succession. He then rocked the two probes together until the whole cylinder rotated. Click! The lid popped up.

The four at the table grinned with anticipation while Molly applauded Paco's feat. The box was lined with the finest white satin, trimmed in purple velvet.

"Hey! It's just costume jewelry," Rachel said. One by one, she lifted out the cuff links, studs, stickpins, and tie tacks. "Nothing valuable at all." She gently turned the open box upside down over a place mat to see if she had missed anything.

"Inspector, why would anyone use such an elaborate and elegant trapping to secrete obviously worthless trinkets?" Avi asked.

"It could be a decoy," Paco replied. He pulled out his notebook and began inventorying the spilled contents.

Molly turned off the burner under her soup pot and ambled over to the breakfast nook. With great care, she picked up the jeweled box and rocked it from side to side. "This thing is too precocious for trinkets, yes, sireee." Cocking her head, she raised the box near her right ear and listened. Rocking the box again, she both heard and felt a heavy piece slide back and forth within. "Gol-ly!" she exclaimed. Setting the treasure back on the table, her plump fingers pressed and prodded the inner walls and floor of the box until she found what she was looking for. She squeezed one end wall. A loud click. The floor of the box popped free to expose a space below it.

"Molly, you are clever," Avi said. "It's a hidden compartment." He removed the false floor panel. "And another key!"

"A weird-looking thing. I wonder what it's to," Rachel said.

Fingering the heavy steel key, Paco said, "My guess is that it's too crude to be a spare front door key to the mansion."

"But it could be the key to the secret room," said Simon.

"We's up to our knees in keys," Molly quipped.

Avi laughed. "Molly, were there any messages for me while I napped?"

"No, Doctor, just another one of those calls for poor Victor. The man wouldn't leave his name or anything, so I just said he wasn't home. It makes me so mad when they do that. They want to remain incarnate."

"What?" Paco asked.

"Incognito," Avi translated for him.

"Oh. Did you get a lot of those kinds of messages for Victor, Molly?" Paco asked.

"Oh, yes, a bunch. Sometimes they'd slam the receiver right in my face."

"Did they ever leave a number for him to call?" Paco was just grasping at straws at this point, but it paid off.

Molly swirled her wooden spoon around and around through the soup before answering. "Last Friday I wrote down a number for him." She moved over to the kitchen wall phone and searched through a pile of notes impaled on a dangerous-looking spike mounted on the small wooden shelf there. "Not here. Oh, I know where it is!" She pushed through the swinging door and returned a few minutes later with a playing card--the two of diamonds--and a telephone number scrawled across it. "I found this in the den the other day," she said, handing the card to Paco.

"It's a 609 area code. Bring the phone book, please." Using the area code map in the front of the book, Paco determined that the call came from southern New Jersey, most likely Atlantic City.

Avi slid into the place Molly had vacated at the table and watched Paco go to the phone, dial eleven numbers, and wait.

"Yes, is Mitch there?" Paco asked. "When will he be back?...Just say a business associate. I'll call back. Thanks."

"Victor's bookie?" Avi asked.

"I believe so. They answered the phone with 'Brodie's!' I've heard the name Mitch Brodie--a biggie with the South Jersey bunch."

"Do you think this was a mob hit?" Avi asked.

"No, sir, I don't. It's not their style. This bunch would rather bruise, break limbs, and stay out of newsprint. Hits are usually the results of mob rifts and conspiracies, not overdue debts. But it wouldn't be the first time persuasion resulted in extinction."

Avi frowned. "I don't follow you, Inspector."

"Sometimes the physical therapy is excessively applied."

"So, you do think it was murder?"

"I'm beginning to think so. And with the key missing, grand larceny at a bare minimum. However, the means or instrument of death remains in question, pending the coroner's report on Tuesday. Of course, Victor's death is my primary concern right now." He traced a circular pattern on the table with his spoon. "But your jeweled key: that's the second problem, and it has me really baffled."

Lenora and Bucky had hardly settled into their room at the inn when they heard a soft tapping at the door. Lenora swung the door back to find Marti standing there with a frozen Cheshire cat grin clear across her face. She reached for Lenora's unwitting hand and slapped a black, unmarked videocassette into it.

"What's this?" Lenora asked.

Marti uttered only four words: "Enjoy! We'll talk later." She did an about-face and headed back to her own room.

CHAPTER 21

LOVE AND LETDOWN

"Caitlin, hang up your sweater and wipe that awful mope off your face." Olivia and her granddaughter had just returned to the Raphael home after dropping off their Marche House passengers at the inn.

"Yes, ma'am."

"You know you were in the wrong back there."

"Yes, ma'am. Does this mean I get the full lecture now?"

"It does, and don't you be so impertinent with me, young lady. I know your poking around had a happy ending. And, yes, we're all thrilled that you found the compartment with the box in it. But, my dear, you can't just go off any which way you please. You can get in big trouble that way."

"Are you ever gonna marry him?"

"Him? Who?"

"Dr. Kepple...Avi."

"I don't know. Stop changing the subject. You..."

"Do you love him?"

Olivia didn't know why the question came as such a surprise, but it did. Yet it seemed so logical. And she knew Caitlin was attempting to wiggle out of a fully deserved dressing down. Olivia didn't have to answer the question, but somehow she wanted to. "Yes, dear. I suppose I do."

"Then why don't you marry him?"

"Because he didn't ask me...Now, for your..."

"Would you?"

"Would I what?"

"Would you marry him if he asked you?"

Olivia became pensive. For a few short moments she dwelled somewhere else, and then she whispered, "Yes." She held out her arms to Caitlin and a very loving conniver snuggled into their fold.

Many minutes passed before Olivia relaxed her grip on her grandchild. When she did, Caitlin, no longer anticipating any punishment, began again.

"What was Granddaddy like?"

"Well, now, he was like the Fourth of July--fireworks, excitement, full of surprises." Olivia's eyes grew wide and wet, her face flexed with new animation, and her voice took on a stronger timbre as she spoke of her husband of forty-five years. "Everyone I knew found him so attractive and athletic. And he left his mark as a man of vision. In a way, he gambled. Not with cards or wheels or sports, but with grand schemes, innovations, things well ahead of their time. He always kept busy; success came too. I'd call him a good husband and father, but he couldn't relax. His heart...we just didn't have enough time together." Olivia could say no more, for the tears had overwhelmed her and the sadness constricted her speech. She tightened her hold on Caitlin once more.

"You loved him a lot, didn't you?"

"To be sure." As soon as Olivia said it, it seemed like such an understatement.

"Dr. Avi isn't much like him, is he?"

"No, dear, he isn't. We love people for different reasons. Sometimes it's who they are and sometimes it's who we are and more often it's where we are in our lives when the magic occurs." She swallowed hard. "I suppose I love Avi for all of his quiet, comforting qualities--his extremely fine intellect, that subtle yet spontaneous sense of humor, and his open, honest friendship." Olivia had surprised herself again, for this description had passed her lips without benefit of forethought.

"Gee!" Caitlin was impressed as well.

"But I'm certain...we will never marry." A deep sadness clung to Olivia's words.

"Why, Grandma? Why not, if you love him like that?"

"Well, I guess the love and the magic did not arrive soon enough in our lives."

"Doesn't he love you?"

"I...I'm sure he does...in his way. Yes, he loves me all right."

"Then why doesn't he ask you?" Caitlin persisted.

"It's a little hard to understand at your age, but when a man and a woman reach a certain time in their lives, they begin to value the companionship and respect aspects of a relationship much more than sharing a whole marriage bed. Avi has been alone for so long now that I believe he prefers the simpler life he's made for himself. He knows he can count on me as a best friend, anyway."

"But...but it's so unfair."

"Fairness is for sportsmanship. As you get older, you'll discover, unfortunately, that life isn't always fair."

The conversation ended with the sharp ring of the telephone. Olivia brushed a tissue across her nose, dabbing up the dampness of spilt thoughts and runny feelings. She answered.

"Hello. Yes, Inspector. We're just about to sit down to a bite of supper. You're welcome to join us if you like. As you wish, in an hour, then."

"What does *he* want?" Caitlin whined. She'd created this special mood with Grandma and resented the intrusion.

"The inspector has a few more questions for me. He'll be here in an hour. We'd better get our supper on the table in a hurry, sweetheart."

"Yeah, I'm starved." Caitlin fumbled with the refrigerator door, swinging it back and forth. "Let's see what Greta made for us. Grandma! Greta left you a note on the fridge door."

"What does it say, honey?"

"It says, 'Some man with a funny accent called. He'll call back later.' How come Greta had to leave tonight?"

"She went to see her sick sister in Oxford over on the Eastern Shore. Her brother-in-law picked her up around four, and he'll bring her back tomorrow night."

"Do we really need to have Greta any more? I'm old enough to stay by myself now when you go out."

"I'm afraid you're not, dear. Your exploits at the museum today proved that you still need a good deal of supervision. Besides, Greta does help me around the house."

"She's kinda old, though."

"Yes, she is. And you know what? She makes me feel young!" Olivia laughed.

"Oh, Grandma." Caitlin laughed too. They spent the next hour pleasantly munching egg salad sandwiches with pimento, German potato salad, and cole slaw. While rinsing the last few dishes, they heard Paco's knock on the kitchen door.

"Come in, Inspector. My, you're the punctual one."

"Yes, good evening, ladies. I'm just coming from Dr. Kepple's place."

Paco winked at Caitlin, and she giggled at his open friendliness. He's such a funny-looking guy, but cute, she thought.

"Oh, I'm curious, Inspector," Olivia said. "Since you were next door, do you know if the Mendelsohns were able to reach a locksmith for the jeweled box?"

"They didn't need one. I was able to pick the simple lock myself."

"Wow!" Caitlin said. "What did you find inside?"

"Yes, Inspector, I'm curious, too."

"Then I'm afraid you're both going to be disappointed, ladies. The beautiful box contained Mr. Marche's costume jewelry. Nothing worth anything. Oh, yes, we found a large steel key in a hidden bottom compartment. Mr. Simon thinks it's to the secret room. Wherever that might be."

"Aw, gee! And I thought I'd found something special, too," Caitlin said.

"Maybe you have, little lady," Paco said.

"Let's go into the front parlor to talk," Olivia said. "I think we can be comfortable there."

"That will be fine, Mrs. Raphael. This should only take a few minutes at the most."

Caitlin followed them to the front of the house.

"Inspector," Olivia said, "do you mind if my granddaughter joins us?"

"Not at all. Now let me see...First, I would like to read Dr. Ahm's letter and listen to old Mr. Aigue's tape for myself, but I needn't take your time with that. I would like to make copies of both, if you wouldn't mind my taking them with me. I'll have them back to you tomorrow."

"That'll be fine, Inspector. I'll get them." Olivia extracted the letter and tape cartridge from her briefcase on the dining room table. As she returned to the living room, she saw Paco leaning forward intently in his chair, his eyes fixed on the oil miniature on the coffee table.

"Mrs. Raphael, this is a most unusual little painting. What a beautiful child. Is it someone from your family? Or part of the Marche collection?"

"Neither, Inspector. In fact, it's rather strange how I came into its possession. You must know Schlem from down at Bubba's Deli."

"Ah, yes, a fine man, too."

"The miniature belongs to him." Olivia went on to explain the significance of the oil and its misbegotten frame. "I believe that the frame is a clue to finding the secret room at Marche House. Note the two distinct renditions of the same pattern."

Paco examined the two pieces of molding forming the lower right corner and saw the significant differences in the engraved patterns. The older part, on the vertical, seemed to him much deeper and rougher hewn than its mate. The newer piece was shallower, but much more precise.

Paco concluded: "I see what you mean. Are you telling me you think they were fashioned by two different craftsmen at two different times?"

"Precisely, Inspector. I'm very excited about this. What most people don't know is that old Isaac Aigue once owned the property where Bubba's Deli is now. He ran a carpentry workshop in a barn that was torn down when the Bubbashlufskys took over."

"And just how do you think this will help you find the elusive room, Mrs. Raphael?"

"The Mendelsohns are meeting me at Marche House tomorrow morning. They're bringing tape measures, a ladder, and a flashlight. We'll be looking for more corners such as this one." Olivia pointed to the frame where Paco had laid it on the table.

"Could you use another hand in the search? The hound dog detective in me simply can't resist such a challenge."

"Of course. We would welcome your help and your professional experience. We should be there by 9:30 tomorrow. Or I could pick you up here at 9:15, if you like."

"I'll be here at 9:15 sharp. And now, back to the business at hand, if I may?"

"Please."

"It's on a subject I neglected to pursue during our first interview, Mrs. Raphael. How would you characterize your relationship with the deceased?"

"I'd say it was almost nonexistent. Mild contempt, if anything."

"And why was that?"

"Avi has made no secret of the fact that his nephew was a wastrel. He considers Victor one of the failures in his life, although I think he's being unfair to himself. Victor needed psychiatric care, all right, but from someone outside the family--someone emotionally detached. And frankly, Inspector..." Olivia lowered her voice to a confidential murmur, "he needed something else no amount of therapy could have given him."

"What was that?"

"A character transplant. He needed to get his head screwed on straight, from an ethical and moral point of view. And that was never going to happen. Not the way he led his life."

Paco nodded. "And what is your relationship with his mother?"

"Freddie is a dear person, but she has a way of keeping others at arm's length. I would say we have a polite friendship. If it weren't for Avi, I dare say we'd be nothing more than casual acquaintances."

Privately, Olivia believed that Freddie resented her closeness to Avi.

The phone rang and Caitlin left to answer it.

"Get the number and I'll ring them back," Olivia called after her.

"On another subject," Paco said, "can you furnish me with all the insurance documents relating to Marche House artifacts?"

"Of course. They're in the filing cabinet in my study. I'll get them for you." Olivia crossed the hall and turned on the light in the next room. A file drawer rolled noisily and then rolled again. The room went dark once more, and Olivia handed Paco a large envelope bearing the insurance company's logo.

"I'm curious to find out if the insurance specifically covers artifacts legally removed from Marche House and stored elsewhere," Paco said.

"You'll find specific riders on just that in the packet. Yes, fortunately, the key is still covered. A copy of Dr. Lord's appraisal and his description of the key are also there."

"Good," Paco said. "Speaking of the key, has anyone else shown an interest in acquiring it?"

"Not really," Olivia said.

Caitlin reentered the room and waited to be noticed.

"Yes, dear, who was that?"

"He didn't say. I told him you were busy and would call him back. He said he would call again instead." Caitlin tilted her head to one side reflectively before continuing. "He sounded kind of funny, though."

"Funny? How so?" Olivia asked.

"Strange, I guess."

"You mean he had an accent?"

"Noooo!" Caitlin drew out the o's. "He spoke perfect English. Yeah! That's it. He sounded *veddy* British." She smiled with satisfaction at her own cleverness.

Olivia became thoughtful. "Strange," she repeated. "I have an idea who that might be. Dr. Ahm's son was supposed to contact me when he got to this country."

"And what would his purpose be?" Paco asked.

"I'm not sure. Perhaps it's just a social call. Then again, he might try to persuade the museum trustees to sell the key. There was some mention in the letter that he would be happy to find a buyer for us."

"I wonder just how anxious they are to get their hands on the key," Paco said.

"Oh, wait a minute, Inspector. Dr. Ahm is not one to get involved in such a nefarious plot."

"Perhaps not, but wilder things have happened where wealth, national pride, and superstition are concerned. Mrs. Raphael, there is one more thing. Might I see the pair of shoes you wore on Friday evening?"

"If you insist, Inspector, but isn't that a rather unusual request?"

"Not in this case, ma'am. There are a number of high-heel footprints that have a bearing on the case, and we'd like to eliminate some of the familiar ones first."

Olivia left him once more and returned with her beige satin pumps. Paco examined the fabric of both shoes for signs of mud, but found none. She gasped as he pressed a near-clear waxlike substance around the heel of one and then the other and unwrapped the impressions they made. "Not to worry, no damage whatsoever," he said.

"I should hope not, Inspector," she said wryly, "or I would expect you to treat me to a new pair."

He smiled, handed the shoes back to her, and dropped the mold into a plastic evidence bag.

"Ah, well, I've taken enough of your valuable time." Paco stood and buttoned up his camel hair coat against the cool autumn night, glad to have retrieved it from the car on the way over.

"Good-night, Inspector."

"Good-night, Mrs. Raphael. You too, young lady."

"Good-night," she echoed. Caitlin stood behind her grandmother, who closed the door after him.

The country air felt good to Paco, a cleansing chill. The dry, crisp leaves crackled and crunched beneath his feet. Walking out of the range of Olivia's porch fixture, there was a three-quarter moon to light his path. Nights like this made him glad he'd retired from the big city. Rural crime came in smaller doses and less frequently, too, although it could be equally tragic and just as impacting when it did occur.

He hadn't reached the front hedgerow when he heard the irritating sound of metal scraping on concrete and stone. He saw Molly over at the Kepple place, dragging two garbage cans toward the street. They were much too heavy for her to lift.

"Miss Molly, can I lend you a hand?" The scraping sound came to a sudden halt, and she looked about to see where the offer had come from.

"Over here, I'm coming," he called. She stood still until Paco took hold of the handles. With his strong wiry arms, he lifted the two cans an inch or two on either side of him and proceeded to the street.

"Having to bring them cans to the street--that kills me to a frizzle, after we pay them high taxes. Don't see why they can't come get 'em like they use ta." She pointed to a spot just inside the gate, and Paco set the cans down.

He slapped his hands together briskly to get rid of the dust and turned to her. "Would you like to take a short walk with me?"

"If you don't go so fast. I saw you walkin'. It's a mile an hour when you get going. That's so strenuous, it'll tucker me in."

He couldn't conceal his smile, but Molly took it for friendliness anyway. "Don't worry, Molly. I'll walk slowly with you. You can set the pace."

"I'll have to get my wrapper on first."

Paco waited at the gate while Molly retrieved her woolly beige cardigan from the hook just inside the kitchen door. He watched her carefully; her steps were quick and steady, but short, absorbing all vertical motion and giving the appearance of someone floating along on air. The woman was no beauty, but then again, neither was he. She obviously lacked a formal education, but she was definitely no dumbbell. Molly continued buttoning up while approaching him. Stopping short, she looked into his eyes and gave him a wide smile. He held his arm out for her and she took it with a flourish.

"You must enjoy walking here, Molly. Good neighborhood, nice houses."

"Yes, most everybody takes good care of their yard. But not those people across the street. Would you look at that? They ran their lawn right into the ground."

"So I see. What's your favorite season, Molly?"

"Oh, me? I like spring 'cuz you can smell the fumes of the lilacs an' everything's a billion greens."

Paco warmed up to the conversation, but he made a conscious effort to keep his tone light. A talented interrogator sometimes had to be sure that skill didn't get in the way of personal relationships. He proceeded cautiously. "Do you have any family, Molly? I mean where do you go when you take a day off?"

"Since my sister passed up, got no real family. I don't like my brother-in-law much, and they never made any children. Course, the Kepples are like family to me. The doctor and Miss Freddie, they're real fine to me and I love being with them. I go shopping, walking, and to church. Sometimes I go to the movies with Greta next door."

"Don't you want more from life, Molly?"

"I'm happy. I got a pillow for my head and a purpose in my life. And what about you? You got any family?"

"Never knew my parents. I grew up in an all-boy's orphanage. From there into the army MP's. No, there's nobody at home but my birds, two sweet-talking macaws."

"You keep birds in a cage at home?" Molly frowned.

"When I'm at work, but when I'm home they have the run of the house."

"I don't like to see birds in captivity. They belong in their own haberdash."

"I assure you I have made a good home for them, and they keep me from being lonely." Paco found himself on the defensive now.

"If you were so lonely, why didn't you marry?"

"I tried that once, but..."

"What happened?"

"She left me. Couldn't stand the rigors of my job. Not knowing when or if I would come home. So she ran off with a plumber."

Molly couldn't resist: "You mean she took the plunge?" Even Paco had to chuckle and then they both began to unwind, at first with nervous giggles and, finally, mutually appreciated laughter.

He patted the chubby arm linked in his. "Molly, you make me feel good."

"Me too! I mean you make me feel good, too." Molly stopped, faced him, and on her tippy toes planted a gentle buss on his cheek. "Thanks!"

"No, thank *you*, Molly." When he took her arm again, he felt her shiver. "I'd better get you home now. You're cold."

Molly walked into Rachel's room to find Freddie sitting on the edge of the double bed. She had pulled one of the drawers out of the bachelor chest and placed it on the floor beside her feet. It was the chest Victor had been using.

Freddie became aware of Molly's presence from the faint moving shadow she cast in front of her. No tears now. Only a thick aura of solemn purpose prevailed.

"Come in, Molly. I've been selecting Victor's clothes for the funeral." Freddie had laid a navy pin-striped suit across the bed. She held up a blue and gold rep tie with a gold tie tack she had given him for his birthday. She ran the tips of her fingers over the suit, smoothing even the finest wrinkle, sensing the final connection to her son, alive no more.

Freddie reached into the drawer at her feet, flipped through a handful of dress shirts, and selected one in pale blue, still brand new in its store cellophane. She held it against the suit on the bed and left it there. The remaining shirts went into a black plastic trash bag at her feet.

"Molly, be a dear and get me the next drawer and return this one to the dresser."

"Sure, Miz Freddie, but whatcha doing?"

"I'm sorting out Vic's clothes and thinking of which charity I'll want to give them to."

"Oh. But you don't have to do this now. There'll be lots of time after the funeral."

"I know, Molly, I know. But I have to keep busy. I don't want to think the thoughts in my head. Ah, thank you, right there is fine." Molly deposited a drawer full of sweaters and casual shirts on the edge of the bed. Freddie unfolded the top two sweaters and checked them front and back before tossing them into the bag. When she opened the third sweater, a folded piece of paper floated to the floor.

"Oh, what's that?" she asked.

Molly retrieved the cream-colored note, bordered in pink roses and written with a feminine hand. She read aloud:

I love it. I'll wear it close to my heart. See you tonight.
Love, R.

The two women looked at each other questioningly.

"Miz Freddie, was Victor seein' someone, somebody in privates?"

Freddie cleared her throat. "I don't know. He never spoke about a girlfriend. I haven't the foggiest notion who R is." Freddie frowned. "I wonder," she said slowly, "what he gave her that she wears close to her heart."

CHAPTER 22

ROOM FOR A VIEW

Lenora pulled open the drapes to let in the bright sunlight after their late afternoon nap. For a man of Bucky's age the nap was essential, and normally she would have snoozed too. But today she found it impossible. She had lain in bed awake for a full hour, her thoughts a chaotic jumble. Why couldn't she relax the way Bucky did? "I clean out my head before I sleep," he often told her when she complained about not being able to sleep. "I take a mental enema." Finding that a distasteful image, she nonetheless envied his discipline and self-control.

She hesitated at the window for a moment. In her black satin slip she silhouetted well-defined features of dignity and elegance with just that hint of imperfection that so enamored her to Bucky. She broke her gaze to the world outside and caught his eyes enveloping her in love and admiration. In her hand she held the videocassette Marti had given her. She lifted it for him to notice.

"Shall we?" she asked.

"By all means!"

Lenora popped the tape into the VCR slot on the TV set and picked up the remote. ON...CH3...PLAY. The screen held the set on a news anchor team for a few seconds and then went mostly white with black noise flecks as the tape advanced to its starting position. Bucky, fully awake now, sat up and slid to the front edge of the bed to see better. His wife sat down beside him.

"What do you suppose is on that tape?" Bucky asked.

"I'm sure I don't know, but Marti Thornberry's up to something. *That's* for sure."

A noise-distorted picture of an empty hallway outside their room appeared on the screen. The noise could be attributed to excessive reuse of the same tape. Cheap condensing lenses found in closed-circuit video cameras caused the remaining distortion. Time/date annotation, 16:00:34 10-25-80, appeared on the upper left of the screen. The monitor revealed no activity in the hall for several minutes afterward.

"Try a little fast-forwarding," Bucky suggested. Lenora did just that, stopping only when new activity appeared in the hall and continuing again when it proved to be of little interest. After about twenty minutes of lurching forward and stopping to view, Lenora began to suspect the purpose of the tape. She then advanced it to 23:45:00 10-25-80 using the fast-forward control in huge leaps. After several minutes an elderly couple traversed the distance from the elevator to their room. Five more minutes passed.

"Keep your eye on the door to room 203," Lenora said. She was now certain about what they would see. She just wasn't sure of the exact time, so she let the machine run in real time.

"203? That's our door," he said.

"It sure is, unfortunately. Just wait."

The door opened slowly and two outstretched white arms preceded the totally nude figure of a woman flailing about, groping for a nonexistent light switch on either side of the door. The figure turned to face the door just as it drifted irreversibly shut, locked.

Bucky's mouth dropped open in surprise. "That's *you*, dearest."

"Yes! I don't even have my dignity on. I told you about this when we were dressing this morning. Last night I could have died altogether. You had your hearing aid off and slept through the whole thing. Gawd, I look awful."

Even though she was wearing a slip now, Lenora instinctively wrapped her arms across her chest to cover herself up as she sat on the bed. Her hands tightly clutched her upper arms, as though it would make a difference to the helpless, humiliated image on the screen.

They watched for some time. She turned to see a grin on Bucky's face, but she couldn't tell if he was enjoying her or her predicament more. He let out a controlled guffaw. Then he couldn't help himself and laughed, actually roared aloud. She smacked him lightly on the arm. "You're enjoying this too much--and at my expense, you dirty old man, you." She rapped him again.

"Okay, okay! I paid for the privilege, didn't I?" The mischievous smile remained on his face.

"If you tell anybody about this, I'll...I'll..."

"Obviously, *you* told someone else. Or *she* did." Bucky pointed to Heidi, who had just appeared on the scene.

"Dear, keep watching and I'll tell you the rest of this grizzly story of mine. If I ever needed a fairy godmother it was at that moment. Believe it or not, Heidi proved to be my saving grace... Hey, wait a minute!" Lenora grabbed the remote, stopped the tape, and reversed it for several moments. She ran it forward again. "I thought so. Look at that thin strip of light in the hall, coming from under the door of the room on the left, 206. See the light disappear when Heidi comes?"

"I see that. Who's in room 206?" Bucky asked innocently.

"Marti and Felix, of course." Lenora slapped the side of her forehead with the palm of her right hand. "I should have known that nosy buzzard was spying on me."

They watched the tape to the point where the night clerk let her back into their room and returned to the elevator. The tape ran on.

Bucky consulted his watch. "We'd better get dressed for dinner. It's 6:45 already."

"Okay, I'll use the bathroom first. I guess you can let the videotape run to the end," Lenora said, closing the mirror-backed door.

Bucky selected a fresh shirt from his suitcase. Still eyeing the screen while he undid the shirt buttons, he suddenly stood transfixed. That stranger now on the screen: he'd seen him in the lobby at the phone booth, arguing with another man, when he'd gone down for a paper Friday evening. The man in the video walked quickly to the far end of the hall and disappeared beyond the camera's range. The annotated time was now 01:45:22. Actually, Bucky recalled, only one of the two men had been argumentative. This man had been exceptionally polite and immaculately dressed, perhaps even in the same suit and solid tie he wore here. The ill-mannered one had bellowed into the phone: "Listen, Moskowitz, I ain't standin' for any more of this crap from you." To the man waiting with him he had said, "Trust me, he'll come around." But the polite one had glanced about as if he were looking for an escape route from his crude associate.

Bucky would have remembered neither man if he hadn't heard the name Moskowitz. He had no idea of the context in which it was used, only the name. Now he wished he'd told the inspector about it. Perhaps he still should. The inspector would probably want to know why he'd waited so long to come forward with this bit of intelligence. Bucky would have to explain that the incident had completely slipped his mind until now. And what exactly was there to tell? Nothing concrete.

He fast-forwarded the tape but couldn't find anything else of interest. So he rewound it and stopped at 11:15:04 10-25-80. He'd just put the tape in PLAY when Lenora came out of the bathroom in a black sweater, long black skirt, and a double strand of pearls that rested atop her breasts.

"You're not dressed yet?" she asked. "What have you been doing all this time?"

"Sorry, I've been fascinated by the tape." Bucky pointed to the screen. "Say, isn't that Derrick Powers leaving room 208?"

"Oh, my God, it is," Lenora exclaimed. "That's the Lords' room. And look at him!" Derrick was carrying a pair of shoes in one hand, a tie and jacket across his arm. He disappeared into room 210 next door.

She sat down on the bed to watch. Five minutes later Ernie Lord, carrying his briefcase, stepped out of the elevator and entered room 208.

"Hah! The plot thickens. This is better than the movies. Too bad there's no sound," Bucky said.

"Yeah. Don't you think Derrick was cutting it kind of close, though?"

Lenora chuckled.

"His type thrives on living on the edge. And the passes he's made at you are typical of a guy who's never grown up."

"Poor Heidi," Lenora said. "I hope she's not serious about that sleaze-bag. She can certainly do better."

They heard a knock at the door. They looked at one another, and when they heard a second knock, Bucky took the remote out of her hand, stopped the tape, and turned off the TV.

"Coming," Lenora called. Bucky moved into the bathroom to finish dressing.

"Who is it?" she asked, standing at the door with her hand readied on the security chain.

"It's me, Marti. May I come in?"

Lenora pulled the chain to its limit. "Yeah, it's you all right. Come to get your first installment of blood money, have you?"

"Blood money?" Marti looked confused.

"Blood money. Extortion. Blackmail. It's illegal. I'm sure you know that, you black-hearted leech."

"Wait a cotton-pickin' minute, Miss Hoity-Toity. Sure I had fun with the tape. Felix too. But extortion? Never. Would I blackmail you and give you the only copy in advance? Think about it." Lenora undid the chain.

"How do I know it's the only copy?"

"It *is* the only copy, I assure you. Now may I come in?" Without waiting for an answer, she pushed through the door. Lenora shut it behind her, but said nothing. She was still seething. It was a concession to even allow Marti in the room.

"And how did you get your hands on the tape in the first place?" she asked, her face contorted in anger.

Marti's eyes darted around the room as she stalled for time. She wasn't quite sure how to answer. "I got it...from the night clerk."

"You got it from the night clerk?" Lenora's voice was tinged with sarcasm. "Marti, there's something screwy about this. Why would the night clerk give *you* a security tape?" Marti didn't answer.

"Well?" Lenora persisted.

"I bribed him for it. I went to high school with Ev and he did me a favor." Her voice rose to a self-righteous whine. "I did it for you."

"Sure you did. Somehow I have trouble believing that."

Bucky reentered the room, wearing a tweed jacket and gray trousers. "Oh, hi, Marti." He stepped warily around her and put his hand on the doorknob. "I'll meet you in the lobby in a few minutes," he told his wife. He left the room without waiting for a reply.

"I don't know what it is with you, Lennie, but every time I try to do something nice for you, you get suspicious and react like I'm trying to get you. It's pure paranoia."

"Something nice for me? And by the way, stop calling me 'Lennie.' You know how I hate that name."

"Yes, something nice. I took that tape out of circulation and gave it to you, didn't I? The only price I sought was a little practical joke. I know you don't think much of me, but to think of me as a blackmailer..."

Lenora's boiling temper subsided to a simmer. She questioned Marti's motives, but the incident was over and done with. What could she do about it now, anyway? Before she could respond further to Marti, there was another knock at the door, loud and insistent.

She looked cautiously through the peephole and opened the door. "Inspector LeSoto! I hardly expected to find you here."

"Mrs. Worthington, Mrs. Thornberry, I'm very sorry to come unannounced. I hope I haven't interrupted anything of importance, ladies. I thought I heard some raised voices. Was I mistaken, or did I hear the word *blackmail*?"

"Harrumph!" bellowed Marti, still angry. "Maybe the inspector would like to view the tape."

"And what tape would that be?" Paco knew he had both women at a disadvantage here and that they would undoubtedly reveal much more than they cared to.

"This tape!" Marti dashed to the TV and pressed the EJECT button on the VCR panel. The cassette appeared like candy from a vending machine.

"You despicable tramp!" Lenora shouted.

"Don't you dare call me a tramp. You're the one who was running around naked," Marti fired back. This was all-out war.

"And I suppose you told the inspector about your affair with Victor?" Lenora gasped at her own words. As furious as she was with Marti, she had not planned on blurting that out. Shooting from the hip, whether dressed or naked, was not her style.

"You bitch!"

"Ladies, ladies! Please!" Paco felt he had let things get out of control.

"Out! Get out!" Lenora said between clenched teeth. "Get out of my room. I don't want to see your face again." She pushed her hand firmly against Marti's back and ushered her out. Lenora excused herself to leave the room, for she was about to cry--something she abhorred doing in public. At the bathroom sink she restored her demeanor with a damp washcloth. She returned to face Paco a calmer being, at least on the surface.

"Mrs. Worthington, I'm sorry, but I'm afraid that I'll have to confiscate the tape now that it has been brought to my attention. I'll examine it for potential evidence, but I guarantee you that any part of that tape that cannot qualify as evidence will be protected by me. It will go no farther, and it will be returned to you afterward. Fair enough?"

"Have I any choice?" Lenora asked.

"You could explore some legal appeals. However, it boils down to the fact that I acquired the tape not as a result of an illegal search, but as a result of potential evidence in plain sight being brought to my attention. You did, of course, invite me into the room."

"Not really, Inspector. I saw that it was you and *allowed* you to come in. There *is* a difference."

"Yes, you're quite right," he answered. "But we're splitting hairs on that, aren't we?" He studied her with his left eyebrow raised.

She knew she'd lost the argument and suddenly felt very dejected.

"Mrs. Worthington, this brings me to the real reason for my coming here. I can assure you it was not to snoop. I came to ask for the volume of your mother's diary that you read at the meeting Friday evening. I would like to copy those passages that might be pertinent to my investigation. I don't have a court order, but I would like your cooperation in this matter. I can have the original back in your hands tomorrow. I can personally guarantee the same confidentiality that applies to this videotape."

"I can hardly refuse, can I?"

"You can, but then I can go to the judge."

"That won't be necessary, Inspector, I'll get it for you."

She went to her weekender suitcase on the folding luggage rack, zipped shut the main section, and flipped it over so that the zippered pocket was now on top. She pulled the zipper tab open and reached inside for the diary, but found nothing. She hesitated a moment, and reached in a second time, sliding her hand inch by inch from one side of the pocket to the other over the entire compartment. She looked up at Paco with a dumbfounded stare, and then turned the suitcase over again to be sure there was no pocket on the opposite side. There was none. She zipped the outside pocket shut, reopened the center section, and poked about in earnest. No diary. She felt sheer panic now.

Paco observed her genuine surprise. "Have you misplaced the diary by any chance? Could it be in a dresser drawer, another suitcase, a briefcase, your car? There are any number of possibilities, I suppose." He watched Lenora's desperate gaze move across the room--darting, scanning--but finding no place to rest.

"No, Inspector. I distinctly remember putting it in there, the pocket of the suitcase. I'm certain someone has removed it."

"Who would have access to your room?"

"I don't know. Friends, hotel help, outsiders? I guess I'm beating a dead horse."

"Mrs. Worthington, if I can have your word that you will provide me with the diary just as soon you find it, I needn't bother you any more today. I'm sorry this has been so difficult for you." Paco waited long enough to see a disappointed Lenora slowly nod her assent. He departed, knowing she would continue her search for a diary she believed someone else had taken.

Paco quietly left room 203 and headed for the elevator, his head lowered as he mulled over the implications of Lenora's missing diary. He stepped out of the elevator into the lobby. Suddenly, a figure sprang from an alcove and blocked his path. His body tensed, and he jerked to a stop. "What the devil!" he muttered. It was Marti Thornberry.

"Inspector! Sorry if I startled you. I wonder if I could talk to you somewhere in private," she said in a low, but urgent tone.

This woman has a real talent for rubbing people the wrong way, he thought. He tried hard not to show his annoyance. "By all means. Let's go over there and sit down." He ushered her to a small grouping of chairs across from the elevator. As Marti began to speak, the aggressive, abrasive edge he had witnessed in Lenora's room began to evaporate into a penitent demeanor. This was a side of the Thornberry woman he hadn't seen before.

"Inspector," she began, "I haven't done anything wrong, and I feel bad that Vic is dead. I mean nobody should die before their time. But I did want to explain something to you. I wanted you to hear it from me and not someone else, especially because Felix doesn't know."

Paco awaited the confession he knew was coming.

"About fifteen years ago," she began almost in a whisper, "Vic and I had an affair. I was already married and it only lasted a few months, but it ended kind of bitterly."

"Why was that?" Paco asked softly.

"I really liked him. He was smooth and awfully good in bed. He seemed kind of glamorous. Felix is a good soul and a decent provider, but he's never been an exciting man and so I got carried away. I didn't know at the time that Vic gambled and couldn't hold a job. And only years later I found out how mean he was to his mother. He..."

Marti knew she'd lost eye contact with the inspector when she followed his gaze to her hands tightly clutching her purse. She released her grip and caught his eye once more. "He dumped me for a younger woman. I got angry with him and have been ever since. But I guess I'm even more angry with myself for falling for such a four-flusher. Now that I look back on it, I'm lucky Felix never found out. It would have wrecked our marriage. I...I assume you'll keep this in confidence. I sure as hell wouldn't want him to know about it now."

"Of course. You have my complete confidence." Marti's confession didn't make Paco like her any better, or trust her either, for that matter. He didn't cotton to calculating women and suddenly felt sympathy for Lenora Worthington. Or for anyone else who made the mistake of incurring Marti Thornberry's wrath.

This was not the first time Ahmed Ahm had participated in a shady deal involving a lot of money, nor would it be the last, he thought. He'd been successful in keeping this aspect of the business from his respected father. He sat in his Hertz rental car at the edge of the parking lot under a big Wye oak. A drizzle had persisted for the last two hours, and his presence in the car, his warm breath, had led to the fogging of all the windows. He sat in blind darkness. He'd arrived there at 11:15, in plenty of time. He pressed the dashboard button for the time. The LED figures revealed 11:40 p.m. He was losing a measure of his nerve and began to fidget.

The package lay on the floor, tucked under the passenger seat, well out of view. A messenger service had delivered the money that morning. A Baltimore branch of a Netherlands commercial banking house, long familiar with Ahm family business transactions, had eagerly obliged him. Two thousand fifty-dollar bills, neatly tied in forty stacks of fifty each, lay waiting for the exchange.

Before Ahmed could reach for the package and abort the plan, the door to the passenger side opened and the dome light shone for a brief instant. A figure in a soaking gray trench coat and a Totes rain cap slid in on the seat next to him. A black knit ski mask hid the stranger's face from Ahmed.

"So what will it be? The painting or the money?" The stranger used a low-level monotone with just a trace of rasp.

"You'll find the package of bills, $100,000, under your seat," Ahmed answered.

The stranger lifted the carefully wrapped package out of a large plastic shopping bag from the inn's boutique, unwrapped it, and sampled each stack of bills by flipping the edges back in succession. "You have done well, my friend. A pleasure doing business with you. Now, if you will remain in your car for another ten minutes, I will take leave of you." The stranger rewrapped the package, tucked it back into the plastic bag, and slipped out into the noiseless drizzle.

CHAPTER 23

IF THE INSCRIPTION FITS
Monday, October 27, 1980

Paco pulled up behind the yellow and black school bus that had stopped in front of the Raphael driveway. He waited while Caitlin climbed aboard, dragging her book bag after her.

Hissss. Paco heard the doors and then the brake of the bus. It groaned, lumbering up the slow road grade and out of his way, enabling his car to turn into a parking space next to Olivia's Lincoln. Olivia, just closing up the house, turned and waved to him.

"Good morning," he said, rolling down the window. "Would you like me to drive?"

"No, Inspector. I prefer to drive. I can drive you as well or you can follow me. Your choice."

"Madam, that is not a choice. It's an invitation, one I accept." Paco popped out of his own car, doffed his tan corduroy cap, and leaped to Olivia's car to open the driver's door for her. Finding it locked, he waited awkwardly for her to unlock it herself.

"You're much too gallant, Inspector. I have trouble remembering you're a policeman." Realizing what she had just said, she added, "But of course, yours is a gallant profession, anyway."

Paco silently eased himself into the front passenger seat. He pulled the zipper down on his roan suede jacket, revealing a plaid shirt in trendy earth tones beneath it. Olivia's warm smile trimmed the embarrassed edge from his awkwardness. A truly classy lady, he thought, in her black slacks and bulky knit dove-gray cardigan.

Paco tried to relax as she backed the long car out of the driveway and efficiently maneuvered the now familiar route to Marche House. He admired and at the same time feared the boldness with which she drove, gripping the knees of his brown corduroy trousers with nervous fingers. Approaching their destination, he saw Simon and Rachel outside on the wrought iron bench waiting for them. The bronze double doors had been left ajar.

Simon bounded to his feet to greet them as they climbed the marble steps to the portico. Rachel grabbed Avi's toolbox, and Paco reached to help Simon with the eight-foot stepladder he'd stowed behind the bench. They set everything down just inside the grand foyer.

"I've got an idea, a theory of where the room might be," Simon announced. "Here, Rachel, hold the end of this at the wall." He produced a fifty-foot steel tape measure from the pocket of his chinos and handed one end to Rachel. The other end he unraveled, walking the room's width at its widest point. "Exactly forty-eight feet four inches," he called out to her.

"I don't have anything to write on or with," she said, turning out one pocket of her jeans.

"An unpenciled editor?" Simon asked.

"Are you going to report me to the editorial police?" she said.

"Not today," he replied.

"I won't either, but I do have a pen," Paco said, quickly jotting down the measurement in his spiral police notebook. He'd decided to take an active role in the search. He might just learn something from this engineer.

"Now," Simon continued as he reeled in the tape, "let's go to the doorway between the library and the parlor."

"I'm ready. Now what?" Rachel asked.

"You hold the tape against the grand foyer wall and we'll get a short wall distance to the doorway...Okay, that's four feet ten inches. Now the other side of the same short wall to the door...four feet eleven inches. Okay! I think we can conclude that it's the same wall as the grand foyer wall on the other side. Now hold the tape at this corner while I walk to the end of the library." Simon pushed a few books to one side on the shelves so he had the full depth of the distance. "Eleven feet one inch. Got that, Inspector?"

"Absolutely, sir."

"Now for a measurement from the grand foyer wall to the rear of the house. Uh-huh...eighteen feet five inches. Very good."

"Does this mean your theory is correct, dear?" Rachel asked.

"Maybe, but we don't have enough information yet. We need a few measurements on the other side of the house."

Simon now led the search party back through the grand foyer to the doorway between the den and the dining room. "I think everyone will agree," he said, "that we are looking at the opposite corner of the grand foyer a foot in from this doorway." Everyone nodded yes.

"Here." Simon put Rachel's finger on the end of the tape again and stretched the tape along the doorway wall to the end of the dining room. "Okay...fifteen feet three inches. Ladies and gentlemen," he said, his voice rising with excitement, "I think we've just found the secret room. Let me see...fifteen feet plus eleven feet. That makes twenty-six. Throw in another foot for good measure, twenty-seven, and subtract it from the grand foyer width of forty-eight feet. I'd say we have a secret room of twenty-one by eighteen feet."

"And it's behind the main staircase in the grand foyer," exclaimed Rachel.

"But the old man was mistaken about the afternoon sun," Paco said.

"You mean Isaac Aigue?" she asked.

"Yes. I listened to the tape and I believe it would've been the morning light," Paco said, noting the sun spilling its rays and colors in through the distorted antique windows onto the oriental rug. "I do believe the creek and bay are to the east of this room."

"Yes, Inspector, they are," Rachel said. She turned to Simon, a wide smile lighting up her face. "I can't believe it. We've found the secret room." She threw her arms around Simon's waist and hugged him tightly. Simon glowed with delight and hugged her back.

"Yes, Rachel," Olivia said. "He's found the room." She paused for effect. "I hate to be the party pooper, but we haven't found our way into the room yet." Olivia sat down in one of the brocade armchairs. "We need to examine more of the clues, don't you think?"

"You're right, Olivia. We're not done yet," Simon said.

"Well, what do we know about the access to the room?" Rachel asked.

"We do know," Olivia said, "that the door release pin is hidden behind a section of molding. And you have to push on that piece or section of molding to get to the pin."

"We'll have to check out every square inch of it. There's a lot of molding to cover on that wall. It not only covers the perimeter of the ceiling," Rachel said, "but it descends down the walls at the corners and edges the chair rails. Maybe we should get the ladder in here."

"That shouldn't be necessary," Paco said. "It's highly unlikely that anyone would design a door release at out-of-reach height. I think we ought to be looking at a height of six feet or less, probably a good deal less. People were considerably shorter eighty years ago. Also, we shouldn't neglect Mrs. Raphael's clues here, either."

"I don't understand. What other clues are there?" Rachel asked.

"Well, I made an interesting discovery," Olivia said. "When Isaac Aigue worked on the room renovations, he had to use a replacement cavetto molding to finish the trimwork. The newer molding is similar, but still recognizably different. The difference can be noted in the depth and straightness of the inscribed wheat pattern, the part decorated in gold leaf. The older molding is rougher and deeper. Irregular, as though hand-carved with a chisel. The newer molding seems to have been made more uniform and shallow with some mechanically rotated tool. Of course, they had no electricity, but, nevertheless, they did have their own version of power tools back then." She reached into her purse and pulled out a good-sized magnifying glass.

"It's great that you thought to bring that, Olivia." Simon was trying to be diplomatic. "But it may not be much help. There must be at least ten coats of white paint and gobs of gold leaf covering the molding since that time." To prove his point, he took a broad putty knife and worked it along the edge of the molding above the chair rail, causing a hairline paint fracture between the molding and the wall. "I wonder whether the spring mechanism will be rendered inoperative by all this paint."

"Forgive me for intruding once more, but I think we're going about this all wrong," Paco said. He had been rummaging through Avi's toolbox and retrieved a flashlight. "May I?" He took the magnifying glass from Olivia and began to examine each length of molding on the pertinent wall.

When he was done, he handed the glass and flashlight to Simon. "I think you'll find that each length on that wall is identical, except for the length on the right between the chair rail and the floor. It doesn't budge, though."

Simon examined the section and agreed with Paco. "This has to be our key in. Figuratively speaking, of course." He looked at Olivia, his expression both eager and deferential, for some kind of approval before proceeding.

"Do try, by all means," she said. Simon knelt in the corner and began to work the sharp putty knife gently under the edge of the entire length of this section. The crack grew as he tapped the end of the knife handle with the open palm of his left hand and guided it with his right hand. He pried and the crack widened. At last he could see under it with the probing light. He pried one last time and then shook his head.

"There's no release pin or any kind of mechanism under here. Just more wood and the securing nails." Simon rose reluctantly to his feet. Beads of sweat dotted his forehead. "And I was so sure."

"And we can't go about tearing up the whole house, can we?" a disappointed Olivia asked.

"Mrs. Raphael," Paco said, "I think we should follow our clues and instincts first and then try to find a logical basis for candidates before assaulting any more of the woodwork. Would that be agreeable, ma'am?"

"I couldn't agree more," she said. "We must take care not to disturb either the interior architectural decor or the furnishings. The guiding principle here is: How easily can we hide any trace of our search? The one small piece of molding we've pried up can be renailed and touched up with matching paint. For starters, let's all probe a bit of the molding in this area to see if any piece is loose or gives way."

The room went quiet as each of them fingered and pressed a section of molding. It took a full ten minutes for Paco to express the conclusion that each of them had reached independently. "I can find no other obvious anomaly in the construction or appearance of that wall."

They sat for several minutes more, and their attention began to wander.

Olivia appeared concerned with a spot on her slacks. Simon rubbed a reddening bruise on his palm, where he'd pounded the putty knife. Paco fiddled with the flashlight. Rachel had been looking out the window, when a fresh thought came to her. "You know, there is another wall like this on the library side."

All four faces regained their former animation. Their enthusiasm mounted as they trooped behind Rachel to the library, where they immediately pored over every inch of the moldings. Here, the moldings ran across the top of the tall bookcases instead of at chair rail level. A plaster relief coat of arms filled the upper portion of the pertinent wall, and short pieces of molding appeared below it. Upon noticing that two pieces were new and one was old, Rachel pressed each in its turn, but none of the three gave way to her pressure.

Simon returned to the den and brought back Avi's tools. He selected a long, thin screwdriver and a small penknife for the tedious and meticulous job of removing all three sections.

"No luck," he announced, shaking his head. "There aren't any door-releasing mechanisms on these pieces." He turned each section over and over, studying the underside of each one, to make sure he hadn't missed something. The disappointment of the group was almost palpable as Simon tapped the pieces gently back into place. Then the four of them moved back to the grand foyer where Olivia and Paco chose to sit on opposite settees.

"All is not lost, folks," said Simon. "I have another idea." He took Rachel by the hand and led her outside, around to the stone patio that extended the length of the house's eastern exposure. There were no windows between the library and the den. There was, however, a two or three-foot space between the top of the first floor and the underside of a balcony that ran below the windows of every bedroom on that side of the house.

"I wonder if any of the first floor rooms has a skylight," Rachel mused.

"Could be," Simon answered. "But we'd have to get the ladder to find that out." With nothing more for them to investigate outdoors, they returned to the grand foyer to join the others.

Coming in the front door again, Rachel became obsessed with the beauty of the staircase. Its graceful sweeping lines virtually hypnotized her. "If only it would lead to the room," she fantasized aloud.

"Perhaps it does after all." Paco sat up straight on the settee; Rachel's fantasy had pumped him up. He got up and moved past the left side of the staircase to the cloakroom, reexamining the molding on the outside as they had all done earlier. Finding nothing of new interest he opened both doors wide. Stepping just inside, he stood motionless. "Bring the light, someone... quick!" he called.

Simon grabbed the flashlight from the toolbox and followed Paco into the cloakroom, hunching forward to avoid hitting his head on the low ceiling. The beam of light entirely filled the tiny room, which was no more than twice the depth and width of a good-sized armoire.

"Notice anything in here?" Paco asked.

"Yeah, there's more of the molding in here. Not quite as many layers of paint, though. Other than that, it looks like the rest of the foyer. The room must have been added afterward."

"I agree. Note also that the left half of the room is trimmed in new molding and the right in old." Paco stepped aside, enabling the two women a chance to see as well.

Almost immediately Simon began probing with his hands. Suddenly, the section bordering the far left edge gave way to his touch, revealing a rectangular hole. He could not see very far into it, because the left wall prevented him from looking deeper. Holding the molding in place with his left hand, Simon felt around the long abyss at the right edge with the fingers of his right hand. Something wooden rattled in place. He traced its shape, hesitated, then retraced it.

"It's a seaman's belaying pin!" he called out triumphantly. He struggled to lift the pin out, but to no avail. He could raise it several inches, but could not extract it from its track, even when he tried slamming it to both extreme positions. "Nothing happens," he said, beginning to feel a crick in his lower back from his almost-crouched position.

Paco edged his way closer, leaning over Simon's shoulder. "Do that again, please," Paco said. "Again! Up! Down! Up once more and hold it there. Good! See this? The large wooden panel? It's pressed tight to the front when the pin is down and it's loose when the pin is up. Wait while I try something." Paco licked the tips of the fingers of his left hand and pushed them against the panel, attempting to slide the panel toward the middle of the room. A fraction of an inch at first, then several inches before hitting another snag. "I think you can let go of the pin now."

Simon withdrew his hand, and the pin clanked to the bottom position. "Hey, Inspector, we're really making progress now, but how about letting me out of this corner? I'm getting all cramped up in here."

"Sure, but I thought you were anxious to figure this out." Paco backed out of the close quarters to let Simon out.

"Yeah, I am. I'll be fine in a minute." He stretched his arms high over his head and rotated his head in a neck stretch. Rachel came to her husband's aid and gently rubbed his lower back, then his shoulders. He slowly limbered up again, but stamped his foot several times. "My foot's asleep."

"You can rub that yourself," she said.

Paco stepped back into the little cloakroom. His shorter frame had no trouble fitting upright inside. Setting the flashlight on the floor, and with the additional room afforded him, he had no problem gripping the wooden panel. It slid back, leaving a three-by-five-foot opening. The others stood at the door watching as he picked up the flashlight once more and trained the light on the opening. "Bingo!" he said.

"Bingo? Is that all you can say, Inspector?" Olivia asked. "What do you see?"

"Yes, please let us in on it." Rachel tried pressing in behind Paco.

"It's a door, a locked door that any prison would be proud to own. Here, see for yourselves." He backed away to let the others have a look.

Rachel took the flashlight from Paco as she entered. She stopped abruptly at the far left corner of the cloakroom. "It's a big old iron door...My God, it must lead to the secret room! You're right, Inspector, it's locked. It won't give at all. I don't see a key hanging anywhere. But there's some space under the door. I'll try to see into the room."

Ignoring the dust balls on the parquet floor and cobwebs woven over the corner, Rachel dropped down on her knees, stretched out flat on her stomach, and shone the light under the door. But she couldn't see more than an inch into the room. She started to get up when the flashlight slipped out of her grip and fell into the space between the access left by the panel and the door ledge.

"Damn!" she cried. Luckily, the light remained on, for it picked up the glitter of another object in the maze of cobwebs. Still on her stomach, straining her whole slender body forward, she retrieved the flashlight. Using it as a tool, she swept away the cobwebs until she felt comfortable reaching for the shiny object. A key! A large steel skeleton key wedged tightly between two rows of stones.

"What's going on in there, Rachel?" When she didn't respond, Simon tried sarcasm. "Are we having so much fun that you won't answer me?" Still no answer. His tone changed. "Rachel? Are you all right in there, babe?"

"Sorry, dear, I'm okay. I think I've just found the door key. I'm trying to retrieve it, but I can't seem to get a decent grip on it."

"Why don't we see if this will fit then?" Simon held out a large crude steel key. "It's the one Molly found in the jeweled box."

Rachel stood up and took the key from him. Brushing the dust from her jeans, she inserted the key in the lock. Before proceeding, she turned to the group and announced dramatically: "Moment of truth, folks." Simon, Paco, and Olivia stood motionless, their eyes fixed on her right hand.

Rachel rotated the key. "It seems to fit," she said. "But I can't turn it very far. I guess I'm not strong enough. Or maybe it's not the right key." With a crestfallen look on her face, she backed away.

"Okay, let me try, then."

Reluctantly, Rachel handed the key and flashlight to her husband. "I so wanted to be the first one in there," she sighed. He smiled.

Simon hunched over and stepped into the cloakroom once more. Strong as he was, the key refused to turn in his clenched fist. "Babe? Could you hand me the hammer and oilcan from your dad's toolbox?"

Armed with these fresh items, he inserted the spout of the can into the lock's escutcheon and squirted oil in every direction. While waiting for the oil to penetrate the lock's mechanisms, he squirted more along the door seams and hinges and began rapping the hammer in the vicinity of the lock. Nothing. He tried again. Still nothing. He rocked the key, rotating it back and forth, and then tried again. A little more this time, More rocking and rattling. The lock pinged as the last ridge of the key passed over its corresponding pawl. Success! Simon pushed against the unlocked door.

It gave way slowly, moving with a horribly loud creak that reminded Paco of the old radio mystery *Inner Sanctum*. The door's movement disturbed cobwebs, dust, and air. A stench arose of matter long decomposed. Stifling, suffocating.

Simon had to get out of there in a hurry. A wave of nausea swept over him.

CHAPTER 24

DUST TO DUST

Simon's chest heaved as he struggled to breathe amid the dust and stench. By opening the door, he had irreverently intruded on the past and broken a precious seal to lives long gone. Now he was being made to atone for it in the last bastion of the forgotten.

"Simon?" Rachel's voice quavered with concern.

"Just give me a minute and I'll be fine," he replied, emerging from the cloakroom into the grand foyer. Rachel rushed to him, gripped her hands about his waist, and studied his face. He was still breathing heavily.

"What? What was it?" she asked. He didn't answer.

"Here, let me have a look." Paco took the flashlight from Simon and reentered the cloakroom.

"I'm coming too," Rachel said.

Before Simon could stop her, she spun around and darted after the inspector, close behind, using him as a shield. He approached the open door to the secret room with almost excessive caution, equating minimal motion with minimal dust. Rachel jerked to a stop, her forward momentum nearly propelling her petite body into Paco's back. He flicked the flashlight on. The beam of light could penetrate only a few feet into the room, as layer upon layer of cobwebs cast eerie shadows from pale gray to impenetrable black. In a slow, purposeful circle, Paco swirled the nearest webs onto the flashlight itself. The effect was minuscule, the task gargantuan.

"Ugh," Rachel said, covering her nose and mouth with her hand. "The smell, it's unbearable." She retreated quickly to the cloakroom.

"So it is," Paco said. "I'm afraid we're going to need some cleaning and ventilating equipment before we can go any farther." He too backed out.

They regrouped in the grand foyer, and Rachel sought out the comfort of her husband. "It's so sinister in there," she told him. "And at the same time I can't wait to see what's inside." Simon nodded.

"Olivia?" Rachel said, her face brightening. "Why don't we drive over to my dad's house and pick up the few things we'll need here. I know there are some good-sized fans in the basement from his pre-air-conditioning days. I could even bring Molly back with me to help."

"Excellent idea, Rachel. Let's go. We'll leave the men here. And, Inspector, I'm going to bring my camera back. This is all terribly exciting, and we need to record it for posterity. Photographs of the secret room will certainly enhance public interest in the museum. Who knows, we might even get the newspapers to do a story."

"Fine with us," said Simon, after seeing no signs of disapproval on Paco's face. "Oh, yeah, could you also bring back some lamps and extension cords for the fans? Long heavy-duty ones, if you can find them."

"Sure, honey," Rachel said.

At the door Olivia looked back and said, "There are a few cleaning things in the kitchen, if you gentlemen want to get started." She pulled the heavy bronze doors shut behind her.

Paco peeled off his suede jacket and carefully hung it over a ladderback chair in the grand foyer. He suddenly felt uncomfortably formal and overdressed, regretting that he hadn't thought to wear jeans. He followed Simon into the kitchen, where they rummaged around until they came up with two straw brooms and a bucket. Paco fished through a drawer and pulled out two clean dish towels. Simon filled the bucket with water, and they carried everything back to the cloakroom.

"Here's a little trick we use in the department," Paco said. He soaked the dish towels in water, wrung them out, and handed one to Simon. Following Paco's lead, Simon covered his nose and mouth and tied the towel behind his head. Paco entered the room first. He hoisted a soaking wet broom up and out in front of him and swept slowly from side to side, wrapping the webs about the broom as he advanced. He cleared a three-foot swath as he went, and Simon illuminated the path and carried the bucket for periodic broom dipping.

"Careful!" Paco warned. "We don't want to disturb anything significant." They avoided a broken chair and edged away from large pieces of furniture, but maintained a direction they thought would lead to an outside wall. Before long, high above their heads at the edge of the farthest wall, they detected a single weak beam of illuminated dust. It did not move with the flashlight.

"That has to be an independent source of light," Simon noted, craning his neck. He raised his broom and, standing on tiptoe, stretched his arms as high as he could to clear the cobwebs and dust away. A two-foot square of filthy glass appeared, covered by a grate--both clogged with debris.

"Let's get out and take another breather," Paco suggested, his voice muffled under the damp dish towel. "Things are still pretty thick in here."

As they retraced their steps to the grand foyer, Simon spoke: "Rachel and I noticed a space between the balcony and the rear wall out back. I'll bet that's where the skylight is located."

"We could go around back and take another look, but we'll need the stepladder."

"I'll grab it. You get the door for me, Inspector."

Searching for the skylight was a tall order for a tall man. Simon's assignment, they tacitly agreed. He climbed to the narrow ledge between the first floor and the balcony.

"Inspector!" he shouted. "We've hit pay dirt, literally and figuratively," he added with a grim smile. "It's not just one skylight, it's three. And they're all a mess." Steadying himself against the house, with his free hand he swept away great clumps of damp, decaying leaves.

"Are those bars on the windows?" Paco asked.

"Yeah, iron bars. Rusting, but still sturdy. Burglar-proofed to the hilt."

Paco handed up one of the brooms, and Simon cleared away most of the remaining debris. The skylight windows led to the secret room below. Flanking the row of skylights were two air vents covered by grates. Simon climbed down long enough to move the ladder. He managed to reach between the bars of the grates and clean out the baffle wells of more decayed muck. Six times the ladder had to be moved before all three windows and two grates were cleared. Now he and Paco were ready to explore the room once more. Coming around the house, they saw Olivia's car parked out front.

"Hi, ladies, were you able to get everything?" Simon asked as he and Paco entered the foyer.

"Sure, it's all on the floor in front of you. But where were the two of you?" Rachel asked. "We kept calling into the room, but no one answered. I was scared."

"Out back cleaning off vents and skylight windows," Simon answered. "Thanks for bringing all this stuff, babe."

"Hi, Mr. Simon. Paco!" Molly stood in the dining room doorway carrying two pails of water from the kitchen.

"Molly! I'm so glad you're here," Paco said. He stepped quickly to relieve her of one of the buckets. She thanked him, but remained quite still, staring at him with her shrewd glassy eyes.

"Something wrong, Molly?"

"Where's your holster, Paco? Where's your gun?"

"You thought all this time that I carried one under my jacket?"

"Of course. Don't all policemen?"

"I used to, dear Molly, when I was on the force in Baltimore, but in my present job I no longer need it. I leave that job to Frank. Are you disappointed?"

She didn't answer.

He cautiously continued. "I had a feeling you might be wondering about it. But I also thought you might feel safer with me if I don't carry one."

She looked relieved. "My sediments exactly!" she said.

Simon and Rachel stood by, watching this little drama with half-smiles.

Simon decided it would be okay to break the spell. "Well, shall we get to work?" he asked.

"Yes, sir!" Paco said with an exaggerated snap of his heels. The two men once more tied the wet dish towels over their faces. In the cloakroom they plugged two lamps into a fifty-foot orange extension cord and carried them into the secret room. Next, they set up both fans in the cloakroom and turned them on HIGH.

The whirring fans spewed powerful shafts of air across the secret room, sending curls and streams of dust into the now-cleared vents. Grimy bands of light penetrated the waving cobwebs and outlined the room's farthest wall.

Olivia chose to remain outside because of her hay fever. "Let's be extremely careful not to disrupt anything," she cautioned once more. "Remember, our main purpose is to probe the room for the precious history it can reveal. Rachel, dear, here's my Pentax. Please take as many shots as you can. I have more film in my purse if you need it." Standing in the doorway, Rachel started snapping pictures immediately.

Molly crossed the threshold and abruptly stopped. "Yuk, it's stenchifying!"

"It sure is," Rachel said. "Let's wait a few minutes until the fans clear out the air." Shortly after, the fans worked their magic and the putrid quality of the air diminished remarkably. Rachel and Molly were able to join the men in the secret room, where Simon had cleared a large area close to the door as a starting place. With three wet brooms delicately manipulated, Simon, Paco, and Rachel methodically punched through the clinging, sticky wall of cobwebs, quickly creating a viable walking space.

Rachel paused for a moment to watch Molly. The housekeeper was flourishing a feather duster with grand sweeps to clear the cobwebs off the walls nearest the door. As if she's Arthur Fiedler conducting the Boston Symphony, Rachel thought affectionately.

Working in silence for another quarter hour, the four of them purposely avoided table and dresser tops, noting that more precise care was required there.

"Hello, what's all this mess?" Molly suddenly asked. She was hunched over, examining the carpeted area near the dressing table. "Plenty of unpleasantness was going on in this room, yes, sireee. Somebody was throwing things." She had encountered broken glass from mirrors and bottles strewn in all directions, as well as combs, brushes, and jewelry. "Miss Rachel, better get your camera over here," she added.

"Right you are, Molly," Paco said. "This debris might be important."

Rachel photographed the disarray--and each intact surface--from several angles to preserve the geometry and position of articles found there. She discovered a grimy fireplace bellows leaning against the hearth. As she cautiously pumped the stiff handles, the bellows kicked up huge puffs of mildewed dust. She coughed and waved her hand back and forth in front of her face. "This is disgusting. I think I'll just stick to my picture-taking," she said, setting it back down against the hearth.

"Here, hon, you need better light." Simon held one lamp high and apart from the other one still on the floor. The obstructing furniture still limited lighting to only small areas of the room at a time.

"It looks like a whole apartment," said Rachel, lowering the Pentax 35mm from her shooting eye. "Everything you'd need is here: a dining room table and chairs, a dresser, a vanity, a writing desk, a settee, and a canopied four-poster bed with a night stand. The furniture is sturdy and functional, but certainly not fancy. Nothing like the elegance of the rest of the house. It makes me wonder if--"

"--if it isn't a jail?" Simon completed her thought.

"Exactly!" she answered. "But for whom? Sophia was dead and Cartier disappeared shortly thereafter."

"Perhaps it was never used," Simon offered.

"I doubt that." Paco's police intuition had picked up unmistakable signs of human habitation in the room: the toilet articles on the dresser, more on the floor. An empty pewter drinking cup and bottle on the table. A woman's brocade slipper beside the night stand. An open book with a quill laid across it and a dried-up inkwell beside it on the desk. He pulled open a few dresser drawers only so far as to determine that they all contained women's clothes.

"Ahhhhh . . . yaah . . . yeeeeeek! It's died dead." The shriek emanated from Molly, shrill, piercing, and prolonged.

"What's wrong, Molly?" asked Paco as he ran to her side.

"What's dead?" asked Rachel. Simon merely stared at the badly shaken housekeeper.

"There's a died body sleeping in that bed over there. I...ah...Oh, no, maybe two," Molly exclaimed as she stepped back and turned away, covering her eyes with both hands.

"I'll be damned, she's right. In fact, there's not just one, but two dead bodies in there," Paco said.

Achoo! Achoo! Loud sneezes caught the group by surprise. Olivia approached the bed. "My God, how gruesome. But how exciting, too," she exclaimed. Achoo! Achoo! "Please excuse me, everyone."

Rachel lowered the camera from her eye. "But Olivia, your hay fever!"

Achoo! "I know, I know," she said, blowing her nose. "But I just can't bear to be left out of this most shocking and extraordinary discovery." Olivia brushed a stray cobweb from her shoulder. "I'm just throwing my hay fever caution to the winds, or to the fans, you might say."

Paco leaned over the bed. He cleared away a stubborn thicket of cobwebs hanging down from the canopy and gently lifted the thick, coarse coverlet. The putrid smell of decomposition penetrated the heavy air. The group moved closer together, as if seeking protection from one another, and watched him in silence.

"It's a man and a woman, and they're both fully dressed. Must be decades after the fact, though." The gray dust had uniformly covered bed clothing and bed occupants until neither was distinguishable from the other except upon closer scrutiny. "I guess now we'll have to treat the room as a crime scene as well as a historical find."

"Why a crime scene, Inspector? Do we know that a crime has actually been committed? Maybe it was a double suicide," Rachel said. She could hardly believe that such a romantic and tragic act transcending several lifetimes could be worth a criminal investigation now.

Meanwhile, a still shaking Molly found her way into the arms of Paco, who was surprised, yet not unwilling. He led her to the other side of the room and sat her down at the desk. His tenderness toward her elicited more than casual glances from Simon and Rachel. They pretended to go on with their photographic work, anyway.

"I'm okay now. Leave me be and I'll be goodly soon enough," Molly whispered. Paco reluctantly left her at the table and then eagerly returned to the two reclining corpses.

"May I use the camera to take a few shots of the bed, please?" he asked. Rachel handed him the camera without comment. He took several shots from each side of the bed, and then one from the end of it. Simon assisted him in gently pulling back the comforter once more, and Paco repeated the shot from the end of the bed. This time they left the cover turned down. As near as the inspector could determine without disturbing anything, the upper reaches of the heads and bodies were skeletally clean. The skulls lay hairless, but the mouths gaped open with teeth intact. The heavily clothed body portions were in various states of prolonged decay and dry rot. Repulsive, but not altogether so, considering the time elapsed. The dust was far too thick and the subjects far too fragile to probe any further.

Paco decided he'd need to borrow a specialized forensics team from Annapolis or Baltimore to handle this properly. He'd found some signs of foul play and struggle in the room, especially the disarray by the dressing table. Under the skylights, he had also noted a broken chair and a badly dented hairbrush. But the corpses were both fully dressed; that part seemed more an indication of double suicide. Perhaps a murder-suicide.

"Keep an eye out for another key in the room, one they could have used to lock themselves in with," Paco said.

Whoosh! Whoosh! Whoosh! All eyes turned toward Molly standing in front of the desk, pumping her elbows in and out as she worked the bellows down onto an open book. They gathered around her for a closer look. Whoosh! Whoosh! She moved the bellows closer this time to a new position and squeezed still another whoosh from its leather lungs.

The scrawny remains of a feather quill shifted to the fold between the spread pages. The faint trace of a graceful, feminine scrawl began to emerge from the utter grayness before them. Molly bent low to the book and used her breath to blow the page to a more readable state.

"The book is hand written," Simon exclaimed.

"I see a date: May 29th, 1913. It must be a diary," Rachel said. She reached out to turn the page.

"Hold it," Paco called out. "I want to get a picture of this." He leaned over Molly's shoulder and took two shots to document their discovery. The intense flash caught the group by surprise, for they were intent on reading.

"Wait, please! Be extra-careful," Olivia warned. "The pages are probably very brittle."

Rachel nodded. With one finger she slowly turned to the next page. "It's blank!" she exclaimed. "So May 29th was the last entry." She carefully closed the pale blue book covers and opened this time to the first entry. She read aloud:

November 13th, 1912

I am alone now. I don't know where except that it is somewhere in the depths of Marche House. All I know is that I must start my diary afresh. I have plenty of paper and ink, as well as a supply of books to read. I am fed decently, three times daily by my husband. He has discharged all the servants except a cook who goes home at night. There is ample water..."

"Inspector, may we take the diary with us?" Olivia asked. "This is such a momentous find, I'd like to read portions of it to the other Historical Society members. We could do it tonight at my house, or Avi's, whichever he prefers. It's really quite fortunate that everyone is still in town for the funeral tomorrow."

Paco thought for a moment. "Why not? We're going to read it anyway, so why not read it in comfort with everyone present?"

"But don't you have to lift the fingerprints from it?" Simon asked.

"No. I wish we could, but the volume is too old. Over the years it's gotten dusty and dried out. The oils from an individual's skin that make it possible for us to lift prints have long since evaporated here in this room. And even if we could lift prints, there's no one alive to compare them to.

"Besides," Paco continued, "I think we've all spent enough time in here today. I don't know about the rest of you, but I'm ready for some good, clean, fresh air."

"Me too," Olivia said, trying to hold back a long series of sneezes. She carried the diary gingerly in both hands.

"Me three," Molly added, chuckling at her own joke.

"Let's leave all the equipment where it is," said Simon. He waited until the others had left. Then he unplugged the extension cords, coiled the ends neatly, and laid them on the floor. The key was still in the door when he pulled it shut behind him. It turned much easier now that the oil had soaked through. He handed it to Paco for police safekeeping.

But Olivia's curiosity overwhelmed her. She settled into a settee in the grand foyer, carefully opened the diary, and began reading page one. After only a few sentences, she suddenly glanced up, aware of the silence and her four cohorts standing expectantly at the front door. "I'm so sorry. I'm keeping you all waiting," she said, laughing. "I just couldn't resist."

"Do you think Daddy and Freddie would mind convening the Society one more time at their house?" Rachel asked.

"Oh, no," Molly piped up. "The Hysterical Society is very important to the doctor." Rachel and Olivia giggled. But Paco was already deep in thought. A double suicide? Or murder?

CHAPTER 25

CONFRONTATION AND RETALIATION

Avi sat in his red leather swivel chair, his back to a bay window bright with early afternoon sunlight. His blue-veined fists gripped the open pages of yesterday's large-type Sunday *New York Times*. On the desk lay the finished obituary he'd written for the local paper: concise and, for Freddie's sake, complimentary; contrived without actually lying. The task had been formidable, because Victor had broken truth and trust with Avi, his mother, and worst of all, himself. Avi wanted to write about all the things Victor could have been and done. At some point, though, he grew aware that he was not alone in the office. He lowered his paper.

Freddie stood in the doorway, leaning on one foot more than the other, her head and left shoulder tilted against the door frame. She had been trying to decide whether or not she should disturb him. His gaze of discovery prompted her to speak. "I'm sorry to interrupt you, Avi."

"Not at all, Freddie. Please come in. Sit, sit!" He indicated a small leather armchair.

"Sit? Sit? You've been spending too much time with the dog, Avi."

He laughed. "Maybe so, Freddie." But he could sense the nervous edge in her voice. When she was wholly settled in and minutes passed and still she had not spoken again, he knew she was wrestling internally; something more was wrong. He would not press her. He crossed his right leg over his knee, leaned back in his chair, and allowed her to perceive this golden patience borne by members of his profession and very few others.

"Last night," she began, "I just had to keep busy. First Molly and I moved the plants out of the den into the sunroom. They were getting kind of peaked in there without benefit of direct sunlight. Then she and I were going through some of Victor's things. This note dropped out when I unfolded a sweater." Freddie reached across the desk and handed the piece of folded stationery to Avi.

"The handwriting is very feminine. I assume you know who R is."

"No, I don't," she said. "That's just the point. I wasn't aware that Victor had someone special in his life. I can't imagine what he gave her in his dire financial state."

"Do you suppose..." Avi stopped mid-sentence to consider the implications of what he was about to say.

"Do I suppose what?"

"I don't care to finish it." He did not want to accuse Victor of anything, especially without proof.

"Do I suppose what?" she repeated.

Avi decided to improvise. "Do you suppose this note is a matter for Inspector LeSoto?"

"Avi, whatever do you mean by that?"

"After all, the key is missing," he said reluctantly.

"Oh, no! On top of everything, you accuse my son of being a thief, too?" Freddie lowered her head so Avi couldn't see her tears. She covered her face with both hands. Her low whimpering filled the air for several long moments.

Avi waited for her to recover and then he went to his sister. "There, there, it's only idle conjecture anyway. Let's just let the inspector sort it all out. He's the professional in that department." He leaned down and kissed his sister on the forehead, and hugged her as well. "I meant him no disrespect, Freddie, especially now that he's gone. Forgive me. I tried to suppress the thought, but I should have known better."

"Oh, Avi, there's nothing to forgive. I know there isn't a mean or disrespectful bone in your body." She looked up at him with two reddened eyes.

Avi pulled a neatly folded handkerchief from his trouser pocket and held it out to her. She gratefully took it from him, opened it, and mopped the flood of tears running down her cheeks. He studied her anguished face. In the two days since Victor's death, dark, puffy pouches had settled under her once bright blue eyes. New lines of grief had carved themselves around her mouth.

"Freddie!" he said. "How would you like to play detective? The two of us, on our own?"

"I can't imagine what you mean," she replied.

"We can do our level best to clear Victor's name. However, there's always the chance that we might find something we would rather not uncover. Are you prepared for that?"

"Yes, but how?"

"Watch me." Avi flipped up a desktop index and dialed a telephone number. "I'd like the room of Felix Thornberry, please...Hello, Felix, this is Avi Kepple...Fine. And yourself? Oh, sorry I interrupted your nap. The reason I'm calling is to determine if Victor knew a certain someone down at the inn. I know you and Victor played cards down there. I'm wondering whether there was one woman in particular...A waitress, you say? A waitress by day, a barmaid at night. Do you know her name, by any chance? Ruby. Ruby Price. Thank you, Felix. You've been most helpful. Freddie and I appreciate your help immensely."

He hung up and looked at Freddie. "That was almost too easy. Well,

Freddie, would you like to meet Vic's mystery woman, Ruby Price?"

"Oh, Avi, I wouldn't miss it for the world. Let me get my purse and jacket."

His spontaneous "therapy" was working. He had given Freddie a tangible mission and stimulated her intellectual juices. She might even contribute to solving the puzzle of Victor's past, Avi thought. He knew that when Freddie prevented her emotions from suffocating her reasoning, her mind could be both sharp and analytical.

Avi went to the front hall closet and put on his suit jacket. By the time he reached the garage access, Freddie had already pushed the button to raise the double garage door. But before they had a chance to reach Avi's Cadillac, Olivia's Lincoln pulled into the driveway and parked directly in front of the garage.

"Daddy," cried Rachel, scurrying out of the back seat. "We found it. We found the secret room. Oh, Daddy...We've got so much to tell you."

"When we get back, Rachel. You can tell us all about it then."

"It can't wait, Daddy. We found another diary."

"It's a great find, Avi," said Olivia. "We thought it would be a good idea for the entire Historical Society to listen to the first reading. We can convene this evening at my place, if you like."

"Nonsense. We have all that leftover food from yesterday. Right, Molly?"

"Yes, Doctor, and new food, too!" Molly struggled out of the plush rear seat of the Lincoln. "Wooee! Uh-uh! That deep back seat of yours is a mite cushy for the tushy, Miss Olivia."

"And besides," Avi continued, "we should stick around the house to receive condolence callers. I think it would be good for Freddie to have everyone here. Would you notify the group and tell them seven o'clock?"

"Certainly! Where are you two off to?" said Olivia.

"We were headed down to the inn to meet someone," said Freddie.

"I'm just plain nosy," said Molly. "Who would that someone be?"

Freddie murmured in Molly's ear: "R. Just plain R." This response left a very excited Molly speechless.

Avi leaned down to look through the driver side window to Paco in the passenger seat. "Oh, Inspector, Lenora called here to tell you that she's found the missing diary. Something about Bucky zipping it up in the wrong suitcase. She says you can pick it up any time this afternoon. She tried to reach you at headquarters, but you were out."

Olivia turned to Paco. "I can run you over to the inn now, Inspector. Avi, I can take you and Freddie too, if you like."

Grateful not to have to drive, his eyesight failing more noticeably these days, Avi held the rear door open for Freddie. On the way, Olivia and Paco briefed them on the secret room and their findings. Avi listened in astonishment and assimilated the extraordinary details. But Freddie was far too distracted by her mission to hear much.

The group split up in the lobby at the inn. Olivia and Paco rode the elevator to the second floor; Paco to the Worthingtons and Olivia to the various members' rooms to invite them to the diary reading.

Avi and Freddie went directly to the restaurant and chose a table near a large window. Finding a nearly empty room, Avi checked his watch--at least an hour before the dinner rush. A lone waitress sat chatting with the maitre d' by the kitchen door. She got up and crossed the room to them.

"Can I get ya a drink and some pretzels?" she asked in a cheery voice, keeping her head turned just enough so that the right side of her face couldn't be seen. "You see, we won't be serving dinner for another forty-five minutes yet."

"By any chance, would your name be Ruby Price, my dear?" Avi asked. The waitress stiffened and looked sideways at him.

"Uh, yes, my name's Ruby...But why do ya want to know?"

"Do you know who I am, Ruby?" Freddie asked in her most nonthreatening voice.

"No, ma'am, I don't. Should I?"

"No, dear, we've never met. I'm Victor Moskowitz's mother."

A second wave of shock took hold of Ruby and her legs almost buckled under her. Avi rose and pulled a chair out for her. "Please join us for a moment," he said.

"Oh, ma'am, I'm so very sorry about Vic, but what do ya want from me?" Ruby lowered herself reluctantly into the chair, her shoulders hunched, tensed almost to her neck, and her eyes watered with anxiety and fear. She sniffled self-consciously. "I can't tell youse anything ya don't know already."

"I'm Dr. Avi Kepple. We just want to ask you a few questions about your relationship with my nephew. Ruby, you would be doing us a great kindness. We would be most appreciative." His gentle voice and sensitive manner seemed to disarm her, and she allowed more of her face to show now. Her hunched shoulders melted back into their normal position on her body. She pulled a hunk of her long, raven hair across her face like a veil so that only her saddened dull eyes showed. The gesture was mechanical, not concocted to hide injury, Avi thought. Nevertheless, he detected the bruises on the side of her face that she had wanted to hide when she first came to their table.

"I don't hafta answer any of your questions," Ruby blurted out.

"Of course not, but we know how much Victor meant to you, and we thought you might be able to help us," Avi said.

"I don't know nothing about Vic's death." Her voice wavered as she struggled with her feelings. "How do I know I can trust you? How do I know you're not going to report me to the police?"

"Is there something to report?" Avi asked.

"No, no, nothing, but I'm scared. And I'm upset, for Chrissake."

"I understand, Ruby, and I'm sure you have a right to be. Of course, the police might want to talk to you at some point, but that's not why Mrs. Moskowitz and I are here. We just need your help," Avi said.

"What about?" Ruby's tone sounded less belligerent now, and she eyed Avi with less suspicion too. His quiet manner and his voice seemed soothing, so respectful. She wasn't used to that. He had a fine way of getting under your skin, she thought.

"Ruby, we know you were at my house Friday night, out front."

"Who says?"

"Several of us saw you standing there. Why were you there?" Avi studied her closely. He was guessing, bluffing, of course, but the monogrammed handkerchief, her reaction, and the salmon-colored lipstick--they all seemed to fit. A comely woman for the most part, he thought, perhaps thirty-five. Strong arms from years of carrying heavy trays. A bit overdone in the cosmetics department and a trifle undersized in the clothing department: the short skirt of her uniform struggling to stay in place on her rounded thighs.

"I, ah..." Ruby's voice cracked, and then she sobbed for several seconds. "I was waiting for him to come out and give me the money he owed me."

"What money was that?" Avi asked quietly.

"The eighty-two bucks he borrowed from me to stake a poker game last Tuesday. He said he would give it back by Friday night. I needed it to pay my rent. I waited four hours for him to come out, but he never showed up." She spoke between the sobs, wiping tears away with the end of her frilly apron. Her thick mascara began to smear and stain her cheeks.

"Why didn't you just come to the door?" Freddie asked.

"You had a lot of people there. I didn't want to make a scene."

"So you just stood out there and smoked half a pack of cigarettes," Avi said.

"So what?" she fired back. "What kind of crime is that?"

Avi ignored her questions. "Oh, yes, the inspector found the butts, and even made plaster casts of your heel prints."

"But I didn't do nothing wrong," she protested. "I feel real bad about losing Vic, but I didn't have nothing to do with his death. I couldn't have."

"You couldn't have?" Freddie asked.

"No. I loved Vic, and he loved me too."

"Did my son actually ever say he loved you?"

"You better believe it," she replied. "And we even talked about gettin' hitched a couple a times, but he...uh, he said...we'd hafta wait till he got back on his feet again."

"Did my son ever give you a gift? Something of value like a keepsake?"

For an instant Ruby thought about lying, but her instinctive reaction gave her away immediately as her hand went to the gold chain resting on her breast. She fingered it lovingly, but remained silent, her lips pressed tightly together.

Freddie tried again. "May we see it, my dear? No one's going to hurt you. We just want to see what Victor gave you."

Ruby played with the chain about her neck. "How do youse know Vic gave me anything?"

Freddie spread the flower-bordered note open on the table before her. "You see, we do know."

Ruby's hand shook as she reluctantly pulled the fourteen-carat gold chain out from her modest cleavage. There at the end of it was a heavy gold and opal ring.

"Victor's college class ring!" exclaimed Freddie.

"He gave it to me," Ruby whimpered. "I shouldn't have to give it up. It's all I have from him."

Avi and Freddie looked at the ring and then at each other. It's not the jeweled key, each was thinking. Did that mean she and Victor were not accomplices? Freddie comforted herself with the answer she wanted; she chuckled and sank back with relief into her chair.

Avi squinted at the ring and looked away, his thoughts folding inward. He felt more disappointment than he cared to show. Ruby didn't strike him as the type to be involved in grand larceny. But that didn't make his predicament any easier. The key was still missing.

"The ring is lovely, my dear, and, of course, you may keep it," Freddie said.

All Ruby could reply was a feeble "Thank you." She simply could not fathom the reaction she had elicited from Victor's mother.

Freddie extended her hand for Ruby to shake, and when the waitress warily decided to take it, they shared a moment's feeling of tenderness. "So you loved my son and now you grieve with me."

Ruby dropped her guard entirely at this point, tossed her head, and her long hair fell away from the partly hidden side of her face.

"That's a nasty cut and bruise you have on your face, Ruby," Avi noted. "Have you had a doctor look at it yet?"

"No, sir."

"How did it happen?"

The waitress opened her mouth but no words came out.

"I can't believe Victor would have done--" Avi said.

"Oh, no!" she interrupted. "Never!" Her voice dropped to a whisper. "It was a guy from Jersey Vic owed money to."

Heavy footsteps. A large man entered the dining room. When Ruby saw him she fairly quivered. "I gotta go now. Gotta get back to work. The kitchen needs me." She pushed her chair back awkwardly as she jumped up. Avi had to grab it to prevent it from toppling.

Pure fright appeared in her face as the stranger approached their table. She tried to turn and leave, but the man clamped his hand down on her shoulder and gripped it tightly.

"Aren't you going to introduce me to your friends, Ruby?" he asked. She wrenched out of his grip and ran, crying all the way to the kitchen door.

"It's none of my business, sir," Avi said, "but that's hardly the way to treat a lady."

"Yer right, mister. It ain't none a your business. My business is wit' dis lady here." He sat down in the chair that Ruby had vacated and pulled it in close to Freddie.

"I'm afraid I don't have any business with you. Nor do I care to have any dealings with such a boor as you. Please remove yourself immediately."

"Oh, yeah? But I do have business wit' you, important business. Missus Moskowitz, your son owed me a lotta scratch...Don't look so surprised, little lady. Fifteen big ones."

Freddie gasped. "I don't know what to say."

"You don't have to say anything, Freddie," Avi said. "I'll take it from here."

"And who do you think you are, bub?" the man asked.

"I'm not your bub. But I am Victor's uncle."

"So?"

"So, Mr. whatever your name is..."

"Ace, Ace Flowers at your disposal."

"So, Mr. Flowers, if you have any legitimate claim against my nephew's estate, I suggest you submit it through proper probate channels."

"What's probate?"

"It's a special court process to settle claims for taxes, creditors, and heirs. But I hardly think there's enough left of Victor's estate to settle any of that."

"Oh, I got a claim all right. I got his markers right here." Ace reached into his coat pocket and pulled out three separate IOU's totaling $15,000.

"I see," said Avi as he watched Ace stuff the folded sheets back into his pocket.

"Don't want no probate. Jes want my dough. Dis lady's got dough."

"The law says she's not responsible for her adult son's debts," Avi continued. "I'm afraid you'll just have to write this off as a loss."

"Quit bustin' in, Mister Uncle. I wanna talk to da lady...alone!"

Avi simply shook his head. "I think you've said quite enough, Mr. Flowers."

"Mitch ain't gonna like dis," Ace muttered.

"Mitch who?" Avi asked.

"Mitch Brodie, my boss. He ain't gonna take dis lyin' down, you know. It's his money."

"Mr. Flowers, let me remind you that Victor's death and a sizable theft as well are still under investigation. I'm sure Inspector LeSoto would be very interested in your whereabouts the evening Victor died. You were seen roughing him up the day before. Perhaps you killed him for the key."

Ace leaped out of the chair and slammed it against the table. "I don't know nuthin' about no murder or no key." He moved toward the door, a gaping hole in his otherwise smooth and tough armor.

Avi called after him, "I strongly suggest you stay away from Ruby Price. I'm sure she'll press charges this time. We'll insist on it."

"Yeah, yeah!" Ace moved faster now.

When he was gone, Freddie asked, "Do you really think he killed Victor?"

"No. No, I don't. He's capable, of course. But if he had, I think he would have been long gone by now and not here pressing you for a gambling debt."

"Do you think he stole your jeweled key, then?"

"It's not likely. For the same reason, although the worth of the key would more than cover the debt. But he seemed a little confused when I mentioned the key."

"Thank you, Avi."

"For what?"

"Oh, for bringing me along to meet Ruby. For getting a look at that hood, the kind of scum that fed off my son's weaknesses. For putting that guy in his place." She paused, her confidence renewed. "I believe Ruby. I think she's telling the truth. You see, Avi, I was right. Victor had nothing to do with the key! I hate to say 'I told you so,' but..." and she laughed, "I told you so!"

Avi didn't answer. He saw no point in upsetting Freddie further, especially the day before the funeral. Ruby did indeed seem to him naive and innocent. Victor had used her as he used everybody else. But Freddie had not produced conclusive evidence absolving her son of the theft.

CHAPTER 26

SOPHIA'S KEY

The early bird specials in the Chandelier Room had already begun to draw an animated crowd of Monday evening diners.

Avi and Freddie waited for Olivia to come and take them home. They sat in silence, emotionally spent from their afternoon in the near-empty dining room. As Avi tried to reassure an anxious Freddie that no one needed their table quite yet, Paco ambled in and approached them. A brown mailing envelope tucked securely under his arm held Geneve's diary.

"Mrs. Raphael will be down in a few minutes. Do you mind if I join you, Doctor? Ma'am?"

"Not at all, Inspector. We'd be disappointed if you didn't," Avi said. "In fact, we'd like to tell you of our encounter with a Mr. Ace Flowers only moments ago."

"Would that be the goon in the black suit I saw entering the elevator just now?"

"Very likely the one."

As he listened, Paco's eyebrows arched and stayed elevated through Avi's entire report. "I'll have to question them both," the inspector said. "Perhaps I can persuade Miss Price to charge Flowers with assault and battery. I'm glad to find out the R stands for Ruby. Your daughter told me this Flowers guy roughed up the deceased on Thursday afternoon. That might be enough to hold him in custody for a few days."

"Very appropriate for that scum," Freddie said. "The very *chutzpah* of him thinking he can intimidate honest people." She gripped her hanky with two hands and yanked on it with a vengeance as she spoke.

"Oh, by the way," Paco added, "I have some news for you both. I checked in with my office just now. The county coroner called and left a message that the deceased has been transferred back to the funeral home as you requested. You can have the funeral tomorrow after all."

"Oh, thank you, Inspector." Freddie dabbed her wrinkled hanky at each damp eye. "It will be just a quiet service at Mount Nemo Cemetery. Only family and a few friends. Everyone is here already."

"If there's anything I can do..."

"Thank you, Inspector," Avi said. "But there is something you're not telling us."

"What's that?"

"The cause of death." Avi tilted his head in readiness for the answer.

"I'm afraid I have to disappoint you there. When I called the coroner's office, he had already left for the day. They informed me that he sent his report via overnight mail."

"Overnight mail?" Freddie wailed.

"Yes. I'm sorry to say the wheels of justice sometimes turn at a painfully slow pace. Anyhow, we'll know tomorrow. Perhaps by noon, if they dropped it in the mail early enough."

"Mrs. Moskowitz, why were your footprints outside the den window Friday night?" Paco suddenly asked.

"I wanted to know if Victor was actually in the room. I suspected that he was hiding from me, so I went to see if the light was on."

"And was it?"

"I couldn't tell," Freddie replied. "I don't think so."

"Well, I hope I haven't kept everyone waiting too long," interjected a pert, froggy voice. Olivia plopped her purse, keys, and doeskin gloves on the table. "I extended an invitation personally to each Society member, and everyone's coming to your place at seven tonight. Oops! Have I interrupted something here?"

"No, not at all. We're sitting here exchanging and digesting information," Avi said.

"It was just that I caught everyone in a pregnant pause," she said. "You can tell me what's new on the way back. Who's ready for the trip home?"

Without replying, they all got to their feet and filed out of the restaurant.

At the Kepple residence that evening, the dinner guests devoured steaming slices of brisket and mashed potatoes steeped in rich brown onion and mushroom gravy. By eight, they'd all gathered in the sunroom to hear Sophia Marche's diary. Olivia, eager to get started, took the first reading herself.

November 13th, 1912

I am alone now. I don't know where, except that it is somewhere in the depths of Marche House. All I know is that I must start my diary afresh. I have plenty of paper and ink as well as a supply of books to read. I am fed decently, three times daily by my husband. He has discharged all the servants except a cook who goes home at night. There is ample water to drink and to bathe with. I have seen no one else in this cool, damp place save him. I am his prisoner, and at times the object of his lust. But I am no longer atop <u>his</u> pedestal of marital bliss. I underline <u>his</u> because the bliss has been his alone for some time now. I feel no pain, no remorse, and I shed no tears.

I have one regret, though. My only child, my dear Hubert, has been taken from me. Cartier told me our darling son is thriving in the care of his new nanny, a Miss Leslie Temple. Hubert has always been raised by nannies whose purpose and plan were strictly dictated by my husband. For some reason I have never understood, Cartier has sought to undo any maternal bonding between my son and myself. And Geneve, my personal secretary, closest friend and confidante, has been sent away. I am lost, abandoned. I am resigned, but I do fear much for my lover, dear Jacques.

Ten weeks ago I wrote my Cousin Elizabeth and told her that I would visit with her at her home in Alexandria while renovations were going on at Marche House. I really didn't want to go away right then, as I was expecting last-minute instructions from Jacques. But I was certainly in no position to argue with Cartier. He had been acting so strange. Not unkind exactly, but so very distant, even when we two were alone.

It all started several months ago when Cartier found the jeweled box, the gift from my beloved Jacques. When I blatantly refused to give him the key to it, he perceived me fondling the chain about my neck and drew the correct conclusion. One yank pulled it from my bodice, a second tore it from my neck, leaving a red line for days afterward. As soon as he opened the box and confirmed that the letters were from my lover, he left the room with the lot. He returned later that day to beat me. He began with the fierceness of earnest jealousy and, to my good fortune, shied from the task, as he could take no satisfaction from it. He left me to my shame. I felt none. I feel none now. My affections are mine alone to give. He confined me to my rooms on the cliff side of the house. Locked me in where no stranger's eye would likely intrude.

He chose to be as quiet then as he is now. He said very little to me other than to make known his wishes. He remained civil enough, but I noticed that he raised his voice at times, as though he wished the whole household to hear something rather trivial. Little did I know that he was plotting my impending disappearance. Oh, he planned his vicious scheme so well!

I heard workmen downstairs, but I had no way of knowing where or what the sounds were about. Cartier had alluded earlier to renovations at Marche House. I had accepted this fact without dreaming it concerned my future lodgings, alas, my whole remaining life.

On September 12th I awoke in my rooms to find my baggage already packed for the journey to Elizabeth's. Cartier had done this completely on his own, and I had no reason to suspect anything. Except, some days later, the baggage left the rooms without me. I remained locked in. He appeared to enjoy my puzzlement, but would take no amount of coaxing to alleviate my curiosity.

On November 3rd he came to me in the night and lifted me out of my bed. It was a day or so after the sounds of construction had ceased. The confusion of interrupted sleep, the sleep mask he kept over my eyes, and the general darkness left me with little concept of the path we took that night. He carried me into an unfamiliar, rather roughly furnished room, one which I did not recognize. A room in my own house that I did not know! He lay with me that night and was most tender. Shamefully, I must confess I found some small pleasure therein, though outwardly I've shown him none of this. I maintain my role as the dutiful wife. I have been here since that night, along with most of my belongings. I have seen no other place nor person except for Cartier.

November 17th

I questioned Cartier this morning and pressed him for any news about my Hubert. He told me that Hubert had grown very attached to his new mother. I became very disturbed about his use of the term "new mother." When I challenged him about it, he declared most matter-of-factly that he had married Leslie Temple, Hubert's nanny, nearly a month ago! I became distraught. I protested that he was already married to me. He said I had been dead for several months. Everyone knew it! And now, for the first time, I understood what the construction was for. He had built a secret room, a hidden room in which to imprison me forever! I was at a loss for words to challenge him and forced to suppress the intensity of my anger, for I had no desire to incur his wrath further.

November 19th

Last night, when Cartier brought my dinner tray, I saw the *Annapolis Journal-Gazette* laid across it. He had graciously fulfilled my morning request to sample events of the world beyond Marche House. He received a long, passionate hug for his trouble. Previously, I had decided to reward him with meagerly portioned out measures of my attentions for any effort on his part to restore me to a more plentiful life, my former life, or (God help me) my freedom. If it is not forthcoming, I will surely wreak revenge of my own upon him. This I swear.

This local newspaper, dated October 18th, I consumed with eager appetite. That is, until I reached a page two article about a sheriff's inquest. I reeled with horror, shock, and anger at the subject of this two-day inquest: "the accidental demise of Mr. Jacques Giraud and Mrs. Sophia Raucheau Marche." I read how Jacques and I had fallen to our deaths when the carriage transporting us plunged over the chalky cliffs at Marche House. Days later, the newspaper said, Jacques's body had been recovered. Mine, after four days, was presumed to be washed out to the storm-wracked bay. Sufficient numbers of my clothing and other possessions were scattered over the site so as to attest to my presence in the ill-fated carriage. My presence was further presumed when Cartier told the inquest that he had hired Mr. Giraud to transport his wife to a cousin in Alexandria. A missing cotter pin linking the horses to the carriage was found rusted and broken just up the drive from the site of the runaway carriage. Thus, the inquest ruled the deaths accidental.

I feel unbearable pain now. Oh, not for my miserable self, but for my lost lover. Though we shared a bed only once, I shall never regret that precious day.

Olivia looked up from her reading and sighed. Tears flooded her eyes. "It's like a gothic novel," she said.

"Would you like me to take over the reading for you?"

"Why, yes, that's very generous of you, Inspector."

"Cartier Marche must have been a very devious, malevolent man to engineer all of that," Rachel said.

"I agree," said Avi. "Then I guess we can conclude that Sophia's letters were destroyed."

"Yes, but thank goodness that beautiful box is intact," said Simon.

"And we found it, thanks to Caitlin's playfulness," Rachel said. "I guess we'll never know whether it was Cartier or Hubert who created the secret hiding place for it in the highboy."

Paco, Rachel, then Marti, then Felix read on through months of seemingly endless passages conveying the decaying will of a woman wronged by a jealous and evil husband.

"Felix," Marti whined, "do you have to ham it up so much? You're spoiling everything."

"What's to spoil?" he asked. But on catching Marti's miffed glance, he handed the diary back to Olivia, with an exaggerated bow in her direction.

"Thank you, Felix, that's very gallant of you," Olivia said, smiling broadly. She opened the book and read on:

May 2nd, 1913

I feel that I'm going mad, and I suppose that's exactly what my husband wants. What does he expect me to do all day, locked in this rough-hewn room? There being a minimal choice of activities within these walls, I have taken to anticipating his arrival each night. I am prudently stingy with my favors now, since it has been some time that I can see any improvement in either my status or my lot. I have prostituted myself to gain more of life's comforts. I am careful, though, not to reverse the barter process. I watch him closely. I analyze his movements, motives, and behavior. I seek the leverage to pry him from his course. I seek the means for my escape. But, most of all, I seek revenge upon him for my debasement. I am obsessed with these three things.

The day's light is gone now. Ah, I hear the big key in its lock. Clink. Turning one revolution. The heavy metal door squeals and scrapes open toward me. Only slightly ajar at first and then all the way when he sees me across the room. The key is still in the lock.

May 3rd

There is new light in the space overhead. I cannot see the sun, but I trust it is there. Cartier is gone now, and I can finish my description of his arrival each night, for it is not prone to change much.

He transfers the key to the inside keyhole, closes the door, and locks it lest I escape while he sleeps in my bed. He then deposits the key in a waist pocket of his trousers. It is one pocket that requires Cartier to inhale deeply before he can access it. Lately, though, he has left these trousers across a chair while he sleeps.

Last night, taking advantage of what I viewed as a lapse in his distrust, I inched out from his arm draped across me and stole to the chair. To my great disappointment the trouser pocket had been emptied. I prayed the key had fallen on the rug and I felt about for it on my hands and knees. But I found nothing. Had he hidden it in one of his shoes? No. What could I do but return to my bed? What had I missed? It couldn't be on his person, for without trousers and blouse, the long bulky key couldn't be in the bed beneath him, and I could account for every other unsightly bulge in plain view. No, nothing in the pillow or its case either.

May 4th

Last night, when I heard the key in the lock, I feigned a deep sleep as I had done purposely and mischievously on so many earlier occasions. But first, I retained a lasting image of the room in my mind's eye, and as I put the sounds of Cartier's movements to it, I knew where he was from the moment of his entry into the room to his climbing into bed with me. The key had to be somewhere between the chair where he lays his clothes and the bed. And when the long, loud snoring sounds told me he was asleep, I stole out of the bed once again to search for the key. I moved the chair and examined its underside. I pulled back the rug and felt along the splintering bare floor. To no avail. I returned to our bed to lie awake and contemplate my failure till dawn's light struck me with renewed determination.

May 5th

It is afternoon now and I am trembling with exhilaration over my success.

This morning after he left I sat down on the floor on his side of the bed to continue my search for the key. I knew the hiding place was within arm's reach of where I sat. I was at first stymied by the paucity of possibilities. I could see clearly under the high four-poster bed. It warranted greater attention. The mattress is framed in wood struts to contain and plump the finest quality goose down. The mattress struts rest on four thick wooden slats running crosswise to the bed, which in turn sit on the shelf of the L-shaped side boards. A new idea struck me.

I crawled around to my side of the bed, lit a small candle, and placed it on the floor as close to the bed as I dared without danger of fire. I then returned to his side and, lying on my back, drew myself under the massive structure to inspect its underside. The flickering candlelight proved more than adequate to the task. A thick coat of dust lay everywhere. Everywhere except for the top of the slat closest to the headboard on his side. That spot was clean! I believe I have found the nighttime hiding place of the key to this prison. Oh, what a triumph!

May 9th

He sleeps now upon the bed as I write. Earlier, upon his arrival with this evening's tray, I welcomed him with all my favors, a hearty, highly satisfying measure to ensure the depth of his rest at a level I needed to execute my plan. I might add that the pleasure of the flesh was not entirely his alone. But the strength of my determination, my hatred of my husband surpassed any pleasure.

I have the key safely in my hand now, but my struggle is just beginning. I have planned painstakingly, passionately, yet not beyond the door itself. As I sit here at the table with pen in hand, I find myself with three painful choices. First, I might pass through that door to a new life far away from Marche House. A meaningless freedom without Jacques, without Hubert, and without wealth or position. Second, I might pass through that door to resume my former life of wealth and position here in this house. I fear they would be roles I could hardly sustain by myself, a manager of a household and business altogether estranged from me. And mother of a child who was taught not to love me.

Both these courses of action would bring me a freedom fraught with guilt for sending Cartier to his death. For I must certainly expose his complicity in Jacques's death and my abduction. Indeed, how else could I explain my return? I cannot carry guilt lightly, no matter how justified my actions might be.

A third choice appeals more to me. I can extract my full revenge and take both our miserable lives in the most docile and genteel way. And that, dear diary, is my decision. I shall push the key under the door outside the room where he cannot reach it. Farther even, with the aid of the folded newspaper...

There! It is done now. Irreversibly gone!

May 12th

I have been incapable of writing for several days. When Cartier couldn't find the key, he turned his rage on me. Because his sweetness and promises fell short of sincerity, he thought he could beat the key's whereabouts out of me. Three times so far he has relented just short of my revealing its hiding place. Needless to say, I have taken to hiding this volume, these guarded words, among the dozen or so books on my shelf.

May 13th

Cartier spends every waking hour searching. Tonight he was convinced the key could not have left the room. He stood the chair upon the table, climbed upon it, and slammed my metal-handled hairbrush against the overhead glass and vents. He could force neither dent nor crack in them.

We have only a pitiful amount of food left--a plate of biscuits I saved from several days' trays, a tiny jar of jam, and a few slices of bread. Water continues to flow from the tap in the porcelain sink, but I don't know how long it can continue. The reservoir must be pumped regularly from the cistern. Cartier sleeps lightly now, so I must be more careful.

May 14th

Today he paced the room quickly and frequently as hunger agitated the growing beast within--striking out, sweeping whole surfaces clear of their offending objects, wildly flinging my clothes out of their drawers. I merely put them back afterward. Each day he continues to search, but no longer with any system or reason.

May 15th

Yesterday, Cartier swept the books from my shelf. Suspicion and curiosity gripped him and he stopped to stare at the titles. Only one, this diary, had no title, so he picked it up to read. He read with increasing interest until, at last, it revealed the key's current resting place. He pounded the desk and swore he would retrieve it. His fury came both from desperation and hunger. He tried positioning a candle's light so as to see beneath the door, while lying prone before it, but the obstinate flame always licked higher than useful. He eventually deduced that moving the candle farther from the door permitted some lesser level of illumination under it. A second candle improved his vision further. He smiled at seeing a lone light reflection (presumably a key, *the* key) not yet beyond eye's reach.

I watched him as he stood up to scour the room for a potential tool. I must admit he was patient making this decision. He selected a wooden chair, which he broke into countless pieces by slamming it to the floor and methodically stomping away superfluous sections. One slat of the broken chair back suited his purposes. From it he fashioned a flat hook, and with this tool of his own making, Cartier resumed his prone position in front of the door. As he slid the hook into place, a splinter on the slat caught on the bottom of the door. He swore loudly and worked it loose again. Taking another angle allowed him to get deeper, but when the slat caught the next time, he clumsily pushed it too far and accidentally bumped the key.

"Damnation! I knocked it to the edge," he shouted to me.

Once more I held out hope, hope that he would fail. For the better part of an hour he tried to snare the elusive key, but each approach from behind tilted the key upward, giving him more of a view of the key than he wanted to see.

"It's teetering," he cried.

I bit my lip until it bled.

"Oh, God! It's gone!" he shrieked. "It's gone over the edge."

He threw himself on the floor, prostrate, flinging his arms wildly and kicking his legs. And then, as suddenly as he started, he went quiet. He turned over and leaned against the door, sitting, staring at nothingness. I saw his face grow from desperate to hopeless. The blood drained from his face as the impact of what he had done set in.

Though far from complete at this point, I saw my revenge take hold. I did not revel in it, for I feared what he might still do to me. I could take no pleasure in it because I too would be its victim. May the good Lord forgive me. I helped Cartier back to bed and he fell into a deep sleep, deeper than I can remember.

May 16th

Cartier slept for twenty hours straight. He lay awake for another five hours without speaking and then he slept again. I occupy my own time with reading, actually rereading the books on my shelf. Only a few hard and crumbling biscuits remain. I feel stomach rumblings all the time now and cramps too. I pray we do not suffer too dreadfully. The water flows only weakly from the tap now. Oh, that this ordeal were over. I'm having second thoughts, but it's too late now.

May 17th

Cartier sleeps much of the time. I know he is hurting because I can see tears in his eyes. Still he says nothing.

May 18th
More of the same. It hurts so much.

May 19th
Cartier awoke today sobbing aloud. He threw his head in my lap as I lay reading. It felt like the most natural thing in the world to stroke his uncombed hair. I am angry with myself because I have trouble hating the father of my child. The husband who wrenched my darling Hubert from me.

May 20th
I never know which Cartier will emerge from sleeping: the vengeful tyrant swinging an indiscriminate back of his hand in my direction or the crying man-child in chaotic tantrum. Or the lump in a catatonic state. Whatever feelings of love or lust that existed before have shriveled with his hunger pangs.

May 21st
The biscuits, the bread, the jam are gone. Oh God, oh for a crumb of something, anything. Only a small jar of water remains. I cannot tell whether the pain has lessened or whether I am more used to it. I am weakened. I cannot read for long. My eyes are sleepy all the time. I nap frequently, but not for any duration.

May 25th
Cartier has become weak and quite docile. I permit him to lie in my arms and cry across my breasts. It is becoming an effort to leave the bed for whatever reason.

May 27th
Cartier has not moved in hours. I cannot hear him breathe. I must assume he is dead before me. My pain, in my head and midsection, comes and goes, sometimes raging and sometimes reduced to a consuming ache.

May 29th
I think I shall not have the strength to return to my pen, so I shall say my good-bye here and now. May God forgive me.

"Gawd, it's the saddest thing I've ever heard," Lenora said, sniffling.

Olivia dabbed flowing tears from her cheeks as she set the diary down, open to the last entry. Slowly she closed the book.

Felix broke the spell. "I don't know what all you ladies are blubbering about. It's no different than the soaps you watch."

"You just don't understand, Felix. It's a woman's thing," Rachel told him.

"Well, if it gets any deeper in here, we'll have to pass out life rings," he retorted.

"I'd like to get the rights to Sophia's story," Danielle said. "I'll bet I could turn it into a best-seller."

"Do it as a play and we can use it as a fund-raiser," Olivia added.

"I'd love to play Sophia," Heidi said. "Such a juicy part."

"You'd make a great Jacques, Derrick," said Danielle.

"I don't like the idea of being bumped off in the first act--nipped in the bud," Derrick said.

"That's not the only place you ought to be nipped, Bud," murmured Lenora.

"If it's still open, dibs on the Jacques role," Felix chimed in.

"Naw, you're more the Cartier type. You already know how to whimper," Marti retorted.

"Sophia Marche was quite an interesting woman," said Avi. "I'll venture she was typical of a woman in her position, particularly in her inability to visualize herself as the head of the household."

"Yes," Bucky added. "And it followed naturally that she would have allowed her child to be raised by a nanny."

"Sophia was dependent, but that was only one side of her. She actually had a multifaceted personality. There was a strong masochistic component, but she had a ruthless side to her as well," Avi mused. "On the other hand, she exhibited courage in plotting and executing revenge on her husband. And, of course, she faced the overwhelming moral dilemma of living with herself as a murderer had she chosen to go on living."

"Agreed, Avi, but fortunately for us, she was an exceptionally articulate woman, or we wouldn't have this remarkable journal," Bucky said. "And that's why she strikes me as appealing and strong. A tragic figure in the end, even in her choice of suicide."

"Darling," Lenora said, stroking his arm, "it's the romantic in you. That's why I love you."

"The diary is a wonderful find," Freddie blurted out. "But please excuse me. This whole subject just brings me back to my own problems." She abruptly stood up. Her voice broke. "The funeral's tomorrow--and I don't even know how my son died!" Without another word, she rushed from the room.

CHAPTER 27

FIRST SERVE, NO ACE

Paco's eyes scanned the bustling kitchen in search of Ruby Price. He'd actually come to the inn to question Ace "Sandman" Flowers. Not finding him, the inspector sought out Ruby for his next interview. He spotted her leaning over the adding machine, totaling tips from the dinner shift. Having accumulated $31.45 thus far, she had planned to go across the hall to complete her evening's work in the bar.

Paco tapped her on the shoulder. Her whole body jerked in hair-trigger response.

"Miss Price, I didn't mean to frighten you. I'm Paco LeSoto, a police inspector hereabouts." He spoke in low tones.

"Yes, Inspector, I know who you are." She glanced around to see who else might be listening. No one. The other waitresses and busboys were rushing about, serving the last few Monday night diners and setting up for breakfast.

Paco cupped his hand under Ruby's elbow and steered her to a quiet area behind the pantry shelves. Although she towered over him by several inches, she allowed herself to be guided out of the kitchen's mainstream.

"I wonder if I might have a few minutes of your time," he said. "I have a few questions I'd like to ask you."

"What for? I didn't do nothing."

"Just routine questions."

She eyed him warily. "Am I under arrest?"

"Oh, no, nothing like that at all. I'm investigating the mysterious death of Victor Moskowitz. I merely want to know a little more about your relationship with the deceased, especially your activity last Friday night."

"Look, I didn't have nothing to do with his death. Do you think this is easy for me? I'm miserable. We were friends and lovers . . . No! More than that. We were gonna get married. Well, not soon, but when he got back on his feet, he told me. We talked about it many times. Once he took me to Atlantic City, just for the day. One of those bus trips. You know, they give you a meal chit and ten bucks to use in the casinos? I was real excited. Vic said he was going to get us started. You know, saving so we could get married. He spent the whole day at the slots. He started out great, won $300 in the first half hour. Said he was gonna put it away for us, for our future. I begged him to quit while he was ahead, but he wouldn't listen. Lost it all. It's a good thing we had round trip bus tickets, or we'd have been stuck up there."

Tears filled her eyes, and in a barely audible voice, she added, "But I loved him anyway." She eyed Paco nervously, as if she expected him to say, What's to love about a bum like that? But he didn't. Still, she felt the need to justify herself. "Yeah, I loved him. I guess it was because we did have lots of good times and he kept promising things were gonna get better."

"I'm so sorry, I know you've been through a lot. How often did you . . . were you and Vic together, Miss Price?"

"Two or three nights a week...days, too, sometimes. We'd been seeing each other for a year almost."

"Can you describe what went on Friday night? Why were you waiting outside the Kepple home for so many hours?"

"So you know about that. I live up the street from them, with Myrtle Cosgrove. She's my aunt. Anyway, I gotta pay rent, eighty-two bucks a month or she won't let me stay. I didn't have it this Friday on account of I gave it to Vic as a stake in his poker game Tuesday night. He said he'd give it back to me on Friday. He was gonna bring it to me here, only he never showed up. That's why I went to the house."

"Miss Price, did you see him at all that night?"

"No, sir. I waited outside in the driveway," she said.

"But why didn't you go in?"

"I knew the house belonged to his uncle, and Vic was only visiting for a few weeks. It would've been too embarrassing to ring the bell. There were so many people around. His mother too. I didn't want to make a scene. Vic would've been really mad."

"Why did you finally give up and leave?" Paco asked.

"I thought someone recognized me from the upstairs window. I saw two faces in the window, so I left."

"If you hadn't done anything wrong, why would that matter?"

"I don't know. At the time it just did."

"Can you tell me anything about your boyfriend's gambling debts?" Paco asked.

"Not really. He wouldn't talk about it. He was always betting the pony parlors and he loved the sports long shots. But poker was his real thing. I think he was into the big boys for about fifteen thou," she said.

"The big boys?"

"Yeah! Mitch Brodie in Atlantic City and his S.O.B. collector, Ace Flowers."

"Ah, yes, the Sandman. And what was it he wanted from you that was worth what he did to your face?"

Ruby's hand flew to her bruised cheek as though the shocking pain had returned. "How...how did you know it was Ace that did this?"

"Let's just say I have my sources. But you haven't answered my question yet." Paco was just fishing, but he obtained the right result in spite of it.

"He wanted to know what nights Vic spent with me down at the inn. I didn't believe him when he said he only wanted to talk to Vic. I knew what he had in mind, that no-good bastard."

"So he hit you?"

"A couple a times. Hard, too!" Her hand went back to her face.

"Just when did this beating take place?"

"After work on Friday night. He was in some kind of crazy mood after talking with that foreigner at the bar. Now *him* I liked."

"Foreigner?" Paco asked.

"Yeah! Like an A-rab or an Indian from India. He talked funny too, like a fancy Brit. I overheard 'em talking about some kind of deal. They mentioned something about diamonds and rubies."

"Do you think this foreigner might be a guest at the inn?"

Ruby thought for a minute. "Yeah, I seen him a couple a times in the bar and elevator."

"What did you mean about Flowers being in a crazy mood?"

"Well, he grabbed my wrist when I came out from behind the bar, but I got away from him."

"Is that when he hit you?"

"No, it was later. He waited for me outside in the parking lot. I was going to my car."

"I don't think a scum bully like Flowers should get away with doing something like that. Do you?"

"No, sir, I don't," she said without expecting the obvious next question.

"Then you surely won't mind pressing assault and battery charges against him." Paco had sprung his trap.

"Whoa! Now just you wait a cotton-pickin' minute. I'm not gonna do that."

"Why not?"

"'Cause I don't want any more trouble from that S.O.B."

"When we get through with him he won't be trouble for anyone. If he goes to trial, he'll surely wind up behind bars. If he skips bail back to Jersey, well, he's gone then, and you're off the hook in either case."

"What if he comes after me later?"

"He won't. This isn't his first offense. He's got too much at stake, and I don't think his boss would like the publicity anyway. My guess is he'll jump bail to avoid that publicity. He'll run with his tail between his legs. However, if he's implicated in any way in the death of Victor Moskowitz, I'll keep him off the streets myself."

"Well, if you think I'll be safe, Inspector."

"I do, my dear, I do. Here's my card. Please call me." He patted her shoulder and left the kitchen. On his way through the lobby, Paco stopped at the desk. He presented his badge and card to the clerk and asked: "Do you have a dark-complexioned male guest staying at the inn who might pass for an Arab, an East Indian, or a Pakistani, by any chance?"

"There's a guy in room 223 that might fit that description." The clerk checked the card file. "Yes, Inspector, 223. He's been a guest since last Thursday."

"Do you have a name for this guest?"

"Yes, sir. Ahm, A-H-M," he spelled.

"Dr. T. T. Ahm of Islamabad?" Paco asked.

"No, sir, Mr. Ahmed A. Ahm of Islamabad, Pakistan."

"I see," Paco said. "And would Mr. Ahm be in his room right now?"

The clerk turned away from Paco and ran his fingers along the second row of boxes on the wall. "I would presume so since there is only one key left for 223."

"Thank you!" Paco said. "May I use your phone? Police business."

"Of course, Inspector." The clerk picked up the desk phone and set it on the counter for Paco to use. He picked up the handset and punched in seven digits from memory. He waited five rings for a pickup and greeting.

"Hello, Judge Mann? It's Inspector LeSoto. Yes, Paco LeSoto...Fine, thank you. And you?...Sir, sorry to disturb you so late, but I'd like to obtain emergency search warrants. I have reason to believe that suspects in the Moskowitz death and robbery case may flee the county. I have a witness who overheard one of them discussing the missing property with another suspect. Yes, Your Honor. I'll pick up the paperwork and be there in twenty minutes." Paco put the phone down and hurried out of the lobby.

Fifty-five minutes later, Paco and Frank Mullins stood in front of room 223 at the inn ready to serve Mr. A. A. Ahm with a search warrant. Frank knocked.

"A moment, please." Ahmed was heard zipping up a suitcase. He came to the door. "Who is it? What do you want?"

"It's the police. We would like to speak with you," said Paco.

A short, trimly built man with dark complexion and gold wire-rimmed glasses opened the door. "Good heavens!" he said, seeing the two police badges extended toward him. He stepped back abruptly. "What could the police possibly want of me? I am but a stranger here."

"Is your name Ahm?" Frank asked.

"It surely is."

"We are investigating a murder and robbery here in Black Rain Corners," continued Frank.

"How dreadful," Ahmed said. "And who was the poor soul?"

"Victor Moskowitz," Paco replied, searching Ahmed's eyes for any sign of recognition. He found none and observed that the Pakistani stood straight, dignified, even elegant in his well-tailored beige suit and matching silk tie.

"I'm afraid I don't know that name. Should I?" Ahmed bowed his head slightly, speaking slowly and respectfully of the dead.

"Perhaps," Paco said. "We thought you might. Does the name Ace Flowers mean anything to you?"

Ahmed shook his head. "I have never heard of him either. What is this all about, sir?"

"It's about your whereabouts last Friday afternoon," Frank replied.

"I'm not sure that I recall that," Ahmed said. "I arrived here on Thursday evening. Let's see, Friday afternoon. Made some phone calls, read my book a bit, and then stopped in the lounge for a spot of sherry."

"Could your so-called spot of sherry have taken place between 4:30 and 6:30?" Paco asked.

"Why, I suppose it could have."

"We have knowledge of a certain conversation that took place at the bar during that time. You were overheard as a party to that conversation." Paco removed the warrant from his shirt pocket and handed it to Ahmed. "This court order grants us the right to search your person, your rental car, and this room. If you will be so kind as to empty the contents of your pockets on the bed, please."

"But...but I'm a respectable businessman, here on legitimate business." Nevertheless, Ahmed took the document he had been served and scanned the legal jargon until he comprehended his vulnerable status.

"And just what is that business, Mr. Ahm?" Paco asked.

"I'm a dealer in objects d'art and rare artifacts." Ahmed began to turn his pockets inside out, allowing the contents to spill out onto the bed. "Surely, there's nothing illegal about that."

"Black Rain Corners is a good deal off the beaten path. Why would you have business here? Raise your arms, please." Ahmed stood in the middle of the room with his arms outstretched while Frank gave him a complete pat-down as he felt for the stolen key and a possible weapon.

"I have a client here. I haven't been able to reach her as yet."

"I'll bet you have," Frank said as he finished with Ahmed. He started searching: night tables, dresser drawers, mattress, pillows, closet. And all the while, Ahmed tried hard not to stare at his garment bag hanging on the closet door. His eyes followed Frank's movements like tracking radar until even Paco knew where he should be looking.

"Would you mind revealing who that client might be?" Paco observed his prey, sensing his tension and perhaps his fear.

"A Mrs. Raphael, Olivia Raphael. I think she's...she's the museum curator. My father asked me to call on her, but we haven't spoken as yet. He wishes to acquire a certain artifact from her."

Paco surreptitiously motioned to Frank, waving off the search of the garment bag. Frank backed away, and Ahmed, having no idea why, sighed in tentative relief.

"Would your father be Dr. T. T. Ahm of Islamabad, Pakistan?"

Ahmed's full attention swung sharply toward Paco. "Why yes, Inspector. How on earth did you know that?"

"Let's just say it has come up in my investigation," Paco replied. "But I'm the one asking the questions now. Would that artifact be a gem-encrusted key, perhaps?"

"Yes, sir," Ahmed replied. "It has been described to me as an exquisite diamond and three matching rubies in a fleur-de-lis pattern, apparently a most interesting and historical piece."

"I will now direct Officer Mullins to search your luggage. Is that garment bag your only piece, Mr. Ahm?"

Ahm nodded in silence.

"Before Officer Mullins searches it," Paco continued, "is there anything you'd like to say to me?"

"Such as, sir?" Ahmed avoided Paco's eyes, walked over to the bed, and sat down. Paco noticed tiny beads of sweat forming on Ahmed's forehead.

Frank went directly to the garment bag hanging on the door and, starting at the top, began unzipping the compartments. His hands felt the typical traveler's accoutrements: socks, underwear, shirts, and ties. Working his way down the bag, he unzipped the largest pocket and removed the only thing in it: a mailing tube for a Playboy calendar. He held it up to the light lengthwise and peered through it. "What have we here? Doesn't seem to be a calendar at all. And sure as hell it's not a key. Looks more like a picture rolled up tight."

Ahmed's back arched. "Key?" he asked. "Why would I have the key? I haven't even been to see Mrs. Raphael yet."

"The key was stolen sometime Friday night from the Kepple home," Paco said.

"I don't know anything about that at all, sir," Ahmed protested. He pulled a handkerchief from the articles on the bed and patted his brow as he watched the officer carefully poke the picture out of its cardboard sheath and unroll it. With both hands, Frank held the large canvas out at arm's length.

Paco fairly leaped to Frank's side and stared at the painting. The canvas revealed an idealized three-quarter view of a young aristocratic beauty in subdued flesh tones. An abundance of soft brown ringlets framed her delicate unsmiling face. A low-cut blue gown fell about her statuesque figure in smooth folds.

"Well, I'll be damned and gone to hell!" the inspector exclaimed. "It's not just any picture. It's the John Singer Sargent painting missing from Marche House!"

"You mean that's Mrs. Sophia Marche?" Frank asked.

"Yes, indeed!" Paco could barely conceal his delight. He turned to Ahmed. "Sir, you have more than just a bit of explaining to do. You're under arrest. Cuff him, Frank. And read him his rights!"

"You have the right to remain silent. Anything you say can and will be used against you in a court of law. You have the right to an attorney..." Frank intoned as he brought out the cuffs.

"Now just a moment, sir," Ahmed said, moving out of Frank's reach to the other side of the bed. "Perhaps we can discuss this in a civilized manner. No cuffs will be necessary. Isn't that picture what you were looking for?"

"Not exactly, Mr. Ahm," said Paco. "We came here fishing for an antique key thief and a murderer, and we found an art thief and a different murderer."

Ahmed jumped to his feet. "I assure you I had nothing to do with any murder. I simply paid for the painting. I say again: I am not a murderer, sir! And I didn't know the painting was stolen."

"Frank, cuff him anyway," Paco insisted. Then turning to Ahmed, he said, "I'm willing to discuss this, but only if you come clean with me, Mr. Ahm. How did this painting come into your possession, then?"

"I bought it from a man," Ahmed said, his voice quavering.

"What man?" countered Paco.

"I don't know. Just a man."

"What's his name? What did he look like?"

"I don't know, I don't know. His face was covered. He wore a ski mask and a gray trench coat." Ahmed sat back down on the bed and loosened his tie. He lowered his head and brought his right hand to his forehead.

"Don't give us that crap," Frank said. "The guy wears a ski mask and you didn't know it was stolen property?"

"I...ah..." Ahmed couldn't manage to get any more out.

"Just how much did you pay for the painting?" Frank asked.

"One hundred thousand in a package of two thousand fifty-dollar bills," Ahmed replied.

"When and where did the exchange take place?" Paco asked.

"Last night in my car about 11:40."

"I think, Mr. Ahm, that you are in a great deal of trouble. As a receiver of stolen goods you will undoubtedly forfeit any monies or property in connection with the transaction. Furthermore, you could be deported from this country as an undesirable. Whether and just how much time you spend in a U.S. prison depends a great deal on your cooperation with the authorities. Before Officer Mullins takes you to the station for booking, is there anything else you can tell us about your accomplice?"

"Like what?" Ahmed asked.

"Like where you met him, for instance," Paco answered.

"We met the first time in the lounge on Friday afternoon at the bar."

"You mean Ace Flowers?" Paco said.

"No, no, not him."

Paco raised his left eyebrow. "Not Flowers? Mr. Ahm, you just told me you'd never heard of Ace Flowers. You lied to me. Are you also lying about everything else you've said?"

Ahmed looked alarmed. Beads of sweat glazed his upper lip. "No, sir, not at all, sir. And it wasn't a lie, exactly. I don't really *know* this Flowers person. We exchanged a few words. But he was such a boor. Got rough with the pub miss, too, so I got up and moved to another stool down the bar. I believe it was the other man, sitting on my left, a taller man, blond, with..."

"Yes, with what?" Paco prompted.

"With a blackened finger... no, thumb it was. I thought he must have hit it with a hammer. The nail was all black." Ahmed nodded his head slowly as he pieced together his fragmented recollection. "I saw it when he poured his beer, Michelob Light, I think. That's all I saw."

"A black thumb, hmm." Paco tried to recall where he'd seen a black thumb recently. "How did you arrange the exchange then?"

"We arrange it?...No *he* arranged it that same night from the bar. He sent a note to my room, slipped it under the door. The note told me how we'd work it, but first I had to telephone the bar number twice and hang up after two rings. If I did that, the painting would be sent to my room the next morning rolled up in a tube."

"And just where is this note now?" Paco asked, arching one brow in disbelief.

"Destroyed it. Flushed it down the plumbing in the W.C.," Ahmed said apologetically.

"I see. Continue."

"The note specified that I had until Sunday night to make my decision. At that time he wanted either the painting back or $100,000 for it. I decided on the latter and arranged with a branch of my father's commercial banking house in Baltimore to furnish the money. They sent it down by armed courier. Still in accord with the note, we made the exchange in my car at the rear of the parking lot Sunday night."

"Was there anything unusual about his voice? Any speech mannerisms, perhaps?" Paco was still mulling over the description of the black nail.

"No. He spoke English with your usual Yankee accent. Nothing out of the ordinary. Quite polite, in fact."

Frank looked at Paco. "Is there some significance to this black thumbnail thing, Inspector?"

"Black thumbnail, that's it!" Paco exclaimed.

"That's what?"

Paco thought for a minute. "You know that second John Doe search warrant I got from the judge?"

"You mean the one you got for Flowers?" said Frank.

"Yeah! Except it's not going to be served on Flowers. The judge isn't going to like this, but I'm going to serve it on somebody with a black thumbnail. Thumb dee dum dum!" Paco grinned from ear to ear. "I now know who stole the painting from Marche House."

Frank cocked his head and looked puzzled. "What did you just say?"

"I said I know..."

"No, before that. Something about 'Thumb dee dum dum.'"

"Yes, what about it?"

"Well," Frank said. "Willard Aigue's last words. He kept repeating the word 'dumb,' or at least that's what we thought he was saying."

"We?" Paco asked.

"Yeah. Me and his wife. She thought that's what he was saying, too. But now that you mention it, I think he must have been saying 'thumb.'" Frank became thoughtful for a moment. "In fact, I'm sure of it, Inspector."

"Well, then," Paco said. "In that case, I think I know who stole the painting *and* killed old Willard. In the meantime--now that you've read Mr. Ahm his rights--why don't you drive him over to the county lockup in Edgewater? Let's see...that should take you about twenty minutes. Meet me back here in an hour, in the lobby. Then we'll pay a call on room 210."

CHAPTER 28

SECOND SERVE, DOUBLE FAULT

It took an hour and a half for Frank to return, and now he and Paco paused in front of room 210. Frank rapped sharply on the door, and the dramatic singsong voice of Heidi Hemming responded.

"Whooo is it?"

"Miss Hemming, it's Inspector LeSoto with Officer Mullins. I'd like to speak with you, if I may."

"Of course, Inspector, just give me a moment." Paco expected her to appear in something hastily thrown on. But when the door actually opened, she stood before them in a leopard-print jump suit and large gold hoop earrings. "Won't you come in? How can I help you, Inspector?"

"Hi, Inspector." Derrick Powers sat on the far side of the bed, pulling a tight white T-shirt over his muscular frame. The slogan imprinted across the front read "THE POWERS TO PERFORM." Derrick stood up and finished tucking in his T-shirt.

Frank noted the black thumbnail on the left hand and thought to himself, Right on, Inspector, right on.

"Actually, it's Mr. Powers we wish to speak with," Paco said. Heidi looked disappointed.

"Well, then," Derrick asked, "how can I help you?"

"Were you in the lounge here at the inn last Friday afternoon, say, around 4:45?" Paco asked.

"I'm not quite sure about Friday, but I do occasionally drop in for an evening draft."

"I remember, dear," Heidi said. "We went down to the lounge and watched the Maryland game for a while. I left to dress about five o'clock, I think."

"If you say so," Derrick conceded. "But what does that have to do with the Moskowitz case, Inspector?"

"Did I say it had anything to do with that case, Mr. Powers?"

Derrick looked confused. "I don't understand. Then why are you here?"

Paco ignored Derrick's question to ask one of his own. "Do you know anyone by the name of Flowers? Ace Flowers from New Jersey?"

"No, I don't know anybody by that name from New Jersey or anyplace else." Derrick's tone of impatience came through.

"I see. Then how about a gentleman from Pakistan by the name of Ahm, Mr. Ahmed Ahm? Perhaps you remember him."

"Look here, Inspector. I don't recognize any of those names. Should I? And I don't know what you're hoping to accomplish with all this nonsense." Derrick's eyes narrowed and he began to push and grind his left fist hard into his right palm. He wanted room to pace, but dared not. Instead, he flexed various muscles--pecs, biceps, triceps--while his mind wrestled with Paco's questions.

"Should you?" Paco watched him intently. "Of course you should. Mr. Ahm remembers *you* quite well. He claims you met socially on Friday and even exchanged gifts on Sunday. Sounds to me like a splendid relationship."

"He's lying," Derrick blurted out with a contorted face.

Heidi shrank from the group and found refuge near the sliding doors to the balcony. The soft-spoken smoothness of her handsome playmate had suddenly turned to ugliness, frightening her.

"I think not, Mr. Powers. We have Ahmed Ahm up on charges of receiving stolen property. Property he claims to have received from you for the sum of $100,000."

"He's a damn two-faced liar," cried Derrick. "He doesn't know who the hell I am."

"How can you be so sure of that, Mr. Powers?"

"I...uh...Are you accusing or arresting me?"

"That, I think, will depend on you and what we find." Paco pulled the court order from his pocket and handed it to Derrick. "I think you'll find this search warrant completely in order, sir. Now, if you will take that chair over there by the drapes, Officer Mullins and I will proceed with the actual search."

Frank started in the bathroom and made quick order of it. Paco began with the triple dresser.

Heidi watched the two men cover the room with a neat precision that left no object unexamined and little evidence of anything being disturbed. She couldn't bear the thought of strangers, especially the police, handling her personal things, but felt grateful that they did it in so impersonal a way.

Derrick folded his arms across his chest and watched the two men with a forced sense of disinterest. He tried hard not to let his gaze rest under the corner of his side of the bed. There he had stashed a canvas gym bag crammed with shorts, T-shirts, hand weights, and fifty dollar bills. Instead, his eyes casually followed the men around the room, spending sufficient amounts of time studying the floor and ceiling to satisfy his own air of detachment. Occasionally, his eyes wandered where they should not.

From time to time Paco observed those eye movements and acquired not only a feeling that there was something to be found, but an area of the room in which it would be found. As he searched, he thought about Ahmed Ahm.

How often suspects behaved alike, so naively revealing what they tried so hard to hide.

Paco moved to the nightstand on the hall side of the bed, Heidi's side. He fingered her romance novel and gold watch. He searched through the drawer and then idly, for effect, flipped through the telephone directory and the Gideon Bible. Dropping to one knee he patted the carpet under that area of the bed. He didn't expect to find anything there. As he moved around to the window side, he detected a heightened attention from Derrick, so he became more deliberate in his rummaging through that nightstand drawer.

Paco sensed a relaxing of Derrick's tense muscles when Frank's arm swept under the bed and yielded nothing. Now the inspector flattened himself out on the floor and flipped the bed ruffle up to survey the entire window-lit area under the bed. There in the corner lay a red gym bag with the black-lettered slogan "THE POWERS TO PERFORM." He reached for the bag and grabbed the handles, when he heard Heidi scream.

"No, Derrick, no!"

Paco had already begun to extricate himself from under the bed, when he felt a sharp pain in his calves. The weight of Heidi's body fell across his legs. The bag was wrenched from his right hand. For an eternity of seconds he had no room to maneuver.

Frank had his back to the scene. He was rifling through the drawers of the mirrored dressing table. Upon hearing Heidi scream, he spun around in time to see Derrick slip toward the sliding doors to the balcony, the gym bag in his left hand. Before Frank could unholster his police issue sidearm, Derrick had dropped the bag to the ground and nimbly scaled the balcony railing in a single bound. He disappeared to the floor below. Frank rushed to the balcony with his revolver out.

Derrick had chosen the unobstructed path toward his car in the parking lot, instead of the cover of the nearby woods. But he sprinted with the determination of a competition to be won.

Steadying his shooting arm with his left hand, Frank fired twice. The first shot was intentionally high. The second struck the tarred pavement all too close to Derrick. He hesitated in fright. Frank stood rigid, poised to fire another shot if necessary. "Freeze!" he bellowed, "or I'll take you down at the knees. Stay where you are! Don't move a muscle!"

On the pavement below, Derrick still struggled with the temptation to escape. Paco took the pistol from Frank and took his own bead on the fugitive, while Frank eased himself over the balcony and dropped to the ground. He caught up with Derrick and quickly cuffed him while canting the Miranda spiel. A crowd began to gather, so Frank scooped up the gym bag and ushered Derrick back to his room with a vicelike grip on his elbow.

"How did you know I took that money, Inspector?"

"We recognized your black thumbnail," Frank interjected.

"Black thumbnail? I slammed my thumb between two barbells. What's that got to do with anything?"

"Old Willard identified his killer by pointing out your thumb," Frank said.

"That's a lie. I never killed anybody."

Heidi quickly came to his defense. "No, he's telling the truth, Inspector. I saw him. Better yet, I heard him yell when he tried to grab the falling barbell."

Paco took the bag from Frank, unzipped it, and rummaged for the missing $100,000. He soon found loose fifties, but no more than $2,500 worth. "Where's the rest, Mr. Powers? Where's the $100,000 Ahm gave you?"

"I don't know what you're talking about," Derrick replied. "I told you I don't know anybody by the name of Ahm."

"Then where'd you get this money from?" Paco asked.

Derrick looked over at Heidi with a sheepish expression. "From her purse. I borrowed it from her purse. I was gonna pay it back. Honest, hon."

Heidi's face transposed from fright to anger as easily as a seasoned actress switches from comedy to tragedy. She groped for her purse, fumbled it open to the cash compartment, and slowly made eye contact once more. She stared at Derrick for some time, shaking her head. "You're nothing but a common thief, a low-life scum of the earth." Her face had a tragic twist. "All you had to do was ask."

"I didn't take it all, hon," he protested. "And I would have paid you back."

"Don't hon me!" she lashed out. "You left me $300. Should I thank you for that? Inspector, get that leech out of my sight before you have another murder on your hands."

"Will you be wanting to press charges, Miss Hemming?" Paco asked, the $2,500 still in his hands.

Heidi released a great sigh and shook her head. "No, just dispose of the garbage that he is. He isn't worth the trouble to prosecute, and I sure can't stand that kind of publicity."

"Since this money is no longer evidence, I believe you'll find better use for it." Paco handed the fistful of bills to Heidi. "Why would you be carrying that much cash in your purse?"

"I had planned to buy one of Lenora's paintings." She tore off the top two fifties. "This is for bus fare. Be sure he's on the next one out of town."

"Yes, ma'am," Frank said, taking off the cuffs. He took the two bills and passed them to Derrick. "We'll drive him up to Annapolis...or just maybe we'll charge him with resisting arrest."

"But what about my stuff, my clothes and things?" Derrick whined.

Paco slammed the gym bag into Derrick's gut, and Frank lifted his Val-Pack from the clothes rail. He shoved Derrick out the door and down the hall toward the elevator.

Her adrenaline spent, Heidi's body collapsed in on itself. She crouched, childlike, trembling in the corner.

"It's all over. You'll be okay," Paco said gently. "Wait here, I'll be right back with someone to stay with you."

He returned with the Worthingtons. Lenora wrapped her arms around a still shivering Heidi, and Bucky approached them a few feet away holding up a short white robe. "Is this the one you wanted, Lenora?"

Lenora nodded. To Heidi she said, "It'll keep you warm when you most need it. I know because you lent it to me the other night. I meant to return it earlier."

Heidi gratefully slipped the thick robe over her jump suit. She quickly kissed Lenora and sought the comfort of her friend's embrace once more.

"Why do I always pick losers?" Heidi asked, sobbing. "They're always looking for the free ride, but this is the first one who was an out-and-out thief."

Bucky said, "You couldn't possibly have known Derrick was a crook."

"He victimized you, Heidi," Lenora said. Heidi nodded.

"And maybe..." Bucky added, "maybe you should look a little beyond the surface of your young men. Be a little less the actress and a little more the real Helga Marche you were trying to escape. And there's no professional fee associated with that advice. I usually charge a hundred fifty dollars an hour."

Heidi smiled in spite of her tears.

Out in the car Paco took the driver's seat. Frank and Derrick sat in back for the twenty-minute drive to the county police station. Paco intended to use the resisting arrest charge to hold Derrick as a material witness in connection with the murder and theft.

Frank said, "You don't know how lucky you are, Powers. That's one generous lady you messed around with. You got anything to say for yourself?"

"Yeah. I don't know what all this is about--the black thumb business. But I'm not the only one who's got one."

"Who else?" Frank asked.

"What's it worth to you?" probed Derrick.

"Well," Paco said, "if it leads to a conviction, we'll drop all charges, including resisting arrest."

Derrick thought for a minute. "Let me have your pad and a pencil, Sergeant." He wrote a name on a clean page, tore it off, and after folding it twice, passed it up to Paco in the front seat.

"Frank?" Paco asked. "Which thumb did he nick? Right or left?"

Frank studied Derrick's cuffed hands. "It's the left thumb, sir."

"You know, Frank, Mr. Powers has a point there. Remember the museum? That bedroom door opened inward from left to right. Try to imagine your left thumb getting caught in the door."

Frank went through a series of contortions with both wrists before admitting, "I see what you mean."

"You're quick, Frank. You'll make your gold shield one day."

"I suppose we do have some unfinished business, sir," Frank said.

Paco nodded. "There's more to put to rest than Victor, my good man."

CHAPTER 29

MOLLYFIED

Tuesday, October 28, 1980

The midmorning October sun severed the overcast sky and penetrated the cluster of fir trees on the hallowed ground of Mount Nemo Cemetery. Then dark clouds closed ranks and unleashed a cold drizzle. The family huddled together, waiting, seated in folding chairs beneath the green canopy erected over the gravesite. Their heads turned to follow the long black hearse as it emerged from the wrought iron entrance gate at the high ground and wound its way slowly and silently down the drive toward them.

So absorbed were they in the hearse's progress that they failed to notice the young woman partially hidden by the fir trees on the hill beyond. She wore a clear plastic raincoat with matching babushka and hugged her body against the raw chill.

“Miss Price?"

She wheeled around. "Inspector!"

"I didn't mean to frighten you,” Paco whispered, stepping closer to her.

"You did a little, but I'm glad it's you. I get the feeling Ace is everywhere watching me."

"Miss Price, I just wanted you to know that I have a bench warrant and bulletin out to apprehend Flowers. We tried to pick him up in his room at the inn, but he hasn't shown up there since yesterday morning. We'll get him, though. You can rest assured."

"Thank you, Inspector, but I can't rest until you put him where he belongs."

"He may have already left the state." Paco thought for a moment before speaking again. "In a way I hope he hasn't. I'd like to nail that S.O.B. for much more than assaulting and harassing you. However, your testimony will put him out of commission for some time."

"I hope I won't have to testify. I hope he's gone and good riddance," she said.

"Can I offer you a ride home from the funeral?"

"No thanks, Inspector, I've got my own car. 'Preciate it, though."

A commanding voice drew their attention to the gravesite, and Paco walked toward the gathering to listen. With the coffin finally in place resting on straps above the deep, gaping hole where it would reside, the funeral began. The family's rabbi said a few prayers. Avi delivered a short eulogy focusing on Victor's potential as a young man. Paths he had taken that had hurt his future. How, in his middle age, he'd tried to stabilize his life--the pity being that he died before he had a chance to do it.

Freddie peeked over the man-sized hanky covering her red nose and damp cheeks to see who was attending. One could hardly call them mourners; there wasn't a teary eye among them. The Historical Society members and a handful of Freddie's and Avi's friends had come out of respect for them. Then she stirred in surprise, cupping her hand over her mouth as though she didn't believe what or who she saw. Rachel, sitting next to her, leaned close to hear what her aunt had to say. Rachel turned too, craning her neck. She nodded several times and then turned to exchange a few words with her husband.

"Where...?" Simon asked. "I see her now. The woman kind of hiding near those trees."

"Dear, please go get her and bring her here," Rachel pleaded. "Now! Please! I'll explain later. And take the umbrella."

As he approached, the woman shied backward a few steps. He called to her. "Is your name Ruby Price?"

Although startled by hearing her name, Ruby responded, "Yes."

"My Aunt Freddie, Mrs. Moskowitz, would like you to join her under the canopy."

"Oh, no, I couldn't do that."

"My aunt said to tell you it would please her greatly if you did."

Ruby relented, nodding her head several times, and reluctantly followed Simon, who held his umbrella for her and allowed himself to get wet. As she took the chair next to his under the canopy, Ruby perceived a momentary look of satisfaction on the kindly old woman's face two chairs away. Three psalms were read, one in Hebrew and two in English. The last one she recognized as the twenty-third.

"And I shall dwell in the house of the Lord forever."

Victor was laid to rest in a simple polished wood casket with no metal trim. Three men spaded mud over it into the grave. The short service ended with the solemn mourners' Kaddish and its chorused "Amen."

Freddie sat longer than the others, and when she finally rose to her feet with Avi's aid, she faced Ruby and stared at her for a few moments, scrutinizing her face. "It is only right and fitting that you, who loved my son, be close to him now, too. We're inviting everyone back to our house for a late lunch. Please join us."

"Oh, no, I couldn't, I mean I shouldn't."

"Of course, you should," Freddie said. "I would be hurt if you didn't."

"Well, okay, thank you. Maybe I can help out in the kitchen."

Freddie understood. It was Ruby's only way to justify being included. "If you wish. Molly, our housekeeper, may very well need you." She grasped Ruby's hand warmly in both of her own. "Thank you, my dear. We're going to stay here for a bit. We'll see you at home."

Ruby nodded, too choked with tears to talk, and wove her way out of the line of folding chairs, through the soggy grass, back to her car. As she tried to coax the aging motor into starting, a slow-moving object caught the corner of her eye: a gray Toyota disappearing behind the fir trees. A chill tremored through her body. She'd seen that car before. But where? As if it understood her sudden fear and need, her engine caught and hummed. The windshield wipers worked double time to keep the road in view. Ruby quickly rounded the bend to the cemetery exit and surged forward. She had to get to the Kepple house.

Molly was laying a lace-trimmed linen cloth on the dining room table when she heard a timid knock at the back door. Expecting Schlem with the deli trays, she was startled to see an anxious-looking young woman.

"Miss Molly? I'm Ruby Price. I, uh, was Victor's girlfriend and, uh, I've just come from the funeral. Miz Moskowitz invited me back here for lunch. I'd, um, be glad to help if you need me. I wait tables at the inn and I'm real good at my job."

"If Miss Freddie invited you, you're sure welcome, yes ma'am. So sorry. I mean about Victor 'n all." As Molly pulled back the screen door, Shana squeezed her furry body with its eagerly wagging tail between the two women. The waitress became the dog's instant friend, and thus won Molly's immediate approval. Ruby giggled and bent down to pet Shana's head. As she straightened up, her thick hair fell away from her face.

"Some pretty bad bruises you got there, Ruby. Looks like somebody picked a mean fight with you."

Ruby nodded and lowered her eyes. "It's a long story," she murmured, peeling off her plastic rain gear.

"I got time," Molly replied. "A minute or two, anyway, until I get ambusheled by the crowd. You can hang that wet coat of yours on them hooks there."

Molly lumbered over to the stove and carefully lifted the lid of the twenty-quart pot. Ducking her head slightly to avoid the rush of steam, she peeked in to check the chicken soup. Yep, she thought, the matzoh balls were ready, just the way Rachel and the doctor liked 'em. She reduced the heat to just below simmer. "Wanna help me make a hot crab dip?" she asked. Molly selected a can of Old Bay Seasoning from the jumbled array of spices in the cabinet.

"Glad to," Ruby said. "They make it all the time at the inn. It's on the 'For

Starters' menu." She began gently sprinkling the hot red-orange spice into a bowl of crab meat and mayonnaise. "Um...the guy who did this to me...he's a mob guy. He was trying to collect on Vic's gambling debt. Thought if he roughed me up, he'd get Vic to pay up."

Molly's watery blue eyes turned to slits and her brow furrowed. "I bet he's that nasty, unrespectful guy who kept calling here." She looked up as she heard a sharp knock at the back door. "That must be Schlem with the trays," she said, wiping her hands on her already grimy apron. But she never got to the door; it had been left ajar when Ruby came in.

Suddenly, a hulking figure with deep-set raccoon eyes filled the narrow back hall. Ruby shrieked, "It's him!"

"I'll teach you to go squealin' to the police!" Ace Flowers shouted, his fist raised. "You think you were hurtin' before? You ain't seen nuthin' yet!"

His unshaven face contorted as he lunged toward Ruby. But in his frenzy, Ace neglected to see the large dog dish on the kitchen floor. His right foot stepped into the plastic bowl, mashing the treat Molly had just spooned into it. The dish slid to his right, pulling his leg out from under him, straining the groin muscle to its limit. "Aww, Damn!" he roared as he tried to regain his balance.

Shana rushed forward, barking thunderously. Her beloved brisket and gravied mashed potatoes squirted out on all sides. Startled by her charging bulk, Ace fell backward, straight into Shana's water bowl. "What the hell is this?" he yelled.

Ruby stood frozen at the counter. But Molly, her moon face cold and determined, marched to the stove. She threw the cover off the soup pot; it clanged to the floor. "Help me, girl," she shouted. Ruby understood. Together they lifted the heavy pot by its handles. Barely avoiding getting burned, they heaved it in perfect rhythm in Ace's direction as he struggled to his feet.

"Aaaahhhh!" he screamed. Scalding chicken soup doused him. Matzoh balls--huge, fluffy, and scorching--pelted his balding head, his thick neck, and face. Ace's arms and legs flailed as steam from the hot soup rose from his black jacket and trousers. He tried to pull himself to his feet for another assault. But this time Ruby was ready. She grabbed the tall metal can on the counter and vigorously emptied the entire contents of Old Bay into Ace's contorted face, most particularly in the direction of his eyes. The stinging spice hit right on the mark.

"Aaaahhhh!" he screamed again, desperately rubbing his eyes with his fists. He flipped himself over and crawled into the hall, then dragged himself to his feet and bolted out the open door.

The women held their breath. Not until Molly heard his car pull out of the driveway did she tiptoe her way through the soup-slopped floor to lock the back door. When she returned to the kitchen, Ruby leaned over and hugged her fiercely. Molly hugged her back without a word. Shana sniffed a matzoh ball, but backed away when her nose touched the heat of it, so she contented herself with slurping up the remains of her brisket and gravy.

But abruptly the retriever raised her head, and her ears perked skyward. She lifted a paw. Her tail stood stiffly out as she listened, alerting the two women. They heard shrill sounds of tires screeching and skidding. A deafening collision. Metal crunching, reverberating. Then silence.

Minutes later, Molly heard the bustle of the returning family. She waddled up the front hall, chicken soup tracks denting the carpet, and threw her short flabby arms around Freddie. "I wanted to be there," she said, "but there was so much to do here."

Freddie smiled weakly, but slid out from the embrace. "There's been an accident right down the street. I have to call an ambulance," she said as she rushed to the phone in the den.

"It looked like quite a bad one. A car hit a tree," Avi said, coming in the door after her. "As if we haven't had enough trauma for one day. And in just a couple hours we'll have a houseful of people here. Are we ready for them, Molly?"

"Yes...and no, Doctor. Maybe you better come in the kitchen. But watch your stepping. It's slickery in there."

"Hello, Ruby," Avi said as he pushed through the swinging door to the kitchen. "Oh, my God!" he exclaimed. Despite Molly's warning, he slid a few inches along the soupy floor. "You must've had a problem in here."

"I'm so sorry, Doctor," Ruby all but whispered. "It was that Ace Flowers guy."

"He dared come here?"

"Yeah. He came looking for me, and we threw the pot of soup at him."

"Oh, my, what an ordeal!" Avi noticed that Ruby had traded in her cocktail waitress image, at least for that day. Her simple white blouse and calf-length gray skirt gave her a sedate, almost virginal look. "Where is Ace now?" he asked.

"He ran out. We heard him drive away."

"Thank God for that. But how frightening, and how brave of you two. I'd better put in a call to the inspector. He'll want to pick up Flowers right away. And, of course, get all the details from you. Come to think of it, he's due here soon, anyway. He's bringing the autopsy report."

A knock at the back door. "It's Schlem," Molly called to Avi. "He's here with the trays of cold cuts and the auxiliaries to go with them."

"No charges," Schlem said, when Molly looked for the bill to sign. He waved and climbed back into his car. "Big mess at the bottom of the lane," he added.

"Molly, are you all right?" Avi asked.

"I'll be fine, Doctor. Ruby's going to help me mop up. And Shanie's licking up. Aren't you, girl? We'll have to make do without the matzoh ball soup, though."

"No matter, it went for a good cause. You're a brave lady, Molly."

"She is," said Ruby. "If it wasn't for her I'd be a dead duck by now." The young woman began sobbing. "I'm so sorry. I made so much trouble here."

"It wasn't your fault at all, my dear. You're both safe. That's the important thing," Avi said.

Twenty minutes passed. Sirens screeched in the distance, grew louder, and whined to a stop as emergency vehicles reached the accident scene down Locust Lane. For the next hour the house remained strangely quiet. The family retired to their rooms to change into more casual wear and to take advantage of the time to rest.

Molly arranged the trays and trimmings in the dining room and left Ruby at the kitchen table with a cup of tea. "You need recoverating, young lady," Molly told her.

But the housekeeper herself had too much time on her hands. She inspected the table and buffet again and again, rearranging and adjusting by whim. In the sunroom she surveyed the rich autumn hues of the condolence bouquets sent there that morning: a bountiful indoor garden enhanced by fresh sunlight and a brightening sky.

The gloomy rain was over and done for now. And when none of the arrangements could be improved upon, Molly's impatience turned to her watering pitcher. She made her way through the house, serving her green prodigies one by one, and wound up in the sunroom, tending last of all to Mrs. Meadows' cactus. Empty pitcher in hand, she left the room. The spider plant dripped water directly on the floor in quick repetitions. The pepperomia pooled about its overflow plate, and a ring of wetness appeared on the rug beside a gurgling philodendron.

"Ahem!"

"Oh, excuse me, Doctor. I didn't see you suspended there behind me."

"I think someone's out front, Molly. It may be the inspector."

The doorbell chimed just then and as she opened the front door, she turned back to Avi. "How'd you know it was him? Is that a part of being mental, too?"

Avi grinned and shrugged. "Ah, Inspector. Good to see you. Let Molly take your coat."

"Good afternoon, Doctor." Paco pulled a large envelope from the side pocket before handing over his camel hair coat.

Molly hung it on the spindled clothes tree beside the door, lingering a moment to enjoy his spiffy outfit: gold turtleneck, blue blazer with brass buttons, and gray flannels. She headed back to the sunroom to set out more chairs for the funeral guests.

"I believe congratulations are in order, Inspector. I read in this morning's paper about the recovery of the Sargent painting," Avi said.

"Why, thank you, Doctor. I would have been here earlier, but I had to drop my sergeant off at the accident scene. Nasty business. A Toyota wrapped itself around that big locust tree at the end of the road."

"Anybody hurt?" Avi asked.

"The driver, but they took him away before I got there. Badly mangled, don't know much more. But I do have some news here." Paco held up the large brown envelope.

"I'm sure you do. I've been waiting for it."

CHAPTER 30

DEJA VU

"The autopsy report, Doctor."

Avi took the envelope from Paco, and just as he started to slide the sheets out, the doorbell chimed.

"Would you get the front door, Molly? Our guests are beginning to arrive."

As soon as Avi turned his attention back to the envelope, the telephone beckoned its turn. He answered in the den and called out to Paco. "It's for you, Inspector. It's your office. They said it's urgent."

He waited until Paco took the phone from him and then walked out into the hall, where he encountered the Lords. Danielle gave him a hug, Ernie a handshake. Both wore solemn expressions. Molly escorted them to the sunroom.

"Miss Freddie's inexposed," Molly said. "Can I get you something while you wait?"

The Lords were about to sit down on the sectional sofa. A puzzled look appeared on Ernie's face. The cactus seemed to be making a statement--gurgling sounds. And then:

"Shissh...blatt...plotzzz...kaplop!"

"Oh, no! My, oh, my!" Molly squealed. The Lords stared at each other in dismay.

Avi raced to the sunroom. There he found the housekeeper seated on the ottoman, her bottom mushroomed over its entirety, her chubby hands covering her face. The walls, the windows, the carpet, the cocktail table--all were plastered with both wet and dry fragments of tough, thorny green fiber. Cactus fiber, thrust from a gaping fault in the trunk. The noble desert plant had exploded. A huge clear puddle had formed at its base.

At first, the shocked grimace on Molly's face seemed cast in stone, and then it slowly melted. When she had gathered sufficient courage to face her employer's stern expression, the two of them broke down and laughed.

"I guess I don't have to restate the obvious, Molly," Avi said, shaking his head. He extended a hand to help her up and she took it, but it was only with Ernie's help that the two men got her to her feet.

Avi hurried to answer another chiming of the front door, and Ernie knelt down to assist Molly in cleaning up. They cautiously gathered up the thorny bits and dropped them into a large glass ashtray. Then Molly left to get a dustpan and whiskbroom, leaving Ernie at the base of the plant. When she returned, he'd taken a seat on the sofa next to Danielle. Molly began brushing debris into the pan at the farthest wall and worked her way back toward the trunk of the cactus.

Paco appeared in the doorway just as Molly paused and frowned.

"What in carnation...Hey, Paco, look at this. It's already been debased," she said. Her gaze was fixed on a shiny slash in the cactus trunk, horseshoe shaped and about five inches high.

Paco knelt down for a closer look. "My dear Molly, you're right. It's almost as if surgery has been performed and epoxy used instead of sutures."

"What a mess," Avi said, reappearing in the room, this time with Frank Mullins. He groaned. "This has been quite a day, Inspector. And you don't even know the half of it. Ace barged his way in here when we were at the funeral. But Molly will have to tell you more about that later."

From his kneeling position, Paco addressed Avi. "I figured as much. Doctor, I have more news for you than I expected when I arrived here. Of course, there's the autopsy report. I don't suppose you've had a chance to read it yet. For all intents and purposes, your nephew died of a heart attack. But with kidney complications, the type that could easily have been caused by a severe beating. Ace's assault on Victor's body could have precipitated the heart attack. The Valium and brandy combination couldn't have helped either."

Molly gasped, her round eyes wide. "My, oh, my! That Flowers weed better get caught. Maybe you can send a sweat team after 'im."

"That won't be necessary," Paco said. "That's what the last phone call was all about. The accident down the road? Actually, it was Flowers' car you saw wrapped around that tree. You say he came here? Apparently, he took the turn out of Locust Lane at too high a speed. He skidded on the wet pavement, lost control of his car, and hit that tree at the bottom of the hill. But there's more. They transported him to the hospital, and my office has just informed me that he died of head wounds he received in the collision."

Paco paused, then continued with a wry smile. "We'll all breathe easier now. And he sure has saved the state a pile of money. An odd thing, though. The hospital said his clothes were wet and his face was partially covered with a reddish-orange powder. They haven't been able to identify it, but the nurse said it smelled something like Old Bay."

Molly gasped again. "Oh, my! Well, you know what they say. Live like a crab, die like a crab cake. Wait till I tell Ruby."

"She's here?" Both of Paco's eyebrows shot north.

"Yup, in the kitchen. Been helping me. Miss Freddie invited her to lunch. And what a help she's been already. You just can't imagine. We circumsized a real disaster."

It was one of the rare moments in Paco's long career that rendered him totally speechless. He understood there was more, much more. But he decided to remain silent for now to pursue his most pressing business. He knelt before the cactus once again while Avi studied the coroner's report.

"What's this about green plant material under Vic's fingernails?" Avi asked.

"I think I'll be able to answer that question shortly," Paco said. With his penknife he sliced smartly through the fleshy fibers of the remains of the cactus trunk. First he traced the perimeter of the healed wound that Molly had discovered in the tough exterior. Next, he cut directly into it. The penknife pinged. Now it had struck an even harder surface. He continued to cut, deeper and deeper, around an object that finally gave itself up to him.

"What the...?" He looked up at Avi and then lapsed into a silence almost crushing in its weight.

"I thought," Paco said slowly, "that I might find your jeweled key in there." Instead, he held up a glittering two-carat diamond, the principal stone from the key, and rolled it around in his fingers. None the worse for wear from its botanical hiding place, the diamond sparkled in the sunbeams that poured through the French doors. "It must have come loose. Of course... there's a cavity in here large enough to have concealed the entire key."

Avi's voice trembled with exasperation. "What the devil's going on? If the key's been in there all this time, where is it now?"

Paco rose to his feet and turned to Molly. "The cavity extends downward toward the exposed rupture wound. When you went for the cleaning tools, did you by any chance leave Dr. and Mrs. Lord alone in this room?"

"Yes, sireee," she replied. "The Mister, he was helping me clean this mess up."

"Inspector LeSoto," protested Ernie. "I don't like the implication. Are you accusing me of having anything to do with the theft?"

"Not exactly, Dr. Lord," Paco answered. "But then you won't mind my clearing this matter up quickly." He took out a folded warrant and served it to Ernie. "This is an official court order permitting the search of your persons, your car, and your hotel room."

"Persons?" Danielle asked. "You mean you want to search me as well?"

"Why, yes, Mrs. Lord," answered Paco. "Why should your husband have all the fun? First you, Dr. Lord. Please place the contents of your pockets on the coffee table in front of you."

Pen, pencil, glasses, key ring, and change all appeared from various pockets. A neatly folded white handkerchief appeared last.

"Frank," Paco instructed, "take the keys and search their car while I continue here." Frank picked up the keys and strode out to the driveway. Paco picked up the mechanical pencil from the table in a gloved hand. With the eraser end, he carefully poked at the handkerchief. It appeared to him to occupy suspiciously more bulk than would be normal. Deftly, he flipped it open. There, on the folds of the white linen, lay the missing jeweled key. A large hole gaped where the diamond had been dislodged.

"My key! Thank God!" Avi exclaimed.

"Dr. Lord, the charge is not theft, but grand theft," Paco said. But before beginning the arrest procedure, Paco whispered something to Molly, and she disappeared from the room.

As Paco finished reading Ernie his Miranda rights, Frank returned carrying a black satin traveling case. "It's all here, sir, the whole take."

"Mrs. Lord?" Paco addressed Danielle. "Would you empty your pockets now, please?"

"I have no pockets, Inspector," she snapped. "Or are you blind?"

"You've got me there, ma'am," he said with just the hint of a smile as he eyed her clinging knit crimson dress. "Then you won't mind extending your right hand, ma'am?"

"I don't understand," she said, but hesitantly held out her right hand. "This is an invasion of privacy, Inspector, and I'll have your hide for it."

Paco ignored her, and as he grasped her hand firmly, Molly reappeared with a cotton ball saturated in nail polish remover. Molly took hold of Danielle's right thumb and rubbed it vigorously until all sign of the gleaming red polish disappeared. The thumbnail retained a dull bluish hue.

"Oh, for God's sake. Now look what you've done!" Danielle said angrily. "You've bruised my thumb."

"I think not, Mrs. Lord," said Paco. "You sustained that bruise when Willard Aigue squashed it in the doorway at Marche House. In addition to charging you with grand theft--the theft of the Sargent painting--I'm charging you with Aigue's death as well....You have the right to remain silent..."

Danielle jerked her hand back, and with surprising strength, shoved Molly's rotund frame in front of Paco. Then, with the agility of a cat, she spun around and grabbed her suede purse. From it she quickly palmed a chrome-plated .32 caliber revolver and pointed it at Paco.

"All of you," she said, motioning with the gun, "get over there by the table. Put your hands over your heads where I can see them. Ernie, collect our things."

Despite the heat of the moment, the tension, the danger, Paco was intensely aware of Danielle's cool, methodical demeanor. He couldn't help but be impressed.

Ernie scooped up the contents of his pockets from the table and stuffed them into the black traveling case. But the jeweled key he treated with respect. Gently, he rewrapped it in his linen handkerchief and tucked it into the breast pocket of his jacket. Then, emboldened by his wife's orchestration of this moment, he pulled back Frank's jacket and lifted the service revolver from its holster.

"Nicely done, Ernie," Danielle said. "I didn't think you had it in you." A broad smile beamed from her perfect white teeth. Triumphant sparks flashed from two intense eyes.

Paco took a calculated risk and began speaking softly: "Mr. and Mrs. Lord, you know you can't get away with this."

"Oh, but we can--and you know it," she countered, her breathing quickening. "A piece of cake in this two-bit burg."

"You're enjoying this, aren't you, Danielle?" The mellow voice came from Avi.

Freddie appeared in the doorway.

"Over there with the rest of them, Freddie," Danielle barked.

"Oh, Danielle, why?" Freddie asked, even as she slowly moved to join the others. "You're a wonderful author. That last book was so good. I loved your characters. So exciting, so real. You didn't have to stoop to..."

"My characters *are* exciting," Danielle answered. "But living through them, vicariously, I'm fed up with it. What about me? I want to live on the edge, know what it's like to have red blood rush through *my* veins. You better damn well believe I'm enjoying this."

"It's not all fun and games, Danielle. There'll be a downside to all this," Avi said. "I don't think you'll be able to handle the guilt. I'm sure you don't want to hurt anybody. Do you?" He slowly reached forward for the gun.

"Get back!" she shouted. Avi retreated. She startled him, waving the gun precariously back and forth in front of them. "I'll use this if I have to. I know what I'm doing. We planned everything."

Paco acted as if she hadn't spoken. "I've checked up on you, Mrs. Lord. Your athletic skill is fairly well known in these parts. It stretches no credibility that you scaled the wall to the mansion. But surely you weren't naive enough to think you could fence a Sargent."

"Ernie already has, and very cleverly," she said.

"He's not as clever as you think. We've already recovered it. But, tell me: why did you have to kill the old man? He couldn't have been a threat to you. He wasn't armed."

Danielle's high cheekbones reddened. Her green eyes narrowed. "That was an accident. I had no intention of killing him. I merely made a move toward him, and he fell backward over the railing."

Paco continued in his low, quiet tone. "But surely you don't think you can fence the jeweled key? Every police department in the country has already been notified about it." Before she could respond, he turned to address Ernie.

"Dr. Lord, why would you want to get involved in a scheme like this? You're a respected professional." But Paco didn't really need an answer. He suspected that Ernie had reached a desperate point in his marriage. Needed to prove to his wife that he still had the balls to be her husband. Even if the scheme meant consorting with a weakling boozer like Victor Moskowitz.

Ernie had lost patience with this goading. "Everyone, stay where you are!" he shouted. His hand shook as he waved Frank's heavy revolver back and forth at each of them. "I'll shoot the first person who comes after us!" He and Danielle backed their way down the hall to the front door.

Nobody dared move until the front door slammed shut. Then the two officers of the law dashed down the hall and out the door. A second slam.

"The crazy fools," said Molly, her watery blue eyes calm. "Them Lords ain't got a prayer. Not with Paco and Frank after 'em."

"Black Rain Two, this is county dispatch. Roger your APB on armed fugitives and acknowledge your hot pursuit of Danielle and Ernest Lord. Units in vicinity of Gander Pointe Inn. Setting up roadblock now."

"Ten-four, dispatch," Paco said into the mike. "I see the block ahead."

"They've turned into the inn," Frank said. "They're running into the lobby." He pulled the police cruiser into the lot and blocked the Lords' abandoned Buick Regal with his vehicle.

"The Lords have entered the inn via the lobby," Paco continued into the mike as Frank fetched a rifle and shotgun from the trunk. "Have your officers move in and cover the rear entrance, both staircases. Caution, they're armed and dangerous."

"That's a ten-four, Black Rain Two."

They entered the lobby just in time to see the elevator doors close on the fleeing couple. Frank dashed up the front staircase while Paco waited for the elevator. Frank emerged through the fire door on the second floor in time to see Danielle unlocking the door to their room. Ernie spotted him and fired a shot in his general direction. The bullet grazed the left wall. Frank ducked back into the fire stairs to wait. He pulled the tactical radio from his belt and requested that the two county officers proceed with caution to the second floor. He peeked into the hall again. It was clear, except for Paco emerging from the elevator. "Take cover till we get backup," he whispered. Police sirens whined in the distance.

When the four officers had grouped up, they converged on the Lords' room from two sides, weapons at the ready. The halls were silent. Suddenly, three shots pierced the silence. The officers flattened themselves against the wall. Paco noted that the door had not splintered from the shots.

Frank saw a cleaning cart on the other side of the staircase. A frightened woman's face poked out from a doorway just beyond. He caught the maid's attention and demonstrated the motions of turning a key. She held up her set of master keys and ducked out of sight once more. While Frank fetched the keys from her, Paco tried the door.

"Police! Open up! Throw your weapons on the floor. Put your hands on your heads and back away from the door. Do it and you won't get hurt!"

The silence that followed stretched into minutes. Frank returned with a tall dresser mirror and leaned it up against the door directly across the hall. There it would provide an excellent view of the Lords' room once the door was opened. He handed the passkeys to Paco, who selected the key marked MASTER and turned it in the lock. From one side of the jamb Paco pushed the door slightly ajar to see if it elicited any action on the part of the room's occupants. It didn't. The nerve-racking quiet continued. Paco moved back beyond the jamb again. He kicked at the door. It swung wide, crashing against the wall.

All eyes jumped to the propped-up mirror. They saw a straight narrow path through the room. A chair beside the dresser held the black satin traveling case. The drapes were drawn. The room was dark.

The two armed backup officers moved in first, in near-perfect tandem, slowly, their guns out in front of them. One swung right to face the bathroom's open door. Nothing there. Frank slipped in behind him to check the shower and waited there. Paco brought up the rear.

The room widened at the corner. The end of the king-size bed came into view. Two sets of feet still in their shoes rested on the end of the bed. One pair, polished black wing tips; the other pair, crimson suede pumps. Legs. Then torsos. Then blood. The officers lowered their weapons.

The Lords no longer presented a danger to anyone. They were both dead. They lay stiffly on their backs. Rather neatly and primly, Paco thought. Frank's service revolver lay abandoned on a chair. Danielle's chrome .32 was still gripped tightly in her right hand.

Avi rushed to answer the door chimes. Friends and colleagues paying respects to the family had come and gone. Several hours had passed since the chase had begun. Paco stood on the threshold looking grim. Avi ushered him into the den without a word.

Paco slowly removed a folded white linen handkerchief from his pocket and unwrapped it. He held out the jeweled key for Avi to see. The missing diamond rested loosely in its original setting.

"I was almost afraid to ask," Avi said, carefully taking the key from him.

"Thank you. But I think I'd better put it in the bank vault first thing in the morning."

"Good idea," Paco said. "We've had enough of the key's destiny for awhile."

"I'm assuming you caught up with the Lords."

"Not exactly, Doctor," Paco said. "In the end they couldn't face retribution." He described the chase and the outcome. "Danielle shot her husband twice in the head and then turned the gun on herself. We found them stretched out on the bed next to each other."

"Dear God," Avi gasped. "Their crimes were just too great to bear."

"Maybe," Paco said. "But I believe it was the prospect of prison, not the guilt."

An eavesdropping Molly stood at the door. "It's *they-ja vu.* Just like Sophia and Cartier Marche. Side by side in their four-poster. Killed dead."

Paco stared at Molly for nearly a minute, appreciating her deeper meaning. With a wave of his hand, he beckoned her into the den. Finally, he turned to Avi and continued.

"Doctor, obviously your nephew conspired with Ernie Lord to carry out this theft. Otherwise, how would Ernie have known the key was in the cactus? Only Victor could have placed it there. I'm very sorry, Doctor. I certainly take no pleasure in breaking this news to you. But I have a feeling you've suspected it all along."

Avi nodded grimly. "And to think I trusted either one of them. Ernie had his own agenda: to continually prove his courage and manliness to his wife. She, on the other hand, had an uncontrollable zest for danger and a taste for the finer things. And I would guess my nephew had his own plans for the key--selling it for a fresh start or perhaps a new stake."

"But you could hardly predict that, Doctor," consoled Paco.

"Of course, Inspector. But I feel somewhat responsible for his becoming a thief."

"I don't understand," Paco said.

"I misplaced the card with the cabinet combination on it. I probably dropped it in the den, and Vic must have picked it up. I never got around to changing the combination the day the cabinet was installed, as I was supposed to. So I created a temptation too great for him to handle in his desperate state. He needed help and I was unable to give it to him."

"Don't blame yourself, Doctor. Some people are just beyond help. They don't have the good sense to follow the right road. In my work I've found--and I'm sure in your profession, too--that some people just go down with the ship."

"You're quite right, Inspector." Avi fell silent for a moment and then said, slowly, "I do have one request of you, my friend."

"I understand completely. For your sister's sake, we needn't mention Victor's role in the conspiracy." Paco looked across the room at Molly, who gave him a big wink.

"So who's the psychoanalyst now?" Avi asked with a tired but contented smile.